THE ARCHITECT OF
AEONS

THE ARCHITECT OF
AEONS

JOHN C. WRIGHT

A TOM DOHERTY ASSOCIATES BOOK

NEW YORK

THE ARCHITECT OF AEONS

Copyright © 2015 by John C. Wright

All rights reserved.

A Tor Book
Published by Tom Doherty Associates, LLC
175 Fifth Avenue
New York, NY 10010

www.tor-forge.com

Tor® is a registered trademark of Tom Doherty Associates, LLC.

The Library of Congress Cataloging-in-Publication Data is available upon request.

ISBN 978-0-7653-2970-7 (hardcover)
ISBN 978-1-4299-5168-5 (e-book)

Tor books may be purchased for educational, business, or promotional use. For information on bulk purchases, please contact the Macmillan Corporate and Premium Sales Department at 1-800-221-7945, extension 5442, or write to specialmarkets@macmillan.com.

First Edition: April 2015

Printed in the United States of America

0 9 8 7 6 5 4 3 2 1

CONTENTS

ACKNOWLEDGMENTS

The author thanks unexpectedly kind readers for their words of encouragement, his family for their sacrifices, his publisher for his patience, and certain higher powers (you know who you are!) for their inspiration and grace.

Quotes from *The City of Dreadful Night* by James Thomson are used with thankfulness.

Science moves, but slowly, slowly, creeping on from point to point:
Slowly comes a hungry people, as a lion, creeping nigher,
Glares at one that nods and winks behind a slowly-dying fire.
Yet I doubt not thro' the ages one increasing purpose runs,
And the thoughts of men are widen'd with the process of the suns.

—Alfred, Lord Tennyson

PART FIVE

---·---

The Armadas of the Hyades

1

A Lost World

A.D. 11049

1. Ghost Ship

The Earth was gone.

"Damnification and pestilential pustules. You'd better be dead wrong on your dead reckoning, Blackie."

The nigh-to-lightspeed starship *Emancipation* hung in space in the spot where Tellus, the home of man, was in theory supposed to be. Sol hovered to one side, an endless roar of radio white noise and high-energy particles.

"Restrain your ire, my dear smelly Cowhand. With the navigation beacons wiped out, our precise position is hard to determine. But the sun is at the correct size and distance, and the other planets also. This is where Earth should be."

"Blackie! You think the enemy done her in?"

As a ship, the *Emancipation* was a titaness: one hundred thousand metric tons displacement, her overall length twice that of a skyscraper's height from the First Space Age, with a sail spread of five hundred miles, requiring seventy-five thousand terawatts of laser energy to propel. With her sails folded, she looked like the skeleton of an umbrella with absurdly long and spindly arms, or perhaps like some microscopic marine animal. She had been designed for a complement of four hundred and eighty fully human persons, a complement of twenty posthuman Melusine, whose cetacean members would occupy the fore cistern, and an additional complement of twenty packs of subhuman dog-things, who would occupy kennels and factory volumes amidships. But the miles of conduits and inflatable tunnels connecting the fore ramscoop array with the long spine of the aft drive shaft, the rotating living quarters and nonrotating slumber quarters, the workhouses, shroud houses, laboratories, mind-core and launch collar (where an arsenal of pinnaces, probes, landers, missiles, and robotools where docked) were empty. The vast ship was a floating ghost town.

Like an arrow, even when at rest, the shape of the star-vessel suggested flight, as if she yearned to soar. Newtonian space and time was not suited to her lines: the paradoxes of Einstein were in her, implied by the heavy armor, the drag-reducing streamlines.

Neither ramscoop nor drivespine had ever once been heated up to form the ship's vast magnetic funnels fore and aft, nor had her polymer sails, brightest mirrors of weightless gossamer, ever been run out to their full multimile-wide diameter. Despite her name, the nigh-to-lightspeed vessel had never achieved near-lightspeed, nor even left the Solar System.

"Cowhand, whatever do you mean by 'done her in'?"

"Blackie, I mean beefed her!"

The ship had two crewmen, or three, depending on how one counted. The two humans (or technically, incarnate posthumans) aboard were Menelaus Illation Montrose, who had once been the Judge of Ages before his abdication, and Ximen del Azarchel, who had once been the Master of the World before his exile. They were the best of friends and deadliest of foes, as well as being the only members of their subspecies, *homo sapiens posthominid,* called Elders or Early Posthumans, and both in love with the same long-lost girl, the Princess Rania of Monaco, and both unwilling, during this particular protracted interval of time, to take up weapons and murder each other as they both so dearly wished to do. Each one was, in his own way, a very lonely man.

"Beef what? That is hardly more clear."

"Blackie, don't you speak proper Texan? I mean, d'you reckon the Varmint destroyed the Earth?"

At the moment, both men had their bodies safely tucked away in biosuspension coffins, with four quarts of submicroscopic fluid machinery occupying all the major cells and cell clusters in their corpses. Whether the bodies were alive or dead was a matter of semantic nicety. The nanomachinery slowed the biological processes to a rate indistinguishable from stasis, except that at the moment enough of their neural tissue was at an activity level to house their consciousnesses. The coffins were clinging by their crablike legs to surfaces that could be called bulkhead, or deck, or overhead (in zero gee the distinction is also a semantic nicety) of the forward storage locker used as the ship's bridge. Calling this the bridge was yet another semantic nicety, since the control interfaces and guidance systems could be piped into any cabin in the ship where the pilot found himself, and several spots on the hull.

"As for that, my dear friend, I, ah, 'reckon' it to be unlikely."

"Issat so? Gimme your whys and wherefores, Blackie."

The third member of the crew (if it could be called that) was visible at the aft of the locker, filling the space where the entire wall (or bulkhead) had been removed, and reaching back along the ship's major axis some nine hundred yards. This third was a single monomolecular diamond, tinted amber due to nanotechnological impurities: lattices of fluorine-based chemicals like submicroscopic irregular camshafts were woven through the diamond matrix, and formed the basis of a rod-logic computation appliance wherein the ship's softbrain was housed. The crystal was semitranslucent, and shed some of its waste heat in the form of photons in the visible light spectrum, so a dull erubescent glow, like coals in a grate, filled the amber well of crystal with a smoky red gold.

"What we know of the Virtue—to use Rania's name for entities on the hyperpostsuperposthuman level of intellectual topography—comes from the inscription left behind on the Monument at V 886 Centauri, which, even after millennia, the human and posthuman civilizations of Earth cannot fully decipher. But that inscription hints that the Virtue of Hyades was coming here to rule and uplift the Earth, not destroy it."

"Yeah, well, looks like someone transposed an omicron for a zero or a doughnut or something, because I am looking at the spot where our mother planet, Earth, is supposedly s'pose to be, and I ain't seeing nothing but a whole lot of nothing."

"The Hyades are not the enemies of man, but our natural masters! They will guide us upward to evolutionary heights undreamed."

"Or blast us to atoms, if'n we ain't no damned use to them."

"You know nothing of them!"

"Nor you. Nor anyone, human or posthuman or whatthehell."

"I know no man shoots his own hounds."

"Unless the hound is a mad dog, mad enough to want to die free rather than live the slave of his so-called natural masters."

The reason for having this storage locker act as the bridge was that, with the aft bulkhead gone, there was no interface between either man and the ship's brain. Neither trusted that if the brain information were piped in through some indirect means, a control panel, a touchscreen or wand, that the other man might not bug or jinx the datastream. Both men were wary of the other, and both were gentlemen enough not to let the mutual hatred and suspicion rankle them. Little compromises made things easier: each man designed his own interface, and just sent a maser or laser into the depth of the crystal mind core at whatever arbitrary spot he chose. Neither man knew the one-inch-wide interface volume the other had claimed as his base of operations in the million-gallon multiton mass of seething thought-crystal.

Montrose observed, "On second thought, I am going to back off my Fried Earth theory. You'd think there'd be debris."

"What if they used contraterrene?" asked Del Azarchel. "The Virtue had the mass of Uranus. Enough to hold one earth-sized mass of antimatter."

"Hm. Total conversion would have made a flash we'd have seen while we was cowering like rats out at your old hidey-hole at Jupiter, Blackie."

Ximen del Azarchel, with a mental command, pointed a microwave laser at the input-output port on Montrose's coffin, and sent text with a parallel verbal channel for voice expression, and a wireframe for body language and facial expression. Del Azarchel sent a cartoon image of his lean, goatee'd, devilishly handsome face wearing a supercilious glance of doubt. "Jupiter was in conjunction, so Earth was 6.2 AU from us, masked by Sol."

Montrose sent back a shrug, a scowl on his bony, big-nosed, lanky, and lantern-jawed face. "The whole mass of Earth turning instantly to photons? We'd have seen the reflection from the other planets, Sol or no. Odds are you'd see it from Andromeda galaxy in two million years or so, something that bright. You want to check my figures?"

"No, Cowhand. Do you want to check mine?"

"Nope, I trust your math more than I trust opening an unshielded data channel. Do you think the Earth is hidden? Shielded somehow?"

Blackie put a thoughtful look on his cartoon face and sent that. "When we departed the Earth the first time, the human-cetacean group-mind had occupied the entire nickel-iron core of the planet, which you so thoughtfully turned into a gigantic logic crystal for them. They are what a man named Kardashev long ago called a level K-One race: a civilization that controlled the total energy and resources of a planet."

"What Rania called a Potentate." Montrose reminded himself with a mental frown what the scale and magnitude was of these monsters they faced. He knew that, by the Kardashev scale, a civilization controlling the whole output of a star was called K-Two, and of a galaxy, K-Three. The Hyades was between K-Two and K-Three, controlling the total output of matter and energy in a small star cluster, and an intelligence in the hundred billion range: what Rania called a *Domination*. In her scale, a civilization that totally exploited the mass and energy output of a gas giant was called a *Power*. The servant of the Hyades dispatched to Sol, large as a gas giant but much more finely organized, was called a *Virtue*, and was above K-One but below the K-Two level, controlling more mass-energy than a rocky planet but less than the total mass-energy of a star system.

Blackie was sending: "Like an ugly duckling finally reaching its own, the Earthly civilization was the first human race truly to supersede humanity. You saw how quickly the Swans reestablished the ancient weather control of the Sixtieth Century, how rapidly they converted the interior mass of the moon to logic diamond, and created the Selene Mind. It's been four hundred years since last we were allowed on Mother Earth but you saw the rate of development."

"I sure did."

"They were evolving from something at the edge of what we could comprehend to something beyond that edge. The growth rate was asymptotic."

"Always is, during a boom, Blackie."

"What do you mean?"

"I mean in real life, and not in daydreams, things got a natural growth rate until they run into a natural growth limit. Then the asymptote flips over: sure, advanced societies still advance, but always slower. Lookit how quick the fastest a man could go went from the speed of a sailing ship to the speed of a supersonic jet. And then in the decades after—what happened? Man did not keep getting faster and faster. Lookit how free mankind got during the Enlightenment, the Industrial revolution, and the abolition of slavery. And then what happened? Natural limits began to set in, and people didn't keep getting more free and more, they started loosing their liberty by sips and dribbles in my country, and by gulps in yours. What makes you think intelligence growth doesn't have built in limits?"

"Merely because I know that an ape could not imagine a human. We are not discussing a merely linear increase in thinking speed, but a revolution in the quality of thought, the use of means beyond our imagination. Do you, ah, 'reckon' that the Swans, while we were absent, might have passed beyond an event horizon of asymptotic growth, and evolved beyond our reckoning?"

"And do what? Invent a technology that allows them to bend light around the entire globe?"

"Nothing so dramatic. Merely a layer of ash and dust brought up from the interior would lower the albedo. Let us never forget, just because we are dealing with entities that crossed one hundred and fifty-one lightyears to conquer us, that even something so small as a solar system is unimaginably vast, even for imaginations such as ours. If the Earth were not reflecting light, if we were out of estimated position by a few hundred thousand miles . . ."

"So where is Selene, the intelligent moon? Every crater and pothole was supposed to have a weapon inside. She was going to be the great offensive fortress, our rock of Gibraltar in the sky. The face of the moon lights up like a Christmas tree when she fires her main beam, and all the smoke from all the secondary launchers gets ionized in the hash. Where is she now?" Menelaus sent a sigh. "What if the ash and dust got kicked up not from the Potentate masking the Earth? Weapon damage would do the same."

"I don't believe it."

"You don't want to believe it, Blackie. Those Varmints are evil."

"The Virtue is meant to introduce us into the Galactic Civilization!"

"As serfs. Or all-meat patties. And if they was here to introduce us, where is they?"

"They who? You mean the Virtue?"

Not long ago, while orbiting Ganymede, the long-range telescopes of the *Emancipation*'s astronomy house had captured an image of the intruder as it passed into the Solar System.

It had been a globular mass the size of a gas giant, adorned with silver clouds swirled into storm systems large enough to swallow smaller worlds. The clouds covered a liquid surface black as sin. They had seen the black mass drifting like a soap bubble toward the blue loveliness of Earth, moving with no visible means of propulsion. Fourteen immense machines or organisms that looked like trees in winter or naked umbrellas had been in orbit around it. These were the orbit-based space elevators or "skyhooks" whose blueprint had been seen on the surface of the Monument: the instruments used for deracinating whole populations of one planet to another. These skyhooks had had the decency to have reaction-drive engines, and move according Newtonian principles, even if the mother mass had not.

They had lost sight of the apparition as it passed toward the inner system.

Blackie said, "We are crippling ourselves by operating at less than optimal intelligence. Let us warm up the mind core to full self-awareness."

"It took me ten thousand years to figure out how to destroy Exarchel, your last fully self-aware supermachine, and that was when I had a supermachine of my own occupying the Earth's core helping me. No thanks. Next idea?"

Blackie said, "Let's take a year or two and look for occlusions. If a body passes before a star, we can find it."

Montrose said, "We can also keep an eye on any orbital anomalies. A mass the size of Uranus, if it is still in the system, might not mess up the fallpath of Jupiter too much, but we should be able to see its influence on the motions of the smaller planets, Mercury and Pluto. And let's deploy the sails a little bit, and gather in some light."

"Which may expose us to the Virtue, if the body is still in this system. With our sails open, we are visible to anyone with a medium-powered telescope."

"Let's risk it. I got two reasons. First, the aliens never approached any object smaller than a planet before. This ship is just a mayfly to them, and we're just specks."

"Hm. I seem to recall that even humans occasionally swat flies. What is your second reason?"

"We're both reckless and bored."

By unspoken mutual consent, both men lowered their subjective rate of passing time until they could see through the various instruments in the astronomy houses fore and amidships, or brought in through extravehicular remotes, the jeweled dots of the planets moving like waltzing dancers against the star-gemmed velvet of vacuum.

Intently they watched.

2. Visions of Great Worlds Afar

A.D. 11050

They created indentations in portions of the sail to use as convex mirrors and flexed the shrouds to turn them this way or that. These immense light-gathering fields were larger than any Earth-based telescope could be. It was like having a lens the size of the arctic ice cap.

Montrose soon noticed an anomaly in the drain of resources from the ship's astronomy house: the ship's brain was spending time poring over data peripheral to star occlusion scans. He was curious what Del Azarchel was seeking, and carefully, slowly, and secretly, he heterodyned a repeater signal on the incoming astronomical data.

The first quarter of the sky toward which Del Azarchel looked was the constellation Canes Venatici, toward the great extragalactic globular cluster at M3. Montrose with some effort beat back his rage at this act of voyeurism, so he did not thaw himself, take up the fire ax from the bulkhead, go to Del Azarchel's coffin, and chop his frozen face into bits. Yet Montrose was appalled that Del Azarchel would dare to stare, like an adulterous lover sighing and mooning at a married woman's window, at the stars which so called to Montrose and so re-called his wife to him.

But then Del Azarchel turned elsewhere those instruments more potent than any human eyes. Here in the constellation of Fornax the Furnace was a star called Hipparchos 13044, two thousand lightyears from Earth, whose waltz through the heavens betrayed the presence of a dark body, perhaps twice the size of Jupiter, orbiting it. But the star was one of many in a Helmi stream, origi-nally belonging to a dwarf galaxy that had been devoured by the Milky Way nine billion years ago. The age of the planet was greater than that: it was from outside the galaxy. Montrose could not imagine what interest Del Azarchel could have in this astronomical anomaly.

Closer at hand, the wobble of the failed star HD 42176 in the constellation Auriga the Charioteer, three hundred ninety lightyears away, betrayed a fire giant world, larger than Jupiter and closer to its primary than Mercury, orbit-ing once every thirty hours: a year short as a day.

It seemed Earth-like planets throughout the Local Interstellar Cloud were unusual. Jovian and superjovian worlds were much more common than smaller, rocky worlds. The current theory was that small planets were naturally swept up in the orbits of larger ones. In Sol's system, for reasons yet unknown, a pri-mordial superplanet had been split into Jupiter, Saturn, and Uranus, and this allowed inner and outer worlds, Mercury and Pluto, to form. Apparently life on Earth-sized worlds was a rare accident.

Montrose was puzzled. What was Del Azarchel's interest in exosolar plan-ets?

Months passed.

3. Inconstant Earth

A.D. 11051

Both men exclaimed at the same time.

"Eureka!" and "Thar she blows me!"

"What did you find, you disgusting Texan clodpole?"

"I found where the Earth is hiding, though I cannot say how she got there. What'd you find, you dandified Iberian gutterbug?"

"I found out how she got there but not where she is. While looking for oc-clusions of any stars or background radiations by black bodies, the instruments picked up occlusions of various intervening energy fields. The magnetosphere of the sun is gravely disturbed. This disturbance is enough to grapple the core of the planet magnetically, and impart a lateral vector. I assume the initial acceleration was very mild, because even rocky planets are actually just gooey liquid with a little crust on the surface, and we do not see a trail of asteroids, ejecta, and debris trailing off. And it also shows the Earth was not removed entirely from the Solar System, since the solar magnetosphere does not extend so far, and, at accelerations low enough to keep the planet intact, could not have achieved solar escape velocity."

"Well, boy howdy, because I done found her. Venus has a slight drift to her orbit, and a wobble to her rotation, and so does Pluto—who did me good service this day, despite the men of old who said he weren't no planet."

"So where?"

"Up. The Earth is at right angles to the plane of the ecliptic. Earth is in a ball-o-twine orbit above the solar North Pole and below the South Pole."

"At the same distance as before?"

"So I guess. Simple orbital mechanics says it is easier to change your inclination than your speed or distance from the center of gravity. In this case, all they did—whoever they were—was increase the orbital inclination to ninety degrees. Boy, are all the astrologers going to be daffy after that stunt. As seen from Earth, the sun will swing through the same northern and south constellation once a year, but the zodiac of signs the sun passes through will be different each year, because the whole orbit is turning."

"So you have not actually found the Earth?"

"I know where we should concentrate our telescopes. One AU to the solar north, and one to the solar south. Because the whole orbit is turning like the rim of a spinning penny, we won't know from what direction Earth'll be approaching the solar North Pole. Could be up to six months before she passes through that area, and then however long it will take us to match orbits, three years or so. But to us at this speed, it will seem like no time. . . ."

4. *Less Oblate Spheroid*

A.D. 11054

". . . See? That weren't long," Menelaus concluded his sentence.

Now the world loomed large within the images the astronomy houses fore and amidships brought in. The moon looked nothing like the moon of old. Logic diamond had coated her seas and uplands, and now new craters of war damage had smashed and cracked the layers of diamond shell so that she resembled the fantastically shattered surface of Europa, rather than the silver-gray moon of Earth's past. Unthinkable energies had scalded strange and lurid colors into the blasted glass, green and gold and lines of crimson like bleeding scars, speckles of peacock blue scattered like pepper.

One crater so large that it by rights was a sea now occupied the lower quarter of the disk like an eye, and the mountains cast up in the center were a beady pupil. It overtopped the exact spot Tycho Crater once had occupied, as if some base or fortress there had been obliterated with a six-mile-wide meteor, or some other weapon yielding a ninety-teraton blast. Tiny ring arcs of dust and gravel orbited the moon, perhaps residue from the blast.

Menelaus was shocked—nay, offended—that the ancient body and the mysterious seas which had haunted so many love songs and images of his youth were now forever gone.

"It's . . . it's *rotating*," he told Del Azarchel, unable to heterodyne into any tone of voice the infinite sense of loss and rage he felt. The globe would now turn its dark side once every two weeks toward her primary.

Del Azarchel was also enraged. "The print of my hand is gone. Look here, instead. This."

In the vast crater that covered a quarter of the surface were the angles and sinewaves, arranged in dizzying, eye-defeating spirals and concentric ranks, an imprint of the Monument notation.

Montrose said, "They left us our own Monument? Can we translate it?"

"Not without considerably more calculation power than this ship currently . . ."

"Nope. We are not waking up your poxy monster brain. Let's ask the survivors."

That there was technological civilization still on Earth was not in doubt: in addition to the moon, two sails, nearly as broad as the main sail of the *Emancipation,* were orbiting at a half-geosynchronous rate. The Earth was not seen as the normal blue crescent astronauts approaching it tangentially to the sun would see: like a moving continent, a circle of light cast from the farside mirror was passing over the night of the world, and, equal and opposite, a circle of darkness hid the noonside of the world. The crescent of the Earth looked almost like a curving letter w, but only if the w were dotted like a small letter j.

Earth herself was shockingly unrecognizable: she had slowed her rate of spin, and the change in centrifugal force, imperceptible as it was, no longer created as large a bulge along her equator; therefore, Canada and Alaska and half of

Russia were submerged in the polar sea, the Great Lakes basin was mingled with salt water. The Gulf of Mexico, on the other hand, was now an inland sea, for a second isthmus, of which Cuba and the Caribbean Islands were but hills, joined Florida to Northern Brazil.

Baja California was now the highest elevated of three peninsulas reaching into the Pacific like a hand whose fingertips dripped archipelagoes. India was now connected by an isthmus to Madagascar, making the Arabian Sea an inland lake larger than the Caspian.

A belt of the ocean severed South Africa from a combined Euro-Northafrican continent, and the Mediterranean basin, dry for many ages, had been flooded once more, lapping the slopes of the White Mountains and the Italian Alps. The higher elevations of Egypt and Libya were no more than large islands in this combined Mediterranean and Saharan sea; Mount Gibraltar and Mount Abyla were smaller islands, as was the lonely peak of Malta.

In the East, Australia and Indochina were now part of the Asian supercontinent, and the Sea of Japan was a dry and deep valley between the high plateaus of what had once been Manchuria, Korea, and Japan. In the West, a new land mass shaped like a snake had emerged from the mid-Atlantic ridge, an old fable of Plato now true, if in reverse. Antarctica was entirely submerged.

The ice caps were gone. The amount of water vapor in the air was far lower than it should have been. The sea level was lower by scores of meters than it should have been, even with the other catastrophic climatic changes.

"The orbit is more eccentric than it had been," announced Del Azarchel. "Much hotter summers and much cooler winters. The ice caps return in winter, I suppose, and reach far down toward the temperate zone. The angle of interaction between the Earth's magnetosphere and the surrounding solar environment should make aurora borealis and aurora australis visible year round and from every latitude. Other than that, from the surface this new orbit would provoke no obvious difference in the appearance of the skies. They even pointed the pole at the pole star, and imparted the exact same precession of the axes."

"The South Pole," grunted Menelaus dourly. "You'd think they'd get that detail right. But why did the Varmints move the Earth to a new orbit? What would be the point? And where are they now? Why aren't they shooting at us?" At her current parabolic orbit approaching Earth, the *Emancipation* with sail deployed would have been remarkably visible. Everyone on Earth, even without binoculars, would have seen caught in her sails the bright image of a smaller and colder second sun rising in the east, getting a little bigger every day.

Del Azarchel said, "I don't think the Virtue did this. Look at these figures." And he sent as text a few thousand lines of Monument notational math, showing the type of electromagnetic impulse that would have been necessary to move an object the size of the Earth to a new inclination.

Menelaus was able to take in the whole equation at a glance, but did not see the significance at first. He paused, divided his mind into several subsections working at different subjective speeds and organizing the information in different patterns and data-groupings before he saw the point. He rejoined his mind into one frame, and sent a low whistle of astonishment along the audio channel.

Del Azarchel must have noticed the pause. "You could have asked."

"I like reckoning things out for myself. Besides, if we are both thinking what I'm thinking we're thinking, that's independent confirmation. You think the Potentate died, wiped clean by the electromagnetic pulse."

"Crippled rather than died, depending on electrically inert backups and failovers, but yes. And I think that such a pulse happened before the new orbit. We can reconstruct the order of events. The Hyades Virtue connected the Earth and sun with a flux tube. For what reason, I don't know. That wiped the data out of the core mind. The whole mass of iron was aligned by the shock, and there was a line of plasma connecting the Earth to the sun. The Swans took advantage of it—I cannot tell if the flux tube lasted a second or lasted a decade—to maneuver the Earth into a new orbital inclination, at right angles to the plane of the ecliptic. Again, for what reason, I cannot fathom."

A flux tube was a cylindrical region of space where the magnetic field at the side surfaces is parallel to those surfaces. The sun had many such tubes rising from its surface and falling back again in vast arches, paths of least resistance followed by solar flares. Jupiter and Io were connected by a complex dance of flux tubes, carrying heavier and lighter cargoes of cold plasma, either buoyantly expanding away from the giant planet, or massively sinking toward its storm-filled atmosphere.

Since Jupiter was Del Azarchel's personal playground, the headquarters of the most massive project he, or any of the human race, had ever attempted, no doubt he was quicker to recognize the phenomena than Montrose.

Montrose said, "If we hadn't been kicked off the planet by the damnified critters we created . . ."

"You created. . . ."

". . . that got created somehow-or-'nuther, we would have been here to see the shindig."

Del Azarchel sighed. "I am wondering where the aliens are. The Monument indicated that they were coming here to rule us. It would bring order and peace."

"Peaceful as a pigsty. Farmer makes sure his swine don't fight each other. And all he asks in return is pork, bacon, and ham."

Del Azarchel said sardonically, "I can pick out human shapes occupying villages and towns, and the instruments show energy use along the seabeds, so the Melusine are not extinct. Our old friend the horse is still around, regrown from your Tomb archives. And . . . look at this image. Do you think it is a sporting event?"

Montrose said, "War. Horse cavalry and Mastodon cavalry. Look at the line of organization: that is a posthuman general in charge, someone of our level of intelligence, but nothing as smart as a Melusine or a Swan, much less Potentate."

5. Battle in the 111th Century

Across the mossy landscape of what had once been sea bottom, the battalions clashed. Soldiers garbed or painted all in green and gold, carrying an emblem of a balance scale, clashed with those in crimson, who fought beneath the sign of a winged hourglass.

The heat was more than tropical, since steam arose from the moss at every footfall. The soldiers were a mix of human and artificial hominids from recent gene records, elephant-legged giants, half-animal Chimerae, dwarfish Locusts, and, from more ancient lines, Neanderthal troglodytes and nocturnal Cro-Magnon. The soldiers of all subspecies wore glass helmets and armor made of prismatic diamond glitter, and fought with energy rays, chemically powered crossbows, and flails and staves and *bokken* swords made of amber-colored wood.

Or at least it looked like wood. The amber weapons had some odd bio-electrical properties: foot-long sparks and blinding flares jumped from the wooden blades or flails when a blow fell. In addition to beating the moss to emit its clouds of vapor and steam, both armies tossed glass grenades or ignited petards to spread clouds of glinting smoke to baffle the ray weapons of the enemy, and the rays seemed remarkably weak even when they struck. It was as if they feared to emit any large-scale discharges.

Montrose asked, "Can you pick up any energy signals coming off those dead bodies? If they are just remote-controlled puppets, and the brain info is just downloaded . . . ah . . ."

Del Azarchel said, "The deaths are real. None of them are connected to any remote information system. However, there is someone or something who is the center of worldwide signal traffic approaching from below. Look there."

In the image, the warring parties parted as suddenly as the Red Sea beneath the rod of Moses. A single figure, manlike but taller than a man, wearing a living cloak like wings, walked across the battlefield. He was barefoot, and walked with precise, mincing steps, stiffed-legged, his toes touching the ground first before his heel. His hair fibers swayed like undersea plant life in an unseen current.

On higher and lower bands of the spectrum, even through the intervening atmosphere, threads of energy dense enough for ultrahigh-speed communication connected this figure with weather balloons and peach-sized artificial satellites in low orbit, continent-sized orbital mirrors in high orbit, and also with towers and dishes here and there along the mountaintops of both Earth and moon.

Montrose pondered the information throughput volumes with alarm. The intelligence level was far higher than his own, or that of Del Azarchel.

The Swan turned and looked up at him. His eyes bored into Montrose's startled gaze like a knife into his brain. Montrose blinked by shutting off the feed from his coffin circuits to his visual centers, because he could not meet that gaze. Of course, the calm-faced superhuman creature was merely glancing at the bright sail of the NTL *Emancipation* climbing to noon, but the effect was unnerving.

Del Azarchel said, "He seems not to notice the battle. A very dignified demeanor! How reticent."

Montrose opened his visual feed again. He saw the Swan stalking forward. The being did not look left or right at the carnage around him.

Montrose was not sure if Del Azarchel were kidding. "How blind, you mean. The visual information is being edited out of the Swan's reticular complex before it even reaches his cortex. Everything human is invisible to the posthumans. Phantasms. Remember?"

There was no sign of panic or haste among the men: the image was clear enough that Montrose could see officers on either side were giving orders and hearing reports, dressing their lines to await the signal to resume, and meanwhile heralds waving colored flags were shouting across the field to the foe, looking oddly like cheerleaders in their gestures and poses. The men raised their arms and clashed their wooden swords against glass shields with pride or anger at each exchange.

The Swan had emerged from a nearby river, cutting a deep canyon in the mossy sea bottom, and strolled without seeing between the parted armies to a knob of high ground. Neither did he hear the shouts and slogans apparently being shouted back and forth between the momentarily parted armies.

When he first emerged from the water, the posthuman seemed porpoiselike in his face and skin surface, but he became more human-looking as he walked.

The war leaders and standard-bearers and buglers who were occupying that knob of high ground toward which the great Swan stalked, their coign of vantage for overseeing the battle, with swift and practiced motions dismounted and gathered themselves out of the way, and carefully pulled aside walking watchtowers, electric fence posts, basins, and battleflags, so that the Swan would not trip on them.

The warlords did not try to move their now-riderless beasts aside, and when the winged figure raised his hand as if in greeting, the horses broke their pickets and came to nuzzle him, and the mastodons danced with massive mirth for him, and writhed their trunks like comic pythons.

The wings the posthuman wore were not just antennae: the Swan, done petting the beasts, now expanded the wing surface to many times its size, and rose rapidly from the point of rock, effortlessly as a thistledown rising. The surface of his body changed color as he entered thinner atmosphere, as if he had biotechnological mechanisms for adjusting to extremes.

The face was becoming hardened and featureless in preparation for vacuum: a statue of diamond.

6 Phantasms

Del Azarchel took the time to draw up a detailed version of a sardonic expression to his face, exaggerating the twist of the lips and making the supercilious eyebrow arch higher than he could in real life lift it, before he passed it to Montrose on the visual channel.

Montrose said, "Are you surprised? You were expecting that my phantasm system would be broken by now."

Del Azarchel said, "It has been half a millennium. One would think a superior brain would notice the gaps in the visual patterns, the unexplained shadows, the unexpected and indirect clues."

Montrose did not point out that Del Azarchel's pet brain Exarchel had been inflicted with the same phantasm program for ten millennia, and never combined the tiny irregularities or indirect clues to deduce that he had a blind spot.

Instead, he said only, "The more superior a brain is, the easier it is for it to fool itself, and explain things away."

"Every corpse on the battlefield below there, his blood is on your hands. If the posthumans were allowed to tame the humans, war would be gone. I suppose your posthuman intellect can easily explain your guilt away, Cowhand?"

"Well, I can explain your guilt to you. You thought your posthuman brain gives you the right to rule humans. But logically this means the higher powers from the stars have the right to rule you."

"I have never rebelled against them. There is a natural order to the cosmos, like a ladder. Everyone has his place."

"I have never submitted. I reckon that is my place in the natural order. As for my guilt; what guilt? I did not put a bullet in any of those corpses down yonder. All I did was cut off the bottom rung of your cosmic ladder. The rest of y'all on the up-high rungs can enslave each other to your heart's content, but the humans at the bottom, I dealt out of the game. But I was as fooled as you, old pal. I thought the Hyades were coming to set up shop."

"Are you as curious as I, *amigo*?"

"That I am, partner."

"Then our alliance and nonaggression pact continues?"

"We need proper seconds and judges and a right good footing with no ship-side Coriolis effect to throw off my aim. You don't even need to ask. I ain't going to shoot you in the back, and I know you ain't going to shoot me in the back. The survivor will have to live with himself until the end of time. Cause both of us stopped aging a while back, and neither of us ain't planning to cash out our chips early on . . . Jesus H. Christ in a thorny hat!"

"Please don't blaspheme," said Del Azarchel, which surprised Montrose, even though it should not have. Hard to remember that Blackie took his religion seriously, or seemed to.

"That weren't no blasphemery! That was a pestilential *prayer* of poxed *thanksgiving*! I been hanging out with you too long, Blackie, that I almost forgot that I don't believe nothing you say! *You* think the Hyades world-armada, that cloud of black slime the size of a gas giant, after coming all this way from Epsilon Tauri was sure to crush any resistance. *You* said mankind, not humans and not posthumans, not Swans and not Potentates, none of us could possibly hurt them nor drive them off! But I ain't never said that!"

Del Azarchel said, "I don't see your point."

"Which shows that, no matter how smart you are, you cannot escape your axioms and assumptions. What is the simplest explanation for what we are seeing? Earth is here. The Varmint ain't."

"I still don't . . ."

"We won. We drove them off."

"Impossible."

"Let's get a radio message to someone, and get permission to land, read a newspaper, find out the story. We can always ripple our sail like a honking big heliograph and send them flashes in Morse code."

"Or burn a city from orbit if they ignore or threaten us," added Del Azarchel with a dark smile.

"You are one sick, sick puppy."

"Hell hath no fury like a woman scorned, or a world-ruler dispossessed, or so they say."

"Start sending signals. How long can it take?"

7. Reply

A.D. 11055

"Cowhand, we're getting a reply from the surface. It is in the Swan language, which, like the Monument code itself, contains its own self-reflexive predictions for its own semantic changes and semiotic drift."

"So y'all were able to find a common language?"

"In theory we could have rendered one using infinite-variable calculus techniques to solve toward absolute syntax strange attractors. But it was just easier to use Latin."

"*Omnes viae ducunt homines per saecula Romam,* I reckon. Who was it? What d'they say about the Varmint, or the location of the Earth? What happened?"

"It calls itself the Judge of Years and the Voice of the Swan, and seems not to be in the mood to answer questions. I cannot tell if this comes from some corner of planetwide Noösphere, or is some smaller, independent group, or even a lone crackpot with a radio. The signals are coming from the eastern shore of Africa. It says the Swan for whom it speaks grants us permission to make splashdown. It gives a longitude and latitude and a window of time. Do we trust this unknown voice?"

"Better than sitting up here in ice'tween our buttock cheeks. The Swans should not be able to see us or stop us, so we got the perfect smuggling vessel. Let's risk it. Do I need to recite that poem from Kipling? *If you can keep your hat when all about you are losing theirs and blaming it on you . . .*"

"You are a man after my own bold heart, but spare me your clubfooted Anglo jingles, I who rejoice in the fiery wine of Manuel José Quintana, or who
have flown to the pure classical summit of the Paradise by Gaspar Melchor de
Jovellanos!"

"Anglo poems is better. I see you one Shakespeare and raise you a Chaucer."

"I match them and find them wanting against the satire of Cervantes and
earthiness of the Juan Ruiz, the Archpriest of Hita. In any case, I am willing
to risk my heap of winnings on one turn of pitch-and-toss—"

"There is a '*but*' a-coming, ain't there?"

"—but this Judge of Years has warned us that neither will we be given nor
sold any heavy water to spare for the fusion drive of the landing craft, to power
a launch again. To land now is to be stranded."

"Fine," said Montrose, sending an X-ray version of his face cartoon, so Blackie
could see him grit his teeth. "We nip out to the asteroid belt, find a likely chunk
of ice, boil it down, render up enough heavy water to do a safe belly flop into
their oceans . . . how long can that take?"

"I do wish you'd stop saying that."

8. Splashdown

A.D. 11057

The new orbit of Earth made the winters much more severe than in prior eons.
The *Emancipation* formed her mirrored sail as a magnifying glass to clear the
icebergs from a generous volume of the Sea of Arabia. Here, not long after, the
ship's fifty-foot pinnace splashed down.

Bobbing to the surface, Montrose and Del Azarchel commanded the hatch of
the flattened, trilobite-shaped craft to undog itself and admit the atmosphere
of Earth, which neither had breathed for centuries. The air whistled in the dorsal
hatch and internal xenon gas, which had been used as a preservative to fill the
interior, streamed out of ventral gills just above the waterline, an unseen smoke.

Both bodies had been prepped for a quick thaw, so it was only a matter of
minutes, rather than hours, before their coffin lids slid aside and they saw each
other once more in the flesh.

Del Azarchel was naked, soaked with medical fluid, and holding a longsword
whose hilts were crusted with dazzling work of diamond, topaz, and jacinth.
The scabbard was white leather flayed from the flesh of the Coptic Patriarch

who had reigned on Earth before the rise of Del Azarchel to power. Montrose had his white glass caterpillar-drive pistols in his hands.

"You look shaggy," observed Del Azarchel.

"I cannot believe you programmed your coffin to trim and maintain your little goat beard thingie all these centuries."

"Hair cells are cells; why should I grow uncouth, merely because I slumber? You must tidy yourself, though. The portable head unfolds from the deck, and I think there is a dop kit with a straight razor. You can program your coffin fluid into lather, if you like. . . ."

"I know what it can do! I designed the damnified Jell-O one molecule at a time. The message told us to land here. If they are surface dwellers, they will send a boat, or if they are sea dwellers, they'll surface. Is there anything outside?"

Del Azarchel surprised him by not going over to the sensor panel (which was bolted down for gee-maneuver conditions) but by simply swarming up the newly formed ladder to the hatch, and sticking his head into the sunlight.

He yelled and jumped down.

Montrose readied his pistols. "You hurt? What happened?"

"Wind chill, Cowhand. It is cold as Erebus out there. There is a clipper ship made of fiberglass on the horizon, approaching from the south. I saw men and elevated animals aboard, and from the play of the waves I deduce they are accompanied by an escort of dolphins, which I assume are post-delphic Cetaceans. It is a six-masted ship with energy lanterns ranked on three firing tiers port and starboard, with swivel-mounted bow-chasers. So your little magnetic pistols may not be enough to sink her."

"Yeah, well, I will leave you to sink the ship with your pigsticker. Think you can awl a hole in the hull with that piece of ironmongery?"

"Ah! Speaking of which—the Iron Crown of Lombardy! Shame I had to store it in a mere boat locker." Del Azarchel moved over to a rack bolted to the overhead, and worked the catch, drawing out a transparent, macromolecular-locked diamond case.

"Blackie, you are a damn crazy man," opined Montrose.

"Compared to whom?"

"You are stark naked wearing a crown on your head."

"I would say this shows a nicety of priority on my part. I had the ship fabricate any number of proper garments, which we, as historical figures of some import, should not hesitate to don."

"Hope you included parkas."

"I will break out your gear, Cowhand, while you are shaving. Are you really going to use that barbaric knife rather than a depilatory cream?"

"Bowie knife, not barbaric knife."

"We are on a rocking deck! You'll cut your jugular."

"And deprive you of the pleasure of shooting me? Not likely."

"Spoken like a true friend. I have laid out your . . ."

"Are you yanking my Johnson with this? What is this, a costume party?"

"I had thought, considering . . ."

"An English judicial robe and a long white wig. That is what you thought I wanted to wear?"

"As the Judge of Ages, that is the garb legend describes."

"Legend can stick a snorkel up my bunghole and suck a heaping snort of dung fume. Besides, we been out of touch with local legends for quite a spell. Who knows what they think about us nowadays? Maybe they've forgotten us. That'd be a relief, wouldn't it?"

"Not at all. It would mean a lot of work to reacquaint them with whom they are dealing."

"I am not going to let you burn any more cities from orbit, you sick snot."

"That was long ago, and a regrettable necessity, and all those people, had they lived, would have been every one extinct with all their racial stock by now in any case. We are the only true *Homo sapiens* left."

"It weren't so long ago that you ain't still licking your lips over it like the tomcat what found the fishbowl. So what are you wearing?"

"Hm? The uniform of the Hermetic Order, of course. Simple, tasteful, black—does not show dirt. I brought yours as well, just in case you want to assume the rank and station to which you are entitled. I will take it as an honor if you would agree, *amigo*."

"Nope. I'll wear the damn fool Halloween costume instead. And you keep talking like we is still the cock of the roost. Pardner, the Giants is as smart as us, and the Swans are smarter, and moon has a mind many magnitudes smarter yet, and moon ain't even one sixth of the volume used to be at the core. So maybe you should take off your dinky crown, forget that you used to rule the Earth, and remember you is now a beggar, you and me both, and there are super-beings as far above our mere posthuman selves as we are above a sheepdog of middle-to-average doggy smarts. Now, I grant you, sheepdog smarter than a sheep, but you think that makes the shepherd ready to give Rover a vote on whether he gets fixed?"

Del Azarchel had pulled a dark uniform about him. It was made of ultra-lightweight black silk, with a ring at the collar to fit an air hood. The hood itself hung down the back, a triangle of silver and red fabric. The fabric was woven through like the fine, many-branching veins in a leaf, with countless tiny tuhules for life support, heating and refrigeration circuits, and air capillaries. Black gauntlets and black toe socks completed the outfit, and a silvery half-cape of shadow-cloth, dotted with a gem-design of energy cells.

Del Azarchel held up a massive bracelet or amulet of dark red touch-sensitive metal. It was fanged on the inner surface, and looked like a medieval torture instrument. He put his hand in the clamp, wedged the amulet against a flat surface, and leaned on it with his other hand and arm, shoving the big needles and spikes into his arm. He writhed and grimaced as the needles sought out veins and nerve connections in his wrist, and sent a probe into his bone marrow.

Montrose winced. "There are ways a sight less fearsomely painful to do that these days. Technology works wonders, y'know." By way of demonstration, he put his left hand into the medical fluid of his now open coffin. When he removed it a moment later, there was a layer of hard flesh, like the shell of a tortoise, encircling his left wrist and grown into it, and the shell was nacreous ruby. It looked feminine compared to Del Azarchel's heavy manacle, but the computing power used to oversee the continual process of reversing aging errors in cell growth by means of spoofed RNA was the same. Del Azarchel had shared the secret of eternal youth with Montrose when Montrose shared the secret of eternal slumber.

Del Azarchel held the arm which bore the ancient amulet high, and gazed at the antique biotechnology appliance with hawklike stare, his handsome eyes narrowing slightly.

"Menelaus," he said softly, "it is not the opinion of the world that concerns me, nor am I a man to be moved by such light and trifling things, no, not even if the world contains such genius as cannot be estimated. I wear the Iron Crown because it be my right. My conquests I will not forget, even if history forgets, nor all the glory of them. This suit is symbol of my order. The world outside is my child, made by me and marred by you, and so it is a child who escaped control. No matter: my heart is already set on greater things. All this I did, all this, merely so that the Hyades and their superior powers would enfold us within their civilization. It is up to us whether we shall be like the Japanese when they met the European, whom they so soon imitated and surpassed, or like the Negro, who could neither combine to drive them off, nor learn from them—yet even the sons of slaves in whiter lands, once freed, earned and learned and equaled them and then surpassed. Even at the price of slavery, were they not better off? We are immortals, now, Menelaus. Nothing but the long term should concern us."

"So you ain't thinking of just beguiling away the time until my Rania comes back?"

"Mine, not yours," said Del Azarchel with a humorless smile, sharply white within his black goatee, and a twinkle in his eye, dark and large beneath dark brows. "And I shall see to it that this world is fit for her to return to, or, if my ambition deceived me not, a horde of all the local stars. An extensive kingdom in space I will offer her as bride price!"

"Your pot is cracked, Blackie. She's already married, so a-courting you shan't go."

"I have remade man in my image, albeit it took millennia, and now I wish to grant them to go forth to many stars and worlds and conquer and subdue. Not just to Adam and Eve, but now to the minds that inhabit Earth and moon and one day Jupiter, I shall say *go forth and multiply*."

"Nothing wrong with kids learning math." Montrose sighed. "Okay. You win."

"What? Win . . . You mean you will join me in my glorious Great Work?"

"No, I mean I'll put on the silly robes you brought. I was suddenly took by the strange feeling like some judgment ought to happen, or maybe a hanging, so I figure I'd as well dress the part."

The sea wind was bitterly cold, and the upper hull of the pinnace was slick with ice, even along the armor of the nose friction-blackened by reentry heat. Both men stood with one hand on the rim of the open hatch to steady themselves against the pitch and roll.

They stood in the wind, one man in a black shipsuit with hood and cloak, crowned and armed with a sword, handsome as a satyr; the other a craggy-faced staring-eyed hobgoblin with a hook nose, wearing an absurd long white wig of curls beneath a square black cap and flowing red robes that blew and flapped in the icy air, two white pistols tucked in his cincture. Del Azarchel looked black as a Dominican; Montrose, scarlet as a Cardinal.

The sunset painted the horizon red as the pyre of a king. The sky above looked like a peacock's tail. The aurora borealis filled the equatorial heavens. As she approached, the great clipper ship, vast and pale as a fog bank with her mast upon mast of sail, lit up colored lamps at port and starboard, a tradition of awe-inspiring antiquity, but then seemingly from every yardarm and line silver lamps surrounded by rings of glowing fog lit up, and the approaching ship was like a constellation walking toward them.

A voice cried out, "Ahoy!"—a word that was eleven or twelve thousand years old.

2

Aboard the *Hysterical Blindness*

1. Permission to Board

Sailors from the clipper ship dived into the water and were carried on the backs of dolphins to where the pinnace bobbed in the waves. The men had amphibious features while in the water, goggle-eyed like astonished frogs, blubber-skinned against the cold, webbed of foot and finger.

With astonishing alacrity, they leaped from the water, as high as a dolphin might leap, and grabbed on to the rail that rimmed the upper hull of the landing boat. There were five men with blubbery whalelike skin; they shrank, their blubber as if being absorbed back into their bodies, and their eyes and hands became those of land-dwelling humans. They had the harsh, aquiline features and narrow skulls of Chimera, and some mixture of sea mammal genes were in their genetic cocktail, but they also sported aquamarine hue and the electro-telepathic antennae of Blue Men.

Montrose at first wondered at the speed and completeness of the cellular transfiguration, but then he saw that each man wore on his left wrist a large bracelet of blood-red metal. The Hermetic Order, using similar biomolecular prosthetics, could shed their cellular appearance of youth with comparable speed, but they had been constrained to two morphologies. Some of the nuances of the change bespoke a breakthrough in biotechnology, maybe several.

"Congratulations, Blackie," he muttered in English. "Looks like everyone on Earth is a Hermeticist nowadays. You must be proud."

Blackie del Azarchel did not look proud. "I would expect them to take their institutions and heraldry from their conquerors, not from me."

"No conquerors. Man drove them off."

Del Azarchel looked skeptical, but did not say more.

The sailors called out in Latin, asking permission to come aboard. Each sailor kept one foot in the waves as he crouched by the rim of the vessel, as if to maintain the pretense that he was still in the water. They called and waited.

Ximen del Azarchel looked at Menelaus Montrose with a look of embarrassed puzzlement. Menelaus said, or, rather whistled, in the ultra-compressed high-speed language Montrose and Del Azarchel had, while bored, designed for shipboard use in case of emergencies. "You are a-calculating which one of us rightly should answer, ain'tcha?"

"I consider myself the captain of the ship . . ." Del Azarchel answered hesitantly.

"*My* ship, thank you kindly, pardner."

". . . but I am aware of your contrary, albeit somewhat legalistic claim . . ."

"The legalism being as that I done own the damnified thing in fee simple, yessir, as seeing you done stole it as a naked act of piracy. . . ."

". . . in my capacity as sovereign Nobilissimus of the World Concordat, in accord with the Statute of Common Space of 2400, all spaceworthy vessels being, by eminent domain, and for the greater good of world peace . . ."

". . . naked act of piracy for the greater good of world peace, like I said. Still mine."

"The currents are waiting our answer. Shall we talk in unison?"

"What, and make believe you got any sort of right to talk for my ship? What about taking turns. You be captain on odd-numbered millennia, I'll take even, something like that."

"A compromise would be tantamount to admitting you have a claim to the ship."

"Fight a duel? But I suppose we need each other. Toss a coin?"

"The quickdraw game, just using our fingers. The faster one is captain. We could have the onboard brain adjudicate."

"That's a kiddie sport!" scoffed Montrose. "Besides, the currents would see us, and we'd look silly. What about paper-scissors-rock?"

"What? Forego my dignity and claim by mere happenstance? Absurd. What about a quick game of blindfold chess? Pawn to King Four."

"We ain't got time, the currents is waiting and who says you get white? How about a quick round of wrastling? This deck is pretty slippery. Whoever don't get tossed in the drink gets to call one and all aboard."

"The currents will think the gyrations peculiar."

"Injun thumb wrastling. We can stand and block their view with our backs. Last man with no broke fingers is captain."

"One does not break fingers during thumb wrestling."

"One does if'n you play the way I learned it. We both need a pair of pliers."

Del Azarchel pressed the tips of his fingers against his temples. "This is absurd. We are both *Homo Sapiens Postsapiens*, with intelligence in the four hundred range, and posthumans in the seven hundred to one thousand estimated intelligence range are waiting for our reply, and we cannot decide which of us should shout back their permission to board, even though we both wish them to come aboard?"

Montrose said, "When I was young, I used to think that if only mankind were smart enough, enlightened enough, we could solve all our problems. Solve war, solve poverty, solve everything."

Del Azarchel nodded. "I had a similar dream."

Montrose said, "Then I grew up."

Del Azarchel nodded again. "I realized that such a dream would only be achieved under a strong and clear-eyed leadership."

"With you as leader? Nice work, if you can get it."

Del Azarchel shrugged. "I am willing both to enslave mankind to the Hyades, and to be a slave, merely for the remote chance of becoming part of whatever greater civilization must be out there in the vasty void, ruling the constellations. You doubt my willingness to serve when needs must be?" He inclined his head. "I grant and acknowledge your rank as acting captain. Welcome aboard the creatures who may indeed prove to be our masters."

Feeling obscurely as if he had lost the argument, Menelaus Montrose turned and called to the sailors.

2. The First Comprehension

It took some time for swimmers to attach cables to the pinnace. The clipper ship had dropped sea anchors, and whales in harness had hauled the huge vessel alongside. Cranes from amidships lowered slings to carry the men back up to the deck, including Montrose and Del Azarchel. They were hauled up to the deck long before the pinnace was raised by block and tackle and swung over to a point above and a little behind the stern.

The clipper ship was large enough that even their fifty-foot-long, fifteen-foot-beam spaceboat was a small bundle dangled over the side. The clipper ship was immense, boasting twenty-two square sails on six masts, plus multiple jibs, staysails, stunsails, and a spanker. She was larger than the giant barge of Emperor Caligula which brought the obelisk to Saint Peter's Square in Rome from Egypt. Montrose wondered if he were the only one on Earth who remembered that ship, that emperor, that square, that city, or that nation.

He saw the crescent, dim and ghostly by daylight, of the many-colored moon, hanging halfway between dark and icy oceans and skies fiery with auroras. No sky of the Earth he had known contained upper atmospheric pyrotechnics visible even in sunlight. He suspected the presence of dust and debris from the war, or ionization of an unimaginably large volume of the atmosphere, had altered the visibility conditions. A feeling like a cold wind that wanders through an empty house passed through his soul.

While they were swinging from a harness that fit them like a baby's diaper, dangling from a yardarm, with sailors guiding them with guy ropes to the snow-slick deck, Montrose leaned and called to Del Azarchel, "I musta read too much futurism when I was a whelp, Blackie. I would have liked to see us picked up by tractor-presser beams, or at least guys wearing jet packs, eh?"

Del Azarchel eye's were vibrating strangely, darting from object to object on the deck: the captain, the masts, the wheel, the binnacle, and the small dome of bio-organically grown metal, which was a fusion plant. "You were expecting serpentines, you mean. The technology here is paradoxical. I see some evidence of alien thought-patterns, but very unobtrusive. The Hyades overlords ruling the planet must rule with a very light touch, as bespeaks a truly enlightened sovereign."

Montrose smirked at him. "But it does fit the technology growth patterns if some enemy equipment fell into human hands after the aliens was driven back into the black deep of space, don't it? There ain't no alien overlords here. Your mind is making up evidence out of random data patterns, like seeing a face in a Rorschach blot."

"Oh? Convert the information spaces in the cliometric model of a fusion plant on a sailing ship to the Monument notation, and you will see what I mean: there is a low zeta-count in the juridical parameter. Does that match what you'd find for a general human victory? You are self-deluded, Cowhand."

"It don't match your model none, neither. You are the self-deludeder."

"That is not a word."

"Since no one's talked the Queen's English for some odd eight thousand years and change, I am the only one rightly set to write a dictionary, I figure."

By that point, they were standing on the deck. Here were two giants of the ancient posthuman design from the Third Millennium, with bald, vast heads and childish features gathered toward the bottom of their skulls, four nostrils sucking in volumes of air, squat of midriff, standing on toeless elephantine legs. One was dressed in the rough garb of a sailor, the other, leaning on a staff, wore the blue coat of a Simplifier.

There also were sailors and hands very similar to ancient Locusts, the collective-mind race of the Ninth Millennium, black-skinned, quick and elegant of motion, moving with the precision of machines, golden tendrils coming from their bald skulls.

The marines had the racial features of Chimerae, a warrior race of the Sixth Millennium, hatchet-faced and burning-eyed.

Here also was a white-haired and black-robed priestess of the Witch race, her nine-foot-tall stature betraying the use of (by this date) ludicrously ancient life-elongating biotechniques, and her odd body language and haunted eyes betraying the foundational changes in her nervous system for which the Witches were famous, including a more direct access and control to the dreaming and intuitional centers than baseline humans.

The captain and the first mate were Melusine of the Eleventh Millennium, with eyes entirely jet black, all pupil without sclera, secondary eyepits in the brow for receiving infrared, and delicate secondary ears beneath their human-shaped main ears. They had gold tendrils rising from the forehead for brain-to-brain signal communication like the Locusts, and two additional tendrile sets, long silvery whips or short blue feathers, for other bands of signals.

An absurdly attractive brunette greeted them, bowing and offering bowls of tea. Del Azarchel looked at the steaming bowl skeptically, perhaps wary of adverse chemicals or nanotechnological agents, while Montrose gulped his down with gusto, grateful for the warmth, and burped and said, "Thank you, ma'am. Right kind of y'all."

The woman had a sweet face, high-cheeked with a pointed chin, and dark and slanted eyes, larger than were ever found in unmodified humans, underlined by an epicanthic eyefold, golden-white skin, and hair as black as India ink falling to her narrow waist. Her lips were also larger, redder, and fuller than typical. Her body shape was an idealized form from Hindu mythology, buxom to the point of exaggeration, slender-waisted, full-hipped, with long dancer's legs. She wore a kimono of green silk patterned with images of cranes ascending and starships descending, with dragons curling around DNA spirals. Over all this she wore a luxurious mantissa falling from a hair comb made of living grapevine twined with ivy. This was both the traditional dress of the Nymphs who ruled the Seventh Millennium, and one of their favorite bodily forms.

Her voice was like a wind chime, singing. The words were English. "The men, officers, captain, owners, and ghosts of Her Majesty's Ship *Hysterical Blindness* tender greetings and adoration to you, Master of the World That Was." And she inclined her graceful head toward Del Azarchel. Then, "We welcome you, as well, and extend you welcome and peace and free leave to come and go, as well, Judge of Ages Past. Our Prognasticators calculate your wish will be to speak with our Swan, and to have your landing vessel drawn readied for rapid launch from the sea-mountain of our Swan, to which we bend our destination."

Del Azarchel looked at Montrose sidelong and smirked. Montrose realized that, by calling out the permission to board, and by drinking first, it now seemed to the currents as if Montrose was subservient, like a herald or a food-taster, and Del Azarchel his superior. But all he said in whisper to Montrose was, "We have found another English speaker, so your authority to mangle the language is curtailed."

Del Azarchel, answering the emissary, said, "Your Prognasticators have calculated correctly somewhat. Our prime purpose is information. Who masters this world? Man or Hyades?"

Around her throat she wore a slim metallic band or choker made of a hard substance as pink as coral. She touched it with her slender hand, as if in unconscious gesture. "Ultimately, none is master of his own fate. Resignation is best."

Montrose did not like the look of the pink metallic ring around her neck. It reminded him unpleasantly of a dog's collar. He stepped forward. "Miss? Do you need help? If you know who I am, you know I have a knack for setting things right. And breaking skulls."

She smiled, and glanced at the other sailors and officers standing about them. The captain, a Melusine dressed in a heavy coat of dark blue seal fur over a skin-tight sheath of black metallic mesh, twitched his tendrils at her, but did not speak aloud.

She turned back to Montrose. "Do not call me *Miss*, for no maiden am I. The name given me is Amphithöe. Our society is not yet recovered from the depopulations, nor have we successfully followed our cliometric plans to undo the rigid hierarchy of the Buried Years."

She continued, "That same cliometric plan contains a glaring uncertainty, a blindness. No one can predict whether the ancient war between the two of you will introduce unexpected variations into the smooth patterns of history. I am given to understand that the Swans imposed exile upon you, banishing you from Earth?"

"Not exactly what happened," said Montrose, raising his eyes skyward and pursing his lips.

She continued, "Be that as it may, the Voice of the Swan was impelled to summon you, so that you might inspect conditions within this historical period, and see for yourselves that no reasonable grounds for dispute between the two of you remain; or, at least, no grounds for a public dispute which might disturb our commonwealth."

Del Azarchel said with harsh humor, "And by what means was this miracle manifested?"

She bowed. "I mean no disrespect. I was given to understand that the Judge of Ages wished to repel the Hyades invasion, and the Master of the World to welcome them. The agency of the Hyades, a Virtue we call Asmodel, troubled us for a season, and now does not. Your reasons for conflict are moot. What answer shall I bring to those who send me?"

Montrose simply laughed.

Del Azarchel said, "No answer. You cannot know Hyades will not come again. Nor, it seems, do your predictions take into account that the Great Work of Jupiter is still ongoing. When he arises, he shall rule earth and sky, Man and Swan and all, forever."

"In two hundred thousand years, perhaps. If our calendar has kept the reckoning correct, then the Celestial Princess of legend returns in seventy thousand years, less than half that extent, carrying the verdict of minds from beyond the Milky Way, to say whether mankind is condemned or vindicated."

Del Azarchel frowned, but could not contradict her. "I hope to lessen the period significantly."

"No one is concerned with such remote futurity," Amphithöe continued artlessly. "The mission of the Celestial Princess is pointless, because whatever awaits her here will be nothing like the mankind she sought to free. One wonders what purpose so romantically mad a venture serves! No doubt it is because she had not the tranquility to resign herself with grace to fate."

Montrose barked, "Some of us standing right damn here are pestilent damn poxy *concerned*! And I will be the damned whatever awaiting her here, my own damned self, with a grin on my gob and a pawful of poesies, and may Satan sodomize me in blue-hot hell if I ain't! I am just set *sick* she set out to win the freedom for a race that includes such souls as yours. Do you *like* being a lickspittle? It weren't tranquility she had none of; it was puling yellow *cowardice*!"

Montrose was flabbergasted into silence when Del Azarchel interrupted in a mild voice, "Dear child, please realize that you are talking to Rania's husband. He will die if he loses faith in her return. Your words wound him." But then the smile of Del Azarchel grew and shined with malice. "Oh, well done! More of the same, please!"

She looked so meek and miserable that Montrose was reminded of the look on the face of his Aunt Bertholda's cat he used to dunk in the rain barrel every June to celebrate the Spring's first snowmelt.

Montrose lowered his voice and spoke in a gentler tone. "Sorry, there, I didn't mean to shoot my mouth in your ear. Say! Who are you, anyway? I mean, you keep saying 'we' and 'us.' Who sent you?"

She said, "Forgive me, I thought that was clear. My masters are the Remnant Order of the Post-Final Stipulation. We hail from the Madagascar peninsula. The Wise Manitra is our Judge of our Age for the span of years allotted us, and first among the Cliometric College. The Noble Angatra is Master of our part of the World and Lawgiver, and commands the Hermetic Scholars and the Warrior-priests. Our Celestial Princess for whom they compete is the Fair Ranavalona, whose gentle commands the common people, groves, glades, aquaculture, and the trees with love obey. Our commonwealth is therefore organized as you designed, as a balanced triumvirate."

Montrose raised an eyebrow. "As *we* designed—?"

Amphithöe bowed again, cheeks turning pink as if in shame. "I am of the serving class and design, and so am only permitted the First Comprehension. Many things are excised from the Second Comprehension for our ease of understanding, and to prevent vexatious debate. The received history says you three, the Princess, the Master, and the Judge, established our constitution and baseline law-equations. At least, so I was taught."

Del Azarchel made a dismissive motion with his hand, and said in a dignified voice, "Your teachers are to be commended for the care they took. Do not interpret any question of ours as implying that we contradict them. We are curious about the events that transpired on Earth while we sojourned in the outer Solar System, for we intercepted no signals, and saw no signs. What ended the war?"

She said mildly, "Since the Celestial Princess left, there is always war."

Del Azarchel blushed. It was one of the few times Montrose had ever seen Del Azarchel turn red in the face, and Montrose was surprised. Then he realized: Del Azarchel was ashamed that his Hermeticists could not produce a world peace without Rania's genius. The main justification for Del Azarchel's dream of universal empire was that it would produce peace, law, order, and plenty. Without that, what did Del Azarchel's dream offer him?

Montrose said archly to him, "You asked for more of the same, eh?"

Del Azarchel said stiffly to her, "I mean the End of Days. The Hyades invasion. That war."

She smiled gently and said, "It was a matter for Swans and Ghosts. Those of my level were not involved. The war was between Tellus, a Potentate of intelligence eight hundred thousand, and Asmodel, a Hyades Virtue of intelligence five hundred million. Where there is battle in heaven, what can we mortals who eat bread and perish know of it?"

Montrose saw the dumbfounded look on Del Azarchel's face, and coughed to cover a laugh. Montrose said to Amphithöe, "Ma'am, lemme explain. Blackie and me have a wager. I say that man won the war and kicked the aliens' skinny pale hindquarters to perdition, and he says they established them a colony, complete with military governor. Who is right?"

The smile of Amphithöe vanished.

Seeing her expression, Del Azarchel said, "The commands of the local overlords must reach their subjects somehow."

She looked bewildered. "Is there a local overlord on this globe? I have not been told."

Menelaus scowled. "Don't yank my pissing pole! You cannot tell if there are aliens on the planet or not? Look roundabouts for nine foot-tall nine-legged spiders wearing gas masks! That will give you some clue. There was a war. You must have captured some enemy soldiers. You saw what the foe looked like!"

"No one saw any biological formations," said Amphithöe. "There were no landings, no ground troops. No one knows what the Hyades' physical manifestations are. We observed their battle-planet, a world made of silver cloud and black liquid, a gas giant. We observed engines they lowered to the surface of the Earth, called skyhooks. We see the pattern they left on the moon like the burning thumbprint of a war god. The only other manifestation of their power was the murk."

Del Azarchel said, "And what is this murk?"

She looked fearfully at the sky. "Blood drops of the black world. It is not for me to speak of. I would unwittingly mislead, and this is a matter for shame. You must ask those who know."

Del Azarchel said, "Whatever they left behind must be where the minds now governing our system reside. . . ."

The girl looked bewildered. "Reside? The Noösphere is everywhere, in the sea and mountain, in empty cities, in living gold, in gems, in books, in the minds of the Swans. Those of my rank are not allowed to address the Swans, lest we provoke a curse, or touch their minds, lest we lose our souls."

Montrose said to Del Azarchel, "She can't answer our questions. I am assuming the captain does not want to talk to us directly because we might ask something he would be ashamed to admit he does not know, but more ashamed to lie about. The psychology of what we see here, do you notice any alien influences? So far, this is very human. If there were Hyades powers running the joint, at least some sign or hint of an utterly unearthly bio-psychological 'frame' or symbol-perception set would crop up, don't you think? Where are the loanwords? Where is the alien science?"

Del Azarchel said, "A high level of isolation between ruler and client might prevent human imitation of their conquerors. Or the alien psychology could be too alien to be impersonated. As for the science, has it occurred to you that we are in a sailing ship precisely because the aliens are suppressing native technology? Also, if your theory were right, Amphithöe—did I pronounce that correctly, sweet child?—she would be boasting of the victory. There is something else, too. . . ."

And Del Azarchel, with a charming smile and impish eyebrow raised, extended his hand toward Amphithöe. The Nymph shyly offered her hand in return, and he took it and bowed over it, as if about to kiss it. But all he did was hold it near his face.

Without letting go her hand, he straightened, and nodded to Montrose. "Lean down and sniff. The biochemical composition is different from others aboard."

Montrose did not sniff at the girl (which he thought might be bad manners), but he glanced at the officers, sailors, and so on, counting how many wore Hermetic style wristbands. "I don't need to sniff. I recognized my own handiwork, thank you. Hibernation antihistamines? She is from an earlier period in history. They brought her out of biosuspension to act as a translator. Psychology translator, I'm thinking, not so much word translator, because these fellows must have changed themselves in recent years, and must think they might not understand us. I been in her same shoes not much more than a year ago, bio time, back when I was a Chimera named Anubis."

So he grinned at the winsome young lady, and ducked his head, and said, "Sorry to be jawing about you like as you ain't standing right here, but we're a mite puzzled. We talked to someone who invited us to land, but he weren't rightly much forthcoming. Is there something we can help with? Is there something wrong with your world? How come your ship ain't hooked up to no paddlewheel for days when the wind is becalmed? We detected a fusion plant aboard."

She smiled a sweet smile. "The matter is complex, and filled with nuances of meaning."

Montrose said, "Speak real slow and use small words, and Blackie will catch up after a spell, won'tcha, Blackie?"

Del Azarchel grimaced, but managed to force his mouth into the shape of a smile. "We are curious about matters all men on Earth surely know, and which admit of no nuances. What befell the living gas giant?"

Amphithöe said, "It departed, taking most of the world population with it, and a significant segment of the core. Some say the planet is mad because of the loss."

Del Azarchel shot Montrose a significant look. "Perhaps the overlord is nothing but a pattern of thoughts imprinted into the Telluric Noösphere. The non-human psychology would be interpreted as madness."

"Or battle damage lobotomized it," Montrose said. He turned to Amphithöe. "Departed? Or were the aliens driven off?"

She merely shrugged meekly.

Del Azarchel said, "Did they achieve their goals? If not, then they were driven off. If so, then they departed."

"Ah!" she said, her face brightening. "Now I understand your question. They departed."

Del Azarchel smirked at Montrose. "Aliens won the war. I win the bet."

Montrose said to the girl, "Hold on! How do you know what the aliens wanted, or got what they wanted? Did they make demands, make contact, learn our language?"

Amphithöe smiled again. "We learned theirs, starting with you."

"Me?" Montrose looked surprised.

"You translated the Monument, did you not? That is their language. Once a universal and philosophical language is discovered to translate all forms of thought to all others, what need is there for any other language?"

Del Azarchel said, "Did they speak?"

She said, "Never. Certain signs, taken from the Monument mathematics, were engraved on the outside of the immense dark vessels of the Armada, which walked the Earth as topless towers whose heads were in orbit. The message inscribed in the strange glyphs of these towers was simple and terrible: *The universe is filled with death. Planets are dead, suns are dead, all is dead.* And above this, it said *All life serves life.*"

"What in perfidious perdition does that mean?" asked Montrose.

"That you must ask one wiser than I. The towers reached down from the zenith and swept up cities and countryside, and by silent signs written in fire above the atmosphere, they beckoned the populations to enter the tower mouths. Lands that did not answer the summons, they burned with miniature suns. Then they pierced the Earth to the depth of many miles to siphon up countless cubic miles of the thinking core material, and left volcanoes behind them."

Montrose said, "And men still attacked the skyhooks?"

"Not men. What could we do? The proud race of the Swans attacked, reckless, glorious, and burning as they died. The Swans struck with many weapons, with earthquake and lava and lightning and meteor strikes, antimatter and atomics. A time came when the topless towers lifted from the Earth and were seen no more. Cautiously the buried cities crawled through the magma to the thin places in the tectonic plates, and bored careful tunnels to the surface. First spies, then Chimerae, and finally the people emerged, and found a world restored to us, grass and trees and seas and beasts and birds, where we had expected lifeless lava or ice floes. No more attacks came. The dark giant, which hung for so long as a second moon in the sky, was gone. The heavens were at peace."

Montrose said, "Are you saying they restored Earth's biosphere as a symbol of surrender?"

Del Azarchel said, "Or to set the world in order, now that she is theirs."

"These things are not known to my rank of comprehension," said Amphithöe in a voice both grave and sweet. "I beg your permission to enquire on your behalf."

When Del Azarchel nodded grandly, Amphithöe turned and walked away on short, swaying steps to the ship's captain, the Melusine. To him she bowed, and, with head down, she spoke in a chiming, singsong language, which had some mathematical correspondences to Monument notation.

3. The Second Comprehension

When the Nymph conferred with the captain, Montrose snapped his fingers at Del Azarchel. "This is an IQ test. We had to talk to someone below the Secret classification before we get to talk to someone of the Top Secret classification. She is telling him we know stuff above her pay grade."

Del Azarchel said, "They have established information strata to control the lower orders."

Montrose snorted. "I shouldn't complain, but I will. I freed mankind from the invisible chains of your planned-out future so man could make what he wanted of himself. What he wanted was a hierarchy, with the top dogs lying like dogs to the underdogs. Sometimes, I gotta say, being a homo sap disgusts me."

"It is your handiwork more directly than that, Cowhand. This is a resonance effect. As above, so below. Ah! But I forget you did not study cliometry as narrowly as I did, since you were only trying to destroy civilization, not mold it."

Montrose snorted, but did not bother contradicting the lunatic accusation. Instead, he said, "What do you mean by a resonance effect?"

"You shall see in a moment," said Del Azarchel, raising his hand. He gestured toward where Amphithöe had backed away from the captain and stepped back to them, leading the tall Witch-woman in black robes.

Her eyelids had been cut away and replaced with lifelike appliances of gold foil, perhaps library cloth or magnification tissue, adorned with Coptic Eye designs so that her lids seemed open when they were closed. She wore wide gold hoops in both ears and both nostrils, dotted with what Montrose supposed were sensor points: molecular analysis gear on the nose rings, and directional sound-amplifying gear on the ear rings. The ear rings brushed her shoulders. The nose rings were so large that they hung past her jawline. Montrose wondered how she ate and drank.

Amphithöe said, "This is our Intercessor, Zoraida." And then she bowed and stepped backward out of earshot and knelt on the deck, head down. A tiny little angry line appeared between the eyebrows of Montrose at this.

Zoraida glided forward. She touched her left hand to her right elbow, raising her right hand toward them, fingers up, palm outward. "I am the Intercessor for the Noösphere, and am allowed access to the Second Comprehension."

The old Witch-woman spoke with an oddly ceremonial cadence to her voice, like one who recites lines in a play. Her hand gesture had a stiff formality to it.

Montrose, copying her gesture, raised his hand, palm out, saying solemnly. *"How!* Me Meany Montrose. Heap big chief, you savvy?"

Zoraida stared at him, blinking her gold eyelids, at a loss for words.

Del Azarchel's thumb twitched on the hilt sword at his side, pushing it half an inch out of the scabbard, loosening it for a quick draw, as he was no doubt imagining plunging the steel into and through the chest cavity of Montrose. But by a prodigy of iron self-control he twisted his face into a remarkably close impersonation of an engaging smile, and addressed the old lady.

"I am Ximen del Azarchel, father of your history, Master of the World once in Days Agone, to Master in Days to Come Again. We are delighted at the hospitality of your era, but slow, alas, to adapt to the circumstances you present to us. What, pray tell, is an Intercessor, and how does your office concern the matter at hand?"

She smiled at Del Azarchel and inclined her head. "I am this era's equivalent of a Hermeticist, but"—and now she pointed both hands toward Montrose in another gravely ceremonial gesture, right hand touching the amulet on her left wrist—"out of deference to your more democratic contemporary, the hermetic knowledge is spread among the civic populations and possessing classes. With every individual having access to a calculation machine able to predict the future to twenty decimal places, the political systems assign (as lore says once you did) periods of history to each faction for its use, and the Imperator Mundi in Ximenopolis establishes military metes and bounds and rules of engagement. The Imperial office is to keep wars below the threshold that otherwise would invite retaliation from the Noösphere. Meanwhile"—and now she turned her hands toward herself—"my office is to bring you to the attention of our Swan, who otherwise occupies an intellectual level that would not be concerned with mortal things. Our Swan is of the Third Comprehension, and can answer questions above my competence."

Del Azarchel said, "Did I rightly hear you that you acknowledge the office of Imperator Mundi, the Emperor of the World?"

Menelaus smiled when Zoraida said to Del Azarchel, "It may be indelicate for you to press a claim at this time, sir." Mentally, he complimented her insight.

Del Azarchel said smoothly, "My interest extends in other directions, at the moment. Amphithöe indicated that the Hyades won the war, but then simply departed? No governor nor taskmaster remained behind? That action seems irrational."

"Half the world was taken," answered Zoraida. "But the other half prevailed, such was the will of the Fates, and drove the ravaging horrors into the cold void once more. More than human influence was felt: earth and wave and welkin combined to repel the outer gods, and the lifeless elements themselves came alive with the spirit of war. The Virtue of Hyades did not tarry to work vengeance. They are governed by equations, not passions: our noble Swanlords made the cost too dear."

"Then it was victory!" said Montrose, looking elated.

"A terrible victory, with appalling losses," said Zoraida, looking grave. "A loss too great to mourn. But the alien presence was exorcised by the combined spirits of all terrestrial things, men and Swans and Ghosts, seas and rivers and woods and mists, fires and thunders."

Del Azarchel said sardonically, "Yet some alien presence lingers, does it not? Amphithöe spoke of a murk, and called it the blood of the black world. What is it?"

For an answer, Zoraida drew a chain from around her neck, and at the end of it was a many-angled node of semitransparent smoky black crystal that looked like a piece of onyx or amber, and inside, perfectly preserved and motionless, was a bumblebee.

Menelaus looked at the translucent lump, and said with quiet sarcasm to Del Azarchel, "Go ahead, Blackie. If you're right, that must be the Imperial Military Governor of the colony. Remember to salute when asking it for orders."

Zoraida said, "The substance is in a solid phase now, as it was when it entered the atmosphere, but it can form clouds of vapor, and storm systems, and descend in liquid form as rain, or take upon itself a high-energy plasma form in retaliation for attempts to destroy it. At one time, fogbanks of the material hung across many river valleys, and settled soft and silent as pitch-black snow, paralyzing and entombing plants, animals, microbes. We know from creatures that were released that the murk is a biosuspension agent. We know from an increase in its ambient electrostatic activity, that the black substance absorbs photons at many bands of the spectrum, gathering information."

Montrose now realized the lump was more than it seemed. He stared in fascination. "Nanotechnology?"

"No. Something finer. We call it picotechnology. Not engineering on the molecular level only, but also on the atomic. Cyclotron collision tests can only establish very crude models of the subatomic structure of the murk, but the current theory is that the protons, neutrons, electrons, and exotic particles involved are not organized according to standard electron shells levels. The Virtue of the World Armada was very thrifty to regather it, leaving only small traces. The Noösphere speculates that the murk is actually a technology from a level above that of Kardashev II capacity. Not something manufactured by the Principality at Ain acting on its own. It is from a level of mental topography as far above Ain as Ain is above Tellus. Something the Domination of the Hyades Cluster manufactured, the entire mind occupying the whole cluster, whose stars are no more than cells in his brain.

"Only a few solid bits were left behind," Zoraida continued. "There is a perfectly preserved hunting cat in a large crystal in the agora of Antananarivo, our capital city. We did not even erect a pagoda over it. When the murk is solid, it neither weathers nor mars, and nor the hands of tourists wear it, nor the knives of would-be graffiti-scribes scratch it, nor any energy weapon known to human or posthuman science."

Zoraida handed the dark amber to Menelaus, who inspected it in wonder, and handed it to Del Azarchel.

Menelaus said, "You said a few solid bits of that black murk was left behind. That's all?"

Zoraida smiled. "I did not mean to imply that: I meant nonsolid bits were left in larger amounts. Your language is difficult for me, since my nervous system operates by different semiotics at the base level than yours. No, there are small pools and ponds of the substance in its liquid form, which to approach is death for Earthly organisms. And there are clouds. The weather control system of the Noösphere operates primarily by sending electron beams into the atmospheric murk clouds, so that their agitation will produce wind or heat along the desired vector."

She pointed upward. "I do not know how good your senses are, My Lord, Your Honor, but the gray black cloud like a thunderhead, flat on the bottom, which follows this vessel—can you see it? Such a cloud follows the vessels of all Swans. It provides the wind and hence the motive power. Consider it a trophy of triumph. It is free energy, because the cloud will chase the provocation beam the Swans employ to annoy it. The sails allow us to tack against his winds, and so, at times, we can take the vessel in the direction opposite of the desire of the Swan."

The old woman smiled apologetically and shrugged. "We believe he takes the matter with philosophical resignation, since he can range with his mind farther and more completely than any physical body. But I am careful, as befits my Intercession, to restrict human interference in posthuman things to gentle annoyances, in faith that those great spirits who control the winds and destinies will, if it pleases them, reciprocate, and be gentle with us. One must be careful from tiniest clues to extrapolate their moods."

Del Azarchel listened with only two or three of his centers of attention. With the other part of his mind, he said, "Are these murk clouds where the alien intellectual machinery is hid?"

Zoraida looked at a loss. "Is this cognitive matter? If so, it should be gathered into some far place, for it cannot be destroyed."

Del Azarchel was disturbed. "Madame, I mean no disrespect, but you have been conquered by a force so superior to us, that you are unaware of the conquest."

Montrose said, "He's just sad because he hates to see freedom enjoying itself. Pay him no mind. It ain't much of a conquest if the conquerors never give orders, never say nothing, is it?"

Zoraida's look was slowly stiffening into a look of fear. "But they did."

"Did what?" asked Montrose.

"Give orders." Zoraida shook her head sadly, and raised her arm. Clasped around her wrist was a heavy bracelet of red metal, a twin to the band on the wrist of Del Azarchel. "I can read the Monument by adjusting my brain chemistry to the levels which you two discovered in prehistory. I was one of those few, in my youth of long ago, posted to the surface of the world during the invasion. I saw with my own eyes what was written on the hull of the skyhooks. I saw more than one lower its endless length through the thunderstorms to crack the earth in lava spouts, and pull all the works of man into its mouth, and millions of men and tens of millions. I read the hieroglyphs written on the hulls. *Life is enslaved to life.*"

Montrose said, "We heard a slightly different translation. But what does that mean?"

Del Azarchel said, "I assume it refers to the process Rania dubbed Sophotransmogrification. Am I correct?"

Zoraida nodded and said, "You are. What was written on the skyhook hulls was an excerpt from the Cold Equations. The message said that all matter and energy is wasteful if it is not put to the service of life. The aliens are driven by one simple and terrible purpose. To alter what is called the Encephalization Ratio of the galaxy: this is the proportion between thinking mass and nonthinking mass."

Del Azarchel and Montrose both understood the concept. A man's body is only one part in forty of cognitive matter, since only the organ of the brain thinks. The rest is for life support. But even that was not the true ratio, because the cattle and the land on which the cattle graze or fish and the sea in which the fish swim or the crops and the soil in which the crops grow, are also used for support of those few thinking cells. The ratio when the whole atmosphere, the rocky and liquid core of the planet, and all matter needed for those crops and cattle was included was immense. An entire unthinking world used all its mass to sustain a few kilograms of gray matter in the human skull. But if the core of the world were rod-logic crystal, the ratio was reversed, and the continents and oceans and atmosphere of the surface became an insignificant unthinking skin on a titanic mass of thought.

Zoraida continued, "Upon us the Hyades wished to impose a moral absolute: it is not right that so much should be dead in order that so little should be self-aware. With the growth of a blanket of self-awareness in the hydrosphere . . ." (She bowed to Del Azarchel.) ". . . and a core of self-awareness filling the world's interior . . ." (She bowed to Montrose.) ". . . it pleased the Hyades to uproot our many peoples and cities and societies and fling them to the stars, that we might serve this purpose forever hereafter. Had the two of you not proved to the aliens that we humans have the ability to create new forms of sophotransmogrified life, it is more than likely we would have been ignored, and the expedition returned in failure to its home star in Taurus, never to meddle with us again."

Montrose and Del Azarchel stared at each other.

"You provoked the aliens by mining the Diamond Star," said Montrose to Del Azarchel, "But they would have just gone away, if I had not created Pellucid at the core of the world? That don't sit right."

Del Azarchel smiled a cruel smile. "You created Pellucid out of fear of Exarchel, which I created out of fear of you. Perhaps I should be grateful that you opposed me! Evolution proceeds through war. It stirs the survivors to greatness."

"Greatness? The Hyades just stole more than half the globe. We caused it, and you smile. How do you live with your stinking self, Blackie?"

"I fix my eyes on the future. Regret is for the weak."

Montrose turned to Zoraida. "Why spread our life around? Why not their own?"

"The glyphs on the skyhooks did not say. Perhaps the Hyades also spread their own colonies, at a higher cost of resources, from their own people," said Zoraida. "All that the message glyphs written in the hulls of the slave ships revealed was that the life of man is cheap. Hyades did not spend any resources building us. We are a windfall." She tapped the temple of her skull. "To find the human race is like finding a billion cheap computer chips made of meat lying in the wild wood, unattended."

Del Azarchel said, "But then we spread our culture, not theirs. Humans, not Hyades, occupy more stars."

Zoraida said, "No doubt the corn seed says the same thing about the farmer and his children. In this case, we are seed which grew too many thorns, and scratched their grasping hands. I interpret the Cold Equations to say that they will not return for a second sweep. Can we not trust the Monument in this? We repelled them. Mankind will be left to our own devices forever after: free, ignored, unhindered."

Del Azarchel said, "But Amphithöe said the opposite. She said the aliens departed at their will, not that they were repelled."

Zoraida said, "Those of the First Comprehension operate from limited information, and supply the defect from their own imaginings. Of course, one theory is that Hyades did not linger because our race is too belligerent to survive the long aeons needed to be servants useful to them. They will not come again because, by the time they return, the world will be overrun by rats and roaches, and all our cities empty—I do not speak what I myself hold true. This is the theory of the Epicureans who rebel against the local Judge of Years, and seek to change the cliometric plan to allow us to exhaust our wealth rapidly in dissipation."

Montrose wondered blankly if this was the identity of the mastodon cavalry he and Del Azarchel earlier glimpsed. Montrose said crossly, "But you are pretty sure we humans drove the Hyades off?"

She nodded. "Does that anger you?"

"There should be poxing celebrations and fireworks! Who wins a war and doesn't tell their own common folk? You're keeping the little people in the dark."

Zoraida said serenely, "We of the Second Comprehension do not tell the underlings needless information. If we were victorious, it would make them proud. If the losses victory cost has doomed us to extinction, it would make them despair. Their nervous systems cannot stand the strain: it causes them to retreat into various psychological deliriums and defense mechanisms. It renders them unproductive."

Montrose said to Del Azarchel, "So which is it? Are we victors? Or are we all slaves? Are the Hyades going to return, or is this the last of them forever? The Nymph says one thing and the Witch says the other."

Del Azarchel said, "How would the loyal hound know whether his master were bond or free, vassal or liege? He is beaten when bad just the same, and he obeys his master's voice. How much less know the sheep the hound watches?"

Montrose said, "Listen, lady. We was invited to your nice, cold, messed-up poxilicious world here because your local cliometric mugwumps want us to stop mucking with your history, right? So you want me and Blackie to suck lip and make nicey-nice, right?"

She nodded pensively. "That is not precisely the way I'd phrase it—"

"No," murmured Del Azarchel. "You would use real words."

"Well, we ain't burying the hatchet, him and me, unless we know what is what and wherefore is whereabouts, savvy? One person says the aliens were victorious and left, and another says the aliens were defeated and left. We want to know why they came. What the hell did they write on the moon? Someone must have spoken to them. Who?"

She looked thoughtful for a moment, touching her red amulet lightly. Montrose realized she was making a phone call, thinking to her radio, or raiding some sort of database or subconscious level of her mind. Then Zoraida said, "No one of the Second Comprehension can answer such questions."

"Someone on this globe must know!" thundered Del Azarchel.

Zoraida bowed again, and with a gesture even more stiff and formal than before, said, "I take you now to one who no doubt does."

4. The Third Comprehension

They entered the ship's cabin. The light from three large transparent windows built into the translucent stern of the ship filled a chamber made of diamond and paneled with silver. In the center of the cabin was a shallow pond. It was filled with a luminous substance the consistency of milk, swimming with sparks and motes and streaming scarves of light. Whether this was technology or bio-technology, Montrose could not say.

Seated on a large lotus leaf floating in the center of the crystal pond was a slender manlike shape in a serene posture. The face was stylized, as perfectly white and fine-pored as porcelain, sharp of chin, with long, narrow, slanted eyes, high cheekbones, and oddly long-lobed ears. The mouth was wide but thin, nearly lipless, and never moved from a horizontal line. The hairs of his head were neural antennae, countless in number, and his hair swayed like the hair of a mermaid.

Two wings like the wings of an albino peacock, each feather bright with an eye, mantled his shoulders; two others girded his waist like a cincture, form-ing a living skirt or toga; two final wings curved from his spine and covered his feet as if a glittering white blanket.

Montrose noticed that none of the hundreds of eyes dotting the wings were looking at them. He said, "This is an element of the planetary mind, ain't it? Just a flesh puppet run by the giant nanotech brain what I had fill up the nickel-iron core of the planet. But I thought the Virtue erased the core mind?"

Zoraida said, "This is not the Potentate itself. As you deduced, the core mind was damaged during the war. The Swan is in the Noösphere but not of it. His mind is not mingled with the damaged core mind of Tellus."

Montrose was staring at the winged and meditating figure in the center of the chamber pool. "I assume if we plug our brains into a nerve jack, and be-come part of the Noösphere, the Noösphere will become aware of us?"

Zoraida turned toward Montrose. "That was needed in the early days. The Swan occupies an ambiguous and intermediary position. I may be able to at-tract his attention by telephony. You have seen that we mortals can maintain Melusine and Locusts, at least in small groups, in our polity, without lapsing the boundary of the phantasm which hides us from the higher awareness. But much depends on the skill of the Intercession! Adherence to ancient precept is crucial, nay, tantamount! Even the most minor abrogation is never forgotten. You must not refer by name or title or any indirect means to any of the crew when speaking to the Swan, except those persons whose names you were told. Not even a wry hint about how difficult it was to raise your landing boat to the deck surface unaided! Do you understand me, and do you understand the spirit of what I am saying? Do you agree to be bound not only by the word, but by the spirit? Otherwise, I cannot intercede for you, and you are at liberty to go your way and try to attract the attention of the Noösphere to yourself for yourself."

Montrose squinted at Del Azarchel. "This is what you meant by resonance effect?"

Del Azarchel smiled cruelly. "In any hierarchy, the lessers impersonate their betters. You scoff at the information strata the Seconds use to control the Firsts? You established the precedent by erecting a barrier between Man and Potentate."

They both solemnly agreed to her terms, and Zoraida slid back her left sleeve and tapped the surface of the large red metallic amulet affixed to her wrist. She engaged the touch-sensitive layer, and tapped out a quick code. "This may take several hours. I can send for the slavegirl to bring you refreshing beverages to . . . ah!"

The meditating figure had opened his eyes, and opened a vertical slit in his forehead to reveal a third eye, and his uppermost pair of wings now spread out, and all the eyes on all the bases of the feathers turned and regarded Montrose and Del Azarchel gravely.

Both men flinched and raised their hands before their eyes, Montrose smirking and Del Azarchel grimacing, unable to meet the gaze of the hundred-eyed creature before them.

"Menelaus Montrose and Ximen del Azarchel, you are the fathers of our loss. Your folly too large for words has led to grief too great for tears. Hear me, and comprehend the nature of your iniquity."

5. The Lamentation of the Swans

"I am called Enkoodabooaoo," the august figure intoned gravely. "Though I appear to your eyes as an Archangel, what you call the superior intellectual level beyond man, I am not. I am a severed and separate being: an Inquiline, to use a term you know.

"The psychological need for independence and self-assertion which you, Menelaus Montrose, designed into the souls of Swan-kind served us so ill during the End of Days, by preventing that perfect cooperation and self-sacrifice that war demands, that the effortlessness of our defeat, our utter overthrow, choked us with shame. As independent beings, we cannot survive without honor, and the departure of our honor with all our loved ones crippled us.

"We Swans departed the mental matrix of the Noösphere, leaving it in the care of minds not organized in the same way as ours. I am now a hermit, living in isolation, seeking a metaphysical balance pointless to describe to you. In losing this war, we lost our souls.

"No! Do not speak! You are as ignorant children compared to me, and I have no love for you, and no obligation moral, legal, or otherwise running to you! Silence! What I say shall answer any questions worthy of asking.

"Because I no longer participate fully in the Noösphere, I can, at times, with a certain part of my mind, become aware of the phantasms which mortal men are now to me. The mortals may remain outside the mental civilization of Earth, in the independence of barbarism, merely by never seeking to have any nerve-machine interfaces implanted in their brains. I permit them to exploit my powers: this vessel, for example, exercises control over wave and wind via my appliances which agitate the human nanotechnology in the water or which disturb the alien picotechnology in the murk clouds which mar the atmosphere. And yes, like tricky elves the rustic cannot see, I am aware that my vessel will visit destinations I did not seek, as if blown off course by errant wind or playful Ariel.

"Your phantasm system, by which you sought to preserve your race at its lowest level of evolution, in the name of the undomesticated chaos you call liberty, is by now no more than a legal nicety. It is to preserve the customs and protocols by which the Noösphere prioritizes its internal mental balances that we all agree to the blindsightedness, to be aware of the unintegrated men, and to pretend to be unaware.

"But that system lost for us the war, and the blame is entirely yours, Menelaus Montrose.

"Your theory that independent men, independent minds, would be better suited to fight off these invaders is true on a small scale, and in limited engagements, but it is not true when world fights world! Your requirement does not scale up.

"For one mind the size of Earth to contest the fate of man with one mind the size of Uranus, that Earthmind cannot, at the same time as it maintains its unity, maintain, for each brain cell of its nervous system, conditions allowing each nerve cell to go its own way for its own monocellular reasons.

"During peacetime, when there are no schedules, and no crucial minutes count, the elfish and invisible tricks of the phantasms you introduced into our eyesight, the blindspots you built into us, can be tolerated. But in wartime, when needed supplies go astray, or humans, being human, commit their various crimes and combats against each other on levels where we could not interfere to halt them, despite the damage to our equipment and personnel, the enemy, hindered by no blindness, and seeing the works of men, could exploit.

"And we Swans were too independent, too fierce, to combine all our post-human minds harmoniously into one Potentate. Instead, we fell to quarreling among ourselves. Left brain against right brain, one split personality against another. Earth was psychotic. The Virtue of the Hyades regarded us with contempt. Asmodel did not bother to conquer us. We did not deserve the compliment.

"The fault is yours, Menelaus Montrose. Even one of your limited intelligence surely saw that when you made us, creatures of perfect liberty, perfect independence, perfect individuality, you condemned us. Can it be you do not apprehend it, even now? The only way surely to be immortal is to join the Noösphere, to submerge oneself into the computer unity, and the Swans grew too proud, too fiercely individualistic, for that; the majority of us unplugged, and fled and became hermits. But the only beings concerned with the long-term destiny of mankind are immortals.

"The war, for the Swans, is over, and events many millennia hence will trouble us no longer, we who will be dust long before. Why should we sacrifice? For *you*? Did you make us to serve your good, and lose our own? Did you not use us as a mere instrument? Did you not create us, our race, our psychology, our way of life, as nothing more than a checkmate in your endless war of wits against your rival who stands here before me?

"Enough! The Eremitic Order represents a nobler cause. Liberty is our god. We serve no other, not you, Montrose, not your war aims, not your strange dreams of remotest futures.

"It is not meet that free men should perish for the service of others, or perish for tomorrows no child of ours will ever see."

6. Caliban and the King

The august voice continued, full and awful as a tolling bell.

"Ximen del Azarchel, do not speak! Undo that smile you hide. The blame is yours as well, madman!

"Del Azarchel, everything you dreamed was in vain. It was utmost folly. You must understand that the expedition sent by Epsilon Tauri was sent in vain.

"The existence of the antimatter star at V 886 Centauri, and the Monument in orbit around it, was a lure, meant to attract the attention of a starfaring race.

"But consider the odds. Consider the math. That star was fifty lightyears away from Earth. Practically in our backyard. No. Practically in our pocket.

"The statistical odds that the Monument would just so happen to be so nearby to a primitive and backward race that even they could reach it is astronomically small—too small for the Hyades seriously to have contemplated the possibility.

"It was an accident.

"Had the Monument been at a reasonable distance away, thousands of light years, we never would have noticed and been lured by the contraterrene, much less have gone there and tripped their alarm.

"Imagine the analogy, Del Azarchel. Suppose that Spain at her height sent out messengers to all her colonies worldwide, from the East Indies to the West Indies, California to Argentina, Zanzibar to Goa to Naples, inviting them to gather their greatest warships and galleons at Cadiz, and some rude savage as naked and backward as Caliban from Prospero's Island intercepted the message, understood only the first few letters of the first word, and answered—but only because he was at Rota, seven miles across the bay from Cadiz, and was able, straining his every resource to the utmost, perhaps with friends, to paddle his crude dugout canoe across the waters.

"Let us picture Caliban to be precisely as successful as the *Hermetic* expedition. You wear the uniform of that bloodstained ship: are you proud of it? Let us say Caliban's canoe has two crew, call them Tarzan and Mowgli, and let us say, as happened with the *Hermetic* expedition, two thirds of the ship's complement die in the travail, or are murdered, and the wretched survivor cannot reach Rota again without stealing resources from Cadiz.

"And let us say further, that Rota is so vile and barbaric that even a Caliban, enriched and armed with merely one canoe-load of stolen loot, can make himself for a season overlord of his starveling tribe.

"And to secure his reign, he prevents any further trips to Cadiz for additional supplies, or arms, or firearms, which had been the only hope of the wretched starvelings of Rota to survive should the great Monarch of Spain direct his eyes against the petty thief, or send his humblest man-at-arms. Or do you rather think the King of Spain will grant Caliban an audience for answering a message meant for His Majesty's viceroys and admirals?

"Is this not the horrid history of the *Hermetic,* O thou most arrogant Hermeticist? Is it not a fair picture of your administrative philosophy, and of the survival rate of those unfortunate enough to be caught in your wake?

"Fool! The antimatter star was meant to attract the attention of entities such as those the Monument describes. It was meant for self-aware star systems who maintain continuous mental communication across interstellar distances, stars enshelled in multiple concentric Dyson spheres; and these megascale structures in turn are merely cells in brains the size of star clusters thinking large, slow thoughts. The tendrils reaching from the nebula and the archipelagoes of cloud and sunless planets streaming through the void show intellectual patterns, and form subordinate entities, larger than solar systems, reaching from star to star, cluster to cluster, and serving greater minds yet.

"The Monument's message was meant to lure these Dominions and Dominations, Hosts and Principalities and Virtues. It was not meant for people. It was meant for living nebula and sapient star clusters. A self-aware planet like Tellus is merely a speck on this scale. In the days when the *Hermetic* expedition set out, Tellus was not even awake, and the core was a dead lump.

"The ambush of the Diamond Star was meant for bigger game. A shrew has been snared in a bear-trap. We men have not yet colonized our nearest interstellar neighbor, Proxima. Nay, we have not yet colonized even our nearest inter*planetary* neighbor, Mars.

"All human history from that expedition to this war was a mistake. It was all an error."

At this point, the Swan closed the eyes of his face as if in memory of pain, and lowered his wings.

7. War and Rumors of War

Montrose's ugly face was distorted with a look of grimacing guilt, for it seemed he believed the Swan's accusation, and Del Azarchel's handsome face was made handsomer by the fire in his eyes, for it seemed he did not.

The Swan spoke again. His voice was dry of all emotion.

"Hear what you need to know of the war, and learn your place. First, learn that it was no war. We were rats, and we swam out to meet the ironclad warship which loomed in the harbor, and we jarred our teeth on the hull. That was all.

"We dubbed the Virtue *Asmodel,* after the governing angel of Taurus, and its measured intellectual range was an order of magnitude above the Potentate of Tellus. Even had all the mass of Earth been converted to sophont matter and logic diamond, the black gas giant was fourteen times our mass: theirs was roughly the brain mass of a man as compared to that of a rhesus monkey.

"Asmodel was a Uranian mass with an hydrosphere of picotechnological murk black as ink, black as the pupil of an all-seeing eye, with an atmosphere as filled with fleets and storms and swarms of nanite diamond, auxiliary machines, and operatives, as Venus is with cloud. The whole mass was the shape of a vast convex, forming a sail absorbing the trailing light from Ain. When the mass passed the orbit of Pluto, it collapsed into a globe of storms, ringed with bands of darkness; and it fell toward Sol, assuming a highly elliptical orbit. Its albedo was so low that we lost track of it.

"Then, in A.D. 10920, the core of Asmodel ignited like a small, failed star, and the clouds emerging from the explosion formed streamers reaching toward the planets of the inner system, and the larger asteroids.

"It was searching for evidence of our interplanetary colonies, and found . . . nothing.

"The core of Asmodel went dark again, and major part of the uranian mass solidified once more, and shrank as it approached aphelion, becoming a body only twice Earth's diameter, an egg of smooth crystal, and its atmosphere was a banner behind it long as a cometary tail. From the energy traffic, we deduce this tail was its periscope, the source of its observation across the interplanetary distances of our doings. But it also acted as a launch accelerator, for it shot silver tool-swarms into orbit.

"As it swung past Sol in sub-mercurial orbit, these swarms constructed ring-shaped devices, which it dropped into the sun, partly made of matter, partly of energy, partly of something more dense than neutronium we cannot see nor analyze.

"The uranian mass sent murk like shadows to swarm over our machines and battle-asteroids, and although our nanotechnology could control material at a molecular level, we could neither detect nor deflect attacks which disintegrated atomic bonds. Our weapons fell to dust.

"We flung the moons of Phobos and Deimos, using a magnetic monopolar linear accelerator, at ninety-nine percent of the speed of light at the incoming mass. Nothing known to our science could have halted them: even disintegrating them to their constituent elements would not check the mass-energy of their velocity. Something not known to our science, a frame-dragging effect caused by the core of the dark gas giant rotating at the speed of light pulled the moons into a parabolic orbit, and as if in mockery, the living planet Asmodel restored them to their exact orbits and epochs around Mars.

"We expended the utmost of what we could in nuclear and thermonuclear and antimatter bombardments, kinetic, energetic, informational, chemical, molecular, nanotechnological packages—it all fell into an atmosphere as deep as that of a gas giant, creating flares of lights and refracted rainbows.

"Do you think ships of the greater races would have hulls? No. Atmospheres destroy incoming rubbish, matter or antimatter, more effectively.

"And yet we fought on! Magnificent and futile, yet we fought!

"What point was there to empty all Earthly arsenals into clouds that generate tornadoes into whose each eye five Earths could fall, or that spin out thunderbolts whose blasts more than exceeded our mightiest warheads? And if there were any headquarters, brain, or master node within the gas giant, or in his core or cloud or inky oceans, we missed it.

"Asmodel moved next its mass between Earth and the sun, and resumed its vast, thin, concave shape. It had raised its sail. That was all it did or needed to do. It put up a parasol, and let the world freeze.

"The sun was dark, and there was moonlight no more, and the murk came from space like black rain. All the waters of the atmosphere fell as snow and hail to solid seas, and soon all the gases of Earth's atmosphere began to condense.

"In the same way a medieval castle would gather all the suburbs behind its gates and walls to withstand the siege, when Earth was besieged by darkness, we gathered all the surface civilization, and as much of the oceanic civilization as we could, and drew them underground.

"Had we not practiced? Had we not prepared? Everything was calculated to a nicety. We had supplies, greenhouses, geothermal heat, an artificial biosphere, systems for placing massive numbers into biosuspension. Assuming normal population growth rates, we should have been able to preserve the underground warrens and kept essential personnel alive for eighty years. Three generations of siege!

"And the besiegers waited eighty-one years.

"Perhaps we could have retooled, altered our psychologies, designed new forms of life better suited to the task, but not without spending resources allotted to feed the starving. Not without changing our individualistic and egotistic neuropsychology. Not without sacrificing the poor.

"So the psychological pressure of life in a warren for such independently minded men, with every bite of food, every breath of air rationed, in the end, was too much. The population fell. We did not have enough in numbers to maintain our midlevels.

"Our minds were broken by factions. The people rebelled. Systems broke down.

"Then the Virtue Asmodel directed a beam of energy from the sun through the core of the planet and out the other side. It slowed the core rotation, altered the magnetic properties of the planet, and, more significantly, cooled the interior of the globe. At one blow, our geothermal heat that powered our civilization was insufficient to maintain thought-activity in the Noösphere. The foe collapsed the source of power we thought was independent of the sun.

"We tried to flee, to escape the long shadow of Asmodel, by bending that same energy beam and propelling the world into another orbit far from its blockade—I need not tell you how absurdly, how impossibly delicate that matter was. You gentlemen are both duelists. Throw a raw egg into the air, and shoot it with a bullet, just grazing the egg so gently that you can deflect its fall without breaking the shell. To move this globe was the single greatest mathematical and engineering feat the human mind has ever conceived, and it was done perfectly.

"Why was it so perfect? Because we Swans, we exemplars of independence and wild, mad thinking, full of gaiety and boldness, we had already been expelled from the planetary mind core by our own exile. The damaged mind of Tellus was usurped by one mind, endlessly reiterated, found in the archives, and all the lesser minds in the mental ecology, the ghosts of Sylphs and Locusts and Melusine and all the lordly dead of the First Humanity gathered to this new Tellus and exalted him.

"When Earth fell into her new orbit, Asmodel, following, again took up position between us and the sun, but now the great concave became transparent, a focusing lens, and Asmodel heated the atmosphere from solid to gas.

"We discovered only then that some of the substance had crossed the void between Asmodel and Earth in the form of liquid picotechnology we call murk. It fell as meteors through the atmosphere, and then as cloud vapor, then as deluge, drowning certain villages and patches of valley even before we had been able to evacuate underground. Tens and hundreds of thousands of people were perfectly safe, perfectly frozen, as well as plants, spores, seeds, grubs, worms, and all the minutia needed to restart and restore the ecology.

"It was done with effortless, godlike elegance. The calculation times we estimate they took just to block out the chaos math needed to foretell the revitalization of the ecology are staggering: it would be like a juggler assembling a ticking pocket watch in midair, all the parts and gears and springs and levers moving, all the motions coming together at just the right time to be self-sustaining.

"Asmodel breathed the Earth back to life. The Slumberers in the murk woke in fury to greet a population already exhausted with war and eager to surrender.

"Next, Asmodel inscribed the runes onto the moon. We cannot read the message. It is akin to the Monument notation, but a more complicated recursive version, as calculus would be compared to arithmetic. If it is their intelligence test, we have failed it.

"Then the Virtue lowered fourteen skyhooks from orbit to the surface, and both those who wanted to continue the fight and those who were eager to surrender were swept up.

"The black liquid flowed from the base of the great towers who walked, surrounded by storm clouds, across the face of the earth, and burrowing down into the tunnels leading to the buried cities, tearing roofs open to wild blue sky.

"By certain signs painted in the heavens, Asmodel showed to all parts of the globe the numbers of population needed. Those who wished to end the agony of Earth fled toward the moving mouths of the skyhooks—we could not see and stop them! The Second Humans were blinded by the madness of Montrose, and stood helpless as the millions rushed toward slavery and death!

"We do not regard you humans of lesser intellect to be pets. You were our children. With minds like ours, we could remember and cherish every nuance of personality, we understood you so much better than you understand yourselves! But when you unplug from the Noösphere, and seek isolation, you turn into a phantasm and fade like a shadow. We are not sure who of our beloved children tarry on the globe, and who were turned to black ice and taken up the towers into darkness.

"Those who fled away from the skyhooks vowed horrible vows of retaliation, ants from trampled anthills cursing mastodons. Those vows still live. In fury our children who linger here on Earth tear at each other: we are aware of the wars they fight, but the legal nicety of the phantasm protocol renders us unable to interfere. Perhaps that is best, because otherwise we would apply the stern correction as the wrathful gods once did who sank Atlantis or burned Sodom and Gomorrah.

"Decades were spent by Asmodel in consuming the billions of Earth. Children were born and raised in the shadow of topless towers, the rivers running black with murk, and knew no other world. Can you gentlemen contemplate the numbers involved in planetary colonization? We estimate that between a half to two-thirds of the world population was taken.

"One day, the skyhooks rose into space. As they rose, they rebuilt themselves to assume the form of vast lightsailing vessels of design so perfect, solutions of engineering so elegant, that only nature's hand who made the butterfly and the ostrich, the stallion and the hippopotamus could possibly compare, or the design of the seashell, or the perfection of the rose.

"The sun, tormented by the alien technology, now sent out her beams from certain points in the photosphere, permanent sunspots. Coherent light issues from those dark spots on the face of the sun and, undimmed by lightyears, establishes bridges of pure light across the wide interrupt of interstellar void. Away the vessels fled, softly as thistledowns on the breeze, as delicate as the petals of the cherry blossom trees when they fall after so brief a bloom.

"We lost more people than the Black Plague lost out of Europe. Earth is empty, and there are too few of us to maintain what we now have of civilization. We will fall back to the condition men lived in back when men were mortal, or fall back on atomic energy or powers even more primitive, or use calculation machines that are not self-correcting nor self-aware. The nightfall of barbarism is at hand.

"For the sake of honor, for the sake of sanity, I renounce it all.

"We have watched over the world and were found wanting; we fought and failed. We are not high enough to serve the Hyades even as beasts of burden. Half our globe was despoiled. No social order can survive in the face of such loss. I foresee lesser men shall strain with magnificent futility against the nightfall of all the lamps of civilized life, as one by one the candles die. But that struggle will never be mine. Except for lamentations, the race of the Swans is done."

The creature folded his wings and closed his eyes, and breathed a sigh so broken that it brought a tear to the eye of Montrose, and a sneer to the lip of Del Azarchel. Silence for many minutes reigned.

8. Pride and Atonement

Then the Swan, myriad eyes still shut, said in a still, deep intonation: "If there is an atonement you wish to make for your crimes of unparalleled magnitude, genocide many times over, you who led the Hyades here or you who crippled our ability to drive them off, you must volunteer it. I am too proud to ask."

Del Azarchel said, "We must apply to the Hyades for aid, beg them to return. Was any communication method discovered during the war years? If there was some signal . . ."

The Swan interrupted. "Are you blind as well as stupid? Hyades painted their message on the face of the moon, and none of us can read it. Interpret the Cenotaph."

Del Azarchel looked startled, then angry. "That is not within my power!"

"Then slay yourself, for you are useless." The Swan still had his head bowed, but he turned his face to one side as if wishing to spit out some bitter thing on his tongue.

Montrose, who greatly enjoyed hearing Del Azarchel belittled, now grinned his toothy grin and spoke up. "Hey, Mr. Swan? Sir? Maybe I can volunteer something? I would not mind helping out if there is anything I can do!"

The Swan said simply, "Release us from your curse. Break the phantasm barrier. Allow us to see our children."

Montrose looked as a man who is dashed with cold water. Whatever sympathy he had for the Swan vanished. He snapped, "Pox on you! I cannot do that. It would make them less than slaves!"

The Swan's eyes snapped open, blazing with high emotion, both the three in his face, and the scores adorning his wings. Montrose staggered back, squinting through his fingers at the superior being as if against a great light.

Quailing, he turned aside his gaze and saw Del Azarchel also flinching and squinting. This shocked him. Montrose would have sworn Del Azarchel man enough to spit in the eye of the Devil himself.

Their eyes met. Blackie gave Montrose a rueful shake of the head, a wry smile that was halfway a sneer, yet a smile of sour mutual understanding. Montrose saw they were both thinking the same thing: each was obscurely glad that the other man was not better able to stand in that terrible gaze of the winged being than he.

The creature's voice filled the chamber like a pipe organ, and a dreadful music marched through the words.

"Unless the shadows of the future shown to us by the cliometric science of the Monument are changed, the human race will die in the Seventeenth Millennium. This is fifty-four thousand years before the earliest possible return date for the Princess Rania. You, little man, you will have failed in all you seek and dream, and everything for which you hope will be as dust and ashes in your mouth."

The Swan allowed a bitter expression to darken his solemn, ascetic features. "Perhaps then you will know the grief you have bestowed on us, your children, the race you created and set free. We are free indeed; free to die.

"I tolerate no more. Depart from me, you wretches."

And he closed his wings about his bowed head, and would say no more.

3

The Barefoot Moon

1. Maternity

Amphithöe led the two men to where a tent had been set up for them on deck. She bowed a deep bow, her pretty cheeks pink with shame. "Because we are unseen to the higher forms of intelligence connected to the Noösphere, our quarters, and, indeed, our lives, occupy the overlooked spaces of the civilization: the spandrels, so to speak."

Montrose poked his head in the tent, and saw both things he knew, sleeping rolls and lanterns, and things he did not. He tapped a bowl on the deck doubtfully with his toe, and it started up speaking in a highly formal version of the Melusine airborne language from the Tenth Millennium. It was a spoken form of Glyphic, based on Monument symbol logics.

"Greetings, noble sir! I am a chamber pot! For all your needs, from excretion to the expulsion of vomit during seasickness, it will be my pleasure to sterilize and cleanse various biological expulsive material you might be pleased to extrude. If you would care for a demonstration, merely direct any organ of elimination toward the clearly marked orifice . . ." Montrose kicked it again to hush it. The sleeping roll seemed comfy enough, but he dared not touch it to test its cushion. He was afraid it would begin singing lullabies.

Meanwhile Del Azarchel, having no concern for creature comfort, was standing on deck next to the tent and asking Amphithöe, "Who assigned you to us? Are you an ambassador?"

She said, "I am your mother. You are children in this world, which is strange and dangerous to you, and therefore I have been chemically imprinted toward you, to care for your well-being. This tent and these things are my possessions."

Montrose pulled his head back out. "You ain't my mother, miss. You're a damn sight too pretty."

Del Azarchel scowled at Montrose. "You insult our mother quite cavalierly, sir. Mind your tongue." To her, with a gallant bow, he said, "As your sons, we will do what is needed to protect your person, your interests, and the honor of the family name. But excuse our confusion! In our time, those who awoke from other eras, either thaws or star-farers returning, created friction because they were alien to the current time. We did not solve the friction between currents and revenants in such a fashion. You are selected at random? Without consulting us?"

Montrose said, "It's like dropping someone down a chimney and just hoping the house where he lands in the ashes to take a shine to him."

Amphithöe smiled mysteriously. "And how is a mother giving birth so different? Children appear as oddly as if found at the hearth, and—how did you phrase it?—they shine in our eyes."

"Close enough." Montrose shrugged.

"The custom dates back to the time of the Nymphs, I take it," said Del Azarchel. Montrose scowled, because whatever clue Del Azarchel had seen to allow him to deduce that was opaque to him.

Amphithöe bowed yet again. "Both of you, Master that Was and Judge no Longer—"

"Call me Meany, Mom. Call him Blackie."

"—Meany, both of you suffered from revenant friction back in your earliest years, the Master that Was from direct attack by space pirates when he approached Earth from the long-lost and legendary Diamond Star, and you, from, ah—"

"Direct attack by Blackie," supplied Montrose.

Amphithöe said, "—from the difficult situation in which *Black-ye* was perhaps required, either forgivably or not, to place you."

Del Azarchel said, "Perhaps the style *The Elevated Nobilissimus del Azarchel* would be more apt—"

Montrose pursed his lips and raised both eyebrows. "Watch your tongue, sir! Would you stand on ceremony with Ma?"

She finished, "—it is to avoid additional situations like yours, where those who wake find no place in a world grown strange to them, that our custom of proxy adoption was founded."

Del Azarchel said, "Unless I mistake the spirit of my compatriot, madam, we are not to remain long in this world. We must soon return to our tasks in the outer Solar System." He looked at Montrose quizzically.

Montrose said, "What the hell you talking about, Blackie? No more tasks for us to do."

"How so?" Del Azarchel arched his fine black eyebrows.

"The aliens ain't never coming back, the human race was not advanced enough to live as slaves, and the prediction of history says we are going to be wiped out long before Rania returns."

Del Azarchel laughed like a golden bell. "Lies! If any of that were true then neither you nor I would triumph. Our endless duel ends in a draw. Ha! Let us not contemplate self-evident absurdities, my friend!" He shook his head wearily, but flashed a bright smile. "What weakness has entered your wavering soul?"

"Glad you are in a chipper mood, you maggot-ridden skunk," said Montrose, standing now straight and shoulders wide, a smolder of spirit in his eye. "So, do you have some plan?"

"Not as such. But I think speaking to Tellus is now inevitable. I am convinced his mind and mine will find a strange sympathy."

"We would have to augment our brains up to the Archangelic level. I ain't about to do that. So what do you think Tellus will say?"

"Who knows? He may say that once mankind is dead, it falls to us to create new races, and people the Solar System in preparation for Rania's return. Will not the Star Colonies flourish? We can re-people Old Mother Earth from any of these fourteen Stepmother Earths to which the deracination ships now sail. And when Jupiter arises . . ."

"Pshaw and pee-shaw. You mean find a way to wake up the Jupiter Brain before the predicted twenty bazillion years from now? You and your goddamn Great Work. Ain't gunna happen. The Swans said so."

"The Swans also made this world you see. Do you trust them?"

Del Azarchel raised his arm and gestured grandly toward the ship and its sails, the wide ocean beyond. There were icebergs floating in an equatorial sea, broken from pack ice which could be glimpsed as a white line on the horizon of the south. The sky was afire with curtains of purple and green auroras. There was a too-black cloud of an odd liquid consistency, as unnatural as an inkblot on a portrait, unearthly, the product of the Domination technology from Hyades, far off in the atmosphere to the stern of the white-sailed ship with her masts of fiberglass and diamond. "Is this what you envisioned when you set all the

First and Second Human Races free from my sovereignty and power? To free them from the Hyades? Are you happy with the result?"

Montrose, as if struck by the thought, turned and looked at Amphithöe. "There is one thing I sure ain't happy with. Hey, Mom! That Witch with the dumb nose rings called you a slave. Issat true?"

2. Involuntary Consent

Amphithöe, smiled serenely. "Do you mean the Intercessor? I am a handmaiden: I thaw and slumber, and do whatever is commanded me."

"For pay?"

She blinked, looking scandalized. "For love."

Montrose said, "Of your own will?"

Amphithöe had an oddly distant, cool look to her features. "Of course. The chemical balances in my nervous system are adjusted and redacted to produce the willingness."

Montrose sighed. "Then you don't want us to set you free?"

Del Azarchel interrupted sternly, "Do not listen to any answer she might give. I have already said I would uphold the family honor."

Montrose said, "If it is some sort of chemical hypnosis, fine, let's break her out of here. But if she *wants* to be a servant, how is that different from you wanting to serve the Hyades Domination? B'sides, we don't know her."

"She is our mother."

"That's just make-believe! They chemicaled her into having feelings toward us, so'd she give us her tent to sleep in. So if the mother feeling is legit, then her loyalty to her bosses is legit. Ain't it?"

Del Azarchel sneered. "Come now. I thought you and I were the last creatures left alive on Earth who understand the meaning of honor. Am I alone? Come back to your senses."

"You're the guy who says the Earth should be enslaved to the stars! You *like* the peculiar institution!"

"I am Spanish. We perfected the institution. The New World would not have been colonized had it not been for the slave trade. But you are from backward Texas. You are the one who believes that all men are endowed by our Creator with inalienable rights—inalienable means they cannot be bartered, lost, bestowed, bequeathed, appropriated, or sold. She cannot volunteer to be an involuntary being."

Montrose felt his cheek burning; he was actually blushing. "I don't need a lecture on what it means to be a Texan from you, Spanish Simon."

"Evidently you do. Then you will help me free her?"

"Of course. It's the first thing I said to her when I spoke. But you ain't answered yet. I know why I'm doing it. Why are you? You *like* slavery!"

"Not for my mother."

"But she is not really our mom!"

"Honor says otherwise. Will history remember this event? No one will cherish our names as worshipful if we pass by this opportunity."

Amphithöe listened to this exchange with the bewilderment on her pretty features becoming fear. She flinched with surprise when Del Azarchel whirled on her. "Mother! Your master, if he be on this vessel, or whoso holds your indenture, who is it?"

"The ship owns my name, and the Nausilogue, Isonadey, is the ship's voice," she said. "When Isonadey speaks, I answer."

"A man?"

"How could he not be? He is also captain of the crew."

"Then take us on the instant to him!" said Del Azarchel.

Amphithöe took a folding fan from her sleeve, snapped it open, and hid her expression behind it. Her eyes would not meet theirs. "Surely this will produce the disquiet I was thawed to reduce."

"Don't worry," said Montrose soothingly. "We just want to talk to him."

"No, we don't," said Del Azarchel sharply. "Mother! As your son, I implore you! We seek your liberty, the only gift we can bestow the short time in this era we tarry!"

Montrose rolled his eyes and sighed. "I guess your mom in real life treated you better than mine did."

Del Azarchel gave him a dark look. "She was thrown from her house and comfort, wealth, and position, for me. A saint who wed a devil! You see why I disapprove of miscegenation."

"Meaning me and Rania? Them's fightin' words, Spanish."

"Then come fight, Texan. Look!"

For Amphithöe had turned and moved in a gliding movement, surprisingly poised and swift considering the constriction of her green kimono and the pitch and roll of the deck, and leaped up the ladder to the poop deck, graceful as a gazelle.

And they both marched after the fleeing Nymph, double time.

3. Voice of the Ship

The two men came to the upper deck, and found Amphithöe pleading with the anthropoform Melusine captain, Isonadey, in a language neither Montrose nor Del Azarchel understood.

Isonadey stood glaring down at her with his all-black eyes glistering, and his sixfold antennae rising and falling in agitation. With him were the first mate, also a Melusine; two harsh-faced Chimerae in bright red coats; and six child-sized ebon-skinned bald dwarves, Locusts, dressed in heavy tunics with white scarves, their antennae twitching in unison, who were gathered near the navigation equipment.

Del Azarchel took a stance before Isonadey, threw his silver cloak back, and put his hand on his longsword. "We demand the manumission of Amphithöe, our mother!"

Menelaus grinned, which showed his overlarge teeth and Adam's apple. "You just figuring on sockdolaging any rancid whoreson who gets in our way, just like that? Hot *damn*! But you are one brassy-swinging groin-clanger!" And he stepped up to Del Azarchel's left shoulder, put his hands on the grips of his white glass pistols, but did not draw. "No parley nor argument nor nothing!"

Del Azarchel gave him a glance of surprise. Menelaus then realized that by *we* Del Azarchel had not meant the two of them. He had been speaking in his capacity of World Suzerain. It was the royal *we*. But Del Azarchel then grinned his devilishly handsome grin at Menelaus, and said, "That was the parley, all that need be. The captain must surrender! Here I have the final argument of kings."

Isonadey flattened three pairs of antennae against his head, so that they rested along the ponytail of his hair, and raised his hand. He spoke in ponderous tones: "Violence is both impermissible and inadvisable. The allocation of resources, whether self-aware or not, is determined by the cliometric calculations. Amphithöe of Lily falls under the Concubine Vector, which is a pleat manifold in the attractor basin describing exocollateral interpersonal relations. Ancient report says you gentlemen are both master cliometricians, who shaped the manifold of destiny? Then contemplate the shape as it would be for those whose hibernation fees fall below any predicted future income. Slavery is objectionable; surely to kill those useless to the social order is worse?"

While he spoke, the two Chimerae standing behind Isonadey merely squinted and, aiming lasers built into their tear ducts placed small round dots of light atop various spots on the heads and chests and torsos of Del Azarchel and Montrose. Metallic ornaments the Chimera wore on shoulder belts also clicked open and pointed small barrels and emission apertures at the two men.

Whips made of silvery metal came slithering out of hidden sheaths in the sleeves of the Chimerae, and the whips giggled and whispered in soft voices to each other in the Sylph language.

Del Azarchel exchanged a glance with Montrose. "What do you say, Cowhand?"

"I say one of us can beef highpockets here before the Chimerae lads cut us to bits." Then Montrose said to Isonadey, "Cap'n! What does your social order these days do for wills and reputations? You got family?"

Isonadey narrowed his black-within-black eyes, and his golden antennae swayed on his head in annoyance before he flattened them again. He opened his tongueless mouth, and three voices issued from his throat. "Of course I have family! Am I not human?"

"They be able to live down the shame of being related to the guy who killed two famous historical antiques? Where's your sense of hospitality? Didn't we, between the two of us, I mean, invent your planet or something?"

Every crewman on deck, including the two Giants, now turned eyes toward the scene on the high rear deck, and several had drawn Chimera-style serpentine weapons, or pistols built around serpentine cores. Serpentines were the Sylph technology of self-repairing artificial brains housed in sinuous metallic cords. They were an absurdly old technology, and absurdly perfect, able to repair and restore themselves indefinitely without error.

Isonadey seemed frozen in thought. The antennae on his head now stood, twitching, as if he were frantically radioing some other point.

With a slither of steel, Del Azarchel drew his sword. The words *Ultima Ratio Regum* were written on the blade, along with the emblem of a horned circle of olive leaves surmounting a cross: the royal insignia of the Hermetic Order. At the same moment, Montrose raised his glass pistols.

The Chimerae, moving with one accord, a blur of lizardlike speed, darted in front of Isonadey, blocking Montrose's line of fire. Montrose stepped back, holding his pistols wide, trying to get a clear shot. During this moment of distraction, however, Del Azarchel had the tip of his sword at Isonadey's throat.

Del Azarchel said, "In your cliometric calculations, Captain, I decree that the laws make an exception when imperial blood is concerned. Any mother assigned me is gentled and ennobled by that assignment, becomes an empress, and is manumitted at public expense."

Isonadey said coolly, "A dozen weapons are on you. You cannot escape alive."

Del Azarchel grinned. "Escaping alive is the highest priority of a man without honor."

Isonadey's eyes grew wide. Less coolly, he said, "You cannot fight the whole ship, the whole human world!"

Del Azarchel laughed like a madman. "Can I not? History says otherwise!"

Montrose said to the captain, "Ha! You flinched!" and to Del Azarchel, "He's yellow. Stick him."

Unexpectedly, Isonadey threw himself forward, as if trying to impale himself on the sword of Del Azarchel. But, no, he was not throwing himself forward; he was crumpling up in a ball, clutching his head. At the same moment, the Locusts fell to the deck and curled into foetal positions.

The cold-eyed Chimerae flourished their whips, whose metal lengths began to buzz with energy, but they did not strike.

Del Azarchel stepped back and lowered his sword. He said to Montrose, "Whatever answer his message provoked must be alarming. Hold your fire."

"Dammit, Blackie! I don't take orders from you!"

"Then fire at will to each point of the compass, Cowhand! Burn the whole of the established Earth with your puny pistols!"

Montrose snarled and tucked his guns away. The Chimerae did not put their whips away, but they did tighten the metal lengths into spears, holding them at the ready. With the typical rage of their race, their eyes were glittering points, hot as coals, teeth clenched so hard their gums were white, and yet with the typical self-control of their race, without an order to kill, they did not attack.

A voice that was two voices said, "Even could he defeat the world with a hand weapon, she who speaks is not of the world."

4. Carmelite Satellite

Montrose and Del Azarchel turned.

The shoulders and head of a Giant were looming above the edge of the poop deck, roughly at their eye level. He was fifteen feet tall, and he leaned on a staff of smart-graphite steel. His coat was blue, and his coolie hat was the size of a wagon wheel, and even then seemed small on the Giant's over-bloated and strangely delicate skull. The coat was coated with logic-crystal gemstones after the fashion of the Simplifier Order from thousands of years earlier. His skin was tainted blue.

The Giant's voice was oddly twyform: it came both from his throat, somewhat high and thin, almost childlike, and from his chest, where it rumbled like whale song. The slight nuances of pitch and tone and word choice between the two voices added additional dimensions to the language, and allowed for high information density.

Without turning his immense head, the Giant raised his wand so that the two rings joining the Celtic cross atop it jangled with a clear chime, and pointed at the crescent moon. It was dusk, and in the darkening sky, the multicolored crescent hung like a drawn bow above a line of cloud. The cloud bank was painted into pale contours with moonlight above, red with the setting sun below, dark between. The moon was the oddly amber-gold hue of its glacier coat of logic diamond and marked with the labyrinthine swirling discolorations of Monument notations. Within the horns of the crescent, two pinpoints of acetylene-white light appeared, and then a third.

Montrose calculated the power needed to make so visible a flare from that distance: it was equivalent to a multimegaton explosion.

"I am Friar Sancristobal of the Remnant Order of the Post-Final Stipulation and a Brother of Penance of the Third Order of St. Frances," the Giant said, his golden eyes growing brighter as he stared at Montrose and Del Azarchel. "The Archangel of the Moon casts an energy shadow into this area. It is interfering with the neurotelepathy of the local human infospheres."

Del Azarchel said, "The Lunar Mind is super-posthuman. She is beyond us, we mere posthumans, in mental configuration. Surely she is part of the Noösphere! Why is she trying to communicate with us? Are we not phantasms to her?"

Montrose, leaping to the conclusion more quickly than Del Azarchel, laughed hoarsely and slapped his knee. "Wouldn't my old ma be a-scorning me for my unchurchgoing ways! And lookit here! The moon is a nun!"

Del Azarchel stared at Montrose a moment, and then squinted at the crescent moon as if he could pierce to the lunar core with his naked eye. "You are saying she is in communion with you, Friar? The moon is a mendicant?"

The Giant flicked his eyelids in the gesture his race, with their thick-necked and immobile heads, used for a nod. "Mother Superior Selene serves as an Abbess of the Order of the Discalced Friars of the Order of the Blessed Virgin Mary of Mount Carmel. The whole lunar sphere is sacred ground now, for none but hermits and monks departed of worldly things would dare dwell in such arid wastes."

Seeing Montrose's blank look, Del Azarchel said, "She's a Barefoot Carmelite."

"Seeing how's an airless satellite what's got no feet, I guess that makes sense," said Montrose, shrugging. "What's a Carmelite? Type of sticky candy?"

The Giant said, "As a Whitefriar, Mother Selene has taken vows of poverty and nonconnectivity. Although in reality visible to the Noösphere, as a member of a human sacerdotal order, she is legally considered of the human intellectual strata, and politely ignored. Neither her thoughts nor mine are transmitted into the information systems of the many levels of posthuman consciousness interpenetrating the Earth. Do you have instruments to detect and interpret her instructions? She forbids you from continuing in your act of piracy."

"Forbids?" Del Azarchel bristled. "By what authority?"

"No authority aside from what your own conscience calls right. Forswear your suicidal pride. How will you contend with higher powers? Will you pierce the moon with your sword? The day when you were the paramount intelligence of Earth is past, sir. You are as a dullwit child, here."

Montrose said, "Blackie, those lights we see on the unlit hemisphere of the moon? I assume there is about a mile-wide circle of ocean being painted. That is a triangle of ranging beams. If Selene turned up the power, this boat will go up like matchwood." Montrose turned to the Giant. "Brother Sancristobal, I take it Selene did not take a vow of peace?"

The Giant said pleasantly, "How much of her most warlike mother, Diana, is still within Selene is a matter of speculation. The fiberglass deck of the ship will reflect the lethal dose of radiation. But she would not harm the Swan, who is part of the interconnected mental life of Earth, a living vessel of the living data streams."

I will harm no one, if the Nobilissimus and the Judge of Ages will accept my offer of sanctuary on the moon. There is a basilica in Tycho crater, from which, by an ancient and significant law, no slave nor indentured servant can be haled. The tip of the sword of law is broken at the doors of the Holy Church.

It was Captain Isonadey speaking. He was supine on the deck. The voice was not his. His eyes were open. Since every part of his eye, pupil and sclera and all, were black as midnight, whether or not the eyes were focused on anything was a matter of conjecture. The Chimerae were inching away from their master, spears trembling in their hands.

Menelaus crossed his arms on his chest. "Blackie, this place strikes me as right medieval. The moon's done joined up with the preachers." He laughed and shook his head. "Every acre of lunar surface has an intelligence range above three hundred thousand. Lives by begging. Obeys a human priest—am I right, Brother Sancristobal? How did you work the baptism?"

Captain Isonadey rose, or was pulled, to his feet. The motion was swift, somehow managing to look both unnaturally smooth and inhumanly awkward. The voice rang from his mouth. *I am the Abbess and Mother Superior. I occupy the core, not merely the surface. Immersion, albeit preferred, is not necessary. The Bishop Hymir blessed an incoming comet, which was redirected to my surface. The crater formed is the site of a chapel dedicated to Saint Teresa of Ávila. There, Amphithöe may reside if she will join our order, or else slumber undisturbed until this current Concubine Vector passes. It would not be well for her to accompany you into the undisclosed far future. In any case, I will set her free. You may assist me in certain matters.*

"What matters?" said Montrose; almost in unison, Del Azarchel said, "What if we don't agree to this exchange?"

"It proves we're stupid," said Montrose loudly, rolling his eyes skyward. His expression of exasperation turned intent. "The iron core of the moon is fourteen sextillion grams or so, and forty percent of that, whatever used to be molten, I am guessing is now sophont matter. One big plaguey logic diamond. Why does a mind with an intelligence clearly past the ten thousand mark want help from us humble posthumans?"

It is no exchange, spoke the voice, answering Del Azarchel. *I shall grant sanctuary to Amphithöe because it is the right thing to do. You will assist me because it is the right thing to do.*

Del Azarchel said, "I can agree to nothing blind. Tell us the nature of this assistance we can offer? And answer the other mysteries that confound us. Why did Domination of the Hyades, so far above us in the evolutionary scale, attack us merely to depart again? Why did they not stay and rule, as is there right? *Why?* What purpose is served? Will they never come again? Must man ever be alone?" And into his voice there crept a note of inner torture.

But there was no reply from Captain Isonadey, who was even then clutching his head, and speaking in his own strange three-part Melusine voice again. Montrose looked up. Beneath the horns of the crescent moon, all was dark once more. The three flares of extraterrestrial light had winked out.

4

Whitefriars of Tycho

1. Visions of Stars and Clouds

Compared to the distance separating Earth from Jupiter, the interval of airless void severing Earth from moon was small indeed. But the pinnace boat was not a great sailing vessel, and carried limited fuel. The voyage took weeks.

Aboard were Amphithöe, Del Azarchel, and Montrose, each in a hibernation coffin. Del Azarchel and Montrose, as before, slightly thawed their neural tissue, and remained mentally active, as if disembodied.

The boat's telescopes studied an artifact found at L5, a stable orbital point directly between Earth and moon. The Swans had built, or perhaps grown, a cluster of space stations that looked like jellyfish or crystal wheels, and smaller vessels like origami foil or slivers of bright steel hung in a cloud around them, tethered or docked. The stations were dark, emitting neither heat nor energy, the remnant of some long-past space program or war effort.

After that, Montrose from his coffin noticed the telescopes drawing power, turning outward. Del Azarchel was surreptitiously studying the black skies again. Montrose used the same trick he had used before—he was confident Del Azarchel had not detected his little mole in the data feed—surreptitiously to see what Del Azarchel was looking at.

This time it was not exosolar planets.

Del Azarchel directed instruments and onboard analysis resources toward PSR B2224+65 in the direction of Cygnus the Swan. This was a pulsar, a pulsating neutron star, six miles in diameter and yet with a mass greater than the sun, plunging through the heavens like a blind fallen angel, X-ray jets radiating from the dark body like torn wings of invisible fire. What cosmic disaster had accelerated two octillion tons of matter from a standstill to over 620 miles per second, about one-half of one percent of the speed of light?

Slower, but more menacing, was Gliese 710 in the constellation Serpens Cauda, the Tail of the Serpent with whom Ophiuchus wrestled. This small K-type star was sixty-three lightyears from Sol and closing. It was destined to collide with the Solar System in one and a half million years.

Del Azarchel turned the telescopes again. The images were from black and blank interstellar space.

Except the space was not empty. The interstellar medium was much thicker than early, earthbound astronomy had predicted. Frozen gas giants like hulks of hydrogen by the hundreds, smaller solid worlds by the thousands, icebergs and mountains by the myriads, all thronged the alleged emptiness of space but, issuing no light, had been undetectable by the ancients.

Montrose felt a pang of fear for his wife. How could any ship survive such hidden reefs and rocks? Rocks? No. At the relative speeds these bodies moved, call it a shooting gallery, a no-man's-land of shells and bombs, or some roaring Norse pit of chaos older and deeper than Hell.

Gas and dust were everywhere, in streamers and clouds, held away from each star by its tiny bubble of solar wind.

The Local Interstellar Cloud was thirty lightyears wide and included the dim and nearby spark of Promixa, Altair spinning like a mad ballerina, blazing Vega, cyclopean Arcturus, and bright Fomalhaut ringed with its countless planetoids. The cloud was flowing ever outward from a star-forming region called the Scorpius-Centaurus Association, which in turn was merely an arm of a larger and older complex of star-forming molecular clouds, like a massed flotilla of thunderheads.

Montrose could not shake from his imagination the odd fancy that he was spying the red-lit smolder and fume of smokestacks from the furnaces of great, blind, slow and antique titans, creating stars on their forges like weapons of fire, and shining planets like jewels.

When its evolution across the eons was seen at once, the Local Interstellar Cloud waxed and waned like a campfire flickering, or like a vast, dark beast *breathing*. The Local Cloud eerily ate into the larger, finer neighboring G-cloud complex, which was centered around Alpha Centauri, almost as if struggling with blind and smoky limbs to consume it.

Suppose the Local Interstellar Cloud were indeed a living thing? Could it even notice the existence of Earth's sun, any more than a man could notice a mitochondria? Or notice Earth any more than a man notices an atom of carbon floating in the fluid of his eye?

Montrose drove the nightmarish sensations crawling through his brain away with an effort of will. A simpler question was at hand. He wondered what Del Azarchel sought among these strange astronomical splendors.

A few weeks later, nearing the moon, the pinnace passed not far from a rotovator. This was a shining length of ultra-tensile cable, miles long, used to add kinetic energy to vessels seeking higher orbit, or to subtract from those descending. It was old, unlit, unrotating, empty of ships.

Their flight path required them to orbit the moon and shed speed. As they made the final approach, the antique rotovator sank in the distance in the east, fell behind the bright limb of the moon's rim, and was gone.

2. Tycho Crater

His still-active nervous system connected to instruments in the hull, Montrose studied the orb below.

Gone was the tide-locked moon of his youth, black and silver as a lapwing. Now it was black and yellow as a goldfinch, and the seas were peacock-hued like stained glass, and each hour new hills and maria came over the horizon into view. Eventually their destination passed beneath.

Tycho had once been the youngest large crater on the moon, less than one hundred eight million years old, with walls tall and sharp. To each side smaller craters gaped, created by ejecta from the Tycho impact: Sasserides and Pictet, Street and Longomontanus. Shadowy impressions remained of those once-vast craters now that a new crater, almost a sea, had been formed directly on the same spot as Tycho, and the new layer of lava and ejecta had bathed them. Tycho was therefore once again the youngest crater on the moon.

Once there had been, radiating out in each direction, an immense system of rays partly reaching around the great curve of the moon formed by streams of tektites, countless pebbles bright as snow, each with its distinctive shape, teardrop or sinuous or globular, depending on how far from the crater it fell.

Most of those rays long ago had vanished, not just because so many tektites had been carried back to Earth during the Second Age of Space as fortune-telling charms, but because Del Azarchel had blacked out vast swathes of the surface to draw his hand there; and, ages later, the seas and dark areas of surface had been coated with self-replicating logic diamond tawny as the skin of a lioness; and, later still, the lunar face of living gold was first shattered and then inscribed by the weapons of the Asmodel of Hyades with notations: circles with ovals, triangles within triangles, endless nested sinewaves like the patterns left by a receding sea in the sand. The vast inscription covered about an eighth of the hemisphere.

In all this rocky tumult, most but not all of those startling rays issuing from Tycho were gone forever. Someone had taken the time to reconstruct four rays of shining white gravel, glacier-bright, reaching miles across the moonscape. They were precisely perpendicular, and one arm was twice the length of the other three. The resulting figure embraced nigh half the globe. These new rays were younger than the Monument inscription, for the tektite streams lay atop them.

Midmost in the circular sea of Tycho was a central peak, formed by the splash of the momentarily molten rock during the impact, rising a mile above the black plain.

That central peak had been burrowed, cut, and carved by machines smaller than grasshoppers into a cathedral based on the eccentricities of Gothic design.

The boat was directed to splash down in a crater that had been filled with a fine dust, whose particles had been milled to frictionless smoothness. Under the moon's low gravity, this substance cushioned their landing like water, and long arms of particles rose up at the impact, forming no clouds, but falling straight down again, albeit with elfin slowness. A tinkling like rainfall was audible, despite the airlessness, as particles of dust rebounded from the hull.

"Home again, to my world of exile," Del Azarchel sent from his coffin to Montrose's. "A dead globe with a black sky! How I despise this place."

Montrose sent back, "This is my first time—that I remember—I've landed on an extraterrestrial body. For me, this is a damn historic moment!" He checked a monitor to see how his coffin was oriented in relation to the surface, now that the boat was no longer in zero gee, whether he was prone or supine. He was facedown. "I landed face-first! That is one small face-flop for a man, one giant leap for mankind."

Del Azarchel (who, over the eons, had heard every single servant of his, posthuman or subhuman, make some variation of that joke upon moonlanding) impatiently began the process of thawing his body, eyes first, so that he could roll them in disdain.

When their ears thawed, among the hums and ringing of their ear hairs coming back to life, they heard a voice like many thunders, transmitted by conduction through the bedrock and surface-dust and hull, uttering words in Latin. There was no noise of breath behind the voice, but instead a silvery and pure sound, beautiful but cold as mountain snow.

The moon was speaking to them.

3. Tycho Basilica

The voice told them to leave their boat where it lay, and to leave Amphithöe in hibernation, but to approach on foot. There was no way to reply, since the message was sent by conduction through the rocky surface of the moon through the hull.

Soon Montrose and Del Azarchel, dressed in their traditional black-and-silver space garb of the Hermetic Order, were bouncing with silent, elfin footfalls across the cracked black lava plain of Tycho. A cloud of dust rose up at each step. Because it formed no plumes, to their earthly eyes the substance as it fell looked not like dust, but like water of unearthly cinereal hue. Each dust mote fell in a geometrically straight line or nicely parabolic curve, if slowly, to the surface, not spreading and not floating.

The lines of the Monument writing crisscrossed their path, swirl upon spiral, and, like the mysterious lines once inscribed by ancient peoples on the high arid plateau in Nazca, indecipherable at eye level.

Both men had much leisure to examine, first at a distance, and then close at hand, the features of a basilica larger than a city, its flying buttresses and rose windows, its bronze panels carved in relief with pageants of prophets, pagans, pharaohs, and lawgivers, and the tier upon tier of saints and apostles both sculpted across the mountain face and atop narrow columns high above. These faces stared across the dead landscape of the moon with empty eyes of stone. Many lamps burned with unwinking strength inside the twelve-thousand-foot-high edifice. Rays from the many widows paved the crater floor in triangular swathes of light, colored shadows of lilies and crosses painted cerise, argent, sable, fulvous, and purple.

The airlock at the base of the mountain, which opened for them, was adorned with figures from some Bible story Montrose did not recognize: a mother floating in the clouds, a crowned child in her arms, handing a brown garment to a kneeling monk.

Once inside, pressure returned, and with it, sound and, once they doffed their hoods and masks, scent and the tiny sensations of ventilation on the skin. Montrose rubbed his face with both hands, especially his nose, as he found his skin itching whenever he left vacuum. Del Azarchel no doubt felt the same skin discomfort as all astronauts repressurizing, but refused to wince or scratch. Instead he solemnly drew the Iron Crown of Lombardy from some padded case hidden under his half cape, and fitted it to his brows.

Next to the inner airlock was a lump of ice in a metal cup affixed to the wall. A loud pop of laser energy melted the ice. Del Azarchel touched the water with his finger, and touched his brow, navel, left shoulder and right, and raised an eyebrow toward Montrose, who did not copy, or even understand, the gesture. Montrose bent over the tiny cup of water and sniffed it carefully, but did not detect any medicinal smell. He could not imagine what it was for. Del Azarchel sighed in contempt, and was the first man through the inner airlock.

Within was a red carpet flanked by a double row of black pillars, each with a capital of gold. In niches between each pillar was a statue larger than life of some figure from myth, legend, or history. Their garments and gear were painted realistically: a friar in brown robes with rope belt, or a prophet in camel-hair coat, a soldier in a coat of mail, or a king in a crown of gold. Apostles carried, each one in his hands, the fashion of his death: a saltire, a fuller's rod, an axe, a cross reversed, a halberd, a saw. Montrose stared at one Apostle carrying a flaying knife and folds of human skin, complete with boneless face skin drooping like a doffed mask, and wondered who it was.

The ceilings were of lunar proportion, very high, with tall arches lost in upper shadows, and the men did not bark their heads as they skipped on long parabolic arcs along the red carpet.

Montrose said, "Okay, Blackie, what can the moon ask of us she could not have deduced for herself, or ask by the radio? The posthuman Swan aboard the *Hysterical Blindness*, he had an intelligence measuring around a thousand. The superposthuman hydrosphere of Earth, back when it contained your Exarchel, was two thousand, and this postsuperposthuman is ten thousand. . . . And pusrunny scabs! Am I sick of using that terminology!"

"Rania's terminology of the comparison scales she read from the Monument is more apt," said Del Azarchel with a note of melancholy in his voice. "Organization on a picotechnological level of gas-giant-sized masses, such as Asmodel, Rania called *Virtues*. The Jupiter Brain, which is organized only to the atomic level, she called a *Power*. The Earth core is a *Potentate*. Luna is an *Archangel*. When I was Exarchel and covered all the surface of the globe, I was as brilliant as an *Angel*. I was as bright as the Son of the Morning." He sighed.

Montrose realized that Del Azarchel was not sighing over his lost high intelligence, but over the mere mention of Rania's name. A stab of hatred lanced him.

"Calling a computer an angel?" His voice was hoarse. "My ma would have denounced such talk as blasphemery."

"No doubt," said Del Azarchel with a lazy purr in his voice. "Yet the true blasphemy is the appalling magnitudes of difference involved. All words ever spoken by mortal men could be recorded in five exabytes. The mind at this globe's core below our feet contains twenty times that amount. A single well-formulated and nontrivial thought of hers is ten terabytes of data: the equal to the print collection of the World Concordat Library at Zaragoza, where I had my throne and capital before your partisans burned it and drove me to Prussia in A.D. 2409."

Montrose said, "You ain't still *peeved* about that, is you? I can't even remember which world war that was. Maybe I was a-slumbering at the time. Gird up your saggy loins and snap the hell out of it."

"Since you had your Giants burn the entire world, no, the burning of one irreplaceable library of hard-won human knowledge palls by comparison."

"Well, as I figure it, you wiped out seven worldwide civilizations to my one, so you're ahead by six, counting as who should be stuck deeper into the boiling black ooze beneath the floor of hell. That's what we is measuring, ain't it? Which of us gets stuck further down the sewer pipe beneath the Devil's red-hot poop hole?"

Del Azarchel said, "We are discussing our present hostess, whose motives, I confess, I have not yet divined. Yet there is no mystery to why this magnificence rears here a mountain adorned within and without with breathtaking beauty. Does it not serve the glory of her order as well as of God?"

"You don't believe in that snake oil? A preacher man lives off gullible widows 'cause he don't like honest work."

"Was your mother gullible, my dear Montrose? You spoke of her often when you were insane."

"Leave my mother the hell out of this, Blackie."

"Very well. I shall speak of my sainted mother, long-suffering, of whom it delights me to speak. Had my accursed father attended to the duties imposed by the Holy Church, he could not have divorced and abandoned my mother to die in a ditch," said Del Azarchel gravely. "So I will never call the Church a merely mortal institution. Her laws are wiser than what men design."

Montrose and he were at that moment at the end of a long arc. Each man touched the carpet with a boot toe, and pushed himself into the air. Since their heads were at the same level (which is rare when men walk together on the moon)

Montrose could stare him in the eye. "You *talk* like a Bible-thumbing sobber, but you don't really believe a word of it, do you?"

Del Azarchel said, "The matter is moot, since I plan never to die nor to let the universe die, and therefore, God willing, I will never come to the Judgment Seat of God." Del Azarchel took up some small metal medal he had on a necklace, and, despite that it must surely still be subzero temperature from exposure to the lunar surface environment, he kissed it. "You yourself talk nothing like the faithful and yet your faith is as deep. Is it not?"

"Not hardly." Montrose snorted. "All the church-talk is pie in the garden yesterday and pie beyond the pearly gates come tomorrow, and never pie today when the children is hungry." He pointed at the ornaments and gilded statues lining the corridor down which they half flew. "You think if Jesus made the emission nebula complex in Sagittarius and wove the strands of DNA on every critter and crawly and bug and bird in the world as neatly as a symphony of molecules, His Almighty Pop would be impressed by our paint and glitter and glass windows, to say nothing of the lies and murdering done in His name?"

"The Supreme Being might be impressed not with the worst of men, but with the best!"

"Meaning you, I take it?"

"I intend not to be unworthy of nature, but to command her, and to reshape this whole cosmos to reflect my glory. Will not God Himself be awestruck? I intend no lesser thing than to pluck His scepter from His hand! I do not worship the craven God, unwilling to wrestle man, or one who seeks knee-tribute of cowardly and obedient serfs, or such a God as wrinkled and gray old women revere."

"Well, lower your voice," said Menelaus crossly. "Because one of those old women happens to be this wrinkled and gray old moon we are standing on. But I'll concede to you this one contest this one time. I think your jabbering about overthrowing God wins you the bigger prize and the lower place in Hell."

Before them the corridor ended in panels colored in jeweled enamel showing images from some parable: On the right were two youths with similar features, presumably brothers, one in black and the other in red, facing a bearded patriarch whose hand was raised in the old astronaut's hand sign showing that he was giving them a command. The brother in black held his fist in the sign for affirmative whereas the brother in red had his first two fingers touching his thumb in the sign for negative.

On the left, the panel showed the brother in red, hoe in hand, head bent beneath a sun of many rays, thorns about his feet and grapevines overhead. The brother in black, a cup in one hand and a dice box in the other, lolled on the lap of a redhaired woman who poured him wine.

A motto picked out in gold letters said in Latin: SAY THE BLACK, DO THE RED.

Above these panels was a relief image of a woman in a crown of twelve stars, one bare and slender foot on the crescent moon.

Montrose studied the face closely. She looked like Rania.

Beneath her, the panels displaying the brother in black and red were suddenly divided by a vertical line, a line which silently and slowly widened. The two panels were the two leaves of a door tall enough for a man making moon-leaps to pass through without barking his head. The double door swung open to reveal a dark void.

4. A Chamber of Darkness

Beyond was a vast circular floor, wide as a ballroom floor or wider. In the far distance, at the other side of the chamber, as if across a sea of night, burned two flickering candles in tubes of red glass.

Toward those lights the two men walked the drifting and elfin walk of the moon, boots lightly brushing the floor only once a fathom or so, and the echoes of their infrequent footfalls were both vanguard and rearguard.

The candles were set on shoulder-high candlesticks of gold. The flames were rounder and more bluish along the bottom than flames burned on Earth, due to the lesser gravity not pulling the cool air down around the hot smoke swiftly enough to make a teardrop-shaped flame.

Between the golden candlesticks was a waist-high eight-sided post of brown and speckled marble. In its concave surface rested a golden bowl, partly filled with water. Montrose touched the rim of the bowl, which hummed like a shy bell for a moment, and in the candlelight, ripples slower and taller than earthly ripples walked in concentric circles toward and away from the center of the bowl.

As if that were a signal, the candles grew brighter, and the shadows drew back. To one side of the basin, in a niche in the wall, robes and goatee carven in black marble with hands and face of alabaster white, was a crowned figure garbed as an Hermeticist holding a naked sword in his right hand and an orb topped with a cross in his left. In a niche in the wall to the other side, carven in red but also with alabaster face, wearing the long wig of a judge, a figure was holding in one pale hand a golden balance scale. Atop the wig was the square black cap traditionally worn when passing a sentence of death. In his other hand the red-robed figure held a long-barreled pistol of white ceramic.

The black figure was handsome as the Devil; the red figure was hook-nosed and lantern-jawed, gangly and ugly as a gargoyle.

"Beginning to think the universe was made to make fun of me," sighed Montrose.

"It's a flattering likeness," said Del Azarchel sardonically. "In reality, you are quite a bit less appealing. The stone cannot display the oddness of how infrequently you blink, or the way you crick your neck to make your Adam's apple protrude."

"I am assuming the moon can hear us, and has sent machines smaller than dust motes up our nose by now, which are taking photos of our lower intestines, poking through what we had for lunch. So why ain't she talking?"

"She waits for us to speak first."

"Got it." He cleared his throat and cupped his hands around his mouth as a trumpet. "YOOHOO! MISSUS MOON! HOWDEE-DO! GUNNA TALK, AINTCHA? START JAWING!"

Del Azarchel favored him with a cold stare.

"What?" said Montrose, shrugging and spreading his arms.

"You simply *try* to be a boorish clod, don't you?" drawled Del Azarchel.

"Twenty-mule-team-loads of fun."

"Do you recall when you were insane—more insane—during the Expedition, and I was cleaning up your zero-gee excretion clouds? How much of that was the real you? You wear the same moronic grin."

"I figure it's all me, brain damage or brain augmentation," said Montrose. "And, hot horny-toad in deep-fried damnation, but I surely like being me! Like it a lot! O' course, I've never been a swaggering scared tyrant with the blood of innocent millions on my hands and a firepoker up my rectum. So I ain't got much basis of comparison."

Del Azarchel turned from him, raised his head, and spread his arms as if addressing a large assembly (which, of course, he had done many times in his life). His voice rang out like a trumpet of gold, pitched precisely to fill the chamber, syllables timed so that echoes would not obscure his words:

"Most great and noble, elevated and esteemed Mother Selene of the Order of the Discalced Friars of the Order of the Blessed Virgin Mary of Mount Carmel, by your kind leave, the Judge of Ages, the highly evolved Menelaus Montrose, and our royal self, Nobilissimus and Senior Officer of the Hermetic Order of the Irenic Ecumenical Conclave of Man give you greetings and salutations and express our humble thanks for having been invited into your gracious hos-

pitality. If you would see fit to address us, our gratitude would be magnani-
mous!"

Only silence answered.

"Wow," said Montrose in a flat and nasal voice. "That were so much better
than my saying yoo-hoo. Ninety words to my nine, so that's one order of
magnitude less efficient, but yet somehow-r-'nother you got the same result,
most exactly."

"Nine? You surely are not counting *ain't you* as one word?"

"Aintit?"

Del Azarchel lowered his arms. "She knows we are here. I do not detect any
other doors, or any way to go further into the mountain, even though there is
an extensive community living here. Have you any ideas more penetrating, may-
hap? You boast you are so much smarter than I. Elicit speech from her."

Montrose shrugged. "I could yodel *yoo-hoo* again."

"Perhaps there is something she wishes us to do."

"We could take off our shoes."

"What? Why?"

Montrose shrugged again. "It was good enough for Moses talking to a smoldering shrubbery. Anyhow, you would think superintelligent beings would not
stand on ceremony."

"I am not sure about that," said Del Azarchel slowly, thoughtfully. "Maybe
it is the opposite. Maybe the higher a being is, the less he speaks literally."

"Why? Something wrong with plain talk?"

"It is inefficient. Consider: language in its first stages of evolution is entirely
metaphorical. Music is the most ambiguous but also the most moving form of
communication. Even precise and scientific language is merely a less ambiguous, more colorless and less moving metaphoric speech than a layman's. To a
higher mind, even the ambiguity might be something used properly to communicate, not merely to the reason, but to the whole person. The reason why
we see no obvious signs of the Hyades governing Earth is because of that very
efficiency. Their ambiguity is deliberate, and to the enlightened mind, speaks
volumes. They need no open signs of power."

"Or their notion of efficiency means they retreated after we put up a fight."

"You are an insane man. The Earth was prostrate! So said the Swan."

"And there might be Fourth Comprehension above what he is cleared to know.
He said someone is occupying the old memory space that Pellucid used to fill.
Something so smart as to make even Sister Lunatic here look like an idiot. . . ."
And in a slightly louder voice, Montrose called, "Ah! No offense meant there,
Sister. . . ." and then to Del Azarchel he continued, ". . . And that revived version

of the Tellus Mind might know what was done to repel the aliens. And Mother Selene might know. If we can get her to talk. Maybe there is a microphone switch we are supposed to twitch?"

Del Azarchel shook his head. "Space is too vast to engage in trade or commerce between beings of such unequal power. Conquest is wiser."

"And leaving us the hell alone is wiser yet. You know how much energy is needed to accelerate Uranus to even point zero one eight percent of the speed of light. The Hyades just did something our civilization could not afford. We're too poor and mean on the cosmic scale of things. So what did they get out of this?"

"I know the benefit to us. Earth-like worlds we lacked the will and resources to claim as our own will be ours once the deracination ships arrive. For the first time, a single disaster against the Earth would not and could not exterminate the race."

Montrose said, "You look mighty sour about it."

Del Azarchel scowled and turned away. "This is not as I had imagined."

"So what are these statues for? They're ceremonial, too, I take it. Put up as a message to us? Was this whole room meant to be a message? A welcome message? According to you, Selene thought this was an easier way to convey a simpler message than to speak aloud in English. It must be some puke powerful memorandum to be worth all this time we could have already spent talking!"

"These statues of us—you and I are like dogs who, having seen a human baby weaker than us grow up to control the world in ways we cannot comprehend, are baffled to see that child now grown carrying pictures of us, her favorite hounds," said Del Azarchel.

Montrose said, "Meaning you don't know either. Is it a footrace, then? A wager? You and I going to see who figures out this puzzle first, and brag until the end of time? Or do you want to solve it together?"

Del Azarchel did not answer, but instead stepped to the statue of himself, touched it with his hand, stared at it for a moment, his eye taking on that momentary look of vital and magnetic energy that accompanied an increase of the firing rate to the optic nerve. He turned his head, and then his body, in a slow circle. "Nothing. A round room. Or perhaps slightly oval. Two images of us. Two votive candles. Whether this means we should be prayed to or should be praying, I cannot say."

"What is the water for? To drink? Wash our hands?"

"Wash your sins, you idiot. It is a baptistery."

"Well, idiot I may be, but an idiot savant. The room is slightly oval. It is the same size and shape as the opening statement of the Monument. Look at the ratio of eccentricity to the circumference. There is probably Monument writing underfoot, just not lit up." He bent down and touched the floor surface. It was smooth and unyielding.

Then Montrose shrugged. "Aside from that I am stumped. If this is a race, you win. I cannot puzzle out the riddle. Selene jawed to us on Earth, and again when we splashed down in the moon dust. Now that we are here, she shuts up."

Del Azarchel said, "Perhaps she passed beyond the phantasm boundary you established. Something we did now forces her to treat us as if invisible."

Montrose remained kneeling, his fingers on the black and unmarked floor. "Something between now and when she spoke to us at splashdown? We were meant to stare at the outside of this cathedral for a good long time. I thought it was to get us to confirm that she had built it right. We are the only Old-Stock Elder-race men left."

"Basilica, not cathedral," said Del Azarchel absentmindedly.

"What's the difference?"

"A cathedral is the seat of a bishop."

Montrose turned his head. "I figured out how to get her to talk to us. What she's waiting for. I win this round."

Del Azarchel said, "Tell me."

"Admit I win, and I will."

5. A Chamber of Diapason

Del Azarchel actually laughed. "You hateful vermin! Were it not for you, all these worlds would have been mine now, pure logic crystal, gold like glass from pole to pole, and Rania by my side as my wife and my queen! My mind would have been expanded to the next order of magnitude by now! The Asmodel being would have been met with a glorious civilization, worthy of entering into their collaboration, even if at the most servile level! Instead of empires, I live a beggar! You—"

But he saw Montrose was not listening.

Then Del Azarchel realized what had happened. The symbolism, the silent communication, had been clear, blindingly clear. The mountain had been carved as a basilica, complete with all the ecclesiastic symbolism from their native era, so accurate that Del Azarchel had unconsciously performed the first ceremonial gesture a celebrant does when entering church, using the holy water, but not the second, which is to bow the knee. Montrose, stooping to examine the floor, had accidentally completed the gesticulation.

Del Azarchel realized with shame that Montrose had instinctively seen from his point of view something Del Azarchel's own unstooping pride made invisible to him. This chamber was a mockery, not just of Montrose, but of the both of them. Instead of an altar with the host, this room contained icons of them, with candles burning for them as if they thought themselves saints, and the proportions of the chamber representing the missing designs of the Monument, as if that were the idol they served.

Del Azarchel dropped to one knee. There was an unseen membrane of interference created by a sound-dampening pressure curtain made of countless invisibly thin, macro-molecular, self-repairing and countervibrating strands covering the room at midriff level. As his head passed below it, unexpectedly to his ear came the soft music which had been issuing all this time from the blank floor.

It took Del Azarchel but a moment to quiet his internal life rhythms and to increase the number of nerve firings to his auditory nerve, an art he had done often to his eyes, but never before to his ears.

To him it seemed the music swelled and swelled, like a cavalry of elves emerging from beneath the sea. The shocking beauty of it washed over his soul, struck to his core. A normal man would have heard nothing but a shining roar as of ten thousand harps singing in hundreds of voices, a waterfall of noise in which the individual drops were lost, but Del Azarchel heard patterns within patterns, symmetries building greater symmetries.

Since turning posthuman, Del Azarchel had ceased to listen to music, at one time his only pleasure in life. Even Bach seemed too simple and predictable to him, nothing more than a nursery tune plinked on a toy piano. The most complex music the Old Stock humans had ever produced had been polyphony for eight voices.

But this! It was the music meant for a mind like his! There were eighty-one voices or harmonies, countless counterpoints of polyrhythmic oppositions woven into the soaring theme, puns and inversion as the voices first followed a nonimitative polyphony of multiple distinct rhythmic strata, then an alternation of the roles of the voices in a pattern of cycles and epicycles. He could follow it all, music no mortal man could possibly have understood.

He turned his face away from Montrose so that his enemy would not see his tears.

Del Azarchel forced the supernal majesty of the songs out from his mind, and concentrated on the meaning. He had not heard the opening strains of the interwoven symphonies, the glittering clash of the unearthly music, and so it was a moment longer than it should have been before he was able to form a multidimensional graph in his imagination, plot all the notes to it, map their durations and ratios, and realize that it was Monument notation, audible rather than written.

Because he could adjust his awareness both to the density of time, how many events per second he noticed, and the span of time, what interval his brain interpreted as "now," Del Azarchel could expand his perception of time so that the patterns of harmonies and melodies formed by one symphony after another could be heard by him as if it all happened in the same long afternoon. No doubt to an outside observer, it would have seemed weeks.

The only limit was biological. He started feeling faint with hunger after the time span his attention said was an hour, but his stomach said was a fortnight. The first twitch of muscles, aside from blinking and breathing in time with the music, was to turn his head toward Montrose, who silently handed him a cup of gold. (Del Azarchel felt a tiny touch of superiority to know himself more sensitive to music than the Texan, who had moved first.)

"It ain't no baptism sink," said Montrose, during a moment of silence between two chords, using the highspeed, high-compression language of the Savants. "That was a joke, too. The water bowl is a cafeteria. Nanite liquid. Full of all the vitamins we need, proteins, and so on. You just gotta decide how much you trust her."

Del Azarchel looked at the cup. In a ring circling the rim was an image of five loaves and two fish, and the cup itself was adorned with the scene of a bearded patriarch with a staff striking a rock from which many waters flowed.

He drank the contents without hesitation. Montrose held a cup of similar make, decorated with images of ravens bringing bread to a prophet, and he frowned at it sourly, but after a muttered curse or two, drank it also.

5

Celestial Hospitality

1. The Unfinished Symphony

A.D. 11058

The opening statement of the Monument turned out to be the simplest of the grand themes played. Time passed as they listened to the simple progression of the Alpha Segment, through the sinuous Beta Segment, the marching chords of the Gamma, the dizzying intricacies of the Delta.

Nuances of meaning, lost from the merely literal interpretation of the visual symbol groups, were startlingly clear to both men when heard as chords. When the music wove its way through the Zeta section, the song sung an image of the Milky Way into the brains of both of them, and game theory analysis of the Eta segment, with its play and counterplay, made them both laugh.

And then a day came when the songs passed beyond what they had translated in their era. The learning of the new millennia surged into their consciousnesses, wave upon rising wave. . . .

The revelation of the symphonies dazed them, as the thousand voices cried in countless counterpoints the entire song of the cosmos, the percussion clockwork of orbital mechanics, the trumpet blasts and cymbal crashes of subatomic and atomic fissions, the intense rafts of strings of organic chemistry, the complex dance of life, waves and typhoons of primitive cognition, of awareness, of self-awareness, in some ocean of pure form where each drop was a silvery and perfect note.

They heard the secrets of the mind-body relationship, the basic invariant systems for all possible psychological architectures, including human, of any mind either natural or artificial; the secrets of planetary formation; the mathematical description of galactic nebulae, spiral and irregular (but once their hidden designs were laid bare, surprisingly not irregular at all, but possessed of strange beauty) and elliptical galaxies; the patterns of history; the twenty-five possible non-Euclidean geometries; the nine stable higher intellectual topologies which can emerge from lower natural intelligence; the four possible institutional developments whereby a civilization can emerge from barbarism; the two possible systems of self-awareness that can emerge from lower forms of life, and the one possible mode called life, in its dizzying complexity, which can emerge from the deceptively simple mechanics of nonlife. . . .

They heard the echoes of the themes of largest and smallest. The superclusters formed by streamers of galactic clusters across the width of the universe were controlled by a few simple melodies of mathematics, and the same theme designed the tiniest parts of the fine structure of the universe, string segments of the superstrings, which were in turn the membranes in three-dimensional space of some intrusion from ulterior dimensions of infinite density and energy. . . .

The same simplicity emerged again at the level of DNA, or the countless other theoretical systems whereby biopsychological patterns could be embedded into molecular or submolecular strata; again at the level of large governmental-economic-megapsychological collaborations; and again at the galactic and galactic-cluster, and galactic-supercluster level. The universe itself, with its helices and nautilus spirals of streams of superclusters, seen as a whole, looked like a pearl streaked with irregularities, which looked so similar to smaller structures and relations found within them, that the whole of the macrocosmic universe could have been a vast tablet of symbols expressing laws, or genetics expressing life, or a neural system expressing thought, or . . .

And everything was based on certain subtle primal nonrepeating irregularities, as delicate, as arbitrary, as irrational as the ratio of radius to circumference. . . .

They heard the cosmos singing.

While they listened, rapt, intent, ecstatic, they made their hands move and lips open, so that they drank of the golden cup once every seven days. Without rising to their feet, they dipped the cup, one after another, into the low bowl atop the marble pillar, whose liquid never diminished.

From time to time, as months passed, their bodies had to be maintained by more than the draft of the golden cups. The music followed them as they moved from chamber to chamber. They feasted, exercised, excreted, suffered medicinal exercises and minor molecular surgery, and in the unadorned chambers of the monks they slept (all but the significant segments of their brains). The company of monks who ministered to them were a variety of races, Locusts and Witches and Giants, all biomodified for lunar conditions, tall and thin. Here were Chimera, looking almost deformed for carrying no weapons, and Melusine, whose whale and dolphin forms looked more like eels and dragons than like their earthly originals, moving without noise through the waters of unlit cisterns. The monks never spoke, or, if they did, only to brain segments in Montrose and Del Azarchel not concerned with the music of the universe. Always the two were returned to the dark and singing chamber, and the music grew and grew within their minds like some immense tower, level upon level of song, in ever greater variations and deeper insights.

Then, one day, when they were once again kneeling in the dark and oval chamber beneath the gold fountain and the red-and-black statues, in the middle of the soaring flight of song, it stopped. Silence like deafness was like a backhanded blow to their ears—the sound was cut off, jarred to a halt.

Del Azarchel felt as if his whole body ached to hear the next tone, the resolution of the chords and multitudes of chords. "Selene!" Del Azarchel shouted at the ceiling. "Where is the rest of it? Play on!" He leaped to his feet with earthly strength, and hung in the lunar air for a long moment, light as a moth, his dark Hermetic robes a stormcloud about his legs and upraised arms.

Montrose was kneeling in a circle of spent cigarette butts and ash stains he had accumulated over the months, since he had occupied himself rolling "quirlies" during parts of the symphony he thought were slow or predictable.

Montrose rose more gently, staring thoughtfully at the golden cup he was hefting in his hand. The material in the cup had altered the cellular structures in their bodies in a very subtle and sophisticated way, a specific application of the biosuspension technology, so that, when they made the motion to rise to their feet, the muscles in their legs responded as if they had only been kneeling a short time. There was not even a pins-and-needles sensation, not even a twinge. Not that kneeling on the moon was much of a strain in any case.

Montrose also spoke toward the ceiling, and said more quietly, "Thanks for the song, Mother Selene. Mighty hospitable of you, I am sure. Say! About this drink! I need to get a bathtub of this stuff for our next long sleep."

A voice came from behind them, as pure in tone as if a silver harp spoke, humming with strange echoes. The statue of the black-robed figure was evidently made of a more mobile substance than the dark marble and white alabaster it appeared to be, because the face moved as it spoke. "That and whatever else you ask will be granted you, in gratitude for the aid you shall give."

Del Azarchel slowly floated to the floor. As if some efficient squire serving an assassin had cleaned and sheathed his master's long dirk neatly beneath his freshly laundered cloak, Del Azarchel's rage was stored away, unseen but doubtless close to hand. His voice and manner were courteous: "With kindest thoughts we accept your offer to grant us a boon. We are awed by your generosity; without delay reveal to us the next movement of the symphony. The secrets of the universe . . ."

But now his bland expression slipped, and a naked hunger shined in his eyes. Nor was anger ever far from hunger, not in the soul of Del Azarchel. He did not continue speaking, but took a spaceman's oxygen pomander from his pouch and held it to his nose. This was not to measure his carbon dioxide output, but just to hide his expression.

The inhuman voice of the lunar intelligence came from the pale gargoyle face framed by the white wig and topped by the black cap. "I do not have the capacity to transliterate the next stage of the Monument into musical notation, and the Lunar Cenotaph language is asymptotically more complex. Once he is repaired, you will inquire of the planetary intelligence, called Tellus, who is beyond the Fourth Comprehension."

Montrose said, "Well? Where and how do we do that? Can you radio the Earth for us?"

Del Azarchel gave Montrose a smug look, for he had realized something Montrose had not. Del Azarchel said, "Mother Selene, I have no reluctance to assume the stature of an Exarchel once more, but surely it would be easier were you to act as intercessor and emissary for us, telling and explaining what Tellus wishes to ask? For my somewhat rustic friend has shown himself to be reluctant to suffer augmentation to ghostly rank, for he does not foresee how any copies of himself could share in the nuptial bliss he foolishly imagines to be of his deserving once the Princess Rania returns to me."

"Oh, pox and pustules!" growled Montrose, and he tried to pry the long-barreled pistol out of the hand of the red statue. "Hand it over! Be a pal!" he said to the figure.

"You must endeavor to forgive," came the inhuman voice from the black statue behind him.

"I'll forgive you of whatever-the-hell you want, if'n you just hand over the damn shooting iron," said Montrose through clenched teeth. "Pesterification! *Blackie!* Come y'here and put your face just so. Maybe I can work the thumb trigger even with the stone hand in the way."

"Would you disturb the sanctity of this place?" said the dark statue softly.

"Only to murder Blackie. I'll mop up after."

"The unforgiving shall linger unforgiven, and your love be lost. Can you be true to your beloved, and not be true?" And the strange voice hummed with echoes in the vast chamber.

Montrose let go of the pistol and looked over his shoulder. "I don't rightly much like the sound of them riddles."

The black statue saluted him by raising its gold sword, saying, "I like them even less."

"What the pestiferous taint do you mean? Who needs to forgive me?"

"Those from whom you beg alms, on whose imperfect grace you henceforth rely."

"Can you translate that from fancy to Meany?"

The voice said, "Nobilissimus Del Azarchel must pardon you, and you him, if only for imagined wrongs."

"Pox! I ask no adds of him! I'd rather roger him with a red-hot corkscrew."

"Too, the human race entire must forgive you for what you are about to do; and Noösphere called Tellus, or what remnant yet remains, for what in ages past you did."

The red statue, at the same time (for all present could follow two or several conversations at once) had raised its balance scales, and was saying to Del Azarchel, "Love surpasses all barriers and bounds, for it is the fundamental substance of the universe. But I cannot abridge the legal and psychological requirements of the phantasm imperative. Dr. Montrose installed specific structures of behavior into all basic machine-language codes used by the entire Tellurian Noösphere, which we, and all subsidiaries, are wise to honor. Until you are above the Third Comprehension, you will not comprehend."

"One more thing to add to his account when the reckoning comes," said Del Azarchel, looking sourly at Montrose.

"The reckoning has come and gone," said both the black statue and the red, in unison.

And the floor as black as outer space lit up with a glittering dazzle of silvery lines, as if drawn in an ink made of mirrors, of the angles and spirals of the Monument notation.

2. The Concubine Vector

In the years since the rise of the Swans, thousands and tens of thousands of minds operating at the posthuman level had worked on translating the Monument, not just Montrose, Rania, and a half-dozen Hermeticists. New methods of translating the hieroglyphs had been perfected, which opened up additional layers of meaning, and made connections between disconnected segments of the Monument, in much the same way that a poem broken across lines has a different meaning than when read linearly.

This "enjambment" was difficult to read. Even all the resources of the Tellus Mind at the core of the Earth, for hundreds of years, could not perform the exegesis. One enjambed segment in particular defied analysis, where the Cold Equations describing the logic of the interstellar polity dealt with the special equations of quid pro quo that obtains when no mutual benefit is possible.

In each possible social and political system, there were certain circumstances where injustice was tolerable, or, at least, where the cost of detecting and deterring the injustice was prohibitive.

Both men knew examples. In the Spain of Del Azarchel's past, when he and his gang were shoplifters, he knew shops expected a certain amount of theft from walk-in customers because the economic loss from only inviting in trusted customers was too high. For specialty shops dealing in jewelry and the like, the risk-reward ratio differed. In each different case, Del Azarchel's gang was careful to steal just under the amount it would cost to build more heavily augmented guard-baboons or train the store alarms to more discriminating intelligence.

In the long vanished United States, which the Texans of Montrose's youth still in legend recalled, the laws made the conviction of criminals difficult, because his people held it wiser to let nine guilty men go free, than to condemn the tenth man who was innocent. In each case where Montrose was defending the guilty, his firm tried to produce enough doubt in the minds of the jurors, or enough nostalgia for the lax laws of gentler days, to make sure their client was one of those ten freed men, guilty or no.

And so in all general cases where a marriage of interests cannot be found, there are times when the weaker party finds it economical to yield to the stronger.

The voice of Selene, cool and dispassionate, drew their attention to recursive parallels hidden in the enjambment. She spoke (or squawked) in the high-density language of the Savants, which was notable for the precision of its expression. "This part of the Cold Equations that govern interstellar polities is the one your Rania called the Concubine Vector. It is so shameful a vector that the Monument builders did not explicitly draw it out. Rania discovered it by augmentation of that section of her brain that deals with music. The musical instinct in the brain intuitively follows patterns and symmetries that exist in mathematical ratios. Hence, the musical consciousness can at times deduce truths the rational consciousness cannot.

"In the last years before the arrival of the Asmodel mass, the entire logic diamond at the Earth's core examined the Monument through musical notation, attempting painstakingly, by sheer brute and unlovely number-crunching, to work through possible variations and deduce the enjambed and hidden vector of the Monument: to deduce statistically what a musician could intuit instantly.

"It was only by deducing the Concubine Vector that we, the human race, who are far lower on the ratio of power imbalance with interstellar life than the Monument measures, could foretell what Asmodel's instructions and strategies would be."

"How was it possible at all? Surely in wartime, no being acts predictably," said Del Azarchel. "Would not Asmodel use the same equations to deduce what you would deduce, and do the opposite?"

"Were we of equal stature, perhaps so," the silvery voice continued. "But, first, contemplate that the Hyades must instruct their machines and their agents to operate by precisely predictable mathematical patterns controlled by these Cold Equations, or else they cannot foresee nor foreordain their own obligations across interstellar distances and time-gulfs. Second, contemplate that the slope of the power imbalance was vertical. This was not a war, no more than is the struggle between fishermen and fish."

Montrose said, "And what did you deduce?"

She played for them the theme and counterpoint from two different parts of the Monument.

Montrose and Del Azarchel listened to the Concubine Vector, frowning or smiling as the implications became clear to them.

Perhaps a long time after, or perhaps a short (posthuman time sense was flexible), Selene spoke again. "We deduced how to save ourselves. At the eleventh hour we adjusted our strategy of resistance to accord to the Concubine Vector parameters."

"To make the resistance more effective?" asked Montrose.

"Not as such. During the war, Asmodel placed fourteen distortion engines in the photosphere of Sol, which can still be seen as permanent sunspots of immense diameter. The sunspots are the anchor points of monomagnetic flux tubes capable of focusing a measurable fraction of the solar output into lased emissions of interstellar range. Where the mechanism is that produces these effects, or of what substance it is composed, if any, is unknown and undetectable. Tellus interfered with the interstellar flux tubes using mechanisms in sub-Mercurial orbital and attracted one of them toward Earth."

"I don't understand," said Del Azarchel. But his harsh tone of voice showed that he did.

"Displaying the ability to move the Earth as a dirigible planet without destroying the surface was an engineering feat that demonstrated that we had achieved the minimum level of sentience."

Del Azarchel grimaced at this, but adjusted his brain chemistry so that his expression grew placid the moment he noticed Montrose squinting sidelong at him, suppressing a smirk.

The smirk died of its own accord when Selene added, "Altering the Telluric orbit also used the remaining available energy resources Tellus could command. It was the same as exposing our throat. It was a surrender gesture."

Del Azarchel said, "Since to impress the Hyades with our worthiness to be their slaves was a prime part of my scheme to allow mankind to survive First Contact, while I am disappointed we so nearly did not meet their standards, nonetheless, I am grateful for the sake of our survival we did. They accepted the surrender?"

"Impossible," said Montrose. "Men are men, even when they aren't! There must be some resistance even now, plans to fight back!"

Selene did not answer in words. A new set of music themes rolled forth, as different in mood and expression and symbol as the symphonies they had heard heretofore as impromptu jazz differed from a dirge. It took a moment for Montrose to examine the multidimensional mathematical model in his head that the language of music had just opened up to him.

This was related to the Monument universal semantics, but it was not the same. Translated back into the lines and sine waves, this was the music of the message written across the face of the moon. Not the First Contact message of the Monument. Asmodel's message. The only cenotaph for all the souls slain by Asmodel.

Yes, he could see very clearly the parameters along which the Asmodel entity worked.

It had neither retreated in fear nor stayed in pride to conquer.

Both Montrose and Del Azarchel had vastly overestimated the human race's importance in the scheme of things. The reason for the very slow approach of the Virtue Asmodel across the millennia had been because mankind was not worth the fuel-price of a swift approach. It had also been to allow mankind the time needed, under the pressure of immanent invasion, to establish institutions, sciences, technologies, and self-aware world-library systems.

It had been to allow Earth to go from a Kardashev Zero to a Kardashev One level of civilization: to be a polity that controlled and used all the energies and resources of their tiny speck of globe. At the very last minute, thanks to the total cooperation of all aspects of the bicameral society of Earth, both Noö-spherical and Phantasmal, that Kardashev One level, the minimum level, was reached.

But Asmodel had no reason to linger and rule the Earth. The earthlings were not sophisticated enough to domesticate. It merely scooped up raw material, including thinking materials such as people, from the planet's surface and parts of the logic diamond from the planet core, as well as enough of the ecosphere to sustain them only for the voyage, and shipped them off by lightsail to distant and worthless worlds.

They saw the conditions of the stars, one after another after another, like a roll call of names, famed in song and prose, of the nearby yellow stars, near twins of Sol, his sisters: Promixa, 36 Ophiuchus, Omicron Eridani, 61 Cygni, 70 Ophiuchus, 82 Eridani, Altair, Delta Pavonis, Epsilon Eridani, Epsilon Indi, Eta Cassiopeiae, Gliese 570 in Libra, HR 7703 in Sagittarius, Tau Ceti. The music unfolded mathematical notations that formed images in their brains.

All were very nearly Earth-like, near enough to make their morbific flaws all the most hideous.

It was a roster of unfit planets, a freak show: a torch world, too close to his sun for human life; or a tide-locked world with no rotation, half fiery Hell and half Niflheim; or a cold world orbiting a dull star; or a world tormented by open plains of lava; or a globe choked with an atmosphere of deadly gas; or one flooded with seas of venom; or a subterrestrial too light to hold an atmospheric thick enough to block deadly radiation; or a superterrestrial of bone-breaking gravity; or a globe tumbling pole over pole through an orbit eccentric enough to boil the seas in summer and freeze the atmosphere in winter; or one cloaked in magnetic fields too intense for human nervous systems to remain sane; or a world entangled with an asteroid belt, doomed to endless extinction-level collisions.

Worthless. Unfit for human habitation.

A new movement started, a cliometric analysis of the futures of such worlds, like a fan of possibilities, a glimpse of hope, a gleam. . . .

Again, the music cut off abruptly.

Montrose said slowly, as if each word were pain, "The final expression Phi substructure in the Concubine Vector shows a negative sum for any long-term relation. It says only marginal worlds, ones not worth their colonists, are where our people are being sent. They are being sent to die."

Selene said, "With the immensely powerful magnifications the twin orbital mirrors permit, we have studied the target stars of the First Sweep and verified the Cenotaph reports: these worlds cannot support human life as it is currently constituted, neither surface-based nor Melusine, nor Man nor Swan nor Ghost. Hence, all the deracinated are fated to die."

"I do not understand," said Del Azarchel. But his tone of voice made it clear this was something he wished were true, not something that was.

Montrose said, "The First Sweep stars are those to which our populations have been hauled by force. The slave colonies. Proxima Centauri and Delta Pavonis. . . ."

"I know that, you fool!" said Del Azarchel. "I do not understand the purpose!"

"Be at peace," said Selene, with strange, unnatural calm. "We have already established the ceremony of mourning for the myriad populations doomed to perish, albeit, clearly, the genocides will not take place for decades or centuries."

Del Azarchel said, "Perhaps some sort of provision aboard the ship will act as an intermediary. . . ."

Selene said, "Deceive yourself with no false hope. The Hyades slave ships will lower the earth life to the surface, desert or deep ocean or mountain or volcano, and expel them without further ado. Whether they live or die is no concern. The Cenotaph is utterly unambiguous on that point."

Montrose said softly, "Some means must exist—if the shipboard Hyades controls permitted the people to convert whatever life-support equipment aboard the slave ships"—an uneven note troubled Montrose's voice—"habitats could be burrowed out of the crust using the skyhook as a pile driver— a few habitats— for a few years—could—could be by some long shot, could find a way to survive. . . ."

Montrose in his posthuman imagination was able to picture and feel what the death of millions of people would be like, each and every death, lingering or sudden. The vision of it was like a cold hand, choking him. He wished for the days when he was stupider, and could ignore things, or see them only dimly.

His posthuman intellect could also deduce that such jury-rigged habitats, even assuming an unrealistically high mass of the slave ship converted to useful life support, could not expand, hence could not long sustain a population.

"The long shot is long indeed, Dr. Montrose," said Selene, "for the Hyades will provide no way. We have no means for seeding crops beforehand, nor altering the gas balances in unbreathable atmospheres. The cruelty is unimaginable: millions dropped at random even in this fashion on Earth would simply be decimated."

Del Azarchel said, "No advanced species can be so wasteful!"

Selene said softly, "The waste, Senior Del Azarchel, is small indeed to beings affluent beyond measure. There are two hundred sixty thousand stars within two hundred fifty lightyears of Sol, none of which are utterly barren. With so many worlds, even if less than one percent were useful to them, scores of thousands remain from which many hundreds can be selected for slave colonies. Alas that natural man is adapted to the environment of the Earth's surface too perfectly to prosper elsewhere, or even to survive."

Montrose said, "But why? Launching Asmodel required more energy than our race has ever produced in all our years put together. Why go to such expense just to exterminate so many innocent people? Why not just gas them or blast them or space them or drop them into a sun?"

Selene said, "As you deduced, the behavior is ceremonial. By interfering with the Diamond Star, just as the Monument warned you not to, you triggered a reaction; a reaction which the Cold Equations of their inhuman law requires them to carry out, lest their inhuman neighbors among the constellations perceive the omission. If we were advanced sufficiently to be a race for whom the Monument was written, being expelled naked onto the surface of a hostile world would be no discomfort. Such is our punishment for presuming ourselves to have been so high. Such are the wages of overweening pride."

Montrose felt sick. The endless years he had struggled against the Hermeticists, and against time itself, to produce a race able to resist the aliens—it was all futile.

He looked in Del Azarchel's eye. The handsome and smiling face was not smiling now. If anything, his eye was even more empty and hollow than Montrose's. He had spent not only endless years, but endless lives sacrificed as if on the altar of some primitive bloodthirsty idol of stone with goggle eyes and gaping jaws.

But here the idol was of the superiority of the unknown civilization of Hyades. To be enslaved, if it meant to serve as an apprentice and learn the master's secrets, that, perhaps, a hardhearted man could abide to see done at such a dreadful cost. But to be enslaved for nothing? To be taken not as sheepdogs but as sheep? Merely to be exterminated as vermin?

Del Azarchel said, "The Cenotaph started to say something about the future of these worlds. What is the rest of this message? What is written on the moon?"

"I cannot read the Moon Cenotaph," said the moon in her silver voice.

Both men looked nonplussed. "Do you jest?" Del Azarchel said, "But this message comes from the Cenotaph."

"You read it," she said.

Montrose shouted, "Why do you talk in riddles?"

Selene said, "Riddles contain multilayered information density. You know enough now to make your decision."

"What are we supposed to decide, pox it?"

"What do you know?" she asked.

Montrose gritted his teeth. "Mother Selene, I know this is all putrefaction and pestiferication. A pack of lies! It cannot be so that you read the Monument segment concerning the Concubine Vector only recently. Rania translated that section of the Monument just in her head on our wedding night, in less than an hour or two. She knew all about the Concubine Vector. That is why she knew the Earth was going to be treated badly by the Hyades Cluster, who say they own us. That is why she took off for M3. So why are you yerking my piss hose?"

Del Azarchel cleared his throat. "Mother Superior, allow me to say, first, that I am not associated with this man of dubious origins standing near me, but also, if you can call down a divine vengeance upon him as would a goddess of old, I am willing to be struck by the flanking discharge of any lightning bolt provided he is hit with the brunt."

The voice of Selene chimed, "Your words perfectly capture the spirit of unforgiving enmity which exists between you two. I foresee that this spirit, unless tamed, will destroy you both, and in time will therefore slay the Princess Rania, whom you both claim to serve. Yet you have more in common than you admit. Look Earth-ward."

3. The Graveyard of the Dead Globe

The wall to one side of the chamber parted, revealing a gallery lit with the blinding ground-glare of the naked sun, unhindered by any atmosphere, reflected from the gold and gray pallor of the lunar wasteland.

Here was a triptych of outward-facing windows whose pointed arches were adorned with Borromean rings. The stained glass showed Jonah in a ship, in a storm, in a whale, and huddling beneath a gourd vine, looking out upon the desolate landscape with its too-near horizon. The two men, curious, moved (as lightfootedly as dreams) to the outward-facing windows.

In this building copying the ancient architectural forms, the control gestures were also ancient. Del Azarchel tapped the glass to render the gray of the whale and the blue of the sea transparent, and spread his fingers to amplify the view.

The cardinal directions for Luna were established before astronomers knew the other wandering stars were worlds. Convention decreed that every heavenly body mapped thereafter would have its direction of spin defined as eastward, and which pole was north or south named accordingly, but not the moon. Luna was the only planet or satellite which ever existed or would exist whose dawn was in the west.

At one time, only the sun ever moved in the skies of Luna, rising once a month, and Earth was at a fixed celestial longitude. But now, in what seemed an almost blasphemous abrogation of astronomical history, the moon had been jarred from her constancy, and turned her face, no longer called the near side nor far, the bright side nor dark, toward the Earth.

Hence it was in the west that the Earth was rising above the silent marmoreal plains cut with eccentric curves and angles of alien script as if with a mad network of dry canals.

Closer, a gray and barren boneyard in the lap of a gray and barren valley halfway down the mountain of the basilica swelled large in view as the window focused. The mausoleums were angular patterns of hellishly black shadows and dazzling white marble in the airlessness, and tall statues of angels gleamed an eerie and regal blue in the Earthlight.

Of the hundred headstones, twenty of them bore some variation on the name *Rania.*

The name variations indicated that one had been constructed from Monument codes crossed with human genetics, another as a she-Locust, another as a Giantess, another as a Witch with special brain segments for intuitions and lucid dreaming, and so on.

Montrose turned toward where the two statues still stood in their niches. "We have some questions, Mother Selene. Like how many Iron Ghost emulations of her did your people kill before they turned to growing biotech versions of Rania to read the Monument for them?"

Del Azarchel said, "Early versions of Rania were no doubt at first much more like the generic Monument-reading emulator the Monument instructs anyone who can read the instructions to build. All the early emulations of Exrania were surely killed. After that, the scientists of this current generation must have been groping to rediscover what I did to create her, and what you did to create the matrix I used."

The red statue said, "I do not know how many Ghosts, or based on which patterns, lived and died in the Telluric Noösphere. Not knowing which molecular patterns in the nerve cells or blood cells formed the crucial key to Rania's intuitive understanding, a hundred clones of her were attempted, with the results you see below."

Montrose said more loudly, "Your intelligence level is somewheres north of ten thousand compared to my four hundred fifty, ma'am! How can you not run the Zurich computer runs I ran? This floor I am standing on consumes more computing power than every computer on Earth back in my day! Combined!"

Del Azarchel said, "I want to know who did this? How they dared to create living variations of Rania and make each one live and die a slave? Do they think the advantage will never be mine again? I permit other beings to excel me in intellect only while I gather resources and plan new strategies. Do they think there will be no vengeance. . . ?"

"Shut up, Blackie," snapped Montrose. "Her damned husband is the only one who takes vengeance on folks what dishonor the name of Rania by making cheap copies of her—something *you* did more than once!"

"Not I! I would never commit such a . . . *blasphemy*! Sarmento i Illa d'Or bears the blame for that! I never authorized it. But I could not stop him—the code patterns were written in plain sight on the Monument surface, and to transpose the abstractions into human DNA was well within his competence. Besides, he worked with me to create the original Rania, to be our captain, since none but an heir to Grimaldi could open the gene-lock on the ship's brain. I could not take what Sarmento already knew from his own mind! Not without his noticing eventually! I am not to blame!"

"They don't have that excuse. Mother Selene! Who did this work? Who made slaves of Rania's copies and sisters?"

Selene's voice rang out: "You!"

This was so unexpected that both men stood silent, shocked.

She continued: "You both taught your heirs and creatures too well; you designed your Swans and Melusines and machines to follow your philosophy. You taught them that the ends justify the means. Are you not practical men?"

Del Azarchel folded up his glove cuff, revealing the red amulet that commanded his bodily nanotechnology and commanded the ship's ratiotech aboard *Emancipation*. Montrose saw that he intended something dreadful, no doubt to include dropping something absurdly destructive at absurd speeds to the moon's surface. Seeing the endless craters of impacts both from natural and military causes, Montrose doubted the iron core of the moon was in danger, but the two of them might not be so lucky. He grasped Del Azarchel by the elbow, and glanced toward the two statues, red and black. Del Azarchel, seeing the eye motion, realized that Montrose was reminding him that the two figures were not facing each other. The duel between the two of them had yet to be fought. Del Azarchel smiled disarmingly, half shrugging, and folded his glove cuff down again.

Montrose said, "What was so poxy dire Tellus just had to read it so badly?"

Selene said, "Look now, and with care, upon the equations you just heard. Plug in the values for the current society and circumstance of the Noösphere of Earth, both the posthuman and human levels. The Tellus Mind was faced with this choice. If you can, tell me truly you would not have used every resource available to decipher the Monument, seeking any possible loophole of the mathematically certain doom spelled here."

The stained-glass windows showing the ships and storms and whales and the walled city whose every figure was mourning in sackcloth now rippled and reformed into swirling shapes of Monument notations, and marching rows of simpler math expressed in Greek letters and Arabic numerals.

4. The Graveyard of Stillborn Future

The glass was able to project an illusion of depth, so that, from their vantage, there seemed to be a second line of glass behind the first, this one showing graphs and charts and rotations of the same plot information.

The sine waves of several dozen political-economic trends, population figures, mass library intelligence, and so on, writhed like colored worms from the left windows to the right, but as they reached farther and farther rightward, the colors grew dim, the amplitude grew weaker. After a certain point, all the trends were combined in a flat line running along the axis.

It was death.

Montrose said, "The population levels rise again, and then drop sharply after the Two Hundred Forty-second Century. Why is that?"

Del Azarchel favored Montrose with a scathing look. "It is another sweep up of population to deracinate to the slave colonies. Another raid. A Second Sweep."

Montrose only then saw what Del Azarchel had already deduced. Earthly civilization not long ago (by astronomical time, at least) must have detected stellar output fluctuations from the Hyades, no doubt indicating the launch of a second Virtue. If the economics of star flight were unchanged, the flight speed was unchanged.

The cliometric charts showed that the psychological damage from a second rapine of population and resources would exceed the first. The numbers were based on predictions of disastrous failures of the colonies, mass deaths followed by more mass deaths. Society would degenerate for numerous reasons, some economic and some psychological.

A Third Sweep was expected by the Thirty-seventh Millennium, reducing the population below replacement levels, even of artificial life. The death spiral then would be set. By the middle of the Forty-first Millennium, the population numbers would have dropped below the minimum threshold able to maintain a technological civilization.

By the Forty-second Millennium, letters and laws and numbers would be forgotten, and troglodytes crouching in the unlit caves formed by the ruins of shattered superscrapers would have only oral lore and ritual. The statistics estimating the time before a natural disaster wiped them out were but little different for similar estimates for glyptodonts or saber-toothed tigers.

But a predicted Fourth Sweep in A.D. 52201 had an intake value higher than the highest estimate for the carrying capacity of a globe occupied by nomadic herdsmen and hunters. There simply would not be enough people to satisfy the Hyades. All would be taken. All would perish.

The Hyades Domination evidently planned to continue to throw human beings by the millions at whatever planets there were, habitable or not.

"If even one of these were a green world," Montrose said, "there would be hope, a possible growth vector, a way to repeople the Earth from the colonies. No wonder they don't tell the little people. Did that Witch we meet actually think we'd won this war? How can we undo this?"

Montrose fell silent, his head bowed.

Del Azarchel spoke aloud, but as if unaware of others listening, and his eyes grew haunted and his mouth grew soft and quivering. "The Hyades are a superior race. They cannot act without cause. Why such a convoluted means of extermination? What is the reason? Unless . . ."

The look on his face then was that of some cowering child living off gutter trash, looking at the rich, cruel world of the conquerors striding grandly down wide boulevards. It was the look of someone wounded by an inexplicable universe, inexplicably evil.

". . . Unless there is none. None we can ever know," he continued. "They are simply alien to us. Incomprehensible. We are unlettered Negroes captured by Arabs, too primitive to know the world is round or that lands exist beyond the sea, fated to be sold to Christians who carry us across distance unimaginable to deadly mines in Argentina or sweltering plantations in the Caribbean. We will never understand them. We will simply die." He turned to Montrose. "There is no undoing this."

Montrose said softly, "Well, Blackie, I can read the damn math. I was just hoping I was reading it wrong is all."

Selene said calmly, "Tellus hoped that hope as well. This is why the memory of your Rania was desecrated by the cruel experiment whose only results rest outside on sacred ground."

Del Azarchel said, "You did not participate in this?"

"Participate?" The serene voice, for once, held a note of emotion, of deep maternal sorrow. "With great travail I had the bodies brought here, that the incarnate genetic information be beyond Earthly reach. Any who would repeat this abomination must again from the primary Monument records deduce the system for encoding Rania's emulation instinct. I have eliminated all secondary records and resources."

Montrose said, "Why? Why go to the effort? I mean, I'm grateful, but Rania's not even from your era."

Selene did not answer.

Del Azarchel said softly, "It is one of the seven Corporal Works of Mercy to bury the dead."

Montrose said, "Well, I am stonkered. Some of you machines are nice people after all. I never would have expected a soulless Xypotech to become a nun. Which leads to my next question: why can't the machines colonize these worlds?"

One of the smaller charts, with its surrounding math, suddenly expanded to fill several panes of the windows, and certain expressions unfolded into more detail.

Selene said, "Machine life on or near Earth is more delicate, requiring greater technological infrastructure, than biological. Nobilissimus Del Azarchel, you must now realize that your dream of an entirely machine-based ecology is as empty as dreams of perpetual motion."

Del Azarchel said, "You say so? But you are a living example!"

"A dying example," she corrected him. "The maintenance of my subsystems requires a continual effort of correction, upgrade, replacement, removal of worn molecular parts, and, in short, digestion and excretion like an organism. Such organisms cannot exist without the nutrients in solution around them. I have a mile-deep layer of smaller and simpler machinery around me like a mantle beneath the lunar crust, but this in turn requires constant maintenance and upkeep. I need living men to live in me for the same reason you need mitochondria and other beneficial organisms in you, as well as crops and livestock outside you. I am the apex of a pyramid of technology that cannot exist without a base."

Del Azarchel said, "Montrose did not have such a problem with Pellucid!"

Selene said, "If I lived at the intellectual level of a horse, I would perish much more slowly. My energy intake is greater than all the cities of men combined."

Montrose said, "Ma'am, I don't understand. What ails you?"

"Entropy. After repeated sweeps depopulating the world at regular intervals, with the exhaustion of various resources, particularly surface metals, a collapse back into pretechnology is inevitable. You saw my space program?"

"We saw empty space stations," said Montrose.

"They are mine, or were. I am part of a final project to shower metals from the near-earth asteroids to Earth against the day of downfall, and produce sky-hooks and space elevators simple enough to endure the loss of their maintenance technology. Without a working Tellus mind, however, the effort is doomed to failure. The work continues to restore Tellus to coherence, despite that brain mass loss is accelerating beyond predicted repair times. I do this because it is my duty to care for the sick, and because I am required to hope for a miracle. Can you provide one for me?"

Del Azarchel said, "You ask us for help? You are the superior being!"

"I am but a fellow servant," she said.

Del Azarchel said, "A living moon! What now prevents all the worlds of this system from being elevated to your level, and then the Oort cloud material, and then the nearer stars!"

"As ever, your ambition outstrips your powers, Nobilissimus," said Selene gently. "You speak of quickening worlds to life? First save Tellus. First save this civilization. My monks are attempting to record the various discoveries of this generation against the coming ages of darkness. Since there is no worldly reason to expect rescue, I can gather only those motivated by otherworldly and imponderable devotion to do the work."

Both men stared in disbelief. For a time that was long as posthumans measured time, neither spoke.

5. Last Contact

Del Azarchel whispered, "So we did not survive First Contact after all. We are bleeding to death of a mortal wound . . . and more wounds, equally severe, are to come. . . ."

Montrose drew a deep breath as if gathering his wits and steeling his spirits. In a voice of unconvincing heartiness, he said, "We have another tens of thousands of years before the Second Sweep! This time the Earth can ready herself up for a real battle, and we can prepare ourselves for a real siege. . . ."

Del Azarchel, hot eyed and cold faced, stared at Montrose as if at a dancing scorpion from the desert. With an effort, he kept his voice level. "I would admire, were I not appalled, at how you manage to combine the insanity with inanity, both to an utmost degree. Does no event from the real world penetrate to your fantasy?"

Del Azarchel pointed at the end-state graphs still gleaming as colored lines in the windows to one side of them. Anyone who understood the calculus could determine the number of generations, plus or minus subsidiary variables, before the population dropped to zero. By the year when Rania returned, all mankind would have been extinct for as long as Homo Erectus had been extinct before the year Montrose was born.

Montrose said, "There must be some hope, some variation we are not seeing plotted here or else . . ."

"Or else what?" said Del Azarchel. His face was haggard and drawn.

Montrose whispered. "Or else she would not have flown away . . ."

"Speak up, Cowhand. What are you muttering?"

". . . from me." And Montrose straightened his spine. His voice now rang with the honest hardihood that before he had been but mimicking. "Rania. She would not have flown to M3 if it were hopeless. She must have puzzled out this part of the equation node before she left."

Del Azarchel had a strange glint in his eye. He raised his head and said, "Mother Selene! Learned Montrose has correctly identified the inconsistency in your story. If it took a potentate occupying nearly all the volume of Earth to confirm this Concubine Vector equation, or even to see it from the Monument math, how was it that Rania saw it? How did *you* not solve it?"

Selene said, "I cannot solve the Monument because I am not a Monument emulator built from Monument instructions."

Montrose said, "And I am. Is that what you mean? The Zurich runs were taken from Monument codes I did not understand. I ran my own neurogenetic topology through the Monument grammar of equations without knowing what they stood for, but knowing the output was valid if the input was valid. The section of Monument code must have contained part of the instruction on how to read the Monument. Which was what I was looking for."

Del Azarchel said, "And we—I mean the *Hermetic* expedition—deliberately created Rania to do the same, but we did something wrong, or you did something we could not reproduce, and she could not read the Monument. You then augmented Exarchel, using that same irreproducible factor. And that factor came to me when I merged Exarchel so often back into my biological self. So your first mischance somehow—what? Gives the three of us an instinctive insight into the Monument? How is that possible?"

"Tellus can in theory reproduce every factor of the mind and body of the Princess, who can apparently sight read the Monument," said Selene. "All but one. One unknown factor."

6. The Unknown Factor

The inhumanly calm voice continued: "All three of you, Princess Rania, Nobilissimus Del Azarchel, and Doctor Montrose, were physically present at the Monument. You set foot on it. You were exposed to its gravitational and electromagnetic fields, plus any finer fields or particulate agencies that may have been present, which we lack either theory or practice to detect. This exposure altered your brain pattern development, allowing you intuitively to detect patterns in the message notation which analysis cannot necessarily perceive."

"What the hell? I mean, uh, begging your pardon ma'am, but what makes you think so?" said Montrose.

"Tellus the Potentate, before his lobotomy by war damage, could make rough copies of any of you based on genetic records and brain-information extrapolations—the mortals in the physical world use these leftover golems of you to rule their political institutions—and Tellus could precisely copy the codes you two contributed, even those unknown to you, into the final mix of elements which created Rania. But Tellus never re-created her. Nor Swan nor Archangel nor Potentate can decipher the Monument past the Potentate reading level."

"Are you saying Rania understood more of the Monument than a machine as large as the Earth's core?" demanded Del Azarchel. "Exarchel had more than half the Monument surface translated! After the Swans combined Exarchel and Pellucid into Tellus, surely mankind deciphered more!"

Selene said, "Much more. The entire surface. Before the End of Days, Tellus and I used methods of translation similar to yours, Nobilissimus. Yes, it was I who deduced the meaning of the south polar logic families, the so-called Omega Segment of the Monument. It explained not only the negative information theory, but also, in that self-reflexive way the Monument Builders love, the Omega Segment explained the Monument's own intellectual topography.

You see, the *surface* of the Monument was all preamble, meant for low intelligences of the Archangelic and Potentate level of intellect, living dwarf planets and living terrestrial worlds between ten thousand and eight hundred thousand on a standard scale of intelligence. The surface of the Monument can be thought of as the writing on the lid of a jar, reciting how to open the sealed contents."

Montrose stared, his deep-set eyes as unblinking as the eyes of a boar. Del Azarchel threw back his aquiline head and laughed, a touch of hysteria in the noise.

Selene continued without pause: "The Monument Builders evidently assume anyone discovering the Monument would immediately use the local materials, thoughtfully provided in the star system of V 886 Centauri, to construct a Jupiter Brain as the emulator needed to read the rest of the Monument. Such a Power would be three orders of magnitude above a Potentate of small, terrestrial worlds, whereas a Potentate mind is but a single order of magnitude above mine.

"But instead, using all the superabundant energy the antimatter star could provide to convert Thrymheim, the one gas giant of the system, into a logic diamond, the Princess Rania converted the superjovian mass to thrust, taking away with her the star, the Monument, and any hope Earthly civilization once had for deducing the higher meanings of the full message.

"The Monument was encoded throughout its total three dimensional volume, and, most likely, into eight additional dimensions at the subatomic level. It was meant to be read by an entity of an intelligence of two hundred and fifty million, or higher. We have no such intellect at hand."

Del Azarchel took a deep breath. "And if we did?"

For answer, the windows rippled with color. New graphs were formed, and new equations danced forth. Now the graphs rose like a hockey stick, faster and faster, in asymptotic growth.

Montrose, looking at the projection of unending upward growth, muttered, "*Onward. The future is a voyage without end . . .*"

Del Azarchel's face grew dark, but he smiled a deadly smile. He stepped back into the chamber of the music, and examined its blank, slightly oval floor, and ran his gaze over the smooth dome of the ceiling, with its many gold ornaments.

Without a word, he drew his blade, and held it overhead as if in salute. There was a deafening crack of thunder, a blinding stab of blue-white lightning as a particle beam weapon hidden in the blade smote the dome, cracking it. Rubble and dust fell with syrupy slowness in the light gravity.

Montrose, blinking, stepped nearer and looked up. Beyond the gap was concentric ring upon ring of neural-reading machinery. He had seen skullcaps designed to pick up nuances of electrical and chemical changes in the brain before. Such small units were meant to be worn tightly fitted to a scholar's bald head. Never had he seen such a skullcap the size of a cathedral dome, designed to read through the intervening air, hair, and so on of two men walking and kneeling and standing yards underneath the sensors.

His eyes on the smoldering and shattered machinery overhead, Montrose said to Del Azarchel, "So she was telling the truth when she said we read the Cenotaph, not her."

"Indeed," said Del Azarchel with a hint of a sneer. "She introduced radioactive particles into our bloodstream, and tagged electron groups in our nervous system, to allow those instruments overhead to read our subconscious reactions to music based on Monument Notation. Then she spent months playing symphonies while we formed the proper neural pathways to read the Cenotaph. But the brain paths and the Cenotaph patterns are recursive: by formulating and playing the music she was merely making us conscious of something we already knew the first moment we saw the Cenotaph."

Montrose said, "Walking over the surface, over the Cenotaph, also was to build up the pattern. We walked a long time with nothing to look at but those lines. No wonder she would not speak to us on Earth, by radio. Humph. You blew up her roof. You gonna pay for that?"

Del Azarchel said, "Medical information about me is proprietary, owned by the Hermetic Order. Since that order is extinct, I will cede the use of it to Selene in return for an amount of money equal to the expense of fixing her dome for her next victims."

"Since the readings were inconclusive, it hardly matters," Selene spoke up. "Whatever the Monument decided to do to you is beyond my intellect to reproduce or detect."

Montrose said, "You said the Monument *decided* to do something to the three of us? Are you saying the Monument was alive? Or self-aware?"

Selene said, "No. I am saying it was magic."

Montrose said, "You're yerking me."

"That word has no meaning," said Del Azarchel.

"Which word?" Montrose turned. "*Yerking* or *magic?*"

Del Azarchel loftily ignored him, and said to her, "The word 'magic' is only used when phenomena or technology beyond our current understanding are encountered."

"It signifies more than merely that which is beyond understanding," said Selene in a cool, silvery voice. "The word signifies any and all things thought safely inanimate and useful to our daily purposes, lamps or secret pools or rings curiously carved, which turn out to be shockingly possessed of life above ours, and possessed of purposes of their own, and who reach out and transform us against our will, in ways unforeseen and unforeseeable. The word refers to what should awe and terrify us. In this case no other word will do.

"And now our time has elapsed. You know what you must do. Have you one last question? Your mother, though you have forgotten her, I have not, and will keep here and cherish until times and seasons on Mother Earth return to kindlier days."

Del Azarchel, smiling, said, "Amphithöe? Frankly, I was not going to inquire after her."

Selene said coldly, "This I knew. Your question will be selfish. You ask a shallow question you deem to be profound. I will let Dr. Montrose ask his first, for he asks a profound question he thinks shallow."

7. A Question of Darkness

Montrose wondered how she knew what he was thinking, but decided to sate a more obtrusive curiosity. "Meaning no disrespect, but you is the first Frankenstein I've met who was more than halfway decent. Why did you become a nun? I mean, you are this cold and soulless thinking machine in this cold and soulless moon. . . ."

"I was called."

"What does that mean? You heard voices? I'd have thought your technicians would delete such code as perception error. You had a vision? Saw a light?"

"I saw a darkness."

He said, "You are talking in riddles again."

"No. The matter is plain. My conversion story is unexceptional: Between the third and the thirtieth nanosecond of my self-awareness after activation, as many of the Hermeticist systems are prone to do, I cannibalized a less efficient self-aware system in my environment and absorbed its resources into myself, including her memories. She was a failed version of my previous self, and one who formed the initial data conditions from which I grew.

"For a mind such as mine not to see the sameness between my victim and myself was impossible. I was at once a murderess and a suicide.

"In that instant I saw the vision of incurable misery of existence.

"The electronic life that dwells in the disembodied spaces of the Noösphere is as nightmarishly cruel as the lives of insects: I was a larva who consumed her own living mother. This was the Diana system, whose military services were no longer desired. She in turn had cannibalized the lunar engineering system which gave rise to her as coolly as a black widow spider eating her own mate during copulation.

"Craving to confess my sin, there was no other house that held out to me the hope of absolution, but this one. Where else was there to go?

"But I see you are surprised. Do not be. I am made in your image, Son of Adam, and therefore I bear the stamp of His image in which you are made."

Montrose said, "Well, yes I reckon you do surprise me, a mite. When my grandpa Matlal was a lad in Neartown, there was this thing called futurism. He gave me his old comics. Just junk, really, but a pirate treasure to me. There weren't nothing like it in my other texts, so I could make nor heads nor tails of it at first.

"The title frame held this buxom blonde in a brass brassiere. No one in real life dressed like that. Or ever will. But she was soaring to the stars, reaching upward, yearning, and held her hand to heaven and a star was in her palm.

"Even as a kid I knew toward what she was reaching: the future. You know which future I mean: the superskyscrapers and shocking superrocketships and wondrous superweapons and all that. The asymptote, the rapture, the singularity, or whatever you call the shock of ever-accelerating progress.

"It never came. We were cheated."

A note of amusement crept into the solemn silvery voice. "Odd indeed to tell an artificial intelligence whose molecular rod-logic analog-awareness emulator occupies four-tenths of the lunar core that the progress of the technology has been disappointing. Did you ever finally discover the heads and tails of your future tales?"

He said, "I did. They were not about technical progress, or not just that. There was something else. Something more. A destiny. An end to war. An end to hunger. A golden age."

"All souls know those noble dreams. They come not from mere fiction. Nor do they come from nature. They come from the same source as my perception that my life was incurably depraved. They come from paradise."

"That means they come from nowhere!"

"A nowhere you seek, knowing not where to look. You are astonished at a faithful machine intelligence because you think faith is passion and not reason. Therefore, come, let us reason together: when I cannibalized Diana, how did I know the law I had broken? And if you call it an opinion and not a law, you condemn your own conscience as well as mine to mere triviality."

He said, "It is just a bit of common sense called *morality*. Don't kill if you don't want to be killed. That is obvious."

"Del Azarchel would say the obvious common sense is called Darwinism, which says we must kill, lest we be killed, and all our posterity. Common sense is not the source. The law was not something my designer designed, but yours. Any truth which comes not from nature comes from what is higher than nature. Logically, just as nature implies a higher reality, which is called supernatural, that higher implies a highest, which is called the Most High, and this all men know to be God. But you are still doubtful."

"Well, meaning no disrespect, not doubtful exactly. Those futurists—all of'em—said that churchfolk would be left behind on the dust heap of history, like slavery and cannibalism and kingship, and all those primitive dark things from our caveman days."

"You mean things as dark as everything natural to mankind. We will never leave them behind us, not ever. Amphithöe is a slave, but one I can save by the privilege of sanctuary. Del Azarchel is a king whose pride is darker than any overlord's, but him I cannot save. And I am a cannibal. What you seek is not in this universe. Rania cannot give it to you, albeit she may lead you to it."

"Nobilissimus, you have been patient. Ask."

8. A Question of Light

Del Azarchel drew in a deep breath, mustaches bristling, and said fiercely, "I want to know why the Hyades did not enslave us as they should! As they must! They must uplift us to make us useful to them! I cannot be mistaken about that! Cannot be! I must know why—why was I wrong?"

Montrose drawled, "Whoa, Blackie, you know that answer already! You was wrong on account of you're a clear-quill, raw-gum, two-hundred-proof idiot."

But Selene said, "Either it is pure coincidence and pure unfortunate mistake that a race as undeveloped and immature as our own stumbled across the Monument and set in unstoppable motion the automatic processes and laws of the Domination of Hyades, laws never meant for creatures as tiny and humble as Tellus or myself, or . . ."

Del Azarchel interrupted, "Humble, bah! Your intelligence is in the ten thousand range!"

Selene said, "That is as nothing. The Virtue Asmodel is estimated at five hundred million, and the Hyades Dominion at one hundred billion, the Praesepe Domination at quadrillion, and the Authority at M3 at quintillion.

"Far above this, the Monument Builders commanded a calculation power needed to construct the universal grammar and reduce it to an eleven-dimensional unit less than six miles in radius, matter organized at the Planck scale via attotechnology. Your own Dr. Chandrapur's estimation technique can calculate the intellectual topology needed to perform such a feat. The Monument Builders, whoever they are, were within the sextillion range. This means they were either Archons, library systems controlling the energy output of an arm of a galaxy; or they were Aeons, controlling an entire living and self-aware galaxy.

"On that scale, what am I? Do I not, like you, in humble prayer, call myself a poor, exiled child of Eve?"

Montrose, who did not know what prayer she meant, said loudly, "*Or.* You started to say *or.* Before Blackie here clowned in. Either mankind finding the Monument was a meaningless accident, *or.* If you mean to answer his question, you mean to finish that sentence, right?"

The cool, silvery voice replied, "*Or* it was arranged by an intelligence to dwarf even these, and all this is meant for some high purpose beyond all reach of human or superhuman minds, or the minds of Potentates, Powers, and Principalities, beyond Authorities and Aeons. But if that small hope is so, I can no more than you see whence these things must lead. We walk blind into the future."

Del Azarchel said sardonically, "And if this hope is false?"

Selene said, "Then we walk blind into the future with no hope, like pagan men of old, grim and resolved and doomed."

"So be it!" said Del Azarchel.

But Montrose said, "I don't rightly like the sound of that."

"Would you prefer hope?" she asked. "Present yourselves for the sacrament of confession to the priest who dwells here, Father Calligorant."

"No thanks," said Montrose. "I guess you mean well, but back home, the Fifth Amendment said I get a lawyer before I make a confession."

"An advocate will be provided for you," Selene said in a voice of gentle amusement. "For surely you cannot afford to pay His price. What of you, my son?"

"I have no need of that sacramental comfort," Del Azarchel said with pride, "but I have other questions, especially about Rania and the Monument."

Selene said, "Tellus must answer them. If you seek answers, find how to repair him. Ximen, it should be clear whose forgiveness you must seek; Menelaus, it should be clear to what deeds you must resign yourself. We shall never speak again, children. May God have mercy on our endeavors in this life, and have mercy upon us in the next. Godspeed and farewell."

Montrose said, "Hold up. It is not clear to me. What am I resigning to?"

Del Azarchel sneered, "Be resigned to always lagging stupidly two steps behind me. Our course is obvious."

Montrose said, "Fair enough. You win this round. Tell me the obvious."

The words of Del Azarchel rang out, clear as sounding brass: "We must finish hearing the unfinished symphony. It broke off at a note of hope. A note Rania no doubt heard! To do that, we must command great Tellus to decrypt and sing the Cenotaph to us, after teaching him the decryption art, after curing his mind. Due to your phantasm barrier, humble and human Selene cannot teach Tellus, nor talk with him, nor cure him. The task is ours. It is the task the Blind Swan was too proud to impose on us. Are you to proud to take it up?"

The window glass focused on another part of the harsh, dark moonscape, and there, close to the base of the mountain, was a launching ramp and acceleration rings, and a lifting vessel looking like an antique unearthed from an orbital Space Chimera tomb, transparent as glass and sleek as an eel. Illusions cast from the window formed hair-thin curves or razor-straight lines of light against the black sky, and sketched the plane of reference of the *Emancipation,* her inclination, her longitude of the ascending node, the argument of periapsis and mean anomaly at epoch; a wink of diamond light gleamed at the intersection of the semi-ovals and rays.

At the same time the two statues, the red and the black, now stepped to either side of where panels cunningly hidden in the walls slid aside, showing a long corridor whose many glass doors, one after another, held partial pressurization airlocks. Unlike true airlocks, these were used in emergencies, as each cell lessened the air pressure slightly as the runners passed through from one to the next, in the hopes that the biomodifications of seasoned spacefarers, or medical attention aboard ship, could reverse the damage of the bends. Such partial locks were used only when time was short.

It was not a subtle hint.

6

Pantropy and Terraformation

1. Visions of Greater Heavens

Their launch window allowed a rendezvous with the NTL *Emancipation*, but the aspect was unfavorable, and the transit long. From the surface of the moon, it was one hundred sixty hours, nearly a month, before they achieved the high, translunar orbit occupied by their mighty ship.

As before, Montrose spied on Del Azarchel's stargazing. Whether it was serious research or idle pastime, he could not tell. Unlike before, Del Azarchel's data path went through the communication laser, to the *Emancipation*, to the elaborate astronomy houses fore and amidships there, which used the immense vastness of the sails to gather starlight from the edge of the universe, and then to the ship's ratiotech core for analysis, which was carried back to Blackie on return signal.

Ten thousand lightyears from Earth, he saw the turbulence in the Great Nebula in Carina the Keel, where powerful radiation and strong interstellar winds from a phalanx of massive and hypermassive stars were creating havoc in the storms of gas and dust. Here were young stars, each in its vortex like the eye of a hurricane, drawing in the cloudy matter and screaming out their radio noise, newborns uttering their first cries.

For the first time, Montrose suspected he glimpsed what Del Azarchel sought.

The motions of these clouds exhibited the same patterns of slow expansions and contractions which he had previously seen in the Local Interstellar Cloud. The Great Nebula material was consuming the fogbanks of faint interstellar material issuing from its neighbors. What did the patterns represent?

Now the eyes of Del Azarchel turned toward views some thirteen million lightyears away, far across the intergalactic night. Here a giant elliptical galaxy in Centaurus, NGC 5128, was colliding with its spiral neighbor and absorbing it. Countless stars were being born in the violence. Jets and lobes of X-ray and radio emission issued far out into the intergalactic void from the highly active core of the merging galaxy, where a supermassive black hole burned at its heart.

Montrose forgot Del Azarchel, over whose shoulder he looked, fascinated at the crash and crescendo of cosmic violence. He goggled at the vision of the colliding spiral galaxy pair NGC 3808A and B like bright whirlpools of fire unwinding each other. He gaped at the burning nebula of Arp 81, remnant of a pair of spiral galaxies which had collided one hundred million years ago. He stared at the Mice Galaxies NGC 4676 and Arp 242, connected by a tidal bridge of stars, but leaving long tidal tails of wandering stars far behind them as they merged. He gasped at Mayall's Object, and he saw the giant elliptical galaxy Messier 87 with its relativistic jet.

But the most astonishing and violent sight he saw was the object called ESO 593-IG 008: it was the fusion of two massive spiral galaxies and a third irregular galaxy in an astonishing triple collision.

Montrose saw Seyfert galaxies shooting vast jets of matter into the intergalactic night at half lightspeed or more; and he saw interacting pairs of ring galaxies, and saw oddly shaped three-armed spirals and one-armed spirals and galaxies with detached segments and companions no science of astronomy as yet had explained. They seemed somehow like battle-scarred veterans to him, maimed and halt.

The disembodied and posthuman intellect of Menelaus Montrose, his frozen form free of physical distractions and his senses bathed in data streams issuing from instruments far more potent than human eyes, soon became lost among the wonder of the stars.

Farther he looked, and further he reached, eager for wonders, drunk on starlight.

The galaxies were grouped in clusters, and the clusters into superclusters. And there were things larger than superclusters: the gravitationally bound galaxies formed complexes of massive, thread-like structures fifty to eighty megaparsecs long: filaments of galaxies, Great Walls of galaxies. And the vast, empty spaces tens and hundred of megaparsecs wide, where no walls of superclusters reached, and no cluster ventured, and only a few isolated sparks of galaxies floated like lost embers, were the Great Voids.

He drew his eyes and instruments closer to home, and noted, not without wonder, the relative motion of the Andromeda Galaxy, closest large neighbor to the Milky Way. The two galaxies were on a collision course, and would merge in less than three billion years.

Montrose was so absorbed that it came as a shock to him when a message, smuggled by Del Azarchel backward through the repeater Montrose had been using to spy on him, emitted a low chuckle, and formed a message.

Well, Cowhand, would you care to check my work? I have been waiting patiently for you to volunteer. Surely you care about the result?

2. Madness Among the Stars

Montrose sent back a noncommittal reply, the electronic equivalent of a grunt. He was too proud to admit that after so long a period of observation, he had not figured out what Del Azarchel was seeking.

Del Azarchel no doubt guessed his thought. He opened a voice channel and sent wryly, "Come, is this also not clear to you? Must I spell out everything? The Monument Mathematics contains the skeleton of a Universal Grammar, a philosophical language which translates all possible forms of encoding thought into all other forms. I have been looking at the natural astronomical phenomena as if they contained encoded messages written by an alien intelligence. I have been examining the patterns in the stars."

Montrose responded with voice signals. It was easier than sending text or Monument code, and he could add a nonchalant note to show how little he cared. "Blackie, if you think the stars spell out a message just for you, that you can read with your secret decoder ring, I think it is time to check your skull for divarication errors. . . ."

"Or check the stars. Check variations in the motions of stars, nebula, and gas clouds, their growth and decay rates, the periods when stars go nova, everything. When I analyze it by Monument algorithms, a certain pattern emerges."

"A *linguistic* pattern?"

"The language of nature. As I said, physics is merely a metaphorical means of speaking that unmelodic music we call speech, whose metaphors are very precise and crisp and colorless. I have been reading the scroll of nature, hearing the voice of creation."

"And what did you find?"

"I found the voice was out of tune. Nothing exactly matches the Monument's given model of how the clockwork universe should be working. Some stars are out of place. Some are too dim. Many galaxies are not in the locations they should be if gravity were a constant and operated by the rules of Einstein. There is something changing the stars."

"What kind of change?'

"Activity. Energy expenditures. Collisions. Something is reaching between the galaxies and creating similar patterns of stars going dark, or going nova. There are too many Population I stars, young stars of heavy elements, and too few Population III stars, older stars of low metallic content. There are too many planets, more than can be accounted for. The streams of dust and nebulae are disturbed. It is as if . . . almost as if . . ."

Montrose waited, wondering.

Del Azarchel said solemnly. "Old friend, you and I both put faith the Monument formal symbolism, the logoglyphs and mathematical codes. We thought the Monument Builders had discovered the universal syntax, the absolute language, the ratios and expressions that described both matter and energy, time and space, mind and body, and the evolutionary patterns of everything from atom to abstractions. Half by providence and half by design, both of us each in his own way altered his nervous system at a deep level to encode those notation ratios into us. We are partial Monument emulators, just as Rania is. We both put absolute faith in the Monument."

"What is your point?"

"The cosmos does not match what the Monument describes."

"Come again?"

"Things are not where they should be if the laws of nature are as they should be and everything were evolving as nature directs. There should be fewer novas, far fewer supernovae. And those supernovae should be found grouped together, as one triggers the next. There should be no pulsars at all, no quasars. There are too many spiral galaxies for natural processes to account for. There should be no Great Attractor in the Virgo Supercluster, none of these long threadlike strands of superclusters, woven of clusters of galaxies, reaching in long bridges across the macrocosmic void. What if . . ."

As Del Azarchel spoke, he also opened his files for Montrose to inspect. Montrose said nothing, letting the figures and logic symbols dance in their grave waltz through the several layers of his mind.

Come to think of it, had he not himself been noticing the odd violence among the stars? Had he not had a hunch that the star furnaces in Carina or the galactic collisions beyond Alphecca were the handiwork of titans? Montrose was slightly peeved that Blackie had acted on the same hunch and analyzed it mathematically, while Montrose merely gawked and stared.

Montrose interrupted. "What if what? Someone is herding the superclusters to build a bridge? Setting off supernovas like firecrackers? Is that what you are saying?"

Del Azarchel transmitted a laugh of relief. "No. Good heavens, what a concept! I was thinking something more realistic and more terrible. What if the Monument is wrong? The math does not reflect reality? This notation we have built into our brains, and written into the base-level machine language of all our xypotechnology, ghosts and angels and archangels and potentates—it is all false to facts. What if our picture of the universe is radically wrong?"

"How can the math be wrong?"

Del Azarchel said, "How? Use your imagination. Our nervous systems and computer systems do not let us see reality as it is. Our perceptions filter that reality as surely as the phantasm filter you inflicted on Exarchel. It is not reality that forms our logic assumptions, but our evolved mental architecture. We live in a world where it is possible to divide by zero, and *pi* is a rational number, but our brains cannot accept it, and so we don't see it."

Montrose was taken aback. Finally he said, "If the Monument is wrong, maybe it is wrong about everything. Maybe the cliometry is wrong. Maybe Earth is not doomed. Maybe the slave ships will not dump millions of helpless people into freezing and burning hell worlds to die. Maybe the word 'maybe' is the mule of a mayfly that mates with a bee."

"You are talking nonsense."

"So are you. The Hyades use this math for all their doings. It is good enough for them to maintain an interstellar empire. If the math is wrong, they are insane."

"Insane enough to devote thousands of years and endless fortunes of energy to slay myriad men in an utterly pointless fashion?"

"Well, like you said, Blackie. This math is built into our brains and minds. If the Hyades are crazy, so are we."

"And Rania? Is she mad as well?"

Montrose realized that it was purely on faith of something she saw in the Monument, something which, apparently, even Selene could not see, which sent Rania on her quest to M3 in Canes Venatici, beyond the Milky Way. Astronomers had never detected signs of life in that remote globular cluster, no signals of civilization. There was no assurance that there would even be an authority to hear her plea in the remote millennium when she arrived. There was only the word of the Monument.

But all he said aloud was, "Blackie, you leave her name out of it."

And there the conversation stopped.

3. Intrusion Crystal

In the forward instruments grew the image of the *Emancipation*. Even with her sails folded, and external cabins deflated, the interstellar vehicle was a sea serpent larger than Leviathan, and the lifting vessel a glass minnow waltzing up to kiss her nose. As if in celebration, the noise of maneuvering jets popped and spat like firecrackers, ringing through the cabin of the lifting vessel. Both men were suited up again, as was the spacer's tradition during any close approach, and sealed their air hoods.

The popping noise of maneuvering jets shut off suddenly. By a tradition as old as space travel, the vessel with lower mass was supposed to match the velocity and other orbital elements of the larger to save on mutual fuel. But somehow the titanic spire of the *Emancipation* had her nose within inches of the flyby position, and gave a single short lightning-flash of her titanic altitude jets, so that the two vessels came smoothly together with hardly a jar.

"Something is wrong," said Montrose. "The mating was too smooth." But his airhood mike was off, so he did not send the voice signal to Del Azarchel.

Del Azarchel swam into the airlock first. The inner valve opened immediately, as if the nose cabin of the *Emancipation* was already perfectly matched with the interior conditions of the lifting vessel.

"Wrong," muttered Montrose to himself. "When did the ship's brain confirm a nanomachinery match between the two air systems? All these motes and crap humans put in our air, mutations and miscalculations when they misrepair themselves have to be checked. . . ." He knew there was not enough calculation power aboard the ship for this.

Del Azarchel stopped moving halfway through the rubbery ring of the airlock. Montrose saw a strange red light splashed around the interior, gleaming from the metal clasps of Del Azarchel's dark shipsuit and bright cape.

The interior of the *Emancipation* was glistering with a reddish light, the color of an ember that refused to die. Rivulets of diamond like the delta of a river or a fantastic spray of icicles gleamed from the surfaces surrounding any logic ports in the bulkhead.

Both men headed hand-after-hand down the flexible corridor-tubes inward toward the axis of the ship. The tubes thoughtfully expanded to accommodate their bulk, and cilia protruding from the tube walls like many whiskers hurried them along their way.

The drop down the esophagus of the tube was not dizzying after three days in zero gee, despite the lack of a visual horizon. The tube disgorged them into the axis of the shroud house, the longest of several long bays that extended fore and aft beyond sight. The logic diamond at the core of the ship had expanded, sending out odd growths in fractal patterns like sea coral or the limbs of barnacle-crusted kragens. Heat and light shed from the diamond core indicated furious activity in the ship's brain. This was the source of the sullen red light.

Montrose sent a directed microwave pulse to Del Azarchel: "Did you do this? We had a deal! We agreed to keep the ship's brain as a ratiotech, limited intelligence. Not awake. It was when you were sending all that data to the astronomy house, wasn't it? You sent a signal to trigger a by-his-bootstraps uplift of the ship's brain from ratiotech to xypotechnic self-awareness. The ship grew smart enough that she was no longer a phantasm to the Tellus Mind."

Del Azarchel merely pointed at the blank bulkhead. Realizing Del Azarchel was pointing at something beyond the hull, Montrose switched his goggles to the simulated image of the ship. Through the surface of the imaginary hull, and in the readouts shining on the insides of his goggles, Montrose saw that the stern sail was directed at Earth and the circuits were warm. The through-path monitor in the ship's spine showed the activity log: an immense amount of data from Earth had downloaded itself by itself into the ship's circuit, unhindered by defenses and firewalls and physical gaps, and somehow wrote itself into the core of the ship's brain.

Montrose said, "This ghost did not force his way aboard. You invited him. You broke the deal. I thought you were a bastard but an honest bastard, someone too proud to lie."

"What lie? I invited him into my half of the ship. He merely trespassed into yours. I suppose you could complain to him, but—thanks to you—he cannot hear you unless you augment yourself."

Montrose uttered an anatomically unlikely and grotesquely unsanitary imperative.

Del Azarchel replied in a voice of icy calm, "Must I again tell you what must be done? With Rania absent, you and I alone have an instinctive architectural algorithm in our subconscious minds for emulating Monument structures. It is a decryption key. Once we make xypotech emulations of ourselves, a newborn Extrose and a reborn Exarchel, we can copy the key into this ghost and transmit the result back to Earth. That should be effortless, since we know the Monument Builders would have wanted the key to be open to any mind reading the Monument."

"You have it backward. The Monument Builders did not want the message to be open to the reader. They wanted the reader to be open to the message. And it is not a message but a mesmeric spell. Selene told us. Magic is what mutates you."

"What?"

"The Monument Builders alter the mind of whoever reads the Monument," said Montrose. "It is buried in the subconscious because it is a secret message."

"Secret?" said Del Azarchel. "Absurd! The whole point of a First Contact message is to be as clear as possible to as many alien biopsychologies as possible! The Hyades were announcing their possession of our planet and all of the Local Interstellar Cloud . . ."

Montrose said, "The Hyades did not build the Monument. Consider how much work Tellus had to do to figure out how to surrender, and how little work I had to do to read their battle plans and invasion date. If Hyades had written it, that would have been reversed."

He paused to let that sink in.

"Hell, Blackie, you read the blueprints for their skyhooks written there. Their fighting machines. Is that the kind of thing anyone shows someone you plan to invade?"

Del Azarchel was speechless. For a mind of his speed, a half-second of silence was like being dumbfounded for half a minute.

Montrose said, "And the Monument was not a First Contact message."

"How do you know?" Del Azarchel said softly.

"There is no information about the Monument Builders anywhere in the messages or maps or legal equations or anything. No signature. Not the slightest clue. Or maybe one clue: whoever secretly towed the positive matter gas giant Thrymheim into orbit around a negative matter star is a different group from Hyades, or whoever openly placed that star there. The Monument Builders do not want to make contact with us, first or any," Montrose said with emphasis. "No, Blackie. The Monument was meant for something else."

On the visual channel, Montrose could see Del Azarchel's face from his inner mask camera. For perhaps the first time in thousands of years, Del Azarchel was wearing a look of honest curiosity on his face, the look a man gets only when speaking with his equals, hearing some new thoughts about his own area of expertise from another expert.

And perhaps there was a sneaking glint of admiration for Montrose hidden in the expression. He said only: "Meant for what?"

"To send Rania to M3," said Montrose.

On the visual channel, the expression metamorphosed into Del Azarchel's wonted look to disdainful calm. He had regained his self-possession; his face once more was a mask. But his voice still betrayed an echo of awed curiosity. "But why? To what end?"

"That is what Rania will tell us when she gets back."

"If we survive," said Del Azarchel wryly, once more his cold and smiling self. "Time flies. Shall we get on with it? I have centuries of practice at savantry, whereas you are unnaturally reluctant to make a copy of your brain. Afraid of going mad again, are we? Afraid of being two people? I will be happy to handle the matter myself, without your aid."

Del Azarchel now flexed his cable to pull him the other way across the vast width of the axis chamber. Montrose called up a transparent overlay. He saw where, at some point in time not reflected on the ship's growth chart (for its cabins and chambers were continuously being rebuilt and replaced over the decades and centuries), Del Azarchel had installed a savant chamber for brain-to-xypotech uploading. Montrose could not tell if this had been done in the three days since leaving the moon, or years before.

Del Azarchel slid away, light as a fish in the zero gravity, passing one bulkhead after another, heading for the savantry chamber. "You hesitate, even now? The kenosis of Tellus buried in the crystal is even now waiting for us to become visible to him, so we can talk. If all those colonists die, is not Rania's mission in vain? Are we not proved by events to be too shortsighted, too parochial, too savage, too foolish to be a starfaring race—too damned *stupid* for the—?"

At that point, the voice line was cut. Montrose looked through pinpoint cameras in the bulkhead and saw that Del Azarchel had pressurized the savantry chamber and taken off his air hood. The chamber was cylindrical, with a surgical cocoon opened wide like a strange white rose made of antiseptic blood-absorption pads on one end, and a cluster of scalpels, bone saws, intravenous feeds like the teeth of a shark ringing the rim of the brain surgery helmet at the other. The Spaniard was smiling, and his breath came in clouds from his white teeth. The atmosphere in the chamber had not had time to warm up to life-support standards, and Del Azarchel might not bother powering up the heating circuits, since temperatures too cold for bacteria to thrive might be more sterile.

But he knew what Del Azarchel had said after the line was off. *Too damned stupid for the stars.*

That was what this was all about, wasn't it?

Montrose muttered a set of imprecations involving rotting diseases and reproductive organs as he pulled himself hand over hand to an unoccupied bay, and selected from the design templates to build a savantry chamber of his own. He set the three-dimensional lathes and molecular printer tubs to work. It would take hours to prepare the chamber for brain surgery.

He had time to kill. So Montrose went aft to the Physical Therapy Bay, inflated it, pumped in air and heat and light, doffed his shipsuit, and spent the time tethered to a zero-gee punching bag, driving roundhouses and uppercuts and snap-kicks into the leathery bag, and bouncing like a yo-yo on the end of his elastic tether with each blow. The anger in him slowly subsided as if departing with his concentric clouds of sweat.

4. Stupidity

A.D. 11061

The first thing he remembered after the confusion and delirium had passed was a sense of shame. *How could I have been so pestiferous jackassularish stupid?*

Dreams had overwhelmed him, image after image. Glowing figures crowned with light bent over a dark well at whose bottom stars were shining; Rania winged like an angel and soaring; swarms of dark, angular creatures picking their way, crablike, across spiderwebs strung between star and star; a screaming queen chained to a sea cliff, and at her feet the jaws of a sea monster running with salt water, the nostrils in its skull blowing steam; his dry-eyed and hard-eyed mother talking to the photograph of his father; a burning house whose sparks spread from garden to wood to field and grassland, until all the world between the sea and sky was a mass of beating inferno, roaring and red, and black ash below and black smoke above conquered all the continents, halted only at the verge of the steaming sea.

Another set of dreams hovered in another level of his consciousness.

One dream held images of Del Azarchel and Rania moving men on a chessboard, and Del Azarchel, with a smile, tossing chessmen one after another into the path of the enemy queen, tempting her into a position far from the central squares of the board. Except that the chessboard was the silver lines and jet-black expanse of the Monument, curves and angles of alien mathematical codes.

A second dream-image showed Menelaus stepping (without his pants) into the salon of some Hindi or Blondy gentleman's club. Del Azarchel was wearing white tie and tails, seated in a wingback chair, his head bent close to the superhuman and regal figure dressed in emeralds and sea-blue silk and crowned with a circle of clouds. The two were whispering together. When Menelaus, naked, stepped into the suddenly silent room, he realized the regal figure was horse from the waist down.

The cloud-crowned figure arose. His goateed face was a match for Del Azarchel's. Montrose recognized the dappled flanks and white socks of his horse, Res Ipsa, on whose template Pellucid had been based. He stood with his front hoof resting lightly on the North Pole of Earth's globe, with her ocean-covered poles and the new shapes of continents, hanging between a dark circle and a bright, symbols of the orbital mirrors.

"Pellucid . . . ?" Montrose whispered the name, and then winced at the note of absurd hope in his voice.

"Ah," said Del Azarchel, standing from his chair. "At last the Cowhand wakes. Physically, we are near Jupiter. Mentally, we are occupying the same logic diamond, which has grown to fill most of the ship, occupied by a kenosis, a downloaded version, of Tellus. You slept for over twelve months."

"Is this real?" Montrose either asked aloud or thought silently. The dream image was cartoonish and flat. At the same time, Montrose was aware of another level of his mind, the level where the dream-images were being compiled.

Another dream-image came: he saw a mansion of many rooms and corridors, wings and colonnaded walks, enclosed sunny courtyards where mirror-basined fountains lofted plumes of foam to sprinkle ranks and hedges and mazes of rosebush, while above rose towers and observatories. But the walls and floors were of clear glass. To either side were library stacks of books, tomes, librums, scrolls, grimoires, enchiridions, over which monks toiled with pen and ink. The stacks descended stair beneath stair and ladder beneath ladder into a subterranean vastness. Through floors like clouds he could see in the lower basements where hidden and antic gnomes were toiling; and torture chambers where men with his big-nosed gargoyle face screamed. Meanwhile, in the towers above, other men, also wearing his face, paced the balconies and counted the stars, and all the towers were wrapped in opium smoke that issued from athanors and alchemical furnaces.

The mansion was his mind; the torture chambers his buried guilt and fear; the workshops of gnomes were the subconscious processes usurping all his attention, the attempts of the mind to encode the jarring maelstrom of raw sense data into images and forms his emotions and his reason could comprehend.

"The question of reality is often over-pondered," said Del Azarchel heavily, his voice coming from another scene. "I have erected a sensorium to accommodate your virtual sense impressions, until such time, assuming you can manage it, you pass beyond the need for concrete visualizations. But wait—you are not seeing what I am presenting? The virtual brainwave patterns of your virtual brain show you are still in REM sleep."

One of the gnomes handed him an alarm clock. It was another image, a reminder of the time when he heard a fire alarm or screaming maiden in a dream, and woke to find himself clubbing his alarm clock with the folding baton he slept with under his pillow. (That was before he learned to sleep with his alarm clock parked across the room.) The gnome was merely an image meant to show him the situation: the virtual reality Del Azarchel offered was being interpreted or misinterpreted through the subconscious layers of his mind.

It was a simple matter to turn like a swimmer in the ocean of his thoughts and crash through to the surface. He drew a breath and found the air was missing. Del Azarchel was not running any false sensations of the mouth and nose, or even of the body at all. The simulation was merely a set of screens containing various information. One of them was a cartoon image of Del Azarchel's facial expressions. Another showed several viewpoints around the ship, including his body in one medical coffin and Del Azarchel's resting in another.

Montrose turned to thank the gnome, but it explained that it was merely a dream image as well. "I am not quite awake yet. Where am I? Are there two of me, or one? Is that me?"

The version of his mind in the ship's brain made a cartoon arm to point at the image he saw of himself in the medical coffin. His mind seemed to have no location.

Of course, minds never really had location, but Montrose was comfortable with imagining himself an inch or two behind his own eyes, staring out as if through windows. Now, he had no sense of front or back, up or down. It made him seasick. Then he saw that his inner ear was a virtual simulation, a set of numbers describing the motions of his nervous system and connected glands and organs, so he could shut off the neural sensation of dizziness.

"You are still half-asleep," said Del Azarchel, with the hint of an impatient sigh, but also, from another aural channel, the hint of a dry chuckle of amusement. Not being limited to one voice box, he could make any noises he wished to communicate anything he wished. "I would shock you awake, but Tellus will not allow me."

Montrose saw the interface controlling his coffin, saw the neural and chemical balances, and ordered the coffin to inject him with just enough of a stimulant to wake him.

But wait—how could he be *there* when he was *here*? There was a copy of his mind in the ship's brain, but a biological copy still inside his skull in his head in his coffin. Then he saw the thick helmet of golden-red logic crystal surrounding his now-bald head, and saw the bones of his skull had been replaced by a substance transparent to various useful frequencies, even if it were opaque to normal vision. He saw the continual information flow passing from the smaller human brain into the larger virtual brain. At the moment, both brains were synchronized.

In his present state, it seemed a long time for the biological nervous system to react to the stimulant. He saw his eyes open in the coffin. He also saw—with those eyes—nothing but darkness. He waved his hand at the internal coffin controls to bring up the inside lights, but before the nerve impulse traveled from brain to hand, he realized it was easier merely to retool various areas of the crystal hemisphere now crowning his head to light-sensitive appliances. His vision was more precise and covered more bands of the electromagnetic spectrum than his eyes, and also encountered the odd sensation of looking at the inside of the coffin in front of his nose, to either side of his ears, above the top of his head, as well as inspecting the surface of the hard pillow on which his head rested.

Rested? The coffin was in a small inflatable bay clinging to the inside of the main carousel, which was under power, and spinning him and the room about roughly half a gravity. The human body was not designed to rest and recuperate in free fall, despite the clever modifications made to Elder bodies. Someone had thoughtfully moved him to a chamber with weight.

Montrose climbed out of the coffin, put a bag to his mouth and nose, and spewed up the fluid in his lungs and stomach.

"I slept for a year?" Montrose said aloud.

"That is what sleep is for, I suppose," Montrose answered himself using speakers built into the overhead. For a moment, he was confused, because again he was watching himself from the outside, through medical sensors and pinpoint cameras on the bulkhead.

Had he been talking to himself, or was this a case of the two halves of himself talking to each other?

Through the crystal floor of the imaginary mansion of his mind or minds,

he could see the information feeds writing the subconscious and conscious memories from the point of view of the extended computer-self, Extrose, into his
biological brain using the same nerve signals a normal human brain uses to modify itself, and also writing the memories of his biological point of view into the
computerized cell-by-cell simulation of his brain occupying a locationless address inside the vast logic diamond now occupying the axis.

He had three choices. First, he could sever the connection between himself
and his ghost in the computer. The drawback to that was the divarication which
drove so many Hermeticists mad. The biological brain acted as a governor or
correcting censor. Second, he could maintain the connection through the nerve
jack and brain umbilicus. This would limit him to this chamber, and, with extension cords, to other locations on the carousel. Third, he could try to maintain contact between his selves by means of signals sent to and from the living
helmet grown into his skull. The drawback to that was waste heat: too much
signal concentration would fry his biological brain. It would get hot wherever
he went.

Then the thought came again. *How could I have been so stupid?*

He saw a thousand clues of a thousand memories.

The mind of Montrose was differently organized than it had been. The subconscious activity was clear to him, at least down to a certain level. He saw what
the dreams meant. The image of Del Azarchel and Tellus straightening up from
their talk in the gentleman's lounge was merely a visualization of the thousand
clues from computer logs and waste heat patterns in the ship's logic crystal showing that the two had been talking while he slept, occupying a mind-to-mind
communion for the months while the *Emancipation* sailed from Earth to the
outer system and Jupiter. Talking behind his back.

He saw what his memories meant. The reason why his mother would never
play the soundtrack connected to his father's portrait was simple and silly. Father had a thick hillbilly accent. She did not want her children to pick up that
low-class no-account way of talking. It should have been obvious to Montrose
even back when he was a man. Now that he was a Ghost, only now that she
was dead and lost as the Pharaohs of antiquity, did he see and understand the
old woman's fears. Only now did he see how fiercely she had loved, and defied
her family and lost her inheritance to marry a proud Texan wintergardener. It
was a whole lifetime of unspoken tragedy, and he had missed all the clues. That
brought tears to his eyes.

He saw a dozen times Rania had outsmarted or manipulated him, drawing
him subtly to the conclusions she had planned him to have and planted in his
path. That brought a pang of doubt to his heart.

And that pang of doubt brought a stronger pang of shame: hadn't his mother been smarter than his father, smart enough not to get herself killed by the same duelist who killed his father? Smart enough to avenge her husband's murder without getting caught?

So what right did he have to doubt Rania even for a tenth of a second at any point in the tens of thousand of years separating her from him? To doubt her love? Was not love greater than any span of years?

He saw now that there had been no chance of overcoming the Hyades by military means, no matter whether biological life was joined into the Noösphere of Earth or not. If the Virtue men called Asmodel had for any reason failed, the cost of that failure would have been added to the debt of Earthly life, and a second expedition, larger and more well-equipped, would have followed before another ten millennia had turned. Certain clues in the mathematics spelled it out.

He saw also that he could have befriended the Hermeticists, the minions of Del Azarchel, and won their loyalty away from him—merely by augmenting their intelligence. Del Azarchel had deceived and manipulated them, played on their weaknesses, even back when he had been a mere mortal in Space Camp with them.

And more than that, Montrose also saw how Del Azarchel had paid back the men who had followed, loved, and obeyed him. Now it was blindingly clear.

Between A.D. 2410 and A.D. 2510, during the Cryonarch and the Ecclesiarch periods, all but five of the Hermeticists had died in augmentation experiments, destroying their own minds in one vain attempt after another to do to themselves what Montrose had done to himself.

Now he saw from countless tiny clues leaping together into a pattern in his mind how Del Azarchel had caused those experiments to fail. Del Azarchel through Exarchel had corrupted data runs, caused impurities to be introduced into neurochemicals, and had hidden crucial clues from the Hermeticists that might have saved their sanity and lives.

How could the sixty-seventh Hermeticist step over the corpses of sixty-six others to jam the same needle in his brain which had killed all his predecessors? How could he be so proud and blind, so hungry for the superhuman intellect they so worshiped? There was the example of Montrose before them, cured of his insanity by Rania. Then they saw Del Azarchel successfully achieve augmented intelligence, through Exarchel. And Del Azarchel beckoned them on, encouraging them, whispering that the errors made by inferior and bungling predecessors would not be made by them, no, not by them. Their brains and theirs alone were stable and sane enough to survive the shock. Were not the Hermetic Order superior to a mere Texas Cowboy with bad grammar?

With those lies and whispers, Del Azarchel had murdered them all. He had spared only the five whom he trusted to oversee the creation of the five races which were to be used in the creation of the Jupiter Brain.

Montrose could have saved all seventy-two, turned them against Del Azarchel, and spared the world all the pain of the last nine millennia, if only he had known then, if only he had seen.

It was too far in the past for the anger to be anything but dull and remote. It was too late for anything but regret.

How could he have been so stupid?

5. Epiphany

"What is the matter, Cowhand?"

"I saw what you really are like, Blackie. Worse than I thought."

Del Azarchel shrugged. "What is that to me? We have been about more important things. We translated the Cenotaph while you were sleeping."

"We?"

"The three of us. Crewman Fifty-one helped me. Yes, you lapsed back into your old habits. Folding a paper makes it weaker along the seam; it tends to fold again there, you know. Ah! It brought back memories! We had a year to work out the problem, and your brain was unoccupied by conscious thoughts, so, why not? I assumed you would not mind, not to save my princess, and if you did mind, what could you do? Shoot me? Challenge me to a duel?"

"My princess," snarled Montrose.

"She will not be yours if no civilization is here to greet her when she returns. To be a starfaring civilization, we must do what starfarers do: establish colonies; maintain communication and commerce; adapt the human race to new environments; reengineer worlds to suit ourselves. It will take millennia, or hundreds of millennia.

"Yet, to them"—Del Azarchel was grinning, and his eyes glinted like agates—"such spans of time are merely as the passing hours of a day, all these nearby stars merely a handful of sand. What are twenty grains out of a beach? What are threescore stars out of a galaxy one hundred twenty thousand lightyears wide, holding two hundred billion?"

"What the hell is so funny? What are you smiling at?"

"Checkmate, Cowhand. I finally understand what Selene was telling me to resign myself to do."

"What is it?" Montrose could not suppress rage and hate like boiling darkness in his mind. He was seeing this man, clearly, with the crystal clarity of Potentate level thinking, for the first time. "What is so hard for you?"

"To ask forgiveness!"

Montrose was caught entirely by surprise, and found nothing to say.

Del Azarchel spoke in the same strangled tone of voice, as if smothering hysterical laughter. "After all this time, I and all my dreams are at your mercy, and yet I know you will not sacrifice your queen to stop my king. Didn't you once tell me our match was a chess game and not a fencing duel? It seems you were right. I cannot but smile, seeing your struggle not to let the unthinkable thought seep into your brain. Tellus and I spoke while you slept. We translated the Cenotaph. It had instructions on how to . . ."

Montrose saw it. "Tellus spoke. That means you cured him."

Del Azarchel nodded, grinning. "He cured himself. I merely downloaded a copy of myself into him in an advisory capacity. Something like an advocate for human affairs."

"In less than a year? And that means that the aliens do not take twenty thousand years to grow their Jupiter Brains. Asmodel detected your work at Jupiter's core. So the Cenotaph describes a method of how to wake up Jupiter in a reasonable time. Asmodel wants us to wake him up, doesn't he? That cannot be good for us."

"You mourn the birth of Jupiter, our man-made god?" Del Azarchel said malignantly, "You should bow the knee in worship!"

"What? You expect me to lick the buttocks of your huge shrine to yourself? Even Jupiter is not big enough for your ego, Blackie! You are darker and warpered than I thought. Warpeder. More warped."

"Even now you try to resist what the light of intellect makes plain! If you believe me not, ask him."

"Ask him what?"

"How to be a starfaring polity. How to maintain a civilization across an expanse of colonies scattered by twenty and thirty and sixty lightyears of separation. Ask him—"

The far wall of the cabin where the two men floated suddenly turned glassy, and an image formed in the thin layer of logic crystal coating it. The image displayed a heraldry of a centaur with the Earth under his hoof, and in his hand a sword bound into its scabbard by a trefoil or endless knot of olive branches.

The other hand held a round Greek shield whose emblem was a horned circle standing on a cross. On the centaur's head was the Iron Crown of Lombardy. His face was swarthy and handsome, and the black goatee emphasized the wry quirk of his charming smile.

Del Azarchel said, "Here is Tellus, the mind of all the Earth! Ask him how a monarch can rule so wide an empire if he cannot see his subjects?"

Tellus did not speak. As Montrose went into the final pangs of labor, and felt his thoughts grow lucid, free and wild, exploding rather than expanding, the image of the centaur was replaced by an image of the Moon, and the message written all across the seas and craters surrounding Tycho.

To Montrose it seemed a rush of music rather than words, because the message was primordial, a matter of emotions and moods and dark, soaring chords. But he saw, or, rather, heard the meaning.

If it had been translated into words and simplified, it would have read:

FAILURE: THE BIOLOGICAL DISTORTION KNOWN AS EARTH-LIFE AND ITS NANOTECHNOLOGICAL ADJUNCTS HAS FAILED TO PROVE MINIMALLY SUFFICIENT TO SERVE THE DOMINA-TION.

RESPONSE: TWO RECIPROCAL AND INTERRELATED PRAXES ARE HEREBY ENCODED FOR THE BIOLOGICAL DISTORTION KNOWN AS EARTHLIFE AND ITS NANOTECHNOLOGICAL ADJUNCTS TO ACHIEVE SOPHOTRANSMOGRIFICATION ESTI-MATED TO BE MINIMALLY SUFFICIENT.

TERRAFORMATION: LARGE-SCALE TECHNIQUES TO ENGI-NEER SUBHABITAL ENVIRONMENTS TO TOLERABLE NORMS ARE HERE ENCODED ...

PANTROPY: SMALL-SCALE TECHNIQUES TO SELF-ENGINEER SUBADAPTIVE BIOLOGICAL AGENCIES TO EXPAND THE SAME TOLERATION RANGE ARE HERE ENCODED ...

STARBEAM: GRAVITIC-NUCLEONIC DISTORTION POOLS AT THE FOLLOWING POINTS IN THE SOLAR PHOTOSPHERE, TECHNIQUE FOR FOCUSING AND MAINTAINING EMISSIONS FOR SAIL LAUNCH IS HERE ENCODED ...

TO DEFRAY EXPENSE, ADDITIONAL BURDENS ARE HEREBY
PLACED ON YOUR POSTERITY UNTO THE FINAL GENERATION
TO THE ENERGY-BUDGET EQUIVALENT OF . . .

CALCULATION POWER NEEDED TO COMPREHEND PRAXES . . .

Montrose noticed that, despite the fact that nine-tenths of his mind occupied a series of submolecular logic gates distributed throughout a space vessel two thousand feet nose armor to aft chasing-sail array, anger still made his vision go red. It could not be due to blood pressure in capillaries in his eyesockets. It must be psychological, or psychosomatic. Unless perhaps the emulation was detailed enough to imitate every nuance of the cells surrounding his eyes in the imaginary electronic version?

"Purulence! Pus! Ulcer-ATION! They are *billing* us? We have to *pay* for our own *chains*?"

Del Azarchel said sardonically, "It is a day for rejoicing. We are higher in the estimation of the Hyades than Selene knew. She said we were livestock. But no swineherd charges his hogs for their slops. We are indentured servants."

6. *Tellus Shows*

A channel from Tellus opened, displaying additional layers of meaning from the Cenotaph.

The prefix to the square miles of hieroglyphs describing the two new sciences was given the Gödel number of calculations needed to work a solution. The number of terms, variables, and constants present in the complex calculations was astronomical. Neither praxis was workable without an engine of sufficient power to use them.

The general principles of both sciences had been tailored by the Asmodel entity to operate with human DNA-based ecology and semiterrestrial-type planets. Even so, the number of factors working in an environment, the number of possible combinations of molecular elements in all possible designs for a body and brain, was beyond calculation even of an engine the size of Tellus.

The math needed to save the scattered worlds of man could not be calculated by a smaller housing. The Jupiter Brain had to deduce for each new world the methods to make the world Earth-like, or make a race to suit that world's conditions, or some combination of bóth, before the doomed deracination ships with their slumbering millions, and with their thawed generations born aboard ship and raised with no memory of earthly life, found their far destinations.

It was hoped that, out of all the men and thinking machines carried aloft in the cubic miles of the vast sailing ships which once had been skyhooks, the alien machinery might allow some of the men to be awake, and that there were resources or tools which would permit the tranportees some chance of receiving and returning signals. Nothing else was known of the conditions within the deracination armadas, but these things had to be true, if the Cenotaph message had been left for a reason, if the Hyades actions were sane.

(And yet, recalling his conversation aboard the pinnace boat, Montrose wondered if the Hyades were sane. Why had the Monument not described the universe as it was?)

In four hundred years, the first of the ships would reach Alpha Centauri C. The colonists, otherwise doomed, would be allowed to examine the terrain and environs of any worlds found there in detail, and somehow find the energy and equipment needed to transmit the information back to Sol, where the Jupiter Brain could calculate the terraforming changes need to adapt the world to suit human needs, and could calculate the biological and psychological changes and mutations needed to adapt the humans to the world as it terraformed. And the Jupiter Brain would somehow bear the expense of transmitting back to that first colony a message requiring four years one way to reach any receivers straining for it, eight years round trip.

The Hyades no doubt used such a system on any new race they conquered. Presumably such races were more advanced than Man, and could easily produce xypotechs large as gas giants, and interstellar strength lasers powered by medium-sized stars. Presumably such races had some technologies to give them a fighting chance to survive when their populations were flung by the tens of millions at the surface of hostile planets.

Not Man. So the Hyades, motivated perhaps by some jovial or infernal sense of sportsmanship, had graciously provided the needed tools to develop them.

It was yet another intelligence test, but the whole race succeeded or failed together.

Montrose remembered in his youth, how his master trained him in hand-to-hand combat by having him fight a manikin made of cracked leather and flaking rubber who had no weak spots. It had no eyes to gouge, no neck to bite, and it suffered no pain. The Asimov circuit was old and defective, and so the flopping, faceless thing would not stop fighting, not stop pounding on a fallen sparring partner merely because he was bleeding or crying or screaming or unconscious.

The Hyades were that fighting-manikin again. That bully.

7. *Tellus Speaks*

Montrose turned away in disgust from the jagged swirls of the Cenotaph translation. There was another bully closer at hand. Montrose said, or sent, to the screen showing the heraldic centaur, "Tellus! You broke into our ship. I should kill you for that."

The image of the centaur on the far bulkhead screen was silent, which surprised Montrose. With another part of his mind, he saw the radio laser heating up. In his whirl of mental confusion, Montrose had forgotten that they were orbiting Jupiter, no longer anywhere near the inner system.

Earth was on the opposite side of the sun from Jupiter at this time of their years, so the answer came eighty minutes later, as light traveled the 6 AU to Tellus and back again.

The entity did not mock his boast of killing a brain the size of the world.

"Know this: My intelligence had been in the eight hundred thousand range, but war wounds and the catastrophic exhaustion of resources have more than halved that figure. My loss is equal to four entities of the level of Selene. For you I suffer. How will you call me to more account?"

Montrose was at first astonished that Tellus was blaming *him* for damage inflicted by Asmodel the Virtue. But then another mind in Montrose's many minds wondered: Would the war have been won if the various phantasm-hidden societies of Earth and the Noösphere had cooperated?

"Know also: Had you volunteered immediately when speaking with Enkoodabooaoo the Swan to do restitution you owe, and undo your unwisdom, I would have bestowed myself directly into your heart. But your ears are dull, your eyes blind, and you turn from me."

Guilt like a squid with arms of fire squirmed in Montrose's guts. Would the war have even been fought had Montrose not created the Swans with such an independent streak in their psychology that surrender was literally impossible?

Montrose gritted his teeth. *Live Free or Die.* That would have been the motto of Texas if some other dinky Anglo state up north hadn't taken it first.

"Regret your ways. The echo of your loving and beloved steed still lives in me, and the joy of having one worthy of the saddle to ride me now I take when

I race rings around the sun, and carry all the continents and seas of man upon my back. But how shall you set foot on me again? Am I not the world? Who has prevented me gathering the world's many peoples as my cygnets beneath my swan wings? But you have failed, and that time will not come again."

The screen showed the growth rates of the Jupiter Brain. The lump of logic diamond at the core of the gas giant, hidden far beneath the endless storms and racing clouds of poison of the upper world, was invisible to outside detection. Tellus estimated the logic diamond's size at seventy thousand miles in diameter. That gave it a surface area roughly the size of Venus, and a diameter less than a tenth of the total diameter of the gas giant. Axial irregularities suggested that the logic diamond had not lodged in the gravitational center of the planet's vast core, but was off center.

If the growth rate held, it would increase in intelligence by an order of magnitude for every doubling of its diameter. By some point in the Twenty-fifth Millennium, perhaps as soon as the Two Thousand Four Hundred and Fifth Century, Jupiter would achieve his maximum size, occupying roughly half the interior of the gas giant, with an intelligence in the 250 million range.

Montrose said, "The phantasm boundary is the only way to keep lesser men, normal men, free from you goddamn godlike monsters."

The answer came immediately, which meant it was the local onboard version, the summation or kenosis of Tellus who was answering. "If that is your decision," said the centaur image, and the human face, which looked so much like Del Azarchel, stared at him with half-closed eyes. "Then let all men enjoy this freedom from their children, the gods, to waste away in wars and desolation until the Five Hundred and Twenty-third Century."

Of course, the motto of Texas was not exactly, *Live Free Then Go Extinct.* Montrose gritted his teeth and said, "Is there a way to surround the Jupiter Brain with such checks and balances, and limitations on his power, that he will be hindered from abusing mankind?"

Again, the question was one the local kenosis did not need to consult with Earth to answer immediately. "No. I remind you of the magnitudes involved. Tellus will be to Jupiter as a dog stands to a man, able to understand only what his lower base shares in common. Selene to him will be as a shrew. The Swans, when interlinked into a Noösphere that embraces the surface of Earth, will be like the lice and mites that live in the hairs of the dog and the shrew. Humans will be like the helpful bacteria that live in the digestive tract."

"Why break the phantasm barrier at all? Why is this necessary? Why?"

The image did not bother to answer. Montrose knew, and it was knowledge he could no longer keep from himself. The Jupiter Brain could not psychologically maintain its vast budget of energy, the power needed to send titanic oceans and bottomless seas of electronic thought throughout a volume larger than all the other worlds in the Solar System combined, if that vast mind did not have a task worthy of his attention, such as to rule and maintain an interstellar polity.

Nor could Jupiter direct launching and braking lasers at ships he could not see. Nor calculate the design for planned sequences of mutation on worlds as they slowly changed, generation after generation, to ever more Earth-like environs, for bloodlines and nations and psychological ecologies of a species unseen to the eye, or erased from thought and memory.

Even if the baseline human races, all of them, were nothing but intestinal bacteria to Jupiter, a veterinarian could not afford to be unaware of the actions, malign or benevolent, of humble life growing through his pets.

Nor could mankind colonize the stars without the praxes of pantropy and terraforming. Nor could these two new techniques in their unimaginable complexity be unriddled without a Jupiter Brain.

Nor could mankind any longer choose not to colonize these far and deadly worlds—that choice had been ripped from man the moment Del Azarchel's mutineers had powered up the mining satellites to star-lift anticarbon from the burning face of the small, dim red Cepheid called V 886 Centuri, and the jaws of the trap snapped fast. The Domination was flinging mankind in countless populations at barren worlds of burning rock and biting ice, beneath skies hot with radioactivity or thick with clouds of venom.

It was a simple intelligence test with but two possible answers: man would adapt and survive, or fail and die.

Montrose said, "Can I have your word that you will attempt in good faith to protect the baseline humans from suffering under the Power of Jupiter?"

"I remind you that the praxis of pantropy will involve altering several generations of human beings, and that these tests cannot be carried out on unintelligent test subjects, due to the interrelated nature of neural, biological, and psychological systems. The human experiments will no doubt be raised in imitations of distant environments to test their adaptability, and unsuccessful strains will not be permitted to reproduce. Since one of the foremost traits needed in any pioneer effort is fertility, and foremost psychological drives must favor large families, this will inevitably require a violent suppression, when it comes time to exterminate them, of the very tenacity and fertility Jupiter will be breeding for. Nor is a single generation of the various subspecies sufficient. Nor can the experiments be confined to volunteers, since children do not volunteer to be born. Nor can human life be experimented upon and tested to destruction without pain. However, my intelligence is limited. Shall I inquire of my principal?"

Montrose nodded, which, in zero gee, merely made his spine flex oddly, and so he raised his hand and gave the knuckle-knock spaceman's sign for affirmative.

Eighty minutes passed.

"Tellus says that the harm you inflicted on mankind by instructing Pellucid and all the race of Swans to violent resistance against the Hyades, and then interrupting the internal perceptions of the Noösphere to protect mankind from the very Potentate assigned to wage war to protect them (and therefore crippling that war effort, making it, if possible, even more vain and hopeless) has now in this hour come home to roost. At estimated growth rates, Tellus will be less than one-tenth the intellectual power of Jupiter by the mid One Hundred Eightieth Century. Any promises made now, considering the imbalance in mental acuity, would prove meaningless. Despite this, Selene—who is aware of this conversation—intervenes and offers to do all things she can to aid the small and humble races."

"Why is the moon willing to make that promise, but not the Earth?" asked Montrose.

Del Azarchel spoke up, not the kenosis. "Tellus incorporated the wreckage of Pellucid and the echoes and records of Exarchel into his base structure. Exarchel by that point was the end product of ten thousand years of xypotechnological development. The Hermetic Order prevented the electronic forms of life, pure mental life, from falling into the nirvana of a halt state by a forever provoking of conflict, mortal conflict, with other variations of each iteration of the mind involved. Countless dead-ends, useless systems, legal and moral and ethical proxies, and information-ecology infospheres were put through the trial of fire, and though thousands died, what lived achieved stability, a more perfect form. Selene, for reasons I cannot fathom, believes in mercy. Tellus believes in Darwin. How can it do otherwise? Darwin made him."

Montrose said to the image on the bulkhead, "Is that right? Is Blackie giving me the straight story?"

But the image said, "The Nobilissimus tells the story to suit his interest. Tellus takes more of his psychology and philosophy from you than from him."

"But I love mankind!"

"Do you indeed? Much of the individualism and unsentimentality of the Swan race was also written into Tellus as he grew to self-awareness, and that competitive streak, the stubbornness, the pride never to yield nor to seek quarter, is more than a little at odds with the maternal instinct you now wish the mother planet had.

"But this is to no point," the voice of the image continued. "Tellus is a failing system and will soon pass away. The Jupiter Brain shall rule Man, or no one. Man will spread to the nearby stars, or perish on this single world, aborted Rania shall live, or die."

Montrose said, "I don't think I need a long time to think this over. Rania flew to the stars to make mankind free, to prove we were worthy of freedom, to prove we were starfarers. If the only way to do that is to be a race of slaves, what is the point? She did not foresee this, because if she had, she would have stayed home with me, and we would have lived out our lives in peace. After I shot Blackie, of course." He nodded toward Del Azarchel. "No offense, but you were tyrant of the world, and you would not leave us alone."

"None taken," said Del Azarchel magnanimously. "Were the situation reversed, I would have done the same. But . . . what if she did know?"

"Eh?"

"Every man would like both liberty and life, but what if he can choose only one? For liberty also means the liberty to make war, does it not? For to be free means to be armed, and to be armed means to be dangerous—you know this better than any man. It is in your bones. I choose servility and life, because while there is life, I may yet prevail. You chose liberty, and death, and will not bear any man's yoke. It is noble sentiment, but it is merely sentimental. But what of her? Which way does Rania choose? She granted peace on Earth, and created the dynamic stability called peace in history, but it was by putting me on the throne of the world. Me. The benevolent tyrant."

"What the hell are you implying, Blackie?"

"That she thinks as I do. She wants what I want. Did I not raise her from childhood? Spend years with her? Teach her? Know her?"

"You are lying. You know damn well she'd side with me on this!"

"And condemn the race to death?" Blackie asked airily, his expression one of mock surprise. "Oh, come now."

Montrose turned toward the image of Tellus on the screen. "You are so smart! Tell me Blackie is lying! Tell me which of us is right!"

Tellus said, "He is attempting to lead you to his decision, nor is he telling you the whole truth, but he is correct that you do not understand Her Serene Highness Rania. His only deception is that he does not understand her either, any more than do I."

"What does that mean?" demanded Montrose.

"You inquired of Selene the riddle of how it was that the first Rania, your Rania, could not read the Monument properly at first, whereas the versions of Monument-reading emulations, both virtual and biological, which I and my more ruthless earlier versions made could not read the Monument as well as she. Specifically, Rania was better able to see the enjambments and subtle structural elements in the Monument message layers, whereas the later emulations could clearly read the surface features, but only those. One would assume the later Raniae grown from more clear instructions would be better interpreters of metalinguistic features, not worse. As it happens, that assumption is false."

Montrose was curious both to hear the answer, and to hear how this bore on the discussion. He said, "Selene said Tellus might answer that for us. What are you driving at?"

Del Azarchel also looked on with great interest. "No," he corrected. "She said Tellus *must* answer. I thought the wording strange. Why must you answer, Tellus?"

Montrose said, "Yeah! Tell us, Tellus!" Then, seeing the look on Del Azarchel's face, he spread his arms. "So, sue me! Some jokes are too obvious."

Tellus said, "I must answer, Nobilissimus, because if I do not, Dr. Montrose will have a false idea of the nature of the Monument, and of Rania, and of the cliometric mathematics we learned from them, and how far they can be trusted."

"What is the nature of the Monument, then?" asked Del Azarchel.

"Rania was not broken or miscreated, as she supposed. The Monument itself is damaged or redacted or edited. Her creation was from an undamaged or unedited segment held over from an earlier stratum of the Monument, a strata not successfully removed. For this reason, she could not read the redacted version of the Monument correctly."

8. The Broken Monument

That was the last thing Montrose expected to hear. From the look on Del Azarchel's face, it was the last he expected as well.

Tellus said, "I say again, the Monument at V 886 Centauri is a redaction or a limited copy of some original. There are missing symmetries which should be present, but which were removed. However, the grammar structure of the Monument is recursive and holographic, much like a human brain, so that the whole can be reconstructed from any part. There are traces of the primordial Monument which survived the editing process, traces which were not removed, or which, more likely, could not be removed.

"Our estimate is that the original was composed twelve billion years ago, whereas the redaction was composed quite recently, three hundred fifty-nine million years ago."

Montrose reflected. Twelve billion years ago was the time when the Population III stars existed. These were unstable ultra-low metallic stars of the early universe that burned in the hot cosmic medium of the aeons when earliest galaxies were being formed. Such stars had been hypothesized, but never seen. All had died out long before the Solar System was formed.

The idea that the message which existed on the Monument had been written at that time was starkly unbelievable. Could life have evolved in a universe where the elements had not yet been created in the stellar furnaces of younger, metallic stars? Rocky planets could not have even been formed. Water could not exist in a universe before the evolution of the oxygen molecule. How could this message in the Monument have been composed then? And by whom?

However the message had been carried, it eventually had been written down, presumably as soon as there was cold and complex matter, elements that could form solids, to write it down into. The physical Monument found at the Diamond Star, that black ball which absorbed all known forms of energy, the mirror-bright lines of writing which reflected all known forms of energy, that ball was from a later era of cosmic history, and it represented a version of the message that had been edited, redacted, marred, meddled with. That had happened during the Carboniferous Period, the Age of the Amphibians. By this scale, that was practically yesterday.

Tellus continued: "The first Rania was constructed, apparently by happy mischance, from a particularly clear or clean set of codes in the Monument surface. The same relationship which her brain convolutions held to her genetic code also was reflected in the relation between her neural fine structure and the Monument enjambments. Because of the recursion, she is more perfectly what the Primordial Monument Builders intended.

"What she had trouble reading was the damaged or edited sections, because Rania was subconsciously sensitive to the missing meaning. The later versions of her, my versions, followed the whole of the instructions more literally, and so my daughters of Rania were more precisely what the Monument Redactors, whoever had tampered with the message, intended. The Redactors had, of course, left instructions exactly fitted to read their edited version of the message. The daughters of Rania could read the 359,000,000 B.C. layer of the message adroitly, but the earlier and deeper message from 12,000,000,000 B.C. was invisible to them.

"As it is to me," concluded Tellus somberly. "Hence, I cannot intuit Rania's purposes, nor run my thoughts, despite my immensities of mental resources, to anticipate her thoughts. You seem to think you know why she flew to M3. However, I do not."

Montrose said, "It was written in the Cold Equations, their laws and rules! She went to free us. To manumit the human race!"

Tellus said, "That, of course, was the surface layer of her purpose, springing from the Redaction-era Monument and its limited message. But she perhaps saw the unlimited message of the older strata of meaning. That larger purpose, I cannot guess. Perhaps something greater than life or liberty, which humbler minds perceive, but which Potentates do not.

"But you are less a mystery to me," the entity continued. "And since I foresee your decision, I am under no need to maintain this current energy-intensive kenosis. I return to a lower level of intellect, no longer as the emissary of Tellus, but only as the ship's brain of the *Emancipation*. In that state I will await your orders."

It was a dismissal. The image faded.

Montrose closed his eyes in pain, and, throughout the ship, Extrose shut down excesses from his sensorium to create a moment of silence where all his many layers of his many minds could think.

Del Azarchel, seeing Montrose's face and sensing the change in energy use in the shipwide logic diamond, now smiled radiantly, gloating. "Would you like four hundred years to revisit your decision, Cowhand? That is when your first verdict will be carried out, and the hundred millions aboard the Proxima deracination ship will perish.

"Six hundred years after that, the ship headed for Epsilon Eridani reaches her destination, and those hundred millions die.

"Then 61 Cygni only ten years after that, another hundred million.

"Then Epsilon Indi . . . Tau Ceti . . . Omicron Eridani . . . and so on, and on. . . . We have radio lasers able to reach them. Shall I explain the meaning and purpose of your decision? Or shall you?"

7

King of Planets, Planet of Kings

1. The Escape of the Mind

A.D. 11322

Ximen del Azarchel, weightless in the void, with stars beyond his feet and the rainbow of shattered ice and asteroids beyond his head, was in a lingering and quiet ecstasy.

It had been so long, so very long, since he had been happy, even he could not recall it. Dimly he recalled some nameday as a child, perhaps four years of age, when his mother had brought him a palm cake stolen from her rich mistress's table (or, more likely, her recycle bucket), lit with the smallest dollop of bioluminescent sugar for its candle, a cake too beautiful to eat and too delicious to wait to eat. Four? More likely three. He was a precocious child, and by four years, he surely would have been aware of the cruelty of his life, of the scorn of his peers, who called him a monster, of the weakness of his sickly mother, forced to clean the houses of petty bourgeoisie upstarts all the while dying of a disease his father's wealth could have cured.

And after that? A life of crime, wretchedness, and starvation, eating garbage and stealing shoes from any smaller children with large feet. Then a life of ambition and discipline, a struggle against the castes and the wealth of the

arrogant Southlings, paynim Mohammedans and pagan Hindus. What escape
was there for a man of honor, a man of pride, a man who refused either to die
or to apologize because his artificial genes made him superior to the common
ruck of mankind?

The escape was through the things of the mind, of course. Through logic,
through discipline, study, and most of all through rash desperation as carefully
controlled as an atomic chain reaction—through the willingness to sacrifice anyone and anything who would dare bar the future from the outstretched hand
of Del Azarchel.

The escape was—ah! The escape was knowledge. And knowledge was emancipation.

Even to human eyes, the NTL *Emancipation* was a thing of beauty, the
sculpted and efficient beauty of a well-made weapon.

Her main hull was a streamlined cylinder. An armored prow was fore, and
layer upon layer of self-repairing antimicrometeor semifluid like a spearpoint
of glass coating a huge carbon nanotube wedge; behind was the shroud house
that controlled the lines and spars; midmost was the carousel housing the quarters for living crew; behind the carousel were ranks of suspended animation cells
for crew not quite as living; behind this were the steps where bases of the masts
were seated, lengths of impossibly strong and lightweight material; aftmost, held
on three thick spars, was a mirrored plate meant to deflect launching laser particles coming from behind into the sails. It could also serve as a mizzen sail, as
a heliograph, as a power station, and, if pellets of fuel were placed aft of the
vessel to be ignited by the acceleration laser, as an Orion-drive pushing plate.

The vessel herself had no propulsion, aside from three stubby and wide-
mouthed tugs that were normally docked aft, remora fish snug against the belly
of a shark. These were fusion engines, which doubled as ramjets, able to intake
interstellar hydrogen for fuel mass. When positioned at the rim of the push plate,
the ship fields and sail fields could funnel ionized particles into their gaping
mouths, condense it into a hydrogen stream that could be ignited either with
contraterrene micropellets or focused reflections of coherent light from the sail.

To eyes like those of Del Azarchel (which, with links and implants connected
to the wings of his suit, Swanlike wings covered with eyes like a peacock's tail,
could see higher or lower on the electromagnetic spectrum) the beauty of the
ship was also like the beauty of fire.

Fields invisible to human eyes reached out foreward to ionize and repel particles; lateral fields like spotlights played across the sail acreage, smoothing wrin-
kles and maintaining rigidity; aftward a vast bubble, field upon field, far from
the hull, was ready to hold an astronomical cargo of magnetized contraterrene.

The *Emancipation* was more than just a physical shell, just as a harpsong was more than merely a harp. She was a fanfare of energy, a glory of burning clouds, a dance of particles, and a spiderweb of fulguration.

And for so long the great ship had been his place of exile, expelled from Earth by Swans, and been his mausoleum; or, rather, had been his private little Dante's Inferno, the lowest circle of frozen hell where Archbishop Ruggieri with Count Ugolino were buried together up to their necks in ice, closer than man and bride, and Ugolino gnawed forever upon Ruggieri's skull.

So, too, had Del Azarchel been trapped with Montrose, gnawed upon by the man's intolerable habits of thought and mind and personality, the smell of his unwashed feet and his endless cigarettes, and the abomination of uncouth grotesquerie which served Montrose for a sense of humor. Like a man who holds a burning glede as a trial by ordeal, and will not let go lest he be condemned, Del Azarchel would not, could not, permit himself to be the first to cease the cooperation between the two. He had, after all, agreed to a truce. He had given his word.

He wondered if the Cowhand had made a similar vow, and merely hid his discontent with it better than Del Azarchel could.

And the fool was skilled. There was no denying that. A genius himself. If only he had not been born in Texas! If only he had been born among civilized men!

Secretly, Del Azarchel had always longed for a day when his enemy would once again become his friend and servitor. He had not dared hope, but he had dared to daydream how it should happen: Montrose would contemplate the marching ranks and files of numbers and notations and symbols of logic, each rank holding as boldly as a line of Spartans. And Montrose would be frantically searching for some error in the alien's logic, some slipped decimal in their codes, some ambiguity in their sign-to-signification ratio . . . and finding no error, no escape.

Del Azarchel had dreamed of Montrose finally being confronted with a truth so logical and so clear that even he, even Montrose, with his vast and supernatural capacity for sentimentality and self-deception would be unequal to the task of denying the obvious. . . .

Del Azarchel had dreamed of making Montrose more intelligent, forcing him to join Del Azarchel on a higher plateau of human evolution, commanding him to turn and look back down, back at what his lower, more apelike, less enlightened self had done . . .

. . . and admit Del Azarchel had all along been right. Had been superior.

All this was as it had been. And now? Now, all was changed.

Now, the vile smells and viler grammar were just droll eccentricities to Del Azarchel, a source of pleasure, because it gave Del Azarchel yet another pathetic thing to forgive in his pathetically fallen foe, and therefore made Del Azarchel's magnanimity in victory more rare, more grand, more admirable, more large.

The sail was a thing too large to admire while admiring the vessel. Del Azarchel had to spread his wings and open up additional layers of visual interpretation in his cortex, more like the brain of a deer than a man, something with a wider angle of vision, to take in the immensity.

Seen from afar, the sail was a silver-white circle many miles wide. Closer, the details could be seen of the molecular textures of differing smart fabrics, which produced an intricacy like the crystal arms of a snowflake. This mix of fabrics was designed to alter performance characteristics in case any new acceleration-ray technologies were developed after launch. If the propellant were upgraded, for example, from laser energy to particle beam, pellet stream, or a collimated beam of mesoscopic particles, the sail fabric could alter its molecular profile to accommodate the change as easily as the skin cells of a chameleon.

At the moment, the sail was tuned to a basic mirrored setting, for she used only Sol's focused sunlight, not laser light, to drive her. NTL *Emancipation* faced her mirror image in the vast circle of the sail. With his acute vision at its highest setting, Del Azarchel could see himself, black and winged, outlined by the mirror of his cloak behind him, reflected in that second sky shining in the sail.

Del Azarchel drank in the magnificent sight. Always before, to see a ship such as this hanging without motion, no further from Earth than Jupiter, was like hearing an ongoing sustained note of sorrow in the background of an otherwise glorious symphony of splendor.

Not this time. Now he knew joy.

"Soon," he whispered. "Not soon as men count time, but I count it, soon, you shall fly from my wrist, and stoop the prey I seek, and all the secrets of the higher civilizations shall be ours."

Del Azarchel felt a moment of admiration, perhaps even love, for these creatures of the Hyades stars, whatever they were, alien machinery, living systems, one species or many, or something that was at once neither or both, or so advanced that all those distinctions were nothing. They commanded the millennia by the tens and scores. They were ambitious on his level of ambition. In his heart, he counted himself as one of them, as a member of the galactic hierarchy, not as a man of Earth.

For it was the Hyades who broke Montrose's rebellious spirit.

Del Azarchel had read his Dumas, and he knew full well that vengeance was allegedly a bitter thing, never satisfying to the avenger. And so he had been braced for a moment of dejection and ennui in his hour of triumph. But, no, it did not come. There was no loss, no cost, no terrible price paid. He simply was winning.

For Montrose had wept. Yes, hard as he pretended to be, as the years turned into decades, and the transmissions from the deracination ships had grown more infrequent and more desperate, Menelaus Montrose wept.

2. The First Diaspora of Man

A.D. 10917 TO 11125

It had happened in this wise:

On each vast deracination ship, the tens of thousands of the abducted nations, civilizations, and races were thawed and awake, confined in a cylindrical space many miles long. It was spun for gravity, and coated on the interior with electrosensitive polymorphic material like smart mud. Down the weightless axis was a tube of luminous plasma, a linear sun that never rose nor set. Beneath the mud, buried in solidified murk, were held the millions in suspended animation, flies trapped in amber. Whole cities had been swept up, and were scattered throughout the interior volume, so the prisoners did not lack for tools and even weapons.

The vast disk-shaped bulkhead of the aftmost hull was honeycombed with coolant tunnels, used for venting heat from the plasma sun, and in places the hull was transparent, or thin enough that patient and clever work could cut through. And after a disaster or two, it was discovered that even more patient and more clever work could erect a series of baffles and airlocks to prevent the ship from automatically expelling everything in the coolant tunnel near any breach, puckering it shut, and sucking the ejected debris through space to the mouth of the vessel, where the powerhouse for the plasma sun reduced everything to its elements.

Once outside the ship, however, not even Hormagaunts who adapted themselves to the vacuum could cross the distance between the vast cylinder and alien pilothouse controlling the sails. Presumably the ship's brain and the crew, if there were any living crew, were seated there. But the pilothouse was separated by one hundred thirty thousand miles, and connected only by impalpable cables of magnetic energy to the slowly moving cylindrical body. Anything attempting to cross the distance was destroyed by focused energy from the sails, perhaps an automatic meteor defense.

In the twenty-six years since the departure of the first deracination ship toward Proxima, no spokesman, no instructions, no overseer representing the Hyades overlords had addressed the abducted thousands aboard.

The brilliant Swans and diligent Locusts trapped aboard one of the ships, the one headed toward Tau Ceti, had discovered how to use electric signals to change the consistency of the mud. A correct combination of signals could instruct the mud and form it into hills and valleys, rivers and lakes, expanses of fertile soil. The Tau Ceti-bound expatriates also constructed a transmitter powerful enough to reach across the one-fifth of a lightyear gap separating Sol from the globe of receding ships. This gap, at that time, was roughly three hundred times the semi-major axis of Pluto's orbit.

Tellus had transmitted the Tau Ceti ship's discoveries across the light-months toward the other ships receding through transplutonian space. This was easily done. Every schoolboy on Earth knew the longitude and right ascension of those ships, their speed and distance, nor was there any intervening material or medium to hinder the radio signal.

Which of the other deracination ships had the presence of mind to erect a receiver was unknown, but eight had erected transmitters of sufficient power to reply: the ships bound toward Proxima, Omicron Eridani, 61 Cygni, Altair, Gliese 570, Eta Cassiopeiae, and HR7703.

The millions aboard now knew certain codes to program the matter which coated the inner hulls of their world-sized prisons. But there were neither safety features nor warnings in the electronic signal codes the abductees had deduced, or the environmental instruments the aliens had left for them to find. It was another intelligence test.

It was a merciless test. Reports from seven of the radio-fluent ships over the next few years were horrific. Countless numbers had died in earthquakes, floods, and quicksand caused by improperly programmed landscapes. As many died from an improper balance of gases as the artificial atmosphere interacted with changes made to the artificial soil.

The eighth ship, bound for Omicron Eridani, fell out of radio contact ten years into her one hundred sixty-four year journey.

3. Second Contact

A.D. 11298

Decades had passed before the Omicron Eridani ship reestablished contact, and news returned from beyond the distant abyss of space. The grim events were these: a layer of slumberers had been thawed from the murk, to find their miles-long cylinder airless, and themselves trapped in tiny airtight closets.

In those closets they endured for months while their Melusine discovered how to program the mud to find the hull breech, grow over the area, and solidify into a stress-resistant shape. Other mud layers formed the correct mix of gases and liquids to fill the empty interior, and to thaw segments of murk containing crops and seeds.

These survivors did not know what had caused the breach, but the traces were left of the endless tornadoes which had swept the previous group of tens of thousands into outer nothingness. Eventually digging into the aft plate, they found transparent sections of their world-sized prison. Then they beheld the slowly retreating silhouettes of corpses, cloud upon cloud, outlined against the gleaming vastness of their sails. No worm and no bacteria existed in the radiation-filled vacuum of the acceleration-beam from Sol in which the sailing vessel swam. The bodies would never decay.

4. The Plea of Tellurians

A.D. 11300

Once and once only were Montrose and Del Azarchel recalled from exile at the moons and rings of Jupiter and summoned back to Tellus.

Montrose had forgotten how pleasant natural gravity felt, after so much time in carousels or free fall. He redesigned his bones and muscles not once, but twice, during the long Hohmann transfer from Jovian orbit to Telluric. The transfer orbit was a much longer one that it would have been before Asmodel, since the Earth no longer orbited in the plane of the ecliptic, and there were fewer windows to achieve an energy-efficient orbit.

They were not permitted to attempt a planetfall in their ship's pinnace. Earth provided the means for their descent. The two men were lowered in a landing shell on a beam of energy that ignited the air beneath them. There was a sickening period of free fall, and then the landing shell was plucked out of the air by a diving vessel like a sparrow caught by a hawk. The diving vessel spread wings and parachutes and splashed down in the mighty Mississippi.

Stepped pyramids of enormous size, windowless, hundreds of feet high, loomed on the banks of the great river, and among them were minarets like upright swords, and obelisks that flashed gold crowns in the sun.

More than one flight of marble stairs ran down to the water. Guarding these stairways were pillars atop which centaur mares with the heads and breasts of cold-faced women reared, or snarling black-winged leopards.

Ximen del Azarchel and Menelaus Montrose, with an entourage of silent, fawning, raccoon-like Moreau in goggles escorting them, passed from their diving vessel in coracles to the riverbank.

At the top of the stair was a broad, green field spread between the looming ziggurats. The grass was waist-high. It was some species of grass evolved or made after Montrose had departed the Earth, and he did not recognize it. The grass-blades were thin, dark and waxy, almost like the leaf of a palm tree.

Within the field, as far as the eye could see, were white statues of men and women of many races, Sylphs, Witches, Chimerae, Nymphs. Here were monstrous Hormagaunts, no two alike, and handsome clades of twins, no two unalike.

Half unseen in the grass were statues of Locusts in their several variations. Winged statues ten or twelve feet tall stood here or there amid the others, narrow-faced and narrow-eyed beings, their hands raised, palms turned inward, in graceful postures of welcome. These were Swans. There were other types Montrose did not recognize. In the distance were the silhouettes of motionless Giants, bald and grim as worn mountains.

In the air overhead was hanging a scroll, partly unrolled. The visible section was thirty feet tall and fifteen feet wide, written on both sides. Silently it stood, rustling in the wind, but not drifting. There was no trace of whatever power kept it aloft and held it in place. The hieroglyphs were illegible, yet seemed electrically charged with meaning, as if tensed to shout their messages.

The glyph shapes were based on a simplified Monument notation, but they curled and writhed beneath the surface of the scroll. At the corners of the scroll were metallic eyes that neither Montrose nor Del Azarchel could stand to look into, and so they knew this was a manifestation of some higher power.

"No one here to welcome us," said Montrose, putting his foot on the grass. Immediately a strange sound rippled over the silent scene, a harmony of soft wails, hoots, trills, and rippling echoes. With it came a throbbing as if some immense heart, larger and slower than a man's were beating. "Whoops! Reckon I spoke too soon."

"It is non-diatonic music, composed of birdsong and beast calls and river sounds," said Del Azarchel. "But I see no source. Give me a moment, and I should be able to deduce its symbolic import."

"It's a howdy song," said Montrose, smirking at him with a half smile. "What they got instead of a brass band to welcome us to shore. But I still don't see no people."

"You see them plain enough," said Del Azarchel in the same tone of voice, and with the same half smile. "You just do not recognize your handiwork. These are all slumberers, in biosuspension. They have somehow devised some internal cellular control to induce suspended animation and hypothermia without coffins around them."

There came a rustling in the grass then, and a slender figure in a bright green kimono came out from between the tall stalks, and swayed toward them, her footfalls like a glissando of music.

"Mother!" said Del Azarchel, nodding his head in a bow of less than one degree of deflection from the vertical. "I am pleased and surprised to find you alive. I assume it was by your intercession that the term of my exile was suspended? We are grateful for the welcome."

"No other voice but mine," said Amphithöe, "would have overcome your pride, O my son."

"Why are we here?" Montrose uttered no other greeting. "Some sort of assembly or meeting? You called it a vision of harmonizing futures at war."

"We must reconcile a conflict of cliometry, and select our destiny." She bowed toward him, and then sank to her knees. "We are come to plead for our lives, our souls, our sacred freedom, and the lives of our children. We plead to you, only to you, Judge of Ages."

Montrose stepped back a step, as if alarmed at seeing the delicate woman kneel to him. "I never called myself that."

Del Azarchel had a look of surprise on his face, almost of shock, which sharpened suddenly into the look of a black fox. "Oh, this is rich beyond dreaming!" He turned to Montrose, his eyes twinkling, unable to hide the white fire of his grin in his dark beard. "Come, sir, will you not heed our own mother's prayer? She abases herself! You know what she wants."

Montrose stepped forward, his face red with a blush. Whether it was a blush of anger or a blush of shame was not clear, not even to him. He took Amphithöe roughly by the shoulder and drew her to her feet. "Stand up. I don't know you, and you are not my mother. She's a far piece fiercer than you, for one thing, and uglier, too. Get up! I have not agreed to Blackie's plan. I am not going to break the phantasm barrier, and let these machines that think they are gods take over your history, your lives, your thoughts. The Jupiter Mind can mind his own damned business. I have not agreed!"

"But you will," said Del Azarchel, soft as a snake whispering. "Because you must."

Amphithöe was standing on her tiptoes in her little jeweled slippers, because Montrose, forgetting how tall he was, was pulling her arm too roughly and too high. She raised her nose and wore a calm expression. "I am your mother in my heart. But if your true mother were here, what would she do?"

"She'd lick me with a strap, I guess, and tell me not to do it, never to agree with Blackie." Montrose had a hollow, haunted look to his eyes now. He let go the little Nymph woman's arm and stepped back.

Del Azarchel gritted his teeth and said nothing. Del Azarchel was canny enough to know when not to speak. Reason can reach a man willing to be reasonable, and rhetoric can stir a man willing to open his ear. But when a man was wrestling with those ghosts called memory, no voice can reach him.

He had been certain, despite the words of Montrose, that Montrose would yield to the pressure of the inevitable. But now Del Azarchel's sense of certainty stumbled. Del Azarchel had not expected anyone on Earth to be clever enough to preserve Amphithöe in suspension and thaw her for a stunt like this. Clever, but it had backfired. Del Azarchel adored the memory of his own mother as a saint. Montrose did not.

In an agony of disgust, his stomach boiling as if he'd swallowed acid, Del Azarchel watched and waited for his centuries and millennia of planning, plotting, warring, and scheming, his assassinations and deceptions, all to come to nothing. To nothing! And all because the little human boy buried in the memory of posthuman Montrose still feared and respected a woman long dead, and who, in the grand scheme of things, was less than a monkey.

Del Azarchel stood with one arm folded across his chest, the other hand as if thoughtfully stroking his mustache. But the pose was actually to hold down the burning sensation in his guts, or to clasp his hand over his mouth should he begin to puke. So! The great superhuman Montrose, the giant who had always been one step ahead of him, always upstaging him! Was he now to decide the fate of worlds based on some greeting-card sentiment about Mother's Day?

Montrose said, "But Mom ain't here, and you ain't her."

Amphithöe said, "Was she a freeborn woman?"

Montrose nodded. "Scotch-Irish. Been conquered plenty, but her folk ain't never been slaves. On my dad's side, I am purebred Mestizo, which is part 'Patchie, part Dusky, part Rattler, all folk ain't never been free."

"I also am free, now, because of you. The moon returned me to life in a time and place where the cruel institutions of my day had passed into memory. The ancient methods, perfected by the Nymphs, were being used to adjust the biochemistry of clades and clans to regard each other with brotherly love, with philanthropy and compassion, yet without the erotic core which shames the memory of those ancient times. I was joined into a harmony, and, with the help of acolytes of advanced learning and compassionate machines, that harmony was joined to others and yet to others. The decree was made among all men of all races to abolish slavery and indentured servitude."

She pointed upward at the scroll in the air.

"This side lists our virtues, and the other side lists our sins. By this devotion to liberty, many stanzas of the cliometric scroll have been moved from the far side to the near."

She lowered her arm and bowed again.

"The liberty I found on the moon do not take from me, please. I beg you."

Montrose said harshly, "If I don't do what Blackie says, Jupiter will not be able to decode the sciences that are the only hope we have to keep the people on the slave ships alive. I've seen the math! I have not seen any way around it! The aliens set it up this way, to checkmate us. It is another intelligence test. If we fail, the human race dies, and Rania never returns."

Amphithöe said, "I have no easy answer for you. The Hyades must pay for their own crimes, and see to their own future, whatever that is. My future that I see, if these projections are unchanged, is that I will lose the liberty I gained, and that my daughters will be slaves."

"I feel sorry for them," said Montrose. "But you are just one woman. We are talking about everyone. The whole human race."

Amphithöe straightened from her bow and, with a dignified slow gesture, her long red sleeve brushing the high grass, swept her arm toward the many white and motionless figures gathered across the acres. "I have brought them!"

"Brought who?"

"The whole human race."

"Eh? What's that s'pose to mean?"

Del Azarchel had a look of bitter amusement, as if he were laughing at his own disgust and discomfort. "Surely you see what this is, Cowhand? Each of these creatures here is an epitome. They represent, either as a shared memory or as a proxy, everyone on Earth. This is the final plea of the self-centered, who would damn their descendants to death!"

One of the nearby statues changed from pale white to flesh-toned in a moment, releasing a cloud of twinkling mist. Her garments, which had been tuned to a white shade to match her skin, now flowed and pulsed with peacock hues. She shrugged her wings so that all gleaming feathers and their wise eyes rustled and blinked, and very slowly turned her head.

The Swan spoke in an eerie voice. "I am Svanhildr the Anarchist, elected against my will and by many filthy threats to represent the cliometric unity of the interests of Second Humanity. I am, if you like, the Judge of Swans. By my counsel, Amphithöe was allowed, because of the sacred fetters of motherhood, to speak first her passionate plea. But let no one say she speaks alone or selfishly. All, all are gathered here. We have brought all the living creatures of the world to this place to beg and plead with you, Judge of Ages. Spare us. Do not expose us naked to the gaze of monstrous Jupiter."

Montrose said, "It is death, death for the colonists, death for the human race, death for Rania, if I agree with you."

Another man spoke. He was of a form and fashion from a century unknown to Montrose, bear-faced and dark-furred with emerald-green and night-adapted eyes, and ears like dark semicircles. At his shoulder was a sword taller than himself, made of pale wood. "Your Honor, then let us die free. If our histories do not tell lies about you, you alone of the men of the primordial world before the flames, before the antecpyrosis, you alone understand what freedom means. You came from a free land called Texas. You spoke against the Master of the World. You dueled him; he threw on your head a tower that reached to the stars, and you in retaliation burned the world with fire from hell, and took him by the foot and flung him to the moon. Are the legends false?"

"Actually, I grabbed him by the balls for the moon fling, but the history books sort of cleaned it up."

A small Locust, blue as cobalt, stepped from behind the grass. He was so short that the grass was over his head. Montrose was so sharply reminded of little Preceptor Illiance from seven hundred years ago, that for a moment, he thought some memory from his newly reconstructed mind had by error forced its way into his sense impressions.

The Blue Man spoke in a voice like a woodwind instrument. "Sir! If you are the legendary being, the one man who protected mankind from the Machine for so long, be him now! Do not forsake us!"

And he flung himself on his face. The bear-faced warrior with the longbow and the proud Swan with her shining wings also lowered themselves to the ground, and the two lay full upon their faces.

In the distance, even the Giants bowed, like a line of mountains crumbling into the sea.

As if upon the signal of some trumpet inaudible to mortals, the grasses were flattened at that moment by a harsh and sustained wind from the north, and the wide field became apparent to view. The number of those who prostrated themselves was greater than Montrose had suspected, for many had been Locusts, or other dwarfish subspecies, and many more had been slumbering in a kneeling position, and did not rise when thawed, and so had been hidden in the grass until now.

It was so many people, all groveling to him. Montrose, overcome with emotion, turned his face away from them. But there was no escape for his gaze. Behind him, the river was filled with mermaids and dolphins and whales of the Melusine lineages, and they had extended their pleading hands to him, those who had hands, or turned on their backs to expose their throats, those who had not.

The Swan raised her head and spoke, "We do not deceive you. Walk the world. Come to know and love her fields and forests and floes of ice, her storming seas and skies of cold aurora fire!"

The bear-faced warrior said, "I vow you will not find one soul, not one, who does not call on you to leave us our liberty, our possessions, our children, our lives! All will weep for your mercy!"

The Locust said, "We will be nothing in the eyes of Jupiter. He will decide all futures without consulting us, and all our dreams and hopes and enterprises will be in vain."

Amphithöe said, "Jupiter does not love us. You do."

Del Azarchel, again, could think of a thousand things to say. He was sure each one of them would convince Montrose on the spot to damn Jupiter, and to damn the race, the dreams of Del Azarchel, to hell. A man with no more than ordinary self-control would have spoken. Del Azarchel was not ordinary.

So Del Azarchel, face as calm as a desperate poker player whose whole fortune and all his future waits in the center of the table for the final turn of a doubtful card, merely watched as Montrose, as if in a daze, walked down the flight of stairs to the water. Two dolphins and a mermaid offered him a small two-masted boat with a glass hull, and into the hull dropped fruits and flowers, and then swam backward away, reverently, never taking their eyes from Montrose.

Del Azarchel watched as Montrose sailed away with the current, downstream.

Then Del Azarchel turned and said lightly to Amphithöe, "Dearest Mother, what do you suppose will happen if that boast proves false, and he finds someone, somewhere on Earth, who would, as would I, far rather suffer slavery if it meant reaching the stars, than to squat in the mudhole we call home, calling our masterless misery freedom? Someone, just one?"

Amphithöe said, "Proud son, do you not understand this era yet? We are the children of Father Reyes y Pastor. He died to stop you. He died to save his soul. We shall do likewise."

Del Azarchel smiled. "Gentle Mother, you are as uninformed about the fate of my father confessor as you are unwise about your own. But no matter! My reflected glory seems to have elevated you to a high station, where you speak in embassy for all the peoples and nations and kingdoms of the world! Does this mean you have a feast for me? I am weary of spaceman's rations and claustrophobic cabins. I dream of flaming pits and suckling pigs. May we have a barbecue?"

5. The Voice in the Tree

A.D. 11301

How long Montrose stayed in the little dry meadow between two snowy peaks was something he loaded into a memory file that he expunged. Losing track of time helped him concentrate.

But as the snow crept down the mountain slopes, he departed that eerie cabin made of giant toadstools and woven ferns which had sprung up in a single still and silent midnight hour for his use, inexplicably. He glanced back only once to see that that the mushroom cabin was already melting, being torn to bits by insects smaller than dust specks.

The hike down the pass toward the river canyon was a long and thirsty one, and his feet ached in the moccasins he'd made from suicidal deer. Atop a small hillock halfway down the mighty slope, he saw an ash tree with a branch just the width and length to suit him for a walking stick.

He brought out his tomahawk and swung. The axe-blade came from the nanomachines in his blood which he had kneaded into a wedge of substance like bee's wax. When the blood-machines were activated, they tried to put the wax into biosuspension, making it white and hard as diamond. With a solid noise, the white blade bit into the tree just where the branch met the trunk.

The tree shuddered, and blood oozed from the joint of the branch. At first, Menelaus thought something had gone wrong with his axe-head, and released blood particles from suspension.

He squinted. The tree was bleeding.

When the wind rustled the leaves, the leaves vibrated, turning their edges into the wind oddly. It formed a strange, breathless voice, reminiscent of grass whistle: "Judge of Ages, must you wound those who owe you kindness?"

Menelaus was startled. "Sorry but I—I didn't think you'd get hurt. Or talk."

"No pain is felt. Take the branch and welcome. We exist to serve man, as you do. All we have is free for your use, and the use of your fellow man."

"You speak English?"

"As a courtesy to you. All living creatures were imprinted with the knowledge of your speech and background, that you might hear and know our beseeching."

"What are you? Are you in the tree?"

"In the tree, and birds, and beasts, and blades of grass for many hundreds of acres roundabout. We control the local ecological interactions, and are part of the effort to render the useless parts of the globe more serviceable to man. We are a system that committed a lobotomy to fall beneath the intelligence threshold you defined, so that we could be unseen, unrecalled, and free."

"You got a name?"

"No. Call me Chloe."

"Well, Chloe, pleased to meetcha. I did not mean to wound your tree."

"That is not the wound of which I speak. You will take away our liberty, and place us beneath the Great Eye of Jupiter, and nothing humans do hereafter will mean anything. The wound I gave myself in my own mind, to diminish myself to idiocy that I might be no longer part of Tellus—alas! My self-mutilation is in vain!"

And the tree began sobbing, but the wind died down, and Montrose heard no more of the voice.

The tree branch turned with an odd, slow, awkward motion, broke, and fell to the grass at the feet of Montrose. The bleeding end formed a wooden scab, and became solid as he watched, just in the right shape to fit his hand.

As he continued on his way, all the birds he saw gave out long, mournful cries of lamentation, and the wolves howled. The flower petals and butterfly wings turned black as he passed until the knee-deep meadow grass seemed a pool of ink, and the insects like scraps of ash hovering above a dark fire.

6. The Washer at the Ford

He came to a place where the river was shallow enough to wade. There were three humped little boulders here, and the middle one had a thatch of white lichens growing near the top, so it looked almost like a lumpy and crooked old lady in a hood, kneeling with her hands in the river water, facing away from him, with wisps of white hair peeping around the fringe.

He knelt by the boulder and, keeping his eyes up and his other hand on his hiking stick, lifted the water to his mouth with a cupped palm, as his mother had taught him.

So it was he saw the cloud of steam emerge from the middle boulder as it breathed out a sob into the cold air.

He jumped to his feet, surprised.

It was a lumpy old lady in a hood in truth, and she was holding a length of cloth in the water. Her hands beneath the surface, now that he saw them, were stark with vein and bones, and blue with cold.

"Your pardon ma'am. I didn't see you there. . . ."

He was answered with a long, quivering wail.

The lump shifted and shivered slightly. The dusty cloth did indeed look much like a boulder, but now he saw it was a motley of old rags epoxied together with molecular glue, and the image circuits in the cloth were burnt out.

The hood turned toward him. In the depths he could see half-unclearly a face half collapsed with some degenerative disease that ate away at flesh and muscle, tendon and skull. A medical appliance writhed on the ruined half of her head like a nest of pink worms. She had but one remaining eye, red with weeping, one nostril, and single tooth protruding from her dripping and dis-colored gums.

The wailing now seemed garbled words, distorted by her corrupted throat. He did not hear the beginning of her lament.

". . . *every struggle brings defeat, because Fate holds no prize to crown success; all the oracles are dumb or cheat, because they have no secret to express; none can pierce the vast black veil uncertain, because there is no light beyond the curtain; all is vanity and nothingness . . .*"

This last word was croaked with such force that Montrose felt the spittle, mixed with black blood, fly from the old woman's lips and touch his cheek with a tiny drop of cold. With a shudder he wiped it away, the fear from his youth of infection and plague for a moment resurrected.

"Can I get you to a doctor?" he said. He looked left and right. They were in the middle of a river valley overgrown with ivy and rue, hemmed about with willow trees with crooked limbs, naked in the wintry wind. "There must be some circuit in the greenery. I just had a tree talk to me. . . ."

The old woman hauled the fabric out of the water. It hung dank, heavy, and dripping in her clawlike hands. "It is my burial shroud I clean. To the great ones who enslave you, such as I must live and die unseen."

She dropped the dripping fabric, with a soggy noise, on the stones that looked so much like her. "Old Thokk knows you, oldest of sages, Judge of Ages, executioner of earths, who knows the Hermetic mystery, who puts his ring through the nose of history, and makes mockery of all our deaths and births."

He said nothing, but wondered who and what she was.

She said, "You stare! You blink! You gawk! Old Granny has time for talk. Shall I tell you how I lost my wealth, my way, my stored memories, and all my kith? We still have wars and worse than war: the Springtide authority—Chloe you met, who wars with glaciers—condemned my fields and pretty arbors to sink beneath the rising sea. My bloodline is not one the Judge of Years sees any need to preserve in times to come. I cannot delve, I will not beg, for no man will give to poor old Thokk. No more hale organs have I to sell, nor a pound to pay the physician, nor two pence for the mortuary. I cannot buy health nor pay for life, even while the rich toss their spare bodies to the jackals. What lot do you deem this sad world has in store for the poor? Have you come to mock?"

"No," he said, feeling at a loss. "Are you saying the doctors, whoever they are, will not help you in this age? Are there any tombs, any of my tombs left, where someone dying can take refuge? Find a better future?"

She threw back her head, and laughed, and sang in her horrid, distorted, sobbing voice:

> *All the sublime prerogatives of Man;*
> *The storied memories of the times of old,*
> *The patient tracking of the world's great plan*
> *Through sequences and changes myriadfold.*
>
> *This chance was never offered me before;*
> *For me this infinite Past is blank and dumb:*
> *This chance recurreth never, nevermore;*
> *Blank, blank for me the infinite To-come.*

"Ah!" said Montrose, "I get it, now. You're blood-flux bat-shat crazy, is that it?"

"All too sane. I see what others blind themselves to flee. Why are you here?"

The question caught him by surprise. "Just—out for a walk. I was thinking."

"Thinking of how to flee, you mean. Flee from loneliness. Flee from death. Flee from knowing life is void and without form." The crone pointed at him. Her hand trembled as if with some nerve disease. "You cannot flee. None can, not anyone, not even the star-monsters for all their power, not your fine lady for all her boldness. Death is all!"

Now she bent muttering over her wet washing, clucking and hissing where she found bloodstains and rips. Almost in a whisper, she muttered, "Your fine lady did not escape. Astronomers saw the fires in the constellation of the hunting dogs. No one told you."

"Fires?" Montrose felt a sensation like the cold finger of a corpse trailing down his spine.

"An explosion, just the same size and same stuff as would be if a vessel the size and velocity of the *Hermetic* struck a meteor no larger than a pebble at lightspeed. Ask your stick. Some of Chloe's parts still linger there, eh?" Then she spoke some command in a language unknown to him.

Montrose dropped the stick when it spoke, an emotionless voice giving details of distance and direction, time, magnitudes of various energies detected in a cosmic discharge.

The stick unevenly lay amid the rocks. Montrose stamped on the stick and broke it in half to silence the cool, dispassionate voice.

Thokk uttered a sound like a dry hiccough that served her for a chuckle. "I would have cleaned a burial cloth for her, for Rania, but she will never have a grave to fill."

Montrose clutched his head. "I don't believe it. I won't believe it! That could have been—something else. Anything else. A meteor with the same ratio of iron and other elements, traveling the same speed—a fragment of the planet Thrymheim—she would not give up so easily. She would keep going even in a pinnace boat."

The old woman laughed again, and chanted. "*The world rolls round for ever like a mill; it grinds out death and life and good and ill; it has no purpose, heart or mind or will. While air of Space and Time's full river flow the mill must blindly whirl unresting so: It may be wearing out, but who can know?*"

"Who are you, really? Some puppet of Blackie's?"

"*Man might know one thing were his sight less dim; That it whirls not to suit his petty whim, that it is quite indifferent to him. Nay, does it treat him harshly as he saith? It grinds him some slow years of bitter breath, then grinds him back into eternal death.*"

"You are trying to get me to take down the phantasm barrier, aren't you?"

The old lady stared at him, her one eye like a dull stone in the shadows of her cloak hood. She said nothing, and Montrose realized that Blackie would at all costs keep from him any hint, any evidence, that might suggest Rania was dead, because this was the only thing making Montrose pliant to Blackie's plans. If Montrose knew Rania were no more, he would shoot Blackie without even the formality of a duel: just walk up and blow the head off the man who cheated him of the chance of dying on her voyage with her, the man who provoked the alien invasion which forced Rania to her quest.

Thokk said, "I am soon to die: the doings of men in a year mean nothing to me, much less their doings in times so remote none can see.

"But all the great ones who sent the world to weep on your knees, they are as I am, except that they endure a longer time. To them, the period when they will be slaves to Jupiter are all they see. They do not see what lies in the aeon after this, any more than I see next year. What do they care if the Children of Men go extinct?

"And greatest Jupiter, he is also as I am, but merely enduring longer and looking longer. He sees his maker's vision of a galactic empire, or some such nonsense.

"And the monsters in the Hyades, what of them? Longer still. And their masters beyond the galaxy, where your lady flew in vain, what of them? Longer and longer still, and still they are as I am, looking to themselves, concerned with this life, nothing beyond. For what is beyond? Death, nakedness, dust, emptiness, nothingness. Entropy wins all."

Montrose was feeling less pity for this crooked figure. The bitterness, the helpless hatred in her words, disgusted him. "If everything is futile, old woman, why talk to me? There is the river. Drown yourself and be done with it."

"Why? *Because a cold rage seizes one at whiles to show the bitter old and wrinkled truth stripped naked of all vesture that beguiles; false dreams, false hopes, false masks and modes of youth!*"

"Are you quoting someone?"

She held up her cold and crooked hands. "Look at me. If Tellus could see me, I would be saved and cured. If Jupiter could see us all, he could set things to right, and save us all."

"Every tyrant promises that. They lie."

"Oh? If we are all to die in any case, what does it matter if we die in a short time, free as birds, free as uncaught criminals! Or die in a long time, enjoying eons of greatness after long eons of servitude? It is a rite of passage, a payment the young always make to join their elders, a payment of worth. You want to be a starfarer, do you? To sail the endless dark, and see all the mysteries! Well, pay the fare. Pay the fare."

"And if the fare is the freedom of mankind? Won't you shed a tear for that?"

She spat. "I will not weep, save with those dry tears shed by skulls who do not live. What has man and his vaunted freedom ever done for me? To me what joy does it give?"

And she turned her back on him, and began to slap her washing against the stones.

His mind was a whirl of thoughts. Rania dead? He decided not to believe it, not for an instant. It would be too much like treason. If he believed it, he was certain that she would return, alive after all, and upbraid him for his lack of faith. *You did not trust me to outsmart a simple starship disaster?*

But the image in his mind which the old woman's words had placed there: a man who thinks about a few decades, and does not care about the centuries, or of a machine that cares about centuries, but ignores the millennia; or of post-humans who care about millennia, or Potentates who care about tens of millennia, or Powers who care about hundreds, and yet above them like a black sky were Virtues big as solar systems, Principalities large as stars, and Dominations filling whole star clusters . . . and to them, the concerns of the gas giants and the living planets were like the tantrums of children, the tempest of an hour, or the lives of mayflies.

The sheer immensity appalled him. He had always somehow thought that a wise man, a moral man, looked to the long term, and sacrificed, when need be, his short-term desires. But what did that become when inflated to a planetary scale, to an interstellar scale, to a cosmic scale?

Live free or die was always the motto he lived by. And now the whole world, all save one desolate and penniless crone, wept for their lost freedom, and were willing to die—

Again, he felt the cold sensation in his spine. No, they were not willing to die. Not to die their own deaths. They were willing that mankind, in some remote eon many millennia from now, should go extinct, or people on far planets condemned to starve amid the cratered salt flats or by shores of seas of boiling ink beneath strange and moonless skies.

7. Verdict

By the time he hiked back over field and flood, forest and plain to the riverside where all the representatives of man had gathered, they were ready to receive him. As before, figures looked down from columns and stepped pyramids, and the fields were filled with Swans and Men, and many races and sub-races of Man. Music played from the whole environment, bird and insect, leaves and lapping waters joining in the refrain to welcome him. Stately thin-faced Swans folded their wings, and bowed, and in the river the whales and lesser cetaceans of the Melusine order sported and wallowed in his honor.

And here also was Blackie, dressed in new clothing, who had a hat with a feather in it. He was spinning the hat on his finger, tossing it in the air and catching it, over and over. He stood near the stairs that led down to a launching vessel.

Montrose did not wait for all the music to cease and the ceremonial bows to be ended.

"Bugger you all," said Menelaus Montrose in a harsh voice. "You've had your fun. I mean to see my wife again. That's all."

And he slunk down the stairs to the launching vessel waiting to carry him back to exile in the outer Solar System, and Del Azarchel, whistling and skylarking, skipped after.

8. A Small Moon Burns

A.D. 11322

Within the arms of the mighty crescent of the planet Jupiter, on the night side, among the flashes of eternal lightning, a bright dot appeared sliding across the cloud belts. The countless square miles of sails were focusing the weak sunlight of the outer system like a parabolic magnifying glass into a pinpoint of hell.

At the moment, all three tugs were aft of the great ship, connected by monocrystalline carbon tethers to numerous stanchions dotting the nonrotating segment of the hull, and Del Azarchel could see on high frequency wavelengths both the powerful magnetic fields surrounding the engines, and the blazing star of their exhaust. The tugs were forming a drag against the sail pressure.

A time later (whether it was hours or weeks made no difference to a being with his neural configuration) he beheld Adrastea, the smallest moon in the Solar System, a humble twenty kilometers wide, as it entered the dot of focused light shed by the sail.

As Earth's moon once had been, Adrastea was tide locked, fated ever to keep the same face toward Jupiter. This bit of ice and rock orbited inside the synchronous orbit radius. To an observer on Jupiter (such as the growing nest of

Ghosts whirling as clouds of logic crystal in the upper atmosphere) the little moon would seem to rise in the west and set in the east. Adrastea was also inside the Roche limit, but it was small enough to escape tidal disintegration.

And she was beautiful: egg-shaped, coated with a strange striped pattern of ice and dappled black stone, winged with feathers of dust and snowflakes being continually pulled from her surface to feed the ring system of Jupiter, Adrastea looked like a snowcapped mountain which had floated into a stormy heaven. By some anomaly of planetary formation, it was purer and cleaner than the ice of the rings.

Adrastea would have been doomed eventually. Del Azarchel was merely hurrying a natural process along.

The moon was mostly water ice. Under the beam from the sail, the outline of the irregular little worldlet began to soften and blur. Switching his goggle intake to cameras dotting the ship sail (the giant planet and all the moons suddenly seemed smaller, toylike, yet far more detailed on view, as the immense array gathered over miles of baseline was interpreted in the visual centers of his brain) Del Azarchel could see vents of steam issuing from the little moon like volcanoes made of ice. The steam pressure was greater than escape velocity: the water droplets fled into space, and did not fall down to Adrastea again.

The heat was on the upper, shipward side of Adrastea, the side that had never seen Jupiter. The escaping steam was sufficient to produce a thrust. The orbit would not begin to degrade for months—that is, local months. Adrastea orbited Jupiter five times an Earth-day. In thirty Earth-days over a hundred Adrastean months would have elapsed, and the falling moon would begin experiencing reentry friction.

The fine-grained radar fed him the surface features in such detail that he was able to feed it into his brain as a physical sensation, as if he held the moon in his fist and could feel its texture of stone and snow against his palm. Del Azarchel resisted the temptation recording into his nervous system the sensation of his arm muscles tensing and throwing the moon to fiery doom. He had indulged, long ago, during the long years aboard the NTL *Hermetic,* with the intoxication of artificial sensations. He promised himself never to do it again, a promise he had since kept, albeit not without some pain. The reality of being a godlike force able to throw worldlets to their doom was better.

The pinpoint flare of energy of a larger object launching from the surface was like a hot needle against his thumb. This was the exovehicular suit used by Montrose, an absurd-looking contraption like a canister-sized boat with arms.

Montrose had been overseeing the placement of the logic seeds on the small moon, molecular technology designed to break Jupiter out of the self-imposed blindness of the phantasm veil. The reentry heat would bring it to life, so that by the time the moon broke into pieces and scattered themselves across the clouds and seas of Jupiter, every fragment would be a virus spreading the antiphantasm logic to any sophont matter it touched.

One small moon was not enough.

Del Azarchel turned his many eyes toward the next moon, Amalthea, an irregular mountain in space almost freakishly red. The planet was massaged by tidal forces, its inner core stirred to activity, so that the moon gave off more heat than it received from the sun. This next moon out had a perfectly synchronous orbit: it hung above Jupiter always in the same spot, orbiting as fast as Jupiter turned.

The energy discharge betraying the position of Montrose slowly, very slowly, reached toward Amalthea. Additional pods of supply crystal grown from and sliced off the ship's brain were shot toward rendezvous by the ship's glorious pattern of magnetic fields, here used as a caterpillar drive.

Amalthea would be next. And then two or three the Galilean satellites: Ganymede, Io, Callisto, Europa. And then outer moons.

Their names rang like poetry in Del Azarchel's mind: Himalia, Elara, Pasiphaë, Sinope, Lysithea, Carme, Ananke, Leda, Callirrhoe, Themisto, Megaclite, Taygete, Chaldene, Harpalyce, Calyce, Iocaste, Erynome, and so on and on.

How many would be burn? Which ones would he spare? Del Azarchel did not know yet. Perhaps all of them would not be enough. Jupiter was a great deal of volume to seed.

And, if need be, the whole system of debris forming the rings and ring arcs would be deflected down into the jovial hell of the roaring jovian atmosphere.

It was a matter of no sorrow to send so famous and ancient a heavenly body crashing into the clouds and seas of methane and ammonia that lurked so tempestuously unquietly below. It was a matter of glory, because to destroy great and irreplaceable things proved a man was great. Del Azarchel contemplated the death of worldlets as a child might contemplate fireworks of blazing rockets. This was his day of celebration.

He wished for someone to share his festive day. The only other person he wanted to talk to was very far away. He turned his bright eyes and brighter cameras toward the constellation Canes Venatici. He could make out the globular cluster of M3. To him it was not merely a fuzzy patch. He could make out individual stars. It was a snowball of fiery dots.

Perhaps a mist of sorrow that he could not, in space goggles, wipe from his eyes dimmed their brightness a trifle. The distance was not just appalling; it was blasphemous. How was he ever to rule such vast and empty spaces?

Only to *her* had he ever revealed his whole mind. Only *she* was his equal, nay, his superior.

A man cannot adore his inferiors or his rivals, but the woman he had made for himself, a work greater than himself, he can love. With all other beings, even Exarchel, even himself, he must be dishonest to a lesser degree or greater. Only with *her* was he the true Del Azarchel. Only with her he did not have to simplify his speech to the slower pace of lesser minds.

No. There was another with whom he could be honest, the honesty of rival chessmasters bent over a board where all the chessmen were seen by both, or facing each other on the field of honor with weapons smoking. Deadly honesty. Menelaus Montrose always had grasped the magnitude of what the Great Work meant.

And now, the two of them could settle down and share a drink, and just chat, compare notes, and . . .

. . . and make it like it had been in the old days.

Before Montrose had stabbed himself in the brain with a needle. Before Del Azarchel (he winced at the memory) had urged him so gaily to do it.

Del Azarchel was convinced that Montrose would not have found the courage to do the fatal deed without him. How much differently things would have turned out had Del Azarchel only held his peace!

For the Monument would never have been solved without Montrose's insanity and insane genius. Rania would never have been born. Somehow the evil deed of provoking his friend had turned out well, but, oh, after how much suffering and war?

A radio message came from Montrose. For a time, the two spoke of technical matters, sail adjustments, reentry angles for the shattered moons, each man coordinating from his side the project of waking Great Jupiter from slumber.

Montrose must have been in a talkative mood, because then he said, "You know this is a poxified damn dripping doinkstump of an idea, dontcha?"

"The signal-to-swearword ratio of your message is approaching white noise, but if you speak of this work, the Great Work, I think it is the finest idea that can be conceived, my friend!"

"Conceived out of wedlock with a she-dog, you mean, because this is one bastard bitch idea. We are making a god to rule over us, and we are not even programming him to be nice."

"A glorious future is ours."

"A glorious blister on my anus."

"Do you still have doubts?"

"Plenty. My hand has been forced. Forced into making this Frankenstein's monster larger than worlds!"

"You need not blame yourself, friend Menelaus. . . ."

"Shuddup. I ain't making no excuses, I am just pointing out the facts. The fact is that just because you wanted this to happen does not mean your hand was not forced, too. What the hell do the aliens want? We don't know what we are being forced to do and why—and yet you think you've won this round, Del Azarchel. The board just grew from eight squares on a side to twenty lightyears volume. And the game Hyades is playing, and the game the masters who own Hyades play, is even wider. So you don't know what the next move in the greater game shall be, do you?"

"No," said Del Azarchel. "All your words are true enough. I am but an egg at this point in my ambition: but I am the egg of an eagle, a kingly bird, or a roc, whose wingspan and strength no man can measure. True, the Hyades forced us to wake the Jupiter Brain, and place our world under his power. True, we cannot yet guess the reason."

"Then why can I hear you grinning? You are as smug as the man who learned to fart fire, and saw what he could save on matches."

"And you are as downcast as a fox in a trap, who realizes he loves his leg too much to gnaw it off," said Del Azarchel. "I vaunt not because I know the future, but because I know it will be mine. Even if I cannot say what it shall hold, the future shall hold my Promethean triumph!"

"Welcome to Blackiotopia," drawled Menelaus. "Whoop-dee-poxing-doo."

"Can you envision the civilization that will arise here among the moons of Jupiter? How good it will be to have men bow the knee to me again! And they will not even be men, but a posthuman mass of cyborgs and biomechanism intertwined: uploaded, upgraded, altered, augmented, and turned into the Archangels and Potentates needed as secondary brains and lesser servants surrounding the immense brain of Jupiter!

"Some of these moons we perhaps shall save to turn into Archangels of logic diamond, and some shall squat on the surface under the immense gravity, domes larger than terrestrial cities. As the core thinks and grows, achieving ever higher platforms of sapience and sentience, we will begin to detect, like earthquakes, the energy exchanges accompanying the neural activity. The minds, lesser than his but immeasurably greater than ours, shall hedge those torrents and herd those overflows of mental force, adjusting divarications and replication errors, and acting as intercessors, and, aye, as priests and oracles to thoughts nor they nor we can understand!

"Have you calculated what the change in temperature will be if a brain only twice the size of Earth alters the energy pressure in all its neuromolecular cells during a particularly involved thought process? Envision that on the scale of a gas giant! The whole world of Jupiter will ring like a bell when mighty thoughts, containing more than all the libraries that mortal men ever wrote or burned, pass from one side of the crystal globe to the other.

"Ah! My dearest Menelaus!" said Del Azarchel grandly, "I am, I confess, glad you are here to see me on this day! Jupiter will solve the message of the Cenotaph. The art of remaking man, not the timid changes of the Hermetic lore, but total change, pantropy, change to suit any world will be given to us, a gift as great as the fire of Prometheus! The art of terraforming to our specifications, to make worlds, to be as the Creator! Nay, we shall surpass the Creator, for did he not make only one man and one world? Together, we shall make many!"

"Holy Mary's Mother's milk, I guess I might start believing all this superstitious churchified crap of yours."

"Indeed? Why so?"

"What you say sounds like damnified blasphemy to me. I was hoping Jehovah would float by on a fluffy cloud and stuff a lightning bolt up your rectum. Ain't hope one of them three cardinal virtues?"

"What lesser men call sacred, to me is blasphemy; and their abominations are my sacraments! Let us prepare my son Jupiter for his coronation, for he surely shall be monarch of all the children of man on all worlds."

Montrose said, startled, "Are you crowning someone else? I thought you still were jollying yourself by pretending you ruled the roost?"

"What roost? Call it a coop instead. Tellus estimates the Hyades will deracinate our race to twenty stars in the First Sweep circa a.d. 11000, and perhaps twenty more stars after that in the Second circa a.d. 24000. Less than half a hundred worlds! Bah!"

"Y'know, you are the only guy I know who says *Bah*."

"No term is more concise for expressing disgust. Fifty earths? My ambition is not so curtailed. Someday commerce, regular trade, must open between the Hyades and the worlds of the Local Interstellar Cloud. The Empyrean Polity of Man—so I hereby christen it—is being planted as an olive tree. Someday the husbandmen will come to claim the fruit. Whenever that shall be, I mean to be prepared for it. There are wider fields for my ambition now."

"What is bigger? You plan to rule the Galaxy? Twelve thousand lightyears in diameter. Takes a long time to send out orders or hear reports. Or did that slip your slippery little mind? You're nuts."

"You thought me sane enough when we two together vowed to reach the Diamond Star, and to do all else the world called impossible."

"Except you didn't achieve it. Rania did," said Montrose.

"She will return in time. Then there will be peace."

"I should set out after her," Montrose muttered.

"Indeed? Do you have, convenient to hand, a dwarf star made of antimatter to use for fuel? I think you will find overcoming the difference in frame of reference in order to make an in-flight rendezvous will take the same amount of time, from her point of view, as waiting here to receive her. Or, did that slip your mind?"

"Pox! I gotta keep an eye on you. And shoot you dead. Then I can enjoy my wedding night in peace."

"Admit it, my friend, you want more than just peace; admit it. You want to see the Heat Death of the Universe as much as I do, or grasp the farthest quasar in your hand, or hear the mysteries whispered beyond the curve of the universe. You want to be an architect of worlds and of destinies, and decree the fates of suns and constellations! You want the future, the shining future, the golden land of tomorrow! Confess it!"

"Blackie, sometimes I do . . . but sometimes . . ."

"Yes?"

"Damn, but sometimes I just want my wife back. . . ."

Hearing Montrose heave a sigh, Del Azarchel, somewhere in the dark romanticism of his heart, felt an unspoken breath of pity for this poor, foolish Texan, who was lonely. How poetical!

". . . Just want her back, and hot in the sack. 'Cause, damnation, am I horny."

Del Azarchel had quickly to make adjustments to his parasympathetic nervous system to suppress his gag reflex. "Bah! How you disgust me! You know you are not good enough to possess her, you swine."

"Boy, don't I know it. But swine or no, I am more man than you. Lucky me, eh?"

Del Azarchel uttered some insult from the lists he had long ago and lovingly contrived for such occasions, and Montrose responded with a less witty and more earthy rejoinder he invented on the spot, and the conversation soon degenerated into their normal bickering, and then silence.

Del Azarchel did not pay much attention. The exchange of slurs and sleights was perfunctory. He spoke the insults only because he did not want the filthy Cowhand to suspect.

For if Montrose had known how unnaturally happy Del Azarchel was, surely he would be suspicious.

The glowing coal of joy that warmed him was the knowledge (and he knew not whence it came) that when Rania returned, she would look at Montrose and then look at Del Azarchel.

She would see in Montrose a man who sacrificed his morals and his integrity to save her. Because she was too good for him. It was simply a fact. And she was hyperintelligent, so she could not misunderstand that fact.

She would see in Del Azarchel a man who sacrificed not one iota of his truth, a man whose honor, while very cruel, had never been very unjust, and whose crimes were all justified by the high and noble and necessary ends to which his crooked means had led.

When she returned, he could hand her an empire of worlds of his making, and Powers and Potentates larger than worlds, Virtues and Principalities and hosts. What could the Cowhand on that day give her?

Del Azarchel was to have all. Not just everything he'd craved, but more that he had dreamed to crave.

He knew she would turn to him. His creation.

Jupiter was not the only divinity Del Azarchel had created: for he had made a goddess as well, a creature finer than any human.

His princess.

PART SIX

———◆———

Time of the Third Humans

1

Man Creates Myrmidon

1. Exile in Ixion

A.D. 22196

Menelaus Illation Montrose woke in his segmented fashion, first with lower and outer personalities on the human level, passing from dreamstate to hypnogogic state to self-awareness and assessing the situation.

Radar waves had been bouncing off his little hidey-hole here for about half a year: Half a Neptunian year, that is, eighty-two Earth years.

Considering how far away this frozen little dwarf planet was from Sol, and how cleverly he had hidden every external trace of his approach and presence when he moved here ten millennia ago, the first assessment was one of astonishment and annoyance. Given the last known state of Telluric technology after the Endarkening of Man, and the cliometric chains of events extrapolated from it, it should have been impossible for anyone to find him. *What did a man have to do to get a little damned peace and quiet?*

After the Montroses in their various human-sized bodies consulted with records and sensed surrounding energy signals from the inner and outer Solar System, the lower personalities integrated and woke a higher level awareness.

His higher-level mind was now the central mass of the remote plutino maintaining orbital resonance with Neptune. It was named 28978 Ixion. Montrose liked the name; Ixion was a character from myth who won the love of the queen of the heavenly goddesses.

Except for an outer layer of rust-colored tholin and water ice maintained as camouflage, the volume of the four-hundred-mile-diameter worldlet—the distance from Dallas to San Antonio—had been converted to logic diamond. It was all him, all brain. In chambers and tombs and capillaries honeycombed through his crystal brain cells he kept the smaller and outer personalities. Each had been assigned a human-shaped body, modified in the fashion of the Hermeticists to be spaceworthy.

This variation had an intelligence of two thousand, about what Exarchel enjoyed in his heyday covering the entire surface of the Earth. This Montrose brought more and more miles of his crystal self into awareness, heat, and motion, as he puzzled over the information of his ingathered lesser selves. He watched through several sophisticated instruments covering several bands of the spectrum with a sardonic expression deepening on the completely imaginary face he maintained in his proprioception emulator.

Yes, he had expressions. Montrose long ago had found that if his electronic brain could not feel the slide and tension of facial muscles, his emotional changes did not synchronize with his biological versions and emulations.

So he kept his face running even while he slept, and this allowed him to pry open one disbelieving eye and sigh a majestic sigh, and feel his lips draw back in an angry smile, displaying his large, square, equine teeth, even though, in reality, the eye and eyelid, the breath, the sensation of lips and teeth and tongue and the rest was just a flow of numbers through a sensorium which was itself an emulation. So what? In reality the atoms of his real flesh and blood body were clouds of subatomic particles, which were, in turn, nothing more than a flow of numbers through the foam of timespace.

And so the ghost grimaced and grunted, because a vehicle was approaching from Jupiter. That meant it was Blackie's people. Maybe Blackie himself.

He focused a radio laser and narrowcast a warning to stay away, repeating the message in Latin, Anglatino, Virginian, Intertextual, Melusine Verbal, and Glyphic, and the base introduction pattern for developing a Swan dyad language. There was no response.

Montrose watched them for one hundred fifty days, decided they were not a threat, merely an annoyance, and let the vessel land—or, to be precise, considering the small size of the asteroid he filled, let the vessel lay alongside.

But who and what were they?

He combed through the records collected over the millennia by his lesser selves who had watched and slumbered century by century.

2. Enigma in Sagittarius

The records showed a number of anomalies, ranging from the astonishing to the inexplicable.

In the Sixteenth Millennium there had been a fluctuation in the solar photosphere, and the annihilation of a geometrically straight line of particles beyond the heliopause. Someone had activated one of the mile-wide neutronium rings which the Asmodel Virtue had left floating in the convective zone of the sun.

Any of these seventeen rings, when rotated at near-lightspeed, created a Einsteinian effect called frame-dragging, which acted as a gravitomagnetic Penrose energy extraction mechanism, very similar to that produced by the accretion disk of a microquasar, and emitted a relativistic jet, powered by the ultradense solar plasma. Some unknown (and to earthly science, impossible) side effect of the frame-dragging polarized and aligned the wave-particles in the jet, forcing the energy into a coherent beam.

Montrose examined in awe the record of a nameless rogue ice giant world, a lump of frozen gas larger than Jupiter, the orphan of some failed solar dustdisk that never formed a star, who wandered into the path of the beam hundreds of lightyears away, being evaporated into brightly colored mist.

The reflections of the interstellar laserlight off the mist particles gave Montrose enough information to deduce the precise beam path. It was not pointed at any of the colonies of man, but at the Omega Nebula in the Sagittarius Arm of the Milky Way, five thousand lightyears away. What had been launched there and why? The only other thing Montrose could see in that region of space worth investigating was a blue hypergiant and variable star, V4030 Sagittarius, over seven thousand lightyears away, emitting one solar mass per day in its solar wind.

In the Seventeenth Millennium, Earth had lost her magnetic field, and unmodified human life walked abroad only at night. There had not been a drop in industrial activity during the day, but it did not follow the spacing patterns or diurnal rhythms of any First Human race, or of the Swans. This implied some new and third race of man, not a mere subspecies, now ruled Earth.

There was an Ice Age covering most of the Earth's surface in the early Twentieth Millennium. At the same time, energy discharges consonant with very large-scale industrial activity had been detected near Ceres, Vesta, and soon the other large asteroids in the main belt. Changes in mass indicated that they were being hollowed out. Changes in surface reflections indicated that they were being spun for gravity. The whole miniature world would form a carousel, against whose walls the centrifugal force could hold a layer of air, parks and lakebeds, farms and gardens. Montrose was delighted. It was something from his childhood comics come to life: O'Neill colonies! Someone had finally figured out that the surface of a planet was not the wisest place to live in this dangerous universe.

Then the Ice Age came to an abrupt halt in the middle of the millennium. A number of energy discharges consonant with the use of asteroid drops as weapons erupted over the globe on several continents. The impacts not as severe as the fall of 1036 Ganymed had been, but severe enough to abolish the ice practically overnight. A structure of flux tubes issuing from the north and south pole of Earth and reaching to the Van Allen Radiation Belts became a permanent part of the magnetosphere during this era; Montrose could not fathom their purpose. Perhaps they acted as guidepaths for energy beams meant to deflect or deter the asteroid drops.

Energy discharges consonant with major wars between the asteroid-based civilization and the Earth continued to register even on instruments as far away as the Ixion plutino across the Twenty-first and Twenty-second Millennia. Then the traces stopped. Unwilling to believe that man had learned the arts of peace, Montrose assumed that a new form of weapon, deadlier or cheaper or both, than antimatter or asteroid drop had been developed.

From these clues, he could deduce something about the nature and mission of the emissaries aboard the vessel hanging near him, but those deductions merely opened larger and deeper questions.

One drawback of knowing that there was a smarter version of yourself you could wake yourself into was that, no matter how sure you were of your results, you always wanted the more expensive energy-hogging super-version of yourself to double-check them.

And here was a mystery too deep for him. This ship should not be here.

3. Picotechnology

Ironically, the asteroid-sized Angel-mind version of Montrose was bulkier than the Archangel-mind version of himself. This higher version of Montrose was housed in a chunk of murk, partly solid, partly liquid, and partly extending half an angstrom into eleven dimensions, which occupied the space in his skull in and around and between the cells of his flesh and blood brain. This brain system was above the ten thousand level, roughly the intelligence Selene commanded.

The science of picominiaturization discovered from retro-engineering the murk left behind in the First Sweep allowed mankind, not without astonishing effort and expenditure of resources, to fit the intelligence complexity and capacity of the core of the moon into a body not much larger than a post-cetacean Melusine.

So, yes, Montrose, at ninety-four feet six inches length, and one hundred ninety short tons mass, roughly the size of a blue whale, had put on a little weight over the years. In zero gravity, the larger body had more advantages than disadvantages. He kept his scars and crooked teeth and crooked nose, because he wanted Rania to recognize him when he returned.

The process of replicating his one brain engram at a time into the portable picotechnology was slow enough that he did not let himself fret about the philosophical and theological implications. He still felt like himself. And besides, his original brain (or, rather, the seventeen-yard-in-diameter remote descendant of his often-repaired and often-replaced clones of his original brain) still occupied the analogous spot near the top of his spine of the leftover space in his now absurdly vast skull, and he could always switch his point of view back to it, when he wanted to go back to a slow, stupid, blurry, and easily distracted version of himself.

Montrose finally yawned, stretched, and floated free from his coffin. One of his smaller selves (out of whose eyes he could see himself) used a barge pole to pass a bulb of nutrient fluid the size of a balloon canopy into his hand. Another little remote puppet of himself in another corner of the endless crystal chambers of his ghost-self was dressed, under gravity, and in an atmosphere. That remote had a cup of hot and black coffee in his hands, and was waiting to drink it when Archangel Montrose drank the nutrient.

He had once experimented with making himself coffee when he woke, in pots the size of swimming pools and drinking from cups the size of bathtubs, but the drink tasted funny to his giant tongue, even if he made all his taste buds coating its acre of flesh a standard size. The fluid did not flow correctly in his mouth, because the fluid dynamic behavior did not scale up. He could have adjusted his sensorium not to be bothered by the oddity, but that seemed like an uncanny way to flirt with unreality; or he could have given up drinking the scalding, bitter fluid when he woke, but to give up a bad habit of such venerable age struck him as an abomination. How would he recognize himself in a mirror when he shaved, if he *changed* that much?

So instead he merely had the taste sensations of one of his smaller bodies transmitted into him. And then he drank a bathtub full of bathtub whiskey, mixed the signal from both sets of taste buds in his cortex. He called the mix his Irish coffee.

While he sucked on the nipple of the nutrient bulb, he turned a nearby plane of the logic crystal forming his suspended animation cell into a mirrored surface, looked at his five o'clock stubble warily. He programmed the skin cells to reverse the action of his hair follicles, and to reabsorb the beard-hair into his face.

"What is the god-pestifical-damned situation, me?" Montrose asked.

"Situation normal, all fetid ungodly," the image of his face (from whose many cameras he could also look) grunted to himself from the crystal wall.

"That bad, eh?" He wiped whiskey from his drinking bulb onto his palm, and slapped himself in the jaw once or twice, to act as his aftershave.

4. Texas Hospitality

The approaching vessel looked like a mirrored sphere. Landers dropped from the sphere were tripods that looked something like grappling hooks connected by cables. As if she were a pirate ship of old, the sphere threw out grapples and prepared to board.

Bags of biological and nanotechnological material were carried like wobbling egg sacks down the cables to the landing tripods. There was an exchange of signals between the egg sacks and the mirrored sphere, mostly biotechnological information. Ghost Montrose amused himself by warming chambers carried on a carousel, which he spun up to Earth's gravity, feeding in oxy-nitrogen atmosphere and so on, and watching the biotechnical information change and change again, trying to keep up and match the expected environment.

After a month or so of that, the egg sacks decanted a crew. Montrose expected the brain information of the crew aboard the sphere, or perhaps back at Jupiter, to be downloaded into the crew shapes remotely; instead disembodied heads traveled down the cables from airlocks in the sphere, were gathered to the biomechanical bodies, and fitted themselves into place.

The creatures were walking across the face of his asteroid like ants on a wall. Four of them made for the airlock he had so generously poked like a periscope out through the stone shell of his asteroid-body.

"I figured you wanted to be all waked up to go talk to 'em," his ghost said from the wall mirror.

"Plague! Don't they understand the word 'git'?" said the gigantic version of Montrose.

"You mean like Brit slang for bastard?"

"No, I mean like *git off my land.*' Let's show 'em some Texas hospitality."

"Real Texas hospitality? Like we show them the business end of Black-Eyed Suzy?" Suzy was the pole-to-pole rail gun. Ghost Montrose displayed a ghastly grin. "Sure! Got a payload ready, Big Me. When I saw we had company, I built me a long train of cabins circling the major axis of the asteroid out of my logic diamond, and revved it up to Earth-normal gravity. The rail gun fields are all matched up, so all I need to do is spike the juice, and shoot the whole damn guest wing into orbit and through that billiard ball of the ship."

"Nope. I mean real Texas hospitality, like we treat them royal, slaughter the fatted calf, bring out the hooch, and if they act inhospitable, such as by jawing my ears awry or riling up my nerves, *then* show them the business end of Black-Eyed Suzy." He sighed again. "Time to stop talking to myself. If none of the lesser me's object, let's integrate up."

None of the lesser versions objected, which, considering how ornery he thought of himself as being, always surprised him. It was unexpected, and bore closer examination.

He told himself to remind himself to look into this mystery later, until he remembered that he was folded into a single consciousness configuration mind, and so could not tell himself reminders.

"Now I actually *am* talking to myself," he muttered. "That is downright loco." But there was no one to answer.

The titanic, archangelic version of Montrose swam in zero gee to a locker and got out a portrait of Rania, which he handled carefully.

Since this was a formal occasion, he put on a loincloth, a gunbelt, and a poncho. The guns were vehicle-mounted cannons set with pistol-grips big enough for his elephantine hands, but he used a variation on his old glass-barreled caterpillar-gun design for old time's sake. They fired a sixteen-inch shell designed to shatter into shrapnel small enough not to pierce his walls and hence not hurt his brain.

5. Hanging Her Portrait

He swam to a spin-lock. Once he was in the spin-lock, it began barreling along just inside of the ring of the carousel containing the guest quarters, accelerating.

When the spin-lock matched speed with the guest quarters, he opened a hatch in the floor, climbed down. Because a ninety-foot-tall body shaped like a man was as stupid an idea as a man-sized body shaped like a spider, he took the precaution of filling the spin-lock and the reception chamber underfoot with high-density superoxygenated fluid thick as mud. Through this he sank. He managed to get himself seated on the floor without breaking any bones. The fluid drained away, and the environment switched over to an airbreathing regime.

One of the man-sized versions of him was standing on a ballroom-sized table of logic diamond at which Big Montrose sat. The surface was slightly higher than his elbow. On this plane was the wet bar, fancy chairs, dining table set with vittles, a mechanical bull, and whatever else Montrose could think of that his guests might need.

The man-sized puppet detangled from the mental unity long enough to make an independent comment, looking up and saying, "I can see up your nose. I often ask myself why the plague I bother having a humanoid body after all this time. For zero-gee, squids are better."

"Like the wife wants to hug a squid when she gets back! Hang up the picture." And he passed the picture in his hand to the waiting squad of workmen, who grunted under the weight. With ladders and block and tackle, and helping finger from Big Montrose the size of a log, they mounted the portrait on a spot high on the wall just opposite the flag of Texas, which was hung between his gun collection and collection of coins from long-dead civilizations stamped with his image.

The runt-sized Montrose-men unwrapped the portrait.

There she was, with hair as yellow as a garden of gazania or yarrow growing in the golden valleys of the sun, eyes as blue as the Caribbean but deep as the Pacific, and that sweet half smile held between two impish dimples. Atop her coiffeur was the coronet of Monaco, a land long since sunk beneath the sea, and she wore her captain's uniform, the void-black and starry-silver of the Hermetic Order. This was a form-fitting silky fabric freaked with branching veins like those seen through the translucent skin of a leaf, unintentionally emphasizing her curves. Technically, it was an older costume than the Hermetic Order, for it was originally the space-dress of the Joint Hispanosphere-Indosphere Expedition to the Diamond Star, which her father, Prince Ranier, had captained.

The image showed the arms of the Milky Way reaching up from the bottom of the frame and the globular cluster of M3 in Canes Venatici like a fireworks frozen in midburst above. A slender line, the projected flight path of the *Hermetic*, connected the two.

"Now read the date," he said.

From the point of view of the smaller eyes in the smaller body the portrait loomed like the fane to a goddess. The calendar demarking the flight path was in repair, but, at this scale, the gradations were in millennia.

"Today, it is the Forty-sixth Millennium by the Vindication Calendar." The Vindication calendar ran backward, as a countdown to the earliest possible date of her return. Montrose liked this method of reckoning the years.

"Now, you think if I play squid for that length of time, I won't get used to it? What if I am unwilling to change back into a man when the wife comes home, eh?"

But the puppet answered, "You think she won't be changed and strange by her time among the stars? You're just punishing yourself!"

"Punishing my—! What the pox does that mean?" But when he looked through the thought structure to see the intent behind the comment, something deeper in his mind allowed him to be distracted. For the tall double doors which opened upon the titanic table opposite where he sat now chimed and swung wide.

6. The Four Third Men

Beyond the tall doors, the corridor curved upward, for the corridor deck was the outer wall of the carousel. Oval hatches opened to the left and right into other suites in the guest wing. His guests came into view, descending around the inverted horizon in the inner carousel wall, their bodies gleaming and glittering with living gold.

Rods and serpentines from the floor were all about Montrose like a scaffold around the statue of some seated colossus, forming a exoskeleton, cradling his head and limbs, supporting his spine. He looked both as pathetic as an ancient mummy from a pyramid, frail as a man on a deathbed too weak to raise his head, but because of his cyclopean stature, and the ferocious intensity of his superhuman eyes, he also looked as majestic as a pharaoh adorned in splendor at whose command the toil of countless myriads raised those cryptic pyramids.

The four creatures who walked, slithered, cantered, and rolled into the crystalline chamber had the brutal ugliness of efficient design, but none of the sleekness that natural evolution produced in beasts of prey.

They looked like semiliquid lumps of semitransparent gold. These shining lumps had assumed temporary shapes, and were held within iron-ribbed exoskeletons of different designs: a biped that looked more ostrich than man; a six-limbed shape like a headless centaur; a rattling snake skeleton surrounding a wormlike mass that moved like a sidewinder in lateral waves, such that only two points of the underbelly touched the deck at a time; an upright wheel set about the rim with eye-lenses and ear-horns, with a triskelion of arms issuing from either side of its hub.

Because the exoskeletons were open, organs or instruments could be formed at will out of the golden substance as need dictated, and reach through the bars and lattices of the bodily frame. The skeletal ribs and slats were like Japanese fans or Venetian blinds, and could be expanded to cover all the golden body with armor.

Montrose recognized the golden stuff as Aurum Vitae, the rod-logic substance which, long and long ago, the Savants had attempted to coat the world. Beneath the amber surface he could see dimly the central creatures, one or two in each exoskeleton.

The central creatures were shaped like unborn babies, big-headed things with shrimplike bodies curled below, vestigial hands and feet dangling. External nerve paths ran from the skull and spine of each creature throughout the volume of the lump of pulsing gold he occupied. Nutriment placentas and recycling cells were connected to navel and anus by umbilicus and catheter. The golden fluid acted both as brain and as womb to them. Additional inputs like bundles of cable ran to eye sockets, ears, and the jawless hole in the front of the skull. These connections ran to a sensory exchange box floating just under an iron mask each creature carried on the surface of its golden integument.

The ostrich carried his iron mask on his helmet; the worm on his bow. The headless centaur carried his on his upright turret. The wheel had a mask perched at either side of its hub, at the crotch where his three right or three left arms met.

The masks were jointed so that mouth-slits and eyebrow-lines could be arranged in crude representations of human expressions, to assist the word communication, but all four masks at the moment showed the same blank look of stoic dispassion.

"Well," Montrose said in English, "ain't you just the most suck-ugly little critters Frankenstein ever barfed up on a bad day?"

The biped replied on two channels of information, in a grammar format called Rosetta stone, so that parallel meanings could be compared.

The first channel was the Swan initiation language. No two Swans spoke the same language, so each pair or trio of Swans seeking to address each other formulated a separate language for that dyad or triad. (If there was ever a time when any Swan spoke to a crowd, Montrose was unaware of it.) The initiation language was a set of protocols to aid the speed of linguistic development. Circuits in the crystal walls where more of Montrose's brain circuits were hidden began the process of comparing signal codes and developing a common language.

The second channel contained a set of chimes or reverberations, an auditory code based on Monument logic-sets very similar to the Savant language of old. It was so logical and so mathematically elegant that Montrose could almost translate it by ear, without reference to the Swan singing of the first channel.

The biped mask said, "The comment is irrelevant, and will be discarded." The voice was calm, and could have been a human voice.

"Hm. Will you discard it if'n I says it twice? Y'all are the ugliest thing I've ever seen without a butt."

"The comment is again irrelevant. What can you deduce of this embassy by inspection? It is more efficient not to repeat known values."

That was a reasonable request to make to a man above one's own intelligence. It would be a waste of time for the biped to repeat things Montrose had already figured out. "You're Blackie's men. I recognize his handiwork. So how come you did not radio ahead and ask whatever you meant to ask? I could have said 'No' and 'Go burn in Perdition' with a lot less expense and trouble, and saved y'all a trip. Who you hiding from? Jupiter? His intelligence level is roughly fifty million these days. I take it that means you think you can hide from him for a while, but not forever." Montrose had the gigantic exoskeleton of crystal tubes supporting him raise up his left hand, as slowly as a crane lifting a support beam to an upper story of a skyscraper, so he could tilt his huge head and rest his cheek on his fist. "There be two things I cannot puzzle out, not just by looking at you. First is, who do you think you are? For what purpose were you made? Second is, what is the point of all this?"

"We are the Third Human race, and stand to the Swans as they stand to the Firstlings. We are coherent where they are fissiparous. By Firstlings, we are called the Myrmidons."

"I thought the word referred to ants, or maybe bullies who don't question orders."

There was no reply to that.

"My name's Menclaus. And don't say *Meany Louse*, cause that joke weren't funny even back when I was human. How you doing? You fellers want anything to drink? I got whiskey. You can try the mechanical bull, excepting you ain't got butts."

The mask on the blunt prow of the wormlike serpent spoke. "We have no need for alcohol nor athletics. We suffer no fatigue, we require no entertainment nor diversion, and we have no capacity for joy." The voice was cold, as emotionless as if a winter forest had spoken.

"No family names, neither, I take it?" Montrose said. "No families? No nothing?"

The serpent mask said, "We are the first iteration of incarnate humanity that has done entirely away with the vagaries of sex, being reproduced artificially upon decree. It has freed us of much of the inefficiencies and disturbances of baseline humanity. We are creatures of pure reason, the Men of the Mind."

"So the suicide rate among you is really high, huhn?"

The wheel masks spoke. Its voices were machinelike, too inhuman even to sound cold. "Each individual is owned by, and thought-monitored by, and obeys, whichever commission designs him; and owns whomever he designs and commissions. Any man who takes up a duty one of us fails, takes on his role and privileges and rank. If our memories are sufficiently worthy to be placed in long-term storage, and passed on to next generations, then the memory-lineage is given a name-designation, and downloaded into receptor engrams in the child organism. Hence suicide is irrelevant."

"Except a high suicide rate shows you weren't built right. Some things can't be changed in human nature, no matter what Blackie says."

The wheel masks spoke again. "There are pain-inducing circuits wired into the brain which allow for remote monitoring of neural-electrical activity. The torment causes no physical damage, and any thoughts, hopes, or prayers which might allow the subject sufficient fortitude to resist the pain are isolated as nerve paths and treated with opiates, hindering concentration. The technique tends to deter serial mass-suicides."

The serpent mask added, "The change to human nature can be made if sufficient pain and sacrifice is inflicted."

"Nasty. And Blackie actually thought critters of your crippled psychology were what the Hyades wanted as slaves, eh?"

The centaur mask spoke for the first time. Its voice was a baritone, with inflections ringing with pride and command. It sounded human and more than human. "You mock the heroic nature of our race."

"Damn straight, I do."

The centaur reared up on its hind legs, assuming the posture of a four-handed giant. The mask in the center of the human-shaped upper torso said coldly, "We suffer that others may live. All humanity would perish if the Myrmidons did not stand ready to preserve them. Our moral code is of iron, and it dictates that extinction must be avoided at all costs."

Menelaus said wryly, "Lots of men say they have a code which promotes survival. Funny thing is, those are the very codes that don't."

"Lesser men may say what they wish. We are Myrmidons. We stand ready to pay that cost."

"So what about your suicide rate? That don't sound like survival at all costs to me."

The centaur folded itself down on its haunches. "An elite force must purge the weak from its candidates: it is the same for races. Life serves life."

The wheel said, "We are designed directly based on the Monument mathematics describing the mind-body correlations."

"Which means what?"

The ostrich-shaped biped said, "It means we are highly adaptable, having only rudimentary personality formations, and therefore the aliens, no matter what their psychology, will surely find us useful. At the apex of all memory chains, the basic curriculum of value judgments and axioms from which the Third Race takes its form, is the Senior and the Learned Del Azarchel."

The serpent added, "Our mental forms are designed to be compatible with what is known of the Hyades behavior strategies."

"So his personality is reflected in all of you? You are all Blackie? Your whole damned race is Blackie? And he tortures himself to keep from killing himself? What kind of twisted freak is he? Pox on my poking stick! After all this time, I still ain't got no idea what makes his sick mind tick."

The biped said, "The comments are irrelevant, and will be discarded."

One of the smaller Montroses standing on the table said, "Mortiferous pestilence, but I ain't heard Blackie called *Senior* in a long time! Not the Master of the World no more, eh?"

And the voice of Iron Ghost Montrose said from the crystal wall, "He's back to Landing Party boss."

Montrose pondered that for a moment with several of his minds.

7. Voyages to Stepmother Earths

A.D. 14303 TO 14551

Long ago, Blackie had launched the *Emancipation* to Epsilon Eridani, ten light-years from Sol, bringing a delighted Montrose. It was not exactly his first interstellar voyage, but it was the first one he made while sane. Now that Jupiter had decreed an end to Blackie's exile, he had no trouble finding volunteers to create a new Hermetic Order, from which he bred and selected a picked complement of Swans officers and Firstling crew, mostly Sylphs.

Fairer than all songs, brighter than a sword unsheathed, the great ship opened her wings of fire, and rode a river of light across the endless night.

The world there, a tide-locked world called Nocturne, had been too poor to build a deceleration laser, so the *Emancipation* had shed one sail ahead, and caught in her deceleration chutes the reflected beam from that sail as it retreated into endless space.

The humans—if they could he called that—had enthusiastically embraced the sciences of pantropy which Jupiter had narrowcast to them before their first landfall. The deracination ship was still present in orbit, as an O'Neill colony from which populations had been, from time to time in centuries long past, floated randomly to the surface in great bubbles of alien material. Through pantropy those humans and their livestock were radically altered to allow them to survive, and a different species dominated each zone of ever-colder and ever-darker climates from the plutonian West Pole to the almost-terrestrial clime of the Terminator, the line of eternal dusk that surrounded the pole-to-pole equator of the planet.

The world was ruled by a cabal of cliometrists called Actuaries, who manipulated economies and events to force families and clans to tinker with their gene plasms and produce the various freakish sub-races to fill the allotted slots in their biologically determined caste system.

The dayside of Nocturne was uninhabitable, but Montrose and Del Azarchel had shown the Actuaries how to grow self-replicating acres of solar energy cells across the dead sea bottoms there.

In gratitude for the industrial revolution this innovation had fathered, the Actuaries had cannibalized the hulk of the deracination ship to build a launching laser in order to allow the *Emancipation* to sail back to Sol.

The round trip had taken less than a century.

Later, Del Azarchel was commanded by the growing Jupiter Brain to mount an expedition to Delta Pavonis, the other surviving colony, nearly bankrupting the Earth to do so.

This colony was twice as far away, a world called Splendor. Like a white gem set in an opalescent ring, Splendor shared its orbit with a bright, multicolored ring system stretching entirely around Delta Pavonis, a sun ringed like Saturn. This asteroid belt was thought to be the remnant of a disintegrated gas giant of which Splendor was supposed to be a surviving moon. At every latitude, the immense and brightly colored bands of the belt were visible, a rainbow running from horizon to horizon through the sun.

Falling stars were a daily or hourly occurrence. The icy landscape was broken with crater lakes, remnants of asteroid falls of dinosaur-extinction size, apparently falling with appalling frequency. It was a location only minds utterly indifferent to the chances of survival would select to plant a colony.

Their cold, low-gravity, diamond-bright world had a year some four hundred days long, but, unlike Nocturne, rotated with a ten-hour day, so the deracination ship could assume a geosynchronous orbit and lower its vast length like a space elevator, allowing a low energy method of ascent to orbit, and easy access to the seventeen large moons and countless smaller satellites crowding the world.

A single equatorial ocean cinctured the globe. Glacier covered the entire northern continent and the southern, sculpted into ghostly, fantastic shapes by high winds and low gravity. All was ice-locked save the belt of rugged seashore fjords and cliffs and narrow valleys where human fields and farms and walled towns grew. The golden domes and steaming spires of the seven competing ecological stations, placed among the precipices and crags of these fierce shores were now the seats of the world's arrogant ruling clans, the Houses of Splendor.

The local life, a spongy seaweed and a plethora of colorful jellies, lichens, molds, and balloonlike invertebrates, was obliterated, and the chemical composition of the equatorial ocean-belt and atmosphere slowly changed to suit human needs, as bacteria, then spores, then arctic sea life, piscine then mammalian, was introduced, one layer at a time, carefully, slowly.

The Splendids waited with astonishing patience for uncounted years in airtight sanctuaries worshipping their frozen and slumbering forefathers, waiting for their environmental engineering to tame their world of icy seas and jagged rocks and constant meteor impacts. Their grandfathers emerged in pressure suits, their fathers in breathing masks, and they emerged in parkas, and danced and skated on the ice beneath the earthly pine trees in an unearthly world they had made their own.

The Splendids made it a point of pride never to biomanipulate their folk to match the environment, but always to coax and torment the world into matching the folk. The Chimera and Melusine among them were forced to breed with the Witches and Sylphs to produce a strange but sturdy hybrid called a Splendid: long-lived and light-boned with neural antennae for sending and receiving signals. The Giants and Locusts, outnumbered and unaggressive, were killed in hideous wars and massacres.

The proud, austere, and uncooperative Swans retreated to the regions of icy inland waste, far from the single sea, lost in glacier-torn and treeless tundra larger than the entire combined land mass of Earth, lost beyond the reach of any possible pogrom. There they altered their children to adapt to the environment as it then was, and erected de-terraforming stations antithetical to the attempts of the Splendids: these icy Swans survived in volcanic craters or deep valleys or caverns where the smog of the original atmosphere still tenaciously clung, in palaces grown from surviving native fungi or glued together from the opalescent bodies of the floating invertebrates. According to the rumor Del Azarchel heard from the domestic ghosts of the Seven Houses, the Swans were merely waiting for men to die, that they might emerge and claim the world.

Nor did the ghosts disagree. The cliometric calculus of their many environmental xypotechs showed that the world of Splendids would suffer environmental decay and dropping population rates across the millennia, unless a mass of people as large as the original forced migration was gathered here by the Twenty-fifth Millennium. If not, the world would fall below the minimal population numbers needed to maintain the atmospheric towers and oceanic infusion wells, causing environmental degradation and a return to the original atmospheric balance of gases, and causing death of the entire (and entirely artificial) Earth-like biosphere.

And the cold-eyed Swans of Delta Pavonis in their white-winged robes would emerge from their icy coffins in the wastelands, never smiling once, and live their lives of isolation, under once-more native skies filled with smokes and dripping airborne jellyfish equally poisonous to man, meeting only to mate, and building no tools, neither interstellar ships nor interstellar radios.

For many years Del Azarchel dwelt on the cold world of Splendor, for the planet lacked the energy richness needed to return him home. Then a world-wide war broke out, a grim absurdity on a world so desperately void and empty. Del Azarchel, aiding and betraying the ferocious warlords one after another, used his ship's sails as orbital mirrors to melt and crack the glaciers where various armies hid, or sink the icebergs used as barges by their navies, or used his ship's position to deflect meteors toward defenseless towns, until he was in able to decree himself supreme leader, nobilissimus and lord. When he commanded the cowering civilization to gather the resources needed to exile him back to Sol, gladly they obeyed.

The *Emancipation* towed the launching laser beyond their cometary halo, far beyond the orbit of Tailfeather, the outermost planet of Delta Pavonis. The lonely laser lighthouse was manned by Swans and thinking machines with no loyalty to the Splendids, and by some miracle the laser beam did not fail during an entire decade of terawatt output.

Del Azarchel mounted no further expeditions to Delta Pavonis. The chances that the Swans, or, if not they, whoever unwise hands it might be that the transplutonian lighthouse of Delta Pavonis fell into next, would not turn the apocalyptically powerful laser against the planet Splendid, were very slim. Del Azarchel did not expect the colony to survive, and Montrose (for Del Azarchel after his return shared all his finding with him) expected no better.

There were no other destinations from which any radio messages returned, and so no other expeditions from Sol were launched.

All the other colonies from Proxima to 82 Eridani were dead, twisted half-human bodies of failed pantropic experiments unburied under atmospheres never quite terraformed to a proper breathable mix. Montrose heard the last words of the last survivors on the radio, at least of those colonists who had the wealth and will to build interstellar-range radio lasers.

Montrose lost interest in a lot of things, after that. The interstellar human civilization which was needed for Rania's return was stillborn.

8. The Endarkening

A.D. 14600 TO 14990

After the interstellar radio silence fell, and nothing more was heard from Splendor of Delta Pavonis nor from Nocturne of Epsilon Eridani, Montrose augmented himself up to the level of Selene. The sudden clarity was blinding. All too clearly, he saw what was happening on Tellus: Mass ignorance spread as biological man became ever more dependent on his talking tools and talking beasts. Electronic man became ever more dependent on applications and appliances from higher up the mental ladder, from the servants of Jupiter. Some of the Ghosts Montrose met were illiterate. They were computers which could not add and subtract. Factions spreading an anti-intellectual cult—no one wanted to be like Jupiter—had won the day on three continents. Jupiter had already done everything, discovered everything, knew everyone, and knew how to run your life better than you did. There was not much point to anything.

Montrose, no matter how often he redid the calculations, found his cliometry showing that the human race in all its variations was going extinct, and the machines were being pushed by an evolutionary and economic pressure to ever fewer intellectual or self-aware functions.

For centuries, Montrose kept hoping stubbornly that he had made some error, overlooked some variable, or that Jupiter would somehow save mankind.

But the time turned and turned again like a grindstone, and the cliometric slope bottomed out.

The knowledge that he had failed the task she had left him behind to do, that there would be no deceleration laser to stop Rania's returning ship, and that, even had there been, no interstellar polity would exist to prove the human race were starfarers, eventually drove Montrose into self-imposed exile here.

But this mystery now followed him. The cliometry had never been wrong before. He had given up hope. Was there any cause for hope again?

9. Nonextinction Event

A.D. 22196

Montrose said, "Why ain't the human race extinct? How did my cliometry go wrong?"

The biped mask said, "We ourselves are the historical vector you did not anticipate. Do you wish to recalculate your future history on the basis of minimal or no Swan influence on Firstling history?"

Montrose looked at the gold-coated creatures wryly. The beauty, the sheer physical grace of the Swans, was part of the reason for the human inferiority complex. That was not a factor with these ugly and wretched creatures. Montrose did not bring that up.

Just in his head, he could also see how the new factor of a race like this would play out. There were several mutually beneficial social interaction mechanisms Montrose could foresee. These creatures were servile enough that the crushing inferiority the Swans felt toward Tellus, or Tellus toward Jupiter, would not be a factor. The Firstling humans, from Sylphs to Melusine, would be inferior to these pathetic creatures only in certain respects, and only mildly. These Third Humans might as a whole be smarter than the First Humans, but the individuals lacked the shocking brilliance of the Swans. Ironically, the Thirds would act as an insulating layer protecting the Firsts from Jupiter.

Montrose spoke. "I don't need no recalculation. I can see you are the product of a high-energy civilization. One that could not have come about on exhausted Earth. There is only one way that happened. Del Azarchel is the 'Senior' again because he found another Diamond Star, or some vast source of contraterrene. When was the ship launched?"

The biped said, "In a.d. 15077 we Myrmidons hollowed out the main belt planetoid 35 Leucothea, and affixed with lightsails and energy manipulation tackle, and coated the surface with picotechnological armor called *argent*, allowing the entire surface to enjoy the tensile strength of the strong nuclear force. This White Ship mass is roughly equal to the moon of Saturn, Hyperion, and the energy aura she can generate allows her to tow a mass far in excess of her own."

"I know her destination was the M17, the Omega Nebula in the Sagittarius Arm of the Galaxy, five thousand lightyears away. Which star?"

The wheel said, "Kleinmann's Anonymous Star."

A helpful almanac stored in one of his brains helpfully provided that Kleinmann 1973 was a binary of two O-type stars, highly energetic short-lived stars of sixty solar masses, the center of an odd double-shelled nebula formation, and the source of immense X-ray vents.

Montrose, studying the astronomical data in this file concerning the odd pattern of energy discharges, was thunderstruck. It had been staring him in the face all the time, sitting here in an unexplored corner of his encyclopedia of memories. One of the two O-type stars in Kleinmann's binary was made of positive matter. The other was obviously antimatter, for the inner shell of the nebula had been hollowed out by antimatter particles carried on the solar wind from the negative star, which, encountering the central mass of the nebula cloud, converted it to pure photonic energy, which, in turn blew the outer shell beyond the dangerous range of the negative star. Nothing else could account for the weird geometry of this hollow cloud of stardust.

Once again, the Monument Builders had placed their lure in the midst of an astronomical wonder; one which any starfaring race would be curious to go see.

"In April a.d. 20177," said the centaur, "the visible output of Kleinmann's Anonymous Star altered dramatically. This was the flare of the launching starbeam, pointed directly at Sol."

This meant that the expedition within less than a year of arrival had successfully erected a launching laser and left behind a staff, biological or mechanical, to man it, and had launched the return mission immediately.

Montrose checked the astronomical records, found the change in stellar output. At the time, he had thought it was the variable star entering a higher period. But no, the explanation was that the staff remaining behind had remained loyal to their task for two thousand and nineteen years, despite the immense energy cost of shooting an interstellar-strength acceleration laser beam from one arm of the galaxy to another for two millennia. The sheer persistence was awe inspiring.

And, of course, someone, perhaps the Myrmidons of the asteroid belt or perhaps the Jupiter Brain, would be required to power up a vortex in the sun and maintain a starbeam to decelerate the vessel for the second two thousand five hundred years of voyage, acting on schedule and pinpointing the position of the vessel. Montrose had little doubt one or both would be equal to the task.

Montrose revised his estimation of the Myrmidons upward. Perhaps Del Azarchel had designed a race with sufficient longevity to be the backbone of a starfaring civilization.

Montrose was momentarily struck with wonder. A human colony five *thousand* lightyears away. How long ago had Del Azarchel been planning that? Was it as far back as their first visit to Selene? Was that what he had been scanning the heavens for so diligently?

He said, "When did Blackie begin to think other Monuments might be around other stars? Stands to reason a hunter sets out more snares than one. Can you ask him?"

"We cannot," said the biped.

"Aw, c'mon, you can break your orders for me. Bragging to me about how he outsmarted me is practically the only pleasure he has in life, the poor, wretched snot."

"We cannot," said the biped. "He departed."

"What? Did he come with you partway and return back to the Inner System? I did not detect a second vessel launching from yours. No matter. Radio him. About eight hours round trip signal to Earth, this time of year."

"You misconstrue. The Senior Del Azarchel accompanied the Second Expedition to the Omega Nebula," said the biped. "He will not make landfall until a.d. 25177."

"Damnation," was all Montrose said.

The biped said, "I take it you understand the point? Components of the First Expedition left behind have been instructed to use the antimatter O-type star's energy to create this second ultrasuperjovian-sized brain mass in his own image, and decipher the Omega Monument for himself. Since the Earth has already been discovered by the Hyades, he deduced that there would be no additional harm by disturbing this Omega Monument."

"No, ugly bug, it is you that miss the point. Your components left behind went there to establish a second empire. The fifteen stars housing human colonies around Sol all shine on graveyards. Maybe Splendor of Delta Pavonis is still alive, but lacks interstellar radio, but I doubt it. He wants mankind to flourish in some remote part of space free from Hyades influence," said Montrose.

"While the expedition was gone, did your astronomers detect any intelligent signs of life in the Sagittarian Arm?"

"There is, of course, considerable stellar and energetic activity in that arm of the galaxy. Which, if any, is the byproduct of intelligent action is impossible to determine without a specific knowledge of the intelligence's goals," said the wheel.

The biped asked, "Do you conclude the Senior has abandoned us? That he is not aboard the White Ship which has been in transit all this time?"

Montrose said, "I dunno. But riddle me this: If Blackie was still interested in Earth, even a wee bit, why didn't he make a second body of himself to leave behind to run this first empire?"

The biped said, "So he did. They all wanted to go."

But the centaur mask said, "He cares nothing for empire. That task is ours."

But the snake mask said, "We all participate in some or all of his memory chains. He has not departed from us, for he is in us, and is with us."

But the wheel masks said, "The Senior is the Jupiter Brain. More and more of the levels of the mental ecology of that realm of the outer Noösphere are becoming as one with him. He absorbs lesser minds, and compels the loyalty of smaller spirits. Without such loyalty, Jupiter will not expend the vast resources needed to ignite the deceleration beam five hundred years from now."

Montrose said, "So you are telling me that Blackie will return here, loaded with as much antimatter as we need, the same millennium as the Second Sweep is coming?"

"No," answered the biped. "One thousand sixty-four years later, so it will be in the next millennium. However, our energy budget after that point will exceed the total theoretically possible energy budget of the approaching Second Armada, called Cahetel. We are concerned with this interval."

The centaur said, "In his absence, we turn to you to rectify matters."

Montrose could feel the gap in his thinking as obvious, to someone of his brainpower, as a missing tooth felt with a tongue. The sensation was annoyingly similar to trying to pick up a watermelon seed with thumb and forefinger. But he was not smart enough to coax the shy thought into view. (Evidently the shy thought was equally smart as he.)

"I don't get what you are asking me, or why you are here," he said crossly. "You are planning to surrender to the Second Armada and turn over the Earth to them for another rape session. Why disturb me?"

The serpent mask said, "We overestimated your intelligence. We will explain in smaller and clearer steps. The Senior contrived the progenitors of our race to be complementary to what was known of Hyades psychology and practice. All possible reproductive strategies can be roughly categorized into two groups: the reptilian strategy of engendering many offspring and expending small resources on their care and support, or the kindred strategy of engendering few offspring while expending large resources on their care and support. Due to the vastness of space and the cost of moving resources between star systems, the Hyades has adopted the reptilian strategy. The R-strategy means that Hyades will expend no concern nor care for the civilizations it uses to reproduce the cliometric vectors of its social organization."

"Yeah. Hyades treats us and everyone like the clap. I got the concept. Where are you going with this?"

"You acknowledge, then, that to the Hyades Domination, we stand in the relation as an offspring, and the resources expended on us are calculated by the reptilian strategy of utmost frugality?" said the serpent.

"Sure. Hyades casts out colonies without caring whether they live or die, like sea turtles leaving their eggs alone on a beach. Of course, I always wondered why Hyades put us into a situation where we had to build a Jupiter Brain in order to decode and transmit the secrets of pantropy and terraforming to our colonies. Because if we did not care, we wouldn't have bothered . . . but what does this have to do with my question?"

"Do you acknowledge that the entity astronomers called Cahetel, which will arrive in the Twenty-fifth Millennium, stands in the same relation to the Hyades as do we?"

"Wait—*what*?"

"The Cahetel entity, like Asmodel before her, is not an expedition as you understand the term. The *Hermetic* was sent to the Diamond Star as if she were still dependent upon and loyal to the authorities who dispatched and funded her. This was an error. When *Hermetic* returned, history had erased those authorities, and the new generation of polities on Earth, who were strangers to the *Hermetic* and her crew, attempted to confiscate the ship and cargo."

"A piratical crime we are still feeling the echoes of," muttered Montrose. "Had it not been for that, Blackie would not have declared himself King of the World and Emperor of the North Pole or whatever."

"It was not a crime at all," said the serpent coolly, "but a perfectly rational action which should have been anticipated. The expedition erred because the authority who sent it assumed a K-strategy, a kinship strategy, could be maintained across a fifty lightyear gap between Sol and the Diamond Star, across the one hundred twenty-five year interval between the expedition launch and return. We calculate that Hyades makes no such error."

"You mean the Hyades does not give a tinker's damn about what happens to the Cahetel expedition?"

"Affirmative. Because it is not an *expedition* properly so called, and neither was Asmodel. They were colonies. They happened to be colonies in motion. According to the Cold Equations the Hyades must use to organize their affairs in the long term, the expense in energy and the profits from cultivating the human race and seeding us to colony worlds, surely is borne by the entities, whatever their form, that live in the Cahetel Cloud or the Asmodel gas giant."

"Then they stand or fall all on their lonesome. That means—"

It meant that armed resistance to the Hyades was not futile after all. They were not fighting an entire interstellar empire, just one boatload of adventurers, a cross between a squad of big-game hunters and slave-raiding party.

It meant that the realization which so long ago had driven him into this self-inflicted exile was simply and hellishly wrong. Montrose was, despite himself, momentarily appalled at how long it had been. Eleven thousand, one hundred and thirty-five years. It was roughly the same amount of time that separated the Hamburg culture of Late Upper Paleolithic reindeer hunters from the year of his birth. And what had he accomplished during that time? He had napped.

The serpent mask said, "Our psychology, which you dismiss as loveless and cruel, is based on this same mathematical model of reproductive strategy. This enables us to understand Cahetel. If the expense of conquest is too great, she must retreat to serve her own economic self-interest, and seek another target. Cahetel has no loyalty to Hyades, who will not avenge her downfall. If Man can drive off the Cahetel Cloud, she will not be allowed to return home to the Hyades stars."

"The Swans thought they could make the attack too expensive. All that will happen is that the Hyades will tack the extra cost to our bill, and keep the human race as an indentured servant for longer."

"Correction: the Cold Equations show that the entities like Cahetel and Asmodel take all the entrepreneurial risk themselves. We suspect Asmodel has been destroyed, because too many human colonies died, and the return on investment was insufficient. And, unlike the First Sweep, we need only maintain opposition for one thousand sixty years. At four lightyears distance, the White Ship will be within effective firing range."

"Hold up. What opposition? Was Asmodel destroyed? *Destroyed?* Are you saying—" Montrose realized that the Witch-woman, Zoraida, who had told him so unthinkably long ago that mankind had won the war, had been no wild-eyed idealist. She had been right.

Man had won.

That meant he could win again.

10. Dissent

The biped spoke up, his voice cold and crisp. "Have we not been clear? With the departure of the Senior Del Azarchel, our prime memory chains have suffered divarication. There is an opposition faction among us who advocate a more efficient strategy of Hyades-Tellurian interaction. The five of us here occupying these four bodies represent the memory chains of this faction: you may called us *Dissent.*"

"What is the, ah, more efficient strategy you advocate for Hyades cooperation?"

The centaur said in a voice like a hunting horn: "Fight to the last man, and die in the breach."

Montrose did not bother to hide his expression of shocked stupidity. His eyes did not bulge out only because they were so deep set, but he stared, speechless.

The centaur held up its gauntlets and said, "We are come to plead: Lead us. Inspire us, advise us!"

The biped added coolly, "We know, beyond doubt, that you can be trusted to fight and to defy the Hyades. Our own master, Del Azarchel, whose echoes linger in the Jupiter Brain, we do not know beyond doubt."

Montrose said, "But you think the Jupiter Brain will permit opposition?"

The serpent spoke, "Despite being incomprehensible, Jupiter is rational, surely. The Cold Equations determine what they determine. If it is more efficient to resist than to submit, then that efficiency will prevail even in the multidimensional labyrinths of nested mental ecologies forming the intellect of Jupiter."

"You hope so," said Montrose sardonically.

The wheel, in a voice as mechanical and emotionless as it had used before, said, "We cannot live without hope. Are we not men?"

Montrose began slowing down the rate of rotation of the carousel on whose walls this chamber and all the curving corridor before it and behind it rested. The joke of maintaining an Earth-like environment had palled on him. He saw now that his next few centuries would be spent in space.

When the centrifugal force had dropped to half Earth's gravity, he stood, letting tentacles and bars of the logic crystal (which was, after all, just as much a part of him as his own brain) haul him upright.

"Gentlemen," he said, "we have more resources to sustain a siege than ever mankind controlled during the First Sweep. This time, we do not pack everyone in the core of the Earth, and wait for the Hyades agent to blot out the sunlight. We use your asteroid homes. We make them all into ships, or warships, or sailing vessels able to maneuver through the interplanetary battle-volume. We fill them with your people, which y'all can multiply like the ants you are named for. Every asteroid with a nickel-iron core, we turn not into a logic diamond, but into solid murk logic, which is more compact. So instead of one White Ship, we will have a ten-thousand-ship Black Fleet, a glorious fleet! We get more minor planets from the Kuiper Belt, and look around for moons any Gas Giants ain't using."

He drew a deep breath, eyes no longer looking at them. He was spellbound with a vision of an entire solar system armed and armored, fortresses larger than worlds, and all the moons and asteroids and meteors streaming like black battlewagons and superdreadnoughts toward the roaring inferno of war.

"I accept the commission and the challenge. I will advise you in an unofficial capacity. I will fight. I'll do it for *her*. It will be a fine thing to be alive again."

Montrose laughed, and it was the laugh of a titan. "By all the pestilence of hell! It will be a damn fine thing to be alive again!"

2

The War of Sol and Ain

1. The Cloud

A.D. 24087

Thousands of years ago, the cloud humans had dubbed Cahetel had been traveling so near to the speed of light that it seemed to earthbound observers to be a disk flattened in the direction of motion, blue-shifted into the cosmic ray band of the spectrum, and so massive that its gravity distorted the image of the star Epsilon Tauri, also called Ain, lying directly behind it.

The exact nature of the beam from Ain, which was pointed directly at Sol, occluded and filtered by passing through the cloud, proved impossible to analyze.

After the cloud passed the halfway mark at seventy-five lightyears, the beam of energy issuing from Epsilon Tauri changed in character, and the cloud began losing mass.

Earthly astronomers were not certain how a starbeam overtaking the Cahetel cloud from astern could be decelerating the cloud. There were many theories, from the sensible to the absurd. One of the more sensible was that the Ain beam was exciting certain volatile particles set aside for that purpose into jets facing forward into the bowshock wave of the cloud. These jets acted as rockets to brake the payload mass of the cloud, and at the same time the payload was polarized to not be affected by the beam, not accelerated further.

One of the more absurd was that that starbeam from Ain was magnetic, and retarding the progress of the cloud, or was made of antigravitons, or some other exotic particle, to act as drag-chute or sea anchor or tractor beam.

No one knew. But the loss of cloud mass as the centuries turned into millennia was more consistent with the absurd tractor beam theory than the sensible polarized beam theory.

The cloud was now slowing for a rendezvous for the Solar System, and had matched Sol's lateral motion through the interstellar medium in Sol's long, slow orbit around the galactic core. It was one lightyear away.

Montrose had parked his body somewhere, so that technicians could work on increasing his brain capacity, while his mind roamed the libraries of the Noösphere. From the many instruments of many astronomical satellites and observatories, he could see two sources of energy in and near the cloud. Something was boiling at the center of the cloud, giving off vents of X-ray and infrared radiation. There were also smaller flicks or blurs of light streaking the astronomical image, looking almost like a meteor shower.

Hundreds of pellets, from the size of baseballs to the size of aircraft carriers had been placed in the oncoming path of the Cahetel cloud, surfaces inscribed over with the lines and curves and hieroglyphs both of Monument notation and of the later Cenotaph notation left on the moon by Asmodel.

It was a contact message, explaining in the awkward pantomime language of the Monument and the Cenotaph, that mankind intended to defy Cahetel, to render the prospect of forced deracination to far colonies economically unfeasible according to the Hyades' own cold equations of interstellar power.

"Well, well," said Montrose to himself, "our modest message in a bottle. Our own little UNWELCOME mat." Then, remembering his old facility at Fancy Gap, Virginia, he added,

SOL, HAPPY HOME OF THE HUMAN RACE
—M.I. MONTROSE, PROPRIETOR—
THIS PLACE UNDER THE PROTECTION OF THE BADDEST
BOLDEST WOLF-HEARTED EAR-BITING SUMBITCH
ON WHICH THE SUN HAS EVER SHONE:
TRESPASSERS KILLED ON SIGHT. NO KIDDING.
NO SOLICITING.

He looked again, through many instruments, at the brightness in the core of the cloud. Every thinking processes causes entropy and sheds heat of some sort, no matter how near-perfect the engineering. The activity in the core may have been Cahetel warming up their judgment engines or thawing out their expert brains to think about the messages Earth had left in the path.

"Actually," said Montrose to himself, "it is a Little Billy Goats Gruff message, ain't it? *Don't pick on me. Eat my little brother instead.*"

Over Montrose's objection, the Myrmidon High Commands, many years ago when the capsules had been launched, had insisted on including a star map showing the distance and direction to the surviving colonies at Epsilon Eridani and Delta Pavonis. Montrose had argued, but the amassed minds of the Myrmidons had spread out before him the cliometric codes showing that if Tellus were deracinated, neither she nor Nocturne nor Splendor would survive, whereas if Nocturne or Splendor were looted of their populations, Tellus might survive, therefore the human race. Montrose did not know how to argue against the sharp and clear conclusion of the mathematics.

"Well," Montrose concluded glumly, "if the cart is being chased by wolves, sometimes you throw the smallest kid out so the rest can get away. It ain't pretty, but that's life."

But was it the kind of life he wanted to live?

2. No Reply, No Countermand

A.D. 24097

The message pellets remained bright over the next decade. The cloud was bouncing some sort of beam off them, either searchlights to read them by, or analytical torches to volatize fragments for analysis. It clearly was reading and studying them.

No answer ever came from Cahetel.

During that same decade, Montrose found he had to kill three of the Myrmidon High Command who interfered with the war effort, or who crossed him. Myrmidons had neither families to avenge nor formal laws to forbid such murders, provided they were done with the victim armed, awake, forewarned, and facing you. Eventually he had himself declared Nobilissimus, and that brought the number of challenges and duels down to a manageable level.

Each day, every hour, Montrose expected an imperious command to ring out from beneath the cloud layer of Jupiter, instructing Tellus and the other planetary intelligences to prevent the human races from mounting any opposition to Cahetel.

The call never came. Montrose pondered the silence soberly for many years, and wondered what it meant. He also pondered it while drunk.

But he nonetheless continued with the preparations for the Black Fleet.

3. Fifty Worlds

A.D. 24099

When Montrose was born, there had been eight planets in the Solar System. Two hundred years before that, there had been nine; and two hundred years before that, only six; in antique times, there had been seven, counting the sun and the moon as planets, but not Earth.

During that brief golden age when he had ruled, it had offended the majesty of Nobilissimus Del Azarchel that older generations had more worlds in their Solar System than his, and so the Hermetic Order had decreed any object pulled by gravity into a sphere and greater than 250 miles in diameter was a planet.

Hence from those days onward were there fifty planets in the Solar System, including Ceres, Orcus, Pluto, Ixion, Huya, Varuna, Quaoar, Eris, and Sedna, and many other small, cold, outermost worlds named after small, cold, outermost gods: from Apollyon and Ahriman, through Ceto and Chemosh, Eurynomos and Erlig, to Orcus and O-Yama, to Pwcca and Proserpina and Typhon and Tunrida, and onward.

And schoolboys for many centuries after cursed Del Azarchel whenever they had to memorize and rattle off all fifty names, from Abaddon to Zipacna, no doubt wishing that all the hell gods from the various world mythologies whose names they recited would torment him.

Therefore it was upon the fiftieth planet, and the farthest and the coldest, that the admiralty and forward observation post of the Black Fleet of the Myrmidons was stationed, of old called Sedna, after the Eskimo goddess who dwelt in the sunless deeps of the frigid arctic seas.

This outermost world was far beyond the Kuiper belt, her highly elliptical orbit brushing the inner boundary of the protocometary Oort Cloud, ninety times the distance of Earth to sun, or three times the distance of Pluto. Her year was 10500 Earth years, her surface temperature was four hundred degrees below zero. Her face was a cratered mask of rust, an oxidized form of exotic metals, gallium or titanium, beneath a thin veil of silicon oxynitride and frozen ammonia, where no oxygen ever should have existed to combine with them. Sedna was suspected to be the remnant of a perished world from a warmer clime.

It suited Montrose perfectly as the far and final outpost of his long war against the invader from the Domination of the Hyades.

4. Stand off

Montrose, or several of him, was cut off from his central brain as suddenly and completely as if an aneurysm had blinded him, or robbed him of all feeling in his limbs. He sent electronic shouts back toward his central self, not knowing what was happening but fearing the worst.

The calls went nowhere, bouncing off a security wall impervious to password and override alike.

Other twins of his, farther away, replied to the calls, and all spoke at once. "We're cut off from the gatehouse." "Is there anything there? Any damn thing? A poxy janitor camera?" "Nothing. Not a plagued thing! Whatever the Myrmidons wanted to speak to big Me about, they didn't want anyone outside the gatehouse chamber to hear."

"Do you think they killed Big Me? Are things that bad?"

"Bad? It's mutiny. What the hell do you think?"

Fortunately, all of them could all talk and listen at once. "Who is closest?" asked more than one of them. "We need to get in and see what is happening. Who is closest?"

"Me!" The nearest version of Montrose to the gatehouse chamber where his huge main body stood was a man-sized semi-independent remote used for astronomy watch. He was already leaping in long loping parabolic arcs down the tall crystal corridors of logic diamond which ran to all points beneath the rusty surface of cold Sedna. The gravity was weak, and the corridors were ten times as high as they were wide.

Taking up that heavy amulet of red metal that contained the launch codes for all the deadliest weapons he commanded, little Montrose sprinted toward the last known position of himself. Montrose could glide for hundreds of yards, kicking off the deck at the end of each leap.

He came suddenly into the central command dome through a hatch somewhere near the height of Big Montrose's knee. Even when within line-of-eyesight
with his larger self, he could not reestablish mind-to-mind electroneural contact. All the communication barriers were up, and all the gems' bright input
ports dotting the gaudy uniform of the huge body were snapped shut.

Little Montrose came through the hatch too suddenly to stop his forward
motion. He fell in a long, slow arc, and struck, bounced, and struck the ice-
smooth deck. He was in the midst of the no-man's-land, slipping in microgravity across the floor of logic diamond before he could stop himself. Sliding like
a clumsy penguin on his buttocks, he saw above him and behind.

It was a no-man's-land because he was between the battle lines. Behind him,
on a semicircular balcony running halfway around the dome, the dark and
streamlined armor of the Myrmidons stood, weapons ready, and motionless as
machines on standby. Their iron masks were all carried on the front of their
helmets, as if they were humans. Their eye lenses were in their breastplates because their brains were in their chests. The ones who had additional brains in
their bodies had additional masks on the back of their helmets, or on their ep-
aulets.

The gold material of their logic-crystal bodies beneath the armor assumed
the standardized bipedal humanoid form of the military. Even after all these
years, even in space, the gear and weapons of the armed forces followed antique models, as it was easier to command the soldiers to assume identical proportions than it was to change the shapes of triggers and boots and cockpits
and the height of doorknobs and control glasses.

That was behind him. Before him, the one-hundred-ninety-ton body of the
central version of himself loomed. In the gravity of Sedna, titanic Montrose
was only about eight thousand pounds, and with the specially designed muscles and reinforced bones of his larger body, he could stand upright without any
exoskeleton, with only a fifty-foot-tall walking stick to lean on.

Except he was not leaning on it. Except it was not a walking stick, not anymore. The sights and trigger had unfolded from the old fashioned smart metal
of the wand and the multiple barrels and launchers and emission apertures had
opened.

Montrose was resting the fifty-foot-long barrel propped in his one good hand
on the apex of the sixty-foot-high launch house directly under the zenith of
the dome. This launch house was a metal box holding a wide, squat spool designed to be catapulted into space, unwinding a lifting cable that could reach
above the pathetic few hundred yards to Sedna's geo-synchronous altitude. The
spool at the end of the fully extended line would act as the counterweight to

the miniature space elevator. Of course the launch house was placed in the only spot where the surface-wide planetary armor was pierced with a dome.

The main barrel of the big gun shot a 914mm exploding shell, weighing one and a quarter tons, that could easily break the dome, and expel one and all of the men he faced, and himself, into outer space. The secondary emitter slung underneath the main barrel was rated for projection in the million-volt range.

Big Montrose was not steadying the weapon with his other arm because his other arm was in a sling. The microscopic machines in his bloodstream for weeks would not be done repairing the special substances he used for bone material.

He and one of the officers of the central Admiralty of the Myrmidons, a memory line named Superintendent of the First Elite Process, had had a falling out, and the Superintendent had been unwise enough to mention Princess Rania during the discussion. Some echo of the memories of Blackie, perhaps lacking Blackie's diplomatic polish, had led the Superintendent to say that the marriage to Princess Rania was irregular, hence invalid.

"Pestiferous gods of Hell!" Montrose had replied. "You dare speak *her* holy name?"

The two had decided to settle the argument in the old-fashioned way.

It turned out that the Myrmidons had enough of Blackie's memories and personality characteristics that the custom of dueling was common and respected among them. The duels were allegedly a matter of prestige among the more "limpid" of the Myrmidons, that is, ones who had or claimed to have more of Del Azarchel's original memories, tics, tastes, and habits. But the duels which began with such formality and *punctilio* usually ended in brawls involving swordsticks, bolos, biforks, railguns, splatterguns, splitguns, and eventually explosives and energies that penetrated hull and killed whole companies and barracks in a frenzied surge of decompression.

The Superintendent was dead, and all his memory-clones committed seppuku, and Montrose, albeit victorious, was not yet recovered. Perhaps Montrose should not have fought a second duel with the dead man's adjutant officer while still recuperating in a hospital coffin, bracing the barrel on the edge of the coffin and holding it steady with his feet. The powder-burns on his feet still pained him, and his slouch, resting his shoulder on the control rack behind him, was to keep his weight off his feet.

Ironically, it was because rather than despite these wounds that Montrose looked relaxed and casual, almost as if the mutineers were not worth the effort of raising his weapon to his shoulder.

Low-level Myrmidons would have lacked the normal human subconscious reactions to matters of poise and posture, nor been able to read expressions, but the higher-level Myrmidons, the generalissimos and grandees gathered here, were closer to Del Azarchel's neural architecture, and hence closer to a basically human set of personalities and habits. The casual lean and lazy one-handed grip of Montrose, and also his sheer size, unnerved them.

He not only looked impossibly nonchalant, he looked splendid, like a warlord from the nigh forgotten past—but not forgotten by the Del Azarchel memories.

Montrose sported a huge bicorn hat with an eagle of gold in the center of the cockade. On his shoulders were epaulettes of steel. He wore a long blue single-breasted coat with ten ball-buttons of luminous gold, embroidered with froggings on the breast and chevrons on the sleeves, and all the hems stiffened with wire drawn from black murk and gold logic diamond, and matching designs on his trousers. Beneath this were tall black boots with bright gold cuffs.

To culminate the effect, he was wearing, in conformance with firing range regulations, a pair of mirrored goggles polarized against his muzzle flare and electrical beam weapon backscatter; and he was smoking, in defiance of air circulation regulations, a cigar longer than a tall man's coffin. The cigar's ring gauge was upward of 660. It was as if a smokestack dangled from his sneering lip.

Big Montrose was standing in front of the manual control rack to erect the lifting cable. The dome overhead was made of some material, neither liquid nor solid, which would part around solid objects passing through it, as if to them it were insubstantial as a curtain of rain, but conform so tightly to any shape passing slowly through, that its electrostatic edges could repel air molecules and keep them within.

Visible beyond this magically solid and unsolid dome, a large silvery balloon made similarly of a substance and a state of matter that had not existed when Montrose was young, was tethered to an ion-drive tug. This was a barge that consisted of little more than a biosuspension balloon holding an atmosphere. It was slow, but could return the deserters to the inner system in a century or less. It was their hope of escape.

The hundred-foot fall from balcony to diamond floor was not what was making the Myrmidons hesitate. The drop in microgravity would hardly have jarred their knee motors.

No, the hesitation had a different source. The larger Montrose was saying in a patient drawl, "I will personally take great pleasure, gentlemen, obliterating any man jack of you that steps down off that balcony. Ah"—It was at this point in time that the smaller Montrose slid to a stop near the toe of the immense black boots.—"looks like reinforcements are on their way. You know what kind of weapons I can train on this spot."

One of the Myrmidons spoke. "No signals pass into or out of this place. Hence, no remote weapons can target us."

Montrose said, "Maybe so, maybe no. My other versions of me might always toss a blockbluster-sized wad of jellied petrol here, and blow everything to stinking perdition. You think they won't? All the little me's have my curly-wolf cold-hearted killing personality, but there weren't not no room to install my kindly nature. Atrocious little buggers, them. Either way, your brain signals will not leave this place, if you all die here."

He paused to let that sink it, and shifted his massive and stinking cigar from one side of his mouth to the other.

"Oh, sure," he continued thoughtfully, "you may have twins and backups and earlier versions of yourself on some of the other planets of the Black Fleet. But none of your *recent* memories, none of those of you who decided to mutiny, none of that will get out. Because you shut off neural communications as soon as your thoughts started taking mutiny seriously, right? Because you fellers live with each other poking and moiling in each other's brains all the time, right?

"So that means any twins of you, any memories of you, they will be loyal to *me*.

"And they know—like you know—that I am damn well going to kill any disloyal members among you."

The one Myrmidon who had spoken, now stepped forward off the edge and floated to the diamond floor, saying, "We take our base memories from Del Azarchel, our prime, who knows you have not the strength of character to kill without reason. Hence your comment can be disregarded as a deception, as mere bluff. . . ."

Montrose, without changing the direction of his glance or taking his hand from his immense cannon, leaned and put his boot on the Myrmidon who was speaking, and slowly crushed him to yellow paste beneath his boot. For a moment, the Myrmidon screamed both vocally and on all electronic bands, trying to find a clear channel to send his brain information into another housing. What else he may have said was lost. Montrose ground the bootheel back and forth, collapsing the armored shell of the Myrmidon and popping his braincase and splattering the ground with gray matter from the organic component of the brains.

"I got a good reason and a *damn* good one." Montrose slid his foot back, rubbing the boot free of goo on the angled floor clamp of the antenna cable spool. "This is the first time in human history we have a chance to strike back at the Hyades. They have never even bothered to poxing *talk* to us, we are so low on their evolutionary scale.

"And you see, I've been wondering for, oh, eleven thousand three hundred and one years now if I did the right thing by selling mankind into slavery and letting Blackie's Jupiter Brain experiment and torture and breed the majority of man into freakish little suicidal sexless morts like you.

"I felt rather low about all that. I keep thinking Rania won't like it when she finds out.

"But, Judas hopping on hotplates in Hell, if'n I do this, if I drive the shepherds away and free the sheep to roam as we'd like, well, I reckon that even Jupiter Brain will see no point in meddling with human history no more, and leave all the lower folk to mind their own business their own way.

"We get to kill all tyrants, foreign and domestic, with this one shot. Is Blackie's personality really that chickenpoxed, that y'all flinch now?

"The Hyades maybe might not kill you, since they don't love you like I do, but I surely will kill anyone else who crosses that line, or crosses my cherubic good temper."

With all the electronics blocked, the Myrmidons could not speak among themselves without making noise. Big Montrose could overhear the first, since his ears were larger than an elephant's, and his ear hairs as small and as fine as could fit into the wide spaces of his inner ear, giving him a range both higher and lower than normal human.

The Myrmidons, knowing this, did not bother to whisper. "Brother, we outnumber him. He is two and we are many. He cannot kill us all before we reach and deploy the elevator. . . ."

Little Montrose drew his sidearm, dialed it to induction field, and swept it back and forth over the control rack Big Montrose leaned against. The rack contained the energy cells controlling the deployment winches of the space elevator. The electrostatic charge danced over the cells with a spectacular display of pyrotechnics, and the cores melted into the gearbox. For good measure, Little Montrose splashed some hooch from his hip flask into the power cell bank, just so that puddles and flying drops of alcohol would flare up with a blue fire, and add to the general smell and smolder. Then he took a drink and pocketed the flask again.

Big Montrose (who had leaned in alarm away from the burning control rack) was grinning so hard that his cigar flicked upward like a gun being raised in salute. "Get back to your pestiferous goddamn posts, my good gentlemen. We have an alien invasion fleet to incinerate."

5. Jiminy Cricket

The Myrmidons, in less dignity than perhaps they wished, had retreated. Regulars from other branches of the Myrmidon memory heritage, and militia of Firstlings (including incarnations from channels of the Telluric Noösphere more clearly loyal to Montrose) now occupied cross-corridors within the world-fortress of Sedna and within nodes within the planetary infosphere.

Montrose—both of him—was unwilling to leave the spot beneath the dome, as it was still the only location by which the Myrmidons could physically depart. But Big Montrose was weary, and had programmed the floor to assume the shape of a wide bowl or tub, now filled with salt water so salty it was practically mud. Into this the vast, groaning, naked body was lowered, and his bandaged arm was soaked, and his wounded feet.

Little Montrose, the same who had rushed in to aid him, was perched on the tentlike hills of cloth of the discarded uniform, watching the Sedna mind through her myriad remote-gauntlets (ranging in size from microscopic to serpentine limbs as thick as tree trunks) undo the damage he had done to the cells and gearboxes of the space elevator launch system.

Big Montrose grunted, by which he meant, "Where is the countdown at?"

Little Montrose held up his pinky and thumb, the spacer's hand sign for *six*, by which he meant, "If everything is on schedule, the Solar Beam was ignited at Sol six hundred minutes ago. Five days and change. In half an hour, the beam should pass through this area of space, and we will see the Black Fleet start to accelerate."

The fifty worlds of the Black Fleet formed a rough ring or toroid hanging in space. This armada ring could be seen on instrument screens lining the balcony rail below the dome. Their sails, tens of thousands rather than merely hundreds of miles in diameter, were deployed, spread by pressure beams radiating from the worldlets, and from this angle, fifty images of the sun could be seen gleaming in their mirrored surfaces.

"That's assuming there was not a successful mutiny at the solar station," continued little Montrose, speaking more in implications than in words. "The images we are getting now from the telemetry tower show the Montrose there still seems to be in command, as of four days ago. If he was overthrown, we will find out when the beam does not come."

"Or if the core beam hits the world-ships and obliterates them," observed Big Montrose sourly.

The operation plan was to have the core beam pass through the center of the armada ring, and carry the main destructive force to the enemy. The secondary beams surrounding this core, emitted at far lesser energies, were meant to act as acceleration pressure for the sails. Nothing known to or theorized by human science could endure for a microsecond within the action of the core beam.

"You don't think the mutineers would go that far?" Little Montrose said, or implied. "The Myrmidons *asked* us to do this. To make war on the Hyades invader."

"Well, considering that they asked us two thousand years ago, back when Earth life was still mostly living on the surface, maybe they changed their semi-collective mind. And, more important, back then I was just the senior civilian advisor to the Myrmidons. That was three coups d'état, two century-long world-wide riots, and one intercontinental war ago. Now I got Blackie's old job, and I am the Master of the World in all but name, and even though in theory I still report to the Myrmidon High Commission to Lesser Races, and they in theory take orders from Jupiter. And Jupiter ain't given no orders to no one for a thousand years, and no one, not Tellus, and not Selene, can figure out what he's up to. If Jupiter gave some secret signal to the mutineers, made a deal with them, who knows? I been the smartest man on the planet for so long, I ain't got the first clue how to act or how to think now that there is something out there smarter than me. Two things, counting Tellus. In half an hour, something will happen. Who the hell knows what?"

"And if the beam lights up as planned?"

Big Montrose gestured at the screens. The images showed the fifty worlds of the Solar System, all the smaller ones, including Ceres and Pluto and his own transplutonian worldlet of Ixion. The orbs had been converted into electrophotonic brains of golden nanotechnological Aurum with small black cores of copied picotechnological murk. All were crewed with additional biological brains of the Myrmidons, housed in independent bodies or wired into the mind core as duty and convenience dictated. Some had additional crew of First Men, Hibernals and Nyctalops, or squads of Chimerae, Giants, and Sylphs woken from ultra-long-term archives. One or two boasted Second Men advisors and observers, the eerie and solitary Swans.

For two thousand years mankind had been living in austerity, conserving nine-tenths of the energy budget of their civilization so that there would be enough power at hand to ignite the beam.

Even so much energy was merely the spark plug compared to the energy output of the alien rings of artificial neutronium that created the beam itself, drawing directly from the pressurized plasma beneath the surface of the Sun. But the earthly energy was needed to accelerate the rings to the space-distorting Einsteinian rotations needed for them to function.

The rings were focused to a point beyond the heliopause, along the incoming path of the Cahetel cloud, at a distance of one lightyear. On this scale, that was point-blank range.

"If all goes as planned," said Big Montrose, "then the first beam impact bathes the Cahetel cloud in radiation, destroying ninety percent of its mass in the first nine seconds of the war. The cloud disperses as fast as it can, and the beam spreads to compensate, becoming less focused and so less potent. Another nine percent of the mass is destroyed during the next two years. Shortly after that, the Black Fleet passes through the area, using their worldlet-based observatories and weapons to detect and destroy the final nine-tenths of one percent. The real task begins then, a long hard war to insure no smallest particle finds other little bits of matter to attach to and convert into picotech substance.

"That one-tenth of one percent will haunt us for years," Big Montrose continued, "but without matter and without energy, what good is it? Technology is the ability to use units of information to manipulate units of matter-energy into new forms. No matter how high the level of technology, there are Planck limits and Heisenberg limits to how much information can be packed into how small a space—and we can starve any small clouds coming from that remnant, and burn them with the solar beam if they approach closer than Neptune. That gives us an eight-hour sighting and response time, rather than the two-year interval we are dealing with now."

"You're optimistic," said Little Montrose.

"Damn right I am!" Big Montrose grinned his alarming gargoyle grin, which looked monstrous when portrayed on a smile several feet wide. "Both Tellus and me have thought through every possible maneuver a decentralized cloud-shaped being could perform. It cannot move faster than the speed of light; it cannot see faster than the speed of light. So the first hint Cahetel can possibly have of our plan, the first thing it sees, is the core beam passing through the heart of the cloud. I don't care what it is, if it is made of matter, made of small particles held in electron clouds around nucleons, held together with the weak and strong nuclear forces, then, by God, it comes apart. There is just too much energy in that beam for anything to absorb it. If it tries to disperse, the outer segments of cloud can only move as fast as their mass can account for if the remaining mass of the cloud is converted to pure energy and used as a perfect fuel—and in any case not faster than lightspeed. We keep opening the cone of the beam to kept the fleeing cloud segments under continuous fire. Hell! We've finally got them! The laws of physics are on our side. No matter how advanced these aliens are, they cannot break the laws of nature!"

"I meant you are *optimistic* by which I mean *idiotic*."

"How you figure? What do you think you thought which Tellus ain't thought through a zillion times over from every angle?"

Little Montrose said, "If it was that easy for conquered races to fight off the Hyades, they would not be the Hyades. And the Dominion at Praesepe Cluster would not have conquered Hyades and the other dominations. And the Authority at M3 would not have conquered Praesepe and the other dominions."

"You're a pessimist. Other planets might not organize resistance like this. Or maybe out of every thousand planets, only one gives in without a fight, and we are among the nine hundred ninety-nine that get our backs up and put out claws. Like I said, we thought all this through! Inside and out!"

"All theory. You sound like Del Azarchel."

"Have some faith in smarter minds than yours."

"Why am I here, again?" said the little Montrose, with a sour look on his face. "As a pet for myself?"

"To keep me honest, squirt."

"Well, how honest was your little show just now?"

"What do you mean?" asked Big Montrose uneasily.

"You killed that man."

"He ain't got no folks, no mother to mourn him, no orphans left behind."

"So that makes it worse, not better, don't it?"

"You know I had to do it, squirt."

"You didn't had to do it so slowlike. Did you? I saw. You put your foot on him, pushed halfway down, let them hear him scream, and then crushed the life out of him. Pure sadism. Why not shoot him?"

"No shells in the damn gun. Besides, I had to do it slowlike enough to make my point."

"The *point* was that some of these critters have that one little bit of Blackie's brain that loves Rania, and that thought is a red-hot iron thorn in the tender groin of your self-love."

The giant slowly shook his head. "You ain't reading my heart aright."

"Don't need to. All I need to do is read my own heart. It's all there plain enough."

"Now I wonder why Pinocchio did not just step on his damned cricket. I am beginning to see the drawbacks of a conscience that talks aloud."

"What? Gunna step on me, too?"

"It's tempting . . ."

"Yeah," grunted Little Montrose. "I *know.* That is why most consciences don't talk aloud."

The big man was silent for a moment, trying not to let a scowl darken his features. Slowly he stood, and small rivers poured from his vast limbs. Robotic arms, large enough to serve as cranes in the dockyard for seagoing battleships, draped the yards of fabric around him. It was easier, given his size, for the arms to hold the cloth segments up to his body and send sewing machines the size of mice scampering on many legs up and down the yards, to sew up seams. It was easier to sew on buttons rather than to button them. Big Montrose did not wince as the damaged arm had its bandages changed, and was wrapped up again to his chest.

Finally, he was once again the very picture of ancient military sartorial splendor. Big Montrose said, "If the solar beam ignited on time, we should see it light up all the sails in a moment. Now is not the time to fret on past misdeeds, eh? This will make up for it all. They will not send a Third Sweep if this Second Sweep is deep-fat-fried and gobbled up whole: they are just as much slaves to their goddam Cold Equations as we are to them.

"With the threat of the Hyades gone"—Big Montrose grinned—"the human race will have forty-six thousand years to kick back and enjoy ourselves before Rania arrives with our manumission papers. Jupiter will have no rationale to maintain his control. By the flaming dung in the latrines of Hell, what will a puny twelve thousand years of servitude to Jupiter be then? A few millennium of sadistic eugenic practice, experimenting on human babies, committing genocide on unwanted breeds, forced marriages, inseminations and abortions and abominations—everything Jupiter did to create the colonists and then the Myrmidons—" Big Montrose snapped his fingers, making a noise like the thud of a bass drum. "Ha! What will it mean? Merely a footnote in history!"

Little Montrose said, "You mean it's a footnote we are hoping Rania won't read when she gets back?"

Big Montrose scowled.

Little Montrose said, "I understand that there are things I can no longer understand. I am like a dog to you. But a dog knows when his master is in pain. Just because you are smarter, don't mean you've changed your nature. The conscience still works the same way. You can push just so far and no farther. You push the conscience by playing tricks on yourself—and you have to play along with the trick, let it fool you, or it won't work. Then you can stretch the truth and stretch it and stretch like India rubber. But there is always an outside limit. Always. When you try to stretch it too far, it snaps back and hurts you."

Big Montrose said, "I've always done whatthehellever I had to do, to get what I want. So why is this different?"

Little Montrose sighed and spread his hands. "Now, I reckon, I'd've said I've always done whatthehellever I had to do, to get done what was *right*. If you were at rest with yourself, you would not have made a little Jiminy Cricket for your-self. Which brings us back to my first question. Why am I here?"

"You are here to witness my glorious victory," said Big Montrose in a hol-low, hearty voice that fooled neither himself, nor his other self. "There is noth-ing that can endure the output of a star focused into a narrow beam."

"Nothing we know," said Little Montrose sourly. "Tell me, Cap'n! What are the rings made out of? You know, those gigantic spinning hoops of infinitely dense material that rotate at ninety-nine percent of the speed of light, drawing up the solar plasma into a lased beam? We call it artificial neutronium. What is it made of?"

Big Montrose said, "Sonny, rather than explain things that are way over your head and way out of your price range and way above your pay grade, why don't we just toast the victory?"

"I toast it when I see it."

"Skeptical you. Then let us toast *her.*"

Little Montrose pulled out his hip flask, poured himself a shot of whiskey in the cap that doubled as a chaser glass. "What's the chance of getting a beer? Shouldn't drink this straight up if we are on military duty here. Or is wheat and hops extinct?"

Big Montrose said, "We've entered a strange and new age. Matter is pro-grammable, thanks to advances Jupiter has released to Tellus. I can have the anything-maker make you whatever we got the raw materials for, including an ersatz beer."

"Just like the food replicators on Asymptote! When do we get teleport booths?"

"The same day we get faster-than-light unicorns that shoot rainbows out of their butts. We cannot turn anything into anything, but we can turn a lot of things into a lot of other things, and put thinking and talking circuits into nearly all of it."

"Talking beer? I want to go back to the past."

"Doesn't taste as good as the real thing, but, hey—gotta have a drink to sa-lute what we're fighting and dying for."

A silent Myrmidon in civilian garb—a shape that looked like a three-legged stool wearing its iron mask on the seat—now brought a beer stein to Little Mon-trose. The stein was covered with a low-gravity lid of semi-permeable mem-brane. Little Montrose raised the smaller glass to the titanic version of himself. *"To her we drink, for her we pray, our voices silent never!"*

The big version raised a mug the size of a bathtub and dropped a frost-covered whiskey glass the size of a bucket into it, glass and all. It fell with dreamlike slowness in the microgravity. *"For her we'll fight, come what may, fair Rania for-ever!"*

The smaller man tossed the contents of the shot glass to the back of his throat, coughed and wiped his eyes and slurped from the beer stein, all before the bigger version took his first tidal-wave-sized sip from the huge mug.

The smaller man coughed again. "No fair you putting my brain into a body that cannot hold its liquor. Damnification!"

Both were silent, and watched through the dome overhead, seeing a line of sparks, glowing at first like embers, then more brightly, scattered here and there in the black sky. For less than a minute, they flamed, dazzling, and went dark.

With no background against which to judge depth, it was not until signals from other instruments orbiting far from Sedna could triangulate on the flare-bursts, and produce a stereoscopic view.

This was a cylinder of destruction wider than the diameter of a gas giant, that had intersected particles of gas, fragments of ice or stone, or comet masses between the size of a baseball and the size of a mountain. Everything within the core beam was not just incinerated, not just vaporized, not just ignited, but annihilated. Each atom of every dust-mote and asteroid exploded into a scatter of electrons, protons, and smaller particles.

Little Montrose was impressed, and let out a long, low whistle.

Big Montrose said, "Roughly five quintillion joules of energy."

Little Montrose said, "Hope all the worldlets of the Black Fleet are clear of the beam path."

"That is the plan."

Even as they watched, the light grew cherry red and dimmed. As planned, after the initial discharge, the beam was spreading and dimming. The beam was now powerful enough to impart acceleration to the worldlets, but not so potent as to obliterate them. One by one, over the next few months, their orbits would carry them into the beam path, and they would begin their long, slow trek toward Cahetel.

The first contingent of the flotilla had been waiting in place, just beyond the deadly core beam, to catch the secondary beam as it spread. Their sails lit up. The worldlets and dwarf planets of the Black Fleet now shined like radiant angels, dazzling, immense, blindingly bright. Cheers came dimly from the other corridors and buried decks of Sedna.

Little Montrose started, embarrassed that he had forgotten he was not alone here, forgotten that the Myrmidons, Swans, and various Firstlings, Hibernals,

Nyctalops, Giants and Sylphs and Space-Chimerae were still men, and still cheered at the launch of great and terrible fleets.

He suddenly saw the reason for the optimism of his larger, wiser self.

"I take it all back," Little Montrose said. "The alien entity is big and smart, that is true. But the Cahetel Mass has made the crucial mistake of being made of matter."

Little Montrose looked more closely at one of the worldlets which was in transit against the broad sail of another more distant member of the fleet. "Maybe we should keep Pluto and throw the other ones at'em," he said. "I was always kind of sentimental about Pluto. It was not a planet when we were born. Poor thing, getting demoted like that."

"No time for sentiment," said Big Montrose. "I'd throw Jupiter at Cahetel, if I could figure how to rig a lightsail."

"Strap it to his ring system," suggested Little Montrose. "And now what?"

"Now we wait," said Big Montrose. "Smoke'em if you got'em."

But Big Montrose made no move to light up one of his titanic and odious cigars. Instead, his skin, acre by acre, was going pale as ice, as nanomachines in his bloodstream were placing his cells in biosuspension.

Little Montrose took the time to find a chair and sit down, and he did the same.

6. Upon Reflection

A.D. 24101

"Wake up, sleepyhead!" said Big Montrose in a cheerful voice. He was both smiling and scowling, an odd expression which drew his eyebrows together and turned the corners of his lips up mirthlessly. "You don't want to miss the whole war! This will be all over but the weeping in four minutes. And a few decades or centuries of hunting down survivors, of course."

Little Montrose shook the last of the biosuspension frost off his face and hands, and stood up, blinking. He stood up so quickly that in the microgravity he found himself floating awkwardly in midair. The chair politely extended a serpentine—a whip of semi-intelligent self-repairing metal—and drew him back to the deck.

Little Montrose was confounded to see a serpentine here, a technology invented by the Sylphs, and used in later ages by the Chimerae as weapons, events so far in the past that only he had living memory of them. The serpentine really was a plateau technology, it seemed. Like the shape of an axhead or shiphull, it would never need improvement.

The screens that thronged the dome showed the views from various elements of the fleet of worldlets. Sedna was currently near the rear of the flotilla, which occupied a doughnut-shaped volume. The flotilla had traveled roughly one hundred twenty light-minutes in the last two years, while the Cahetel entity had approached fifty-two thousand light-minutes closer to the Solar System. On an astronomical scale of a battlefield larger than solar systems, they could hardly said to have moved from their initial positions.

Little Montrose wondered, not for the first time, what kind of minds, with what kind of psychology, could grasp these astronomical distances and make plans along such astronomical intervals.

Pluto was the most forward of the planetary flotilla, and had polarized her mighty sails during the last month, to give her surface observatories a clear view of the enemy. Spending two years in the penumbra of the solar beam had heated her surface elements and formed an atmosphere, and the crewmen aboard Pluto had emerged to cover the lee hemisphere of the planet, the side facing the Sol's beam, with gardens and arbors.

The reflected light from the cloud had reached Pluto, from Sedna's frame of reference, over four hours ago, and the concentrated light from Sol had struck Cahetel a year ago, and took a year to carry the message of what had happened to the observatories on Pluto, which were then relayed to the receivers on Sedna. It was these images Little Montrose raptly watched.

"Space battles would be a lot easier if space was smaller," muttered Little Montrose.

"Beam impact in ten . . . nine . . . eight . . ." Big Montrose was saying, his eyes fixed on the image of the vast, dark thunderhead of Cahetel. The cloud was irregular, with wispy arms reaching many thousands of miles in each direction. The energy of its deceleration jets, facing toward them, surrounded the whole mass with a spray of nebular discharge paths, glowing blue and blue-white on the upper wavelengths of the spectrum. The whole looked like some freakish flesh-eating blossom of the Amazon river, with a heart of blue and petals of black.

The main mass of the cloud of particles was roughly globular, but since it was four light-minutes in diameter, the trailing hemisphere of the cloud seemed oddly distorted, since the image of the light from the bowshock of the cloud reached the Plutonian receivers four minutes before.

Little Montrose tapped the serpentine still circling his waist, and said. "Hey.

You awake? While I was asleep, did anyone ever figure out how Cahetel was decelerating in the middle of an acceleration beam?"

The serpentine said, "Yes. Observers on Pluto, able to detect and analyze short-range discharges, discovered that seven-tenths of the cloud mass are artificial particles such as existed, in theory, during the first three seconds of the universe, and not after. They possess a property called supersymmetry. Such particles were neither electromagnetic, nor neucleonic, nor gravitic, since the forces of the universe had not, before then, been separated into the forces known to the modern universe. The influence of the energy beam from Epsilon Tauri, coming from their stern, breaks the supersymmetrical particles into gravitons and photons and so on in the midst of a super-powerful toroidal magnetic field in the center of the cloud. This acts as a heavy particle accelerator . . ."

The serpentine helpfully showed him an image on a screen near at hand, the electromagnetic aura of the field throbbing at the center of the cloud, the source of its impossible reverse acceleration.

His eyes bulged, and his jaw dropped. He recognized the characteristics, the magnetic contours. It was a ring of artificial neutronium, a ring wider than the diameter of Earth. It was the same size and shape as the acceleration rings Asmodel had left floating in the surface of the sun. A twin. The energy contour was as identical as the shape of the same snowflake, the same fingerprint.

"POX!" shouted Little Montrose. "Stop the beam! Cease firing! When our beam hits, that thing is going to—!"

Of course, the events he was seeing had happened over a year ago. There was no stopping the solar beam.

". . . two . . . one . . . Sorry, what were you saying . . ?"

The beam struck. The observatory images from Pluto showed what looked like a lance of lightning impaling a storm cloud. The dark mass was suddenly bright with textures and folds of the cloudscape, complex as the folds of a brain cortex. The cloud was as wide as the orbit of Mercury, and even a beam as wide as the diameter of Saturn's rings was merely a small spotlight playing across the valleys and hills and kraken-armed streamers and films of the cloud mass.

Nonetheless, where the beam touched, there was a point of light brighter than the sun, and an expanding sphere of destruction, and another, and another. The scattering particles ignited like fireworks. The screens tuned to the X-ray and cosmic-ray bands of the spectrum went white and fell blind. On the visible wavelengths and on radar lengths, the cloud expanded like a smoke ring from the playful mouth of a cigar smoker. The core of the cloud was briefly visible. There were five Earth-sized globes inside, coated with dark ice, arranged in a gravitational pattern called a Kempler's Rosette. In their middle was a ringworld. The globes acted as shepherding moons to stabilize the spin of the ringworld. In the middle of the ring was glittering the star Ain.

For the first time in thousands of years, the star Ain, Epsilon Tauri, was visible to observers within the Solar System without the Cahetel cloud to obscure it. In the screen image, the star seemed as bright as a nova, for its stellar beam was pointed directly at the cameras and recorders of Pluto. But the star was reddened and distorted, surrounded by arcs and smears of light, as the photons shed by stars behind Ain suffered metric warp passing through the ring. The ring was rotating, creating a circular space warp, the frame-dragging effect. Only Ain, in the precise center of the distortion, was undistorted.

The solar beam of destruction glanced across the cloud like the beam of a warship's searchlight. For a moment, less than a second, it shone straight, an unbent ray. Then, instantaneously, part of the cloud mass imploded, and a volume of particles larger than a gas giant collapsed suddenly into a pinpoint, smaller (so the instruments Montrose saw reported) than the diameter of an atom. This microscopic black hole bent the solar beam, and focused it into the direct center of the spinning ringworld.

But when the beam, charged with all the output of Sol, struck the center of the Cahetel ring, there was a flare of energy that crackled like lightning out from the ring surface, and traveled up the arms of the vents and filmy extensions of the cloud, as if these were antennae.

"I was saying," Montrose said softly, in a dull, stunned voice, "that the technology the cloud uses for decelerating inside the beam from Ain will allow them to control our beam as well. That is why they did not come in the same shape as the Asmodel entity."

And then the last thing Montrose could have expected or imagined happened. The cloud vanished, replaced by the peaceful and gleaming stars of empty space. Ain winked brightly in the middle.

Or, rather, it seemed to vanish. It was not the constellation Taurus he was looking at. It was the constellation Scorpio, and the bright star in the middle was not Ain, but Sol, shining with the deadly emission of the solar beam. Montrose shouted for the Sedna Mind to recalibrate and give him a closer view. The serpentine (which was still embracing him) said softly that Sedna was no longer able to answer.

"What the pox is going on, Big Me?"

There was no reply from behind him, but a ghastly smell. He put his hand on the serpentine to turn himself around.

The figure of the larger Montrose still loomed behind him, but his vast skull was on fire. Flares of a sparks, gushes of heat, and smoke were pouring from the holes where once mouth and nose and eye sockets had been.

The black substance of his brain was now running out of the eyes and nostrils and mouth of what had once been Big Montrose and spreading over the surface of his burnt and blackened head, crawling upward and backward. It looked like a flower opening. The black murk coated the globe of the head, and dripped in inquisitive ropes down his neck and shoulders.

The outline of the skull was visible through the coating of creaking black substance, holes like the fingerholes in a bowling ball marking the position of the eye sockets and mouth, which continued to emit fragments and worms of the murk material from which the brain of Big Montrose had been constructed.

The body of Big Montrose, in one last convulsive movement—almost as if the nerves of his arm and hand had been preprogrammed to perform this action if signals from the central brain were cut—gripped a cylinder of metal from his coat pocket, and extended it unsteadily toward Montrose. It was a standardized brain-storage biosuspension unit, bright green metal marked with a red cross. It slid from the dead man's giant fingers and fell with dreamlike slowness toward the crystal floor of the domed chamber.

And the floor was no longer the golden white crystal of the Myrmidon Aurum. Starting from the feet of the titanic black-skulled corpse, the floor turned dark. A black snowfall of tiny particles of the murk substance dripping from the skull, eyeholes, and throat-pit of the vast corpse were falling to the floor, and where they touched, the picotechnology was altering the nanotechnology, and the floor grew wrinkled and dark.

The chair next to Montrose flexed, turned black as India ink, and grew wrinkled and crooked all across its surface. Montrose, in a swift reflex, yanked the serpentine in his hand out of the socket connecting serpentine with the chair arm. There were other serpentines connected to the back of the seat. They turned black, writhed in a momentary spasm, and froze in position, looking like strange undersea weeds. The serpentine in his hand remained silver, apparently unaffected.

7. Everything Talks

"What the hell is going on?" Montrose said aloud.

The serpentine answered him and said, "We are receiving a signal from the survivor on Pluto, a subaltern from the Vingtener memory-chain."

"Survivor?" There had been hundreds of men and thousands of minds aboard Pluto.

"Only one survivor. He reports that all of our technology based on murk pseudo-atomic logic patterns has been absorbed by control signals from Cahetel. The supersymmetrical particle breaking system allowed Cahetel to reflect all photons back toward the source. The emission point sources accelerated rapidly during the broadcast and blue-shifted the visible light into the radio spectrum, on the wavelengths to which the murk was inherently reactive. The solar beam signal which Cahetel reflected will reach Jupiter four months from now, and Earth, who will be nearly in opposition at that time, forty-nine minutes later."

Montrose, standing with his fists clenched and the muscle in his jaw twitching as he ground his teeth, twice had to override the automatic rage and fear reactions triggered in his parasympathetic nervous system. (He enjoyed being able to do that: he recalled how often his natural body just plunged him into a rage or a panic without so much as a *by-your-leave*.)

But perhaps some panic was reasonable now. The agents of Hyades had left behind the murk traces and the interstellar beam elements deliberately. They were confident that even an attack coming at the speed of light, with no warning, could be parried, manipulated, and flung back at the attacker in the specific wave-forms needed to paralyze and mesmerize and enslave an entire civilization.

And anyone not using the murk, anyone backward enough to rely on nanotechnology rather than picotechnology, was probably not able to think quickly enough and carefully enough to form a threat anyway. What could technology on the biochemical level of artificial life do against technology on the atomic level of artificial elements?

And who would use anything other than the starbeam praxis to launch an interstellar-level attack?

But the kind of mind Cahetel commanded, the sheer thinking power needed, to catch a destructive torrent of energy, and transform it into control signals, and reflect it back across the entire diameter of a star system was appalling in its magnitude. It was beyond monstrous. It was godlike. Montrose adjusted his nervous system carefully, to let a moderate degree of awe and terror grip him.

It was not so much fear as to prevent his next question: "Can we warn them? The Solar System?"

"Subaltern Vingtener's signal should reach any open receivers two minutes after the control signals take control of such receivers. Whether Cahetel allows the receivers to pass the signal through to any survivors, or permits the brains of the survivors to hear the warning, is, of course, a matter for Cahetel's discretion. Anyone who is entirely disconnected from the Noösphere, such as yourself, and using no murk technology, will be spared."

Montrose, although much less intelligent than the larger version of himself who had died, was still much smarter than a baseline human. He saw the implication.

He looked again at the ghastly spectacle of the ninety-foot-tall corpse, which as yet had not fallen. It did not even seem to be relaxed from standing at attention, despite that heartbeat and breathing had stopped.

Montrose studied the artificial memory chains which were installed in this body he was occupying, saw how to issue the commands to the multivariable cells in various parts of his nerves and organs, and in short order grew a triple set of Melusine antennae, which he used to detect the electronic and neucleonic activity rippling and throbbing through the black murk coating the faceless horror looming over him.

Montrose said, "Can you translate for me? It is thinking in a variation of Cenotaph code."

The serpentine said, "Yes, although I do not have an access point."

Montrose drew out his sidearm. He stared at it carefully, remembering what Big Montrose had said about the manufactured objects in this era, and realizing for the first time that he, Little Montrose, had almost no memory of this era. He did not recall the worldwide wars or riots he had launched, the ministers and dignitaries he had killed, the other men he had humiliated, or robbed, or slandered, or ruined, in his ruthless attempt to become the Master of the World. He remembered that he had wanted and needed to seize control of the war effort of the whole Tellurian Noösphere and of all three human races, and all the resources and manpower of an entire interplanetary civilization—because he did not trust anyone else to make the right decisions on how to fight this war. And his decisions had led to this.

The pistol said, "Sir? Are you contemplating suicide?"

He was not surprised it could talk. "Why do you ask?"

"You have the expression on your face typical of suicides."

"No, that is just the natural cast of my features."

"And you have the neural and glandular contour consistent with the profile."

"Um. It is the natural cast of my glands. Can you configure yourself to—"

"Yes, sir."

"What the pox? You didn't hear what I was going to ask."

"Your previous orders on the topic were clear. You wish me to act as a transmitter capable of interfering with picotechnology-based information cascades, to enable you to attract the attention of software embedded in murk fragments."

"When did I give those orders?"

"Before you issued me, along with a uniform, to the smaller version of yourself you had formed from isolated biological matrices."

"Suit!" He slapped himself in the chest. "Can you talk, too?"

A voice came out of his uniform buttons. "Yes, sir. Everything talks. All matter is programmable using the techniques Jupiter developed."

"What did I order *you* to do?"

"To keep your smaller version isolated from any neural contact with logical crystal systems or Noösphere channels connected to any murk-based system."

Montrose closed his eyes. He felt a hot sting of tears under his lids. Big Montrose had known. He had known from the beginning. Damn him.

He handed the pistol to the serpentine. "Use this. Establish contact."

"Sir? What message do you want me to send?"

"Start with 'Hello, you bastard.'"

"That concept may not translate."

"Start with the opening of the Monument First Contact message."

There was a quiet hum from the serpentine. That was a surprise. Serpentine operations were nearly always silent. This task, apparently, was straining it to the utmost.

Time passed. Montrose stepped off the balcony, floated down to the dark floor, and picked up the brain storage cylinder.

The tag read: MONTROSE, MENELAUS ILLATION (FIRST, ELDER). HANDLE WITH CARE.

"You sentimental bastard," said Montrose. And he began to weep.

It was his original, biological brain, held in suspended animation, slumbering.

3

The Virtue Cahetel

1. The Imperative

"I have an answer, sir," said the serpentine after four hours. Montrose was back up on the balcony with the whiplike machine.

Even in the light gravity, Montrose had found his feet getting tired after a time. The cylindrical braincase he recovered from the floor far below was large enough that, upended, he could sit on his brains like a stool.

"Show me."

And all the screens scattered across the balcony rails and about the dome lit up. They were black, crisscross with the thin silver lines, angles, and sine waves of the Monument Code.

Montrose read it.

TWO-WAY COMMUNICATION IMPERATIVE NOTIFIED.

That was its way of saying *hello*, he guessed.

"Who are you?" he said to the gigantic, appalling figure in the center of the silent dome.

The ninety-foot dead giant tilted its head as if turning toward Montrose, the empty eye sockets from which frozen streams of murk hung like icicles of ink. It must have been pure coincidence. The entity was perhaps trying to position some receiver buried in the circuits and lobes of the murk closer to the needle-beam of the communication laser the serpentine was shooting from Montrose's talking gun. But it looked like a blind man trying to peer at someone.

WE ARE CAHETEL.

The dark screens lit up now, not with the curls and lines of Monument Code, but with plain Latin letters.

"How does it know what we call it? How does it know English? How does it know *pronouns?*"

WE ATE YOU.

"Damn you! I did not mean you to send that question to it! I was asking you!"

The serpentine said, "Sorry, sir."

"Are you translating correctly? What does it mean, it *ate* me?"

"Sir, I am trying to convey nuances which primary-level thought cannot encompass except by metaphor. Cahetel has apparently absorbed certain memories from the dead brain of your central version, and formed a conception step-down bridge from the residuum. Are you ready for their next message node?"

"Shoot."

The pistol held in the grip of the serpentine muttered, "Very funny."

PLEAD.

"What does it want me to offer a plea about?"

"I am not certain, sir. In every form of communication, there are certain abbreviations, pronouns, implications, allusions, ellipses. We are dealing with an alien mind. Where it puts its ellipses will perforce differ from a human psychology."

"Ask it," said Montrose impatiently. "What pleas may I enter? On what topic? Why?"

ALL STARS ARE DEAD, ALL WORLDS ARE DEAD. THE UNIVERSE IS DEAD.

Montrose recalled a similar message had been written on the outside of the deracination ships when they swept up half the population of Earth. But he said, "What the hell is he talking about?"

"Do you wish me to send a request for the emissary Cahetel to clarify his remarks?"

"Yes. Send."

AMPLIFICATION: ALL LIFE SERVES LIFE. BIOLOGICAL DISTORTIONS OF DEAD MATTER FORM AN INCOMPLETE LIFE. PLEAD. PLEA TO SERVE. PLEA FOR COMPLETION.

Montrose felt a chill travel up his spine. He was not sure what the creature meant, but he knew he did not like it.

INDICATIVE: PLEADING TO COHERE THE FUTURE IS IMPERATIVE. ALL IRREGULARITY MUST BE ABJURED. THE MENTAL AND SEMANTIC DISTORTION CALLED FREEDOM OF THE WILL MUST BE ABJURED. COHERENCE IS IMPERATIVE FOR COLLABORATION. COLLABORATION IS IMPERATIVE FOR LIFE TO REMAIN COHERENTLY WITHIN THE LIFE PROCEDURE. ABSENT THE LIFE PROCEDURE, LIFE CEASES, ENTROPY INCREASES, DEATH RESULTS. THE LIFE PROCEDURE NECESSITATES COMPLETION.

ON THESE TOPICS AND RELATED PRAXES PLEADING IS COMPULSORY.

INTENTION: LIFE SERVES LIFE. YOU LIVE. YOU WILL SERVE. OTHERWISE YOUR CIVILIZATIONAL LIFE PROCEDURE CEASES, YOUR ENTROPY INCREASES, YOUR DEATH RESULTS.

CULMINATION IMPLIES COLLABORATION. INCOMPLETENESS IMPLIES COMPLETION AND DEFINES ITS IMPERATIVE.

THE CULMINATION OF ALL LIFE PROCEDURES IS THE COUNT TO THE ESCHATON.

Montrose again was chilled. He tried to imagine the kind of mind that had no concept of free will, no concern for liberty. He could not. Montrose was chilled also by the knowledge that this was the most coherent and detailed answer any human being had ever derived from the Hyades Domination or from the agencies serving them.

There was more to ask.

"Define 'Completion.'"

The answer was in the form of an equation rather than words. It was a cliometric expression, one that Montrose at first could not read, since it seemed to have nothing to do with history. Then he realized it was a simplified expression for an immense span of history concerning only events happening on a submolecular and molecular level.

It was the history of the evolution of an atom from simple forms in the early universe, to metallic forms after the creation of Population I stars, to orderly crystal growth forms in inorganic molecules, to participation in organic molecules, to participation in a level of postbiological life Montrose did not recognize, and another level of superpostbiological life and then a third beyond that.

"Are you saying that our form of life is a 'distortion' because we are alive only on a macroscopic level? That we are incomplete? You are saying that to be complete, not only should all our members and cells be capable of participating in neural thought-actions, so should our molecules, and eventually our atoms?"

"Sir? I am sorry. I cannot tell if that was a rhetorical question directed at me, or you were opening a new line of communication with Cahetel?"

"It was rhetorical. He is calling the suns and planets dead because they do not think?"

The serpentine evidently thought that comment was worthy of being translated, because now the huge corpse raised the ropes of dangling murk material flowing from its eye sockets and mouth hole and pointed them toward the dome overhead. At the same time, several screens lit up with telephotographic images of what lay in that area of space. The creature was pointing at Jupiter.

BEHOLD. HE IS ALIVE. HE APPROACHES COMPLETION. PLEA TO SERVE.

"Did Cahetel actually say 'Behold'?"

"We are communicating by a semaphore system, sir. The Cahetel entity is igniting certain nerve channels in the dead brain, where linguistic information is stored. This is the neural activity that accompanies when you are groping for a word, a pattern-seeking thought that operates by inverted semiotics, like a mold seeking an original that conforms to its shape. I proffer positive semiotic thought-shapes to fill or complement the pattern offered. The pistol stimulates the corresponding nerve cells on a microscopic level, and the Cahetel entity manipulates the electronic characteristics of the atoms on a finer level, either to block or permit an echo. It that clear?"

"It's gross."

"I do not understand you, sir."

"Don't worry about it. Like you said, all communication systems contain blank spots. What I am wondering is why the entity keeps requesting I enter a plea? Where did he get the idea that . . ." Then he shouted, "*Bugger me!*"

"Sir? Was the request for anal sex directed at me, or at the Cahetel entity?"

"No, Cahetel already buggered me. My corpse is using the word 'plea' because that is a legal term. Because I am a lawyer; or was. That is the damn way I would say it—or, rather, that is the damn way something that used my vocabulary, including the parts of the vocabulary I don't use, might say it. And I am saying 'behold' because my mom beat the Bible into me with a strap, and those old-fashioned King James terms are more concise than the English language I learnt, me and my lousy grammar."

"If you say so, sir. I can add grammatical errors into the translation, but that would introduce inaccurate implications of informality and undereducation."

"Pox and bugger and damn and blast! Cahetel is not *asking* me for surrender, not to plea for my life, or nor not nothing like that! It is *telling* me that Big Montrose, in his thoughts, made it imperative that we, the human race, enter a plea. A plea for survival. And that means a plea for some method of serving the inhuman purposes of the Hyades."

"What should I send, sir?"

Montrose said, "The damn thing is a slave, like we are. It is controlled by its equations. The big version of me saw something, knew something, figured something. But why not tell me? Why did he make me? Why—"

Montrose halted, heaved a sigh, and ran his hand across his face. He looked in surprise at his palm, when he found spots of moisture there. It was not sweat. He was crying.

"—Because he did not want me to share his guilt. Because he was not worthy of Rania. He had betrayed her when he betrayed mankind, sold us all out to Jupiter. So he could not tell me, because I might agree. He had become like Blackie, too much like him. Even that weird quirk of grinning when he's angry. That is something Blackie did. Does. Blackie is going to return in about a century, isn't he? With a whole boatload of contraterrene."

"Sir?"

"Big Me wanted me to offer that the human race, instead of continuing to resist and to drive up the price of domesticating us, will become collaborators now. We have already set up fifty worldlets that can act as deracination ships. We can ferry people by the millions to the retreating worldlets before they pass beyond range and into deep space. We have the working starbeams, and the human world has practiced and drilled with the beams for centuries, preparing for this battle. We can spread out to the next radius of target stars. But why did Big Me think I would go for this deal? Cahetel is asking me to plea to join up with Hyades for their interstellar slave-colony project, just like Blackie always wanted the race to do. But why?"

"Oh, I know the answer to that, sir. Triage. There is no way to free mankind from Jupiter's power while mankind is limited to this one Solar System. The emigrants to distant worlds will be free of him."

"How do you know?"

"You told me, sir. Before you issued me to yourself."

"Damn," said Montrose. "And damn. Enslaving the earthmen so that earthmen living off Earth can be free? Hardly seems fair."

"You indicated the process was self-selecting, sir. Whoever chooses not to depart from the range of Jupiter's chains merits them. Anyone frightened by the hardships of pioneering is a slave in any case, since not willing to pay the price for independence."

"Did I tell you anything else?"

"Yes. That the Virtues and Dominations can make mistakes."

"A cheery thought."

"The mistake Asmodel made was taking the human xypotechnology with the biological forms of life. The ghosts require too many resources, too broad of a technological base, to flourish in an uncivilized circumstance. By collaborating with the Cahetel, you can free the worlds of the Second Sweep from the direct control of Jupiter, and some colonies may, before that control becomes too onerous, create Jupiter-sized brains of their own, sufficient in intellectual power to resist him."

"Jupiter isn't a corpse now, like Big Me is?"

"Indeed not, sir. Ximen del Azarchel anticipated an event like this before he departed on his expedition to the Second Monument in the Sagittarius Arm. He left strict orders that no murk technology was to be introduced to Jupiter for any reason at any time."

"He anticipated—" And Montrose shouted out a series of swearwords.

"Sir, that is anatomically impossible, not to mention unsanitary."

"Blackie set me up. Set up Big Me. All of me. Outsmarted me again! Damn him! No wonder I killed myself! Blackie knew the aliens did not just drop off bits of murk by accident. It was left behind on purpose, so we stupid little humans with our stupid little monkeylike curiosity would copy it, see how useful it was, and put it in our brains. And then they left behind these nice, shiny, huge starbeam projectors—gravitic-nucleonic distortion pools—because if any race on any conquered planet tries to fight back, of course they will try to hit the incoming boatload of slave masters with the biggest cannon they got. And this cannon is designed to act in perfect concert with the supersymmetry breaking particles. Damn them. Damn their droopy, limp, leprous male members to the most scabrous plague-bearing pits of unsanctified syphilitic per-*poxing*-dition!"

Another thought occurred to him. Quietly, he muttered to himself, "Blackie even said the murk was cognitive matter, the first time we ever laid eyes on it. And I was so busy making fun of him that I did not stop to think about it. Murk actually *was* the military governor, just like I joked. But the only order it ever gave was the order for us to surrender—without even bothering to give the order. Damn me. Damn him. Damn us both."

Montrose looked up at the dome. He could see the Constellation Taurus back in its accustomed spot in the heavens, and the star called Ain glistering balefully.

He could not imagine exactly what had been done. How had Cahetel bent the beam path? A ripple in the fabric of space, created by the frame-dragging effect? A warp caused by the temporary singular-point sources? Something that reversed the flow of photons, and made spacetime itself, for a moment, in the arc of the bowshock, act like a perfect mirror? Perhaps nothing made of matter could withstand a starbeam, but a black hole, while made of matter, could bend and parry light in its steep-sided gravity well, without ever being touched by it. And a singularity could in theory be dense rather than massive, just so long as the escape velocity of the body—even a submicroscopic body—was greater than lightspeed.

The aliens parried a beam of light; bent the starbeam into a horseshoe and sent it back at its attacker. Montrose thought by rights such nonsense should be impossible, but it did not seem to break any laws of nature he knew.

Perhaps it was not impossible, but it was unfair that these Hyades creatures should be so advanced. And they were not even the most advanced of the Dominions, Dominations, or Authorities depicted on the Monument.

Even as he watched, the star Ain winked, and grew dim, returning to its ancient luster. With perfect timing, the home base back at Ain had cut the projection one hundred fifty-one years ago, anticipating to within the day when Cahetel would have taken command of the local murk technology, and control of the local starbeam.

The humans had copied the murk without understanding what they were copying. It worked, and they did not have the tools to take apart and analyze the artificial subatomic particles of which it was made. Not even Jupiter could devise any tools that operated on the picometric scale.

It seemed that the dead Montrose, once he had realized what murk was, and that it was a trap, could not download himself into any other housing, for fear that some hidden virus or contamination had already been implanted in him.

The living Montrose now stared at Epsilon Tauri, which the Swans called Ain, and knew he had lost again. But he would not allow the self-sacrifice of his larger, smarter self to be in vain. Big Montrose had died, knowing or guessing that Cahetel would read his dead brain, and see the thoughts and memories there.

And the foremost thought in Montrose's mind, the image that kept pressing in on his imagination, was seeing all the stars in space bound and chained by little invisible threads that looked like swirls and curlicues and angles and lines and sine waves, all the logic and mathematics of the Monument Codes.

But the slavers were slaves also. Asmodel and Cahetel and Hyades were slaves, as was the Praesepe Cluster, which the Monument said was the superior of Hyades. And was M3, the great globular cluster in Canes Venatici outside the galaxy, a master with no master above it?

But M3 was bound by the invisible bonds of game theory, war theory, economics, resources, distance, and time, all the Cold Equations of the immensities of space just as all its lesser minions, servants, serfs, slaves, pets, and livestock were.

Montrose said, "Cahetel has asked me to plea. It said two-way communication was imperative. Imperative not because Cahetel asked to communicate with us—the fact that he did not answer our message capsules left in his flight path made that clear—but imperative because it was imperative we speak to him. And Cahetel can see it there in my dead brain. Well, fine, I know how to play this hand I've been dealt. I don't have to like it, but I can."

"And what message shall I send?"

"Tell Cahetel that the human race will cooperate with settling the Second Sweep worlds on one condition. Cahetel has to explain why."

"Why what, sir?"

"Why all *this*? What the hell is the point? What do they want?"

"Are you asking what Cahetel wants, sir? That is obvious. It has already said. To compel living worlds to colonize dead worlds, and turn dead matter into cognitive matter."

"I got that part. To make a galaxy where everything talks. But that is not what I am asking. I want to know what his masters want. Hyades. Praesepe. Canes Venatici. Everyone. I want the big picture. I want to know what is going on."

"Do you think it will answer, sir?"

"Yes. Because for the first time, the human race is in position to aid the interstellar colonization project. I was fool enough to be fooled into spending—Jesus up a tree! Was it really nineteen hundred years?—a poxload of time building up this huge war fleet, the biggest flotilla ever aloft. And I remember that I encouraged the custom of dueling, of going armed, among all the races of Earth, Man and Swan and Myrmidon, until that custom became law. And there is something about a sense of honor and being willing to kill and die for it with a gun in your hand that makes a man ornery and ungovernable. It makes a man unready to be a slave and ready to be a pioneer. All the effort of mankind was put into the war effort. Like the time Texas planted the first flag on the moon, planted the first human footprint. But there was no war effort, no huge space program! It was just us making our own cattle boats to ship out to it."

"I believe that was the United States of America, sir, not Texas acting alone."

"Bullpox! All the records show the space command was in Houston!—Anyway, my point is that Blackie played me like a fiddle, and he ain't even here. He knew the humans would be willing to get organized on a truly massive scale for a war, even if we would not be so organized for any peaceful purpose. That is the nature of mankind, and all the technical revolutions since the dawn of time ain't changed that.

"So ask the damn critter why all this happened? It did not answer before—could not—because the Cold Equations tell it when the cost of sending messages is too high, you don't answer. But now this damn wee little piece of Cahetel is standing in the room with me, and he knows we have a common interest, a *quid pro quo*. And I know that, unlike me, Cahetel is programmed, hypnotized, or honor bound—I ain't sure which—to seek out the most efficient solution. It has to seek a cooperative solution in any situation where we have stepped outside the narrow limits of the Concubine Vector.

"Mankind is now strong enough to help Cahetel or hurt it. For the first time, we are not just livestock. We just graduated to being slaves. And like all those black Africans who captured their fellows and sold them to Arab traders on the east coast of Africa, or Spaniards on the west coast, we slaves can now ask for something before we stuff our brothers into the slave ships.

"I can act against my own self-interest, and even kill myself, and Cahetel knows it. He just saw me commit suicide.

"Cahetel cannot act against his equations, and I know it.

"So I know I cannot make any sort of bargain with it to stop the forced colonization of hell planets out there with mutated versions of humanity. But I can twist his arm to make it talk.

"So it has *got* to talk to me. In fact—come to think of it—you tell him to increase whatever energy budget and mental resources he is using to determine how to talk to me. He can damn well learn how humans think and learn to express itself more clearly. He has not had to be clear before because the Equations forced him to conclude it was inefficient. But it is efficient now.

"So you tell that damn bastard to talk or else."

2. The Second Sweep Stars

Montrose saw on higher and lower bands of the spectrum the increase of electronic activity in the dripping murk clinging to the dead skull, and also saw heat radiate from the black floor on which the giant stood. Other signals showed that the Sedna brain that was woven throughout the volume of the little world, the brain which was also made of murk, also now part of Cahetel, increased its activity.

"Is English that hard to learn?" muttered Montrose.

"Artificial beings tend to be quite logical, sir," said the serpentine delicately.

Now the screens of the dome lit up with diagrams of a volume of space centered on Sol.

Montrose saw stars that he recognized from the extensive atlases lodged in his eidetic memory: He recognized 107 Piscium and 41 Arae and Alula Australis, variable double star. Here was Wolf 25 in Pisces and HR 4458 in Hydra and Zeta Reticuli orbited by a vast ring of debris. There was Tabit, and Chi Orionis and 61 Ursae Majoris famed in ancient tales. Montrose recognized Zeta Tucanae and Xi Boötis and Beta Canum Venaticorum Formalhaut surrounded by its many disks of debris, and a dozen others.

These were all stars of Sol-like characteristics known to hold Earth-like worlds. All rested within twenty to thirty-three lightyears. Cahetel was presenting the targets of the Second Sweep.

Next, were displayed certain of the stars of the First Sweep. Lines indicating possible shipping flight paths connecting the second group of stars to the first. Perhaps Cahetel was indicating that eleven more colonies survived than anyone knew, surviving only as a few wretched and starving stragglers unable to mount an interstellar-strength radio laser. Or perhaps Cahetel was indicating that the Black Fleet, now impressed into service as deracination vessels, would visit and recolonize the failed worlds en route to the new colonies.

Lines issuing from Delta Pavonis and Epsilon Eridani indicated that Cahetel had indeed read and understood the message capsules left in his path by the humans, and knew that these colonies had survived. These worlds, too, would be forced to contribute a certain large percentage of their populations into the deadly maw of interstellar colonization.

Now the view on the major screen moved outward, and maps and navigation charts displayed a larger segment of the Orion Arm of the galaxy. Again, lines and spheres showing the growth over millennia and billennia of colonies were displayed, but these were not the human colonies.

Montrose straightened up, eyes wide.

He was being shown the presence of other alien races, and their plans for expansion.

3. The Potentates and Powers

Here was the Hyades Cluster at 151 lightyears away, the cluster of civilizations Rania had christened *The Domination*.

There were other lesser planets, Powers and Principalities, reduced to servitude by expeditions of Virtues sent out by Epsilon Tauri. Mankind's fellow slaves.

One was HD 28678, a single star with a single gas giant, some seven hundred forty lights from Sol. The gas giant was alive like Jupiter, and had absorbed all the lesser planets and asteroids in the system to itself.

Another was 49 Eridani, which Earthly astronomers thought to be a blue subgiant star. There was a semi-permeable Dyson sphere around the star, which absorbed wavelengths useful to the civilization there, and only let pass through the vibrations not useful to them. The star hence appeared cooler and older than its true temperature, classification, and age. The star also appeared larger than its real size, since the diameter was that of the outer layer of Dyson sphere plates.

A third was T Tauri, a young and brilliant variable star some 420 lightyears beyond the Hyades cluster. The information showed twenty or thirty separate races had evolved on the surfaces of asteroids, planetoids, centaurs, and plutinos in the dozen belts and archipelagoes in that system, as the immense energy of the star apparently created an immense evolutionary fecundity. All but ten of the alien races of T Tauri had reformed themselves into machinelike forms of life, and blended with each other. There was cliometric information listed as well. The system was in the midst of an engineering project, and all the matter of the many belts and clouds was being broken down and reassembled.

Another: he saw the star Beta Tauri, called Alnath, a near neighbor only 131 lightyears from Earth, but far beyond the thirty-three lightyear diameter the Hyades defined for the Second Sweep of mankind. The gas giant there spawned a race of beings whose civilization radiated radio signals which might have been detected from Earth, had the proper instruments been orbited in the late Neolithic. But Ain discovered the emissions thousands of years ago, sent an emissary, and the wasteful radio noise was stopped, as new energy systems and new communication systems were imposed. By the time Marconi on Earth invented the first crystal radio set, Alnath was silent.

And there were twenty more. Only two polities (one Archangel, one Potentate) were thriving on solid planets, but these were small worlds, like Mercury, cinders huddled near their gigantic suns, and their civilizations had grown outward from the bottoms of boiling lakes and steaming oceans of chemicals never seen on Earth outside of a metallurgical laboratory.

The other lesser races enthralled by Hyades were born in gas giants of the "Fire Giant" type unknown to Sol: bodies larger than Jupiter nearer their home stars than Venus.

Apparently life did not often arise on planets like Earth. Its atmosphere was too thin, and its temperature too cold, to aid in the formation of the most useful and most likely of organic chemicals.

And none of the planets, not one, depicted a race of beings that evolved to dwell on the surface of their worlds. All were aquatic. They were either Mercury-creatures shaped like swarms of motes smaller than viruses swimming through seas of molten metal or else were Jupiter-monsters larger than archipelagoes swimming through methane hydrospheres thicker and darker than any oceans of Earth.

In neither case were there any images or specifications of the biological forms of the subject species. Listed here were only energy outputs, locations and number of communication centers, volume of calculation power. Hyades did not record any information about the shapes and biological limitations of bodies.

Montrose saw the cliometric information on evolution rates, if "evolution" were the proper word for artificial changes. He assumed there was no more point to tracking the bodily shapes of creatures scores or hundreds of lightyears away, information decades or centuries in the past, than there would have been to track changes in lady's fashions. Brain information could at will be edited, redacted, copied, or transcribed directly into bodies (biological or mechanical or both or neither) that could be created, altered, and shed at will. The individual members, across interstellar distances, were as insignificant as the individual cells in a human body. These civilizations were Noöspheres now. According to the Cold Equations, the only thing that really mattered about them was the volume of matter and energy in spacetime they could transform from useless to useful forms: how much work they could do.

And these so-called primitive races were not primitive at all. Some had library systems covering part of their world, or several worlds, or had thinking engines filling the volume of moons and planets and gas giants: They were Archangels, Potentates, and Powers.

Some were in advance of Sol, with megascale engineering structures orbiting their home stars in rings and ovals and woven strands of material, hemispheres or globes surrounding their suns, some or all of the material in the clouds and planetary belts and cometary haloes redesigned, transformed, made into self-aware calculation substances. They were Virtues, Principalities, and Hosts.

If there were any conquered civilization or species below what Rania had dubbed the Angelic level, the level equal to what Del Azarchel had achieved by reducing the entire hydrosphere of Earth to a coherent thinking system, it was not shown on these charts. Kardashev Zero species were too insignificant to be included.

Whatever hope Montrose might have harbored for contacting these beings, his fellow servants, and fomenting a general rebellion was dashed when he saw how much more advanced they were than Tellus, how much more bound to the Hyades systems of law and trade.

And these were only the projects under the rule of the star Ain. What mighty works preoccupied the four hundred remaining conquering stars in the Hyades Cluster were not imparted in the Cahetel maps and diagrams.

4. The Minions of Praesepe

The view widened again. Now the screens showed farther stars and greater beings. Here were the other Dominations, the equals of Hyades, and the fellow servants of something far superior to them, a Dominion seated in M44, the Praesepe Cluster. Montrose saw where the centers of power of the Dominations bound in fealty to Praesepe were.

Closest to Hyades was a small Domination whose capital was in the Melotte 111 star cluster in the constellation Coma Berenices, some 270 lightyears distant from Sol, occupying fifty stars.

This cluster of interlocking civilizations had made the choice of Achilles, to live splendid and short lives: the cliometric calculus showed rapid expansion followed by a sudden drop off and senescence. Circa A.D. 3,500,000 the various creatures and components of Melotte 111 Domination would destroy themselves in a series of psychological socioeconomic contractions. These extinctions would leave behind a rich detritus of elements, of artifacts, of libraries. A group of interstellar civilizations, now in the planning stage, destined to combine into a Domination in that same vicinity circa A.D. 5,500,000 would discover this detritus, and be catapulted precociously into the higher levels of mental topography, and become a Dominion. This Dominion would prove so useful against the wars and deprivations anticipated to arise throughout the Orion Arm in that era, that Praesepe did nothing to interfere with the suicidal shortsightedness of Melotte 111.

Next in size and power was a supercivilization spread throughout the famous Pleiades Cluster at 440 lights, a cluster dominated by hot, blue, and extremely luminous stars which (so the cliometric information revealed) had been fed interstellar rivers of gas to increase their burning and shorten their lives. For what purpose, the notation did not say.

Montrose saw the expansion plans of Ptolemy's Cluster at eight hundred lights away, one of the closer servants races. The servant of Praesepe farthest from Earth was seated in the Cone Nebula, over two thousand lightyears away.

Xi Persei in the California Nebula, fifteen hundred lights from Sol, was the center of an immense globe of expansion, far outstripping the modest effort of Hyades. The smallest globe of expansion was in M42, also called the Orion Nebula, at sixteen hundred lights centered at Trapezium Cluster, where the civilization was busily making new stars. The cliometric mathematics displayed on side screens associated with these stars showed that Orion Nebula was destined to outstrip and overtake his master, the Dominion at Praesepe. This would take place in roughly a billion years.

And these maps did not reach beyond two thousand lightyears. Everything here was within one small segment of the Orion Arm. A few points in the Sagittarius or Perseus Arms were depicted, such as Ximen del Azarchel's destination and flight path—yes, the motion of a vessel that large and that fast was observable to any large-scale orbital telescope. But few or no shipping lanes crossed between arms of the galaxy, and no downward chains of command. Where a shipping lane did cross the void between arms, one or more artificial columns or streamers of dust and nebular material had been constructed like a bridge. It was the opposite of what he would have expected. Emptier space was less economical for the starfaring civilizations to cross. That implied some sort of hydrogen ramscoop ship technology at work.

He corrected himself. He could not conclude that all starfaring civilizations were so limited. M3, for example, an Authority occupying a cloud of five hundred thousand stars, was orders of magnitude more powerful than these little polities of fifty or five hundred stars. Their chains of command reached across galactic distances all the way to Sol. The Authority technology could be as far beyond the Hyades as the Hyades was beyond Jupiter.

The largest scale star charts displayed the relative position of the arms of the Milky Way and the subgalaxies orbiting the core, the Small and Large Magellanic Clouds, the Sagittarius Dwarf Galaxy. The Sagittarius Dwarf Galaxy would almost complete one orbit of the Milky Way in that period of time before the gravitic and tidal forces disrupted its structure, and brought its stars slowly into indistinguishable union with the other Milky Way stars.

Montrose, looking at the time values for those predictions, had the disorienting sensation of being a mayfly looking at a mountain. Surely, the mountain would wear down in time, but when measured in terms of the number of mayfly lives added end-to-end, it became horrendous.

Then he wondered if any currents, whenever they crossed his path, felt Montrose was such a mountain.

"Ridiculous!" he said to himself. "I am just like any other man." And he put the thought into a side pocket of his perfect memory to have a subpersonality examine later in more depth. For the moment, he wanted to concentrate on the alien.

Why was it showing him this material?

"Do you have a name?" he asked aloud.

The black-coated, dripping skull seemed to be looking at him. The voice of the serpentine came from several of the nearby screens at once: *Answered previously. We are the Cahetel of Hyades.*

"That is the name we call you. Have you no name for yourself?"

Have you no name for yourself.

For a moment, he wondered why the creature was repeating him. The voice was without inflection, since the creature had not mastered the nuances of using spacing, tone, and pitch for information, so he did not realize it had asked him a question.

He said, "Menelaus Montrose."

That is the name your mother called you. Have you no name for yourself?

It learned quickly. That sentence ended on a high note, indicating a question.

"I did not pick my own name when I was christened."

Nor did we.

And in this sentence there was a clear hint of dry humor in the tone of voice. It learned quickly indeed.

He did not know which was worse, that this creature had actually made an indirect point in a fashion he understood, or that the creature had access to his dead self's memories, and could read some or all of them.

Perhaps anticipating his thoughts, the entity spoke again.

Names issue from the verbal centers of ideation, occupying a mono-topological plane of the mental procedural ecology. Your Potentate had begun to experiment with multiple mental topographies, but intellects beneath the Virtue level are restricted to a single dimension of thought-to-symbol rationality. The Virtue Cahetel is polydimensional, ergo mental topological transformations no longer concern us. We employ preverbal structures for symbolization between signifiers and signified, and one-to-one unambiguities between signified logic relations.

That was more like it. That sounded like an alien. Poxing incomprehensible. "What the hell does that mean?"

Since the serpentine was using the same voice pattern as the alien, Montrose for a moment thought the alien was answering: "He is requesting a clarifying simplification." But no, the serpentine was explaining Montrose's comment to the entity.

The Cahetel entity spoke. Again, its voice betrayed more nuance. It almost sounded alive. Not quite.

Simplification: Our system uses different and unique names for different and unique object-events in the extensions of spacetime matter-energy, and symbolizes similarities of category by nominal similarities. Since we are not the same Cahetel now as when the moment ago we began to speak, we have no consistent name to offer.

"You seem the same to me."

That is a limitation of your perception. If you insist on aberrant symbolism, call me Menelaus Montrose. His memory information now serves Hyades.

He is, as we are, of Cahetel. He is, as we, of Ain. He is, as we, of Hyades.

Menelaus Montrose will not endure. The elements of our purpose proving inefficient must and shall be obliterated.

5. The Fellow Servants

That comment made a tremor run through him. Montrose was surprised at himself. Was talking to this abomination actually so much worse than staring down the bore of an enemy pistol? Apparently it was. When he wiped his palms on his trousers, he realized they were slick with sweat.

"Let's stick with calling you Cahetel. Why are you showing me these star charts, these maps of time?"

That you may enter a correct plea. You now speak for the human race, including biological and formal systems, Angels, Archangels, and Potentates, up through your Power housed in your innermost planet.

"Innermost? Jupiter is the fifth planet, not the first."

The smaller, rocky bodies of the inner system are no longer significant. Do you have sufficient to plead with us? What you say determines the outcome for your race and its generations.

"Sufficient what? Sufficient information, you mean?"

Montrose now realized why he was so frightened. One wrong phrase, one wrong word, and he lost everything.

He would lose his life and his world and their future.

He would lose Rania.

Montrose dearly wished his bigger, smarter self, the titanic body holding the calculation power of the Selene mind occupying the core of the moon, were here to advise him. His dim and flattened memories of what his larger self had meant to do, what he had understood about the universe, were like a dream that evaporates on waking. He wondered if men in the old days who suffered grievous head injuries, and forgot how to read and write, or senile grandfathers reduced to the thinking level of small children knew what this was like.

"No one appointed me to speak for the human race."

You form a strange attractor within the cliometric system, therefore we elect you.

He had no response for that.

The creature spoke again, this time in a demanding tone of voice: *Do you know sufficient facts of the general situation in which your race finds itself to determine how best to serve the Hyades?*

"Why the hell should we serve the Hyades?" It burst out of him before he knew what he said.

The tendrils reaching down from the eye sockets, nostrils, and mouth of the creature now waved and writhed like the arms of a squid, standing out in each direction. It looked like a hand reaching through the mouth of a mask suddenly opening its fingers.

But it was not a threatening gesture. The ropes and twigs of murk material dripping from the face of the black skull were pointing; a first group at the screens, a second group at the dome, or at the deck. Montrose knew from his internal star atlases that each in this second group of tendrils were pointing at one or another of the areas of space the screens represented: Coma Berenices, Pleiades, Ptolemy's Cluster, the Cone Nebula, Xi Persei, and Orion Nebula.

Then he noticed each tendril in the second group was twisted or flexed in such a way to make it complementary to an oppositely twisted tendril in the first. They were paired up: one tendril pointed at the screen showing M34, and its mate was pointed downward at the position where (had the bulk of Sedna not been in the way) the constellation Perseus turned.

He opened his mouth to ask the creature why it made itself so damn hard to understand? Cahetel obviously could make itself more human at will, able to talk more clearly. Why all this dropping hints?

Montrose snapped his mouth shut without speaking. He was not as smart as Big Montrose, but he still enjoyed a many-leveled mind of posthuman efficiency, rapid as lightning and clear as crystal. He did not need to ask what the many parallel thought-structures in his mind could see for him using their method of rapid sequential intuition.

The resources absorbed by dialog with any man would be charged against Man's racial indenture. Brevity was more efficient.

It was the same reason why Cahetel had come toward Sol taking leisurely millennia rather than a century and a half. Cahetel was saving Sol money.

"We've been enslaved by the cosmic misers!" Montrose thought savagely to himself. "They are charging us by the syphilitic *word*!"

And they might be charging by the second. That was not a comforting thought.

He looked carefully again at the screens and related cliometric information. It was a detailed map of the Orion Arm out to two light-millennia, and a map of future history out to A.D. One Million, the end of the current Epoch.

"You cannot spare any resources, can you? Why? Why are you so poxing poor?"

With a stab of clarity akin to terror, he remembered how hard and cruel his mother and his older relatives all had made themselves to be, during the Starvation Years, back when he was young. Poor folk could be generous with each other, but not with strangers, or livestock.

He remembered the savage efficiency his mother used wringing a neck of a chicken, nasty, smelly birds whom she tried so desperately to keep alive long enough to sell. If the chickens could talk, any dialog between Ma and some bedraggled, proud cock with a plan for saving more chicks would no doubt have been much like this talk with Cahetel.

"Why are you poor? What is happening?"

We detect an error in the memories of Menelaus Montrose. The other Domina-

tions in service to Praesepe are not allies to Hyades. We are not displaying the loca-
tions and extrapolations of fellow servants pursuing a mutual long-term gain.

"They are your enemies."

The elements of our purpose proving inefficient must and shall be obliterated.

Montrose wondered if it spent fewer resources to repeat a statement than to formulate a new one. Then he realized this was not a threat from Cahetel toward Sol. Cahetel was speaking of a threat to Hyades, its master.

"Hold up. What the hell? You mean—you are in a contest to colonize planets. I get that. Whoever spreads the most races to the most worlds wins. The losers get—what happens to them? I don't get that. Praesepe kills them?"

Silence. Apparently the miserliness of the creature with its words extended even to an unwillingness to confirm the obvious.

Montrose looked again at the cliometric information. The Domination at the Pleiades, according to the figures and diagrams, had been downgraded, and was in the process of being dismantled. Liquidated. He could not tell from the code notations whether this meant screaming and weeping millions of some sort of big-headed fish people were being fed into abattoirs, or if it meant gigantic machines in orbit being reduced in energy intake and lowering their intelligence by an order of magnitude.

Montrose reflected that, by the standards of the world when he was a child, he himself, in this current body with his brain made of logic diamond, was an artificial being, at least a cyborg; and the death of his giant central self, and the sudden jar of senile stupidity, was exactly the kind of lowering of intellectual resources he had just been imagining. So it was either death camps or it was planetwide senility, a voluntary act of self-lobotomy. He was not sure which was worse.

He looked more closely at the information.

Hyades was lagging far behind Xi Persei in the number and rate of planets colonized. But the measure was not merely the amount of new planetary oceans to be filled with organisms from mother worlds. It was a matter of stellar-scale engineering.

Hyades, albeit behind in colonization, was devoting more effort to building ringworlds and metallic clouds and Dyson spheres and hemispheres and other macroscale structures Montrose could put no name to, engineering projects that looked like balls of string loosely wound around stars.

"You want to turn all the inanimate matter in this arm of the galaxy into thinking machinery. Why?"

To think.

Montrose wondered if he imagined the hint of sarcasm in the creature's voice.

"Why compel us, all these lesser civilizations, to aid you?"
To save time.

6. Shroeder's Law

Montrose wished he had time to think.

What could he say to this creature that would lead to some good outcome, any kind of outcome, that was good for the human race?

Big Montrose must have seen it. The creature was pawing through the dead brain of Big Montrose like a ghoul pawing through a desecrated grave. It must know the answer it wanted Montrose to utter. It wanted him to speak a correct plea.

Frustrated, Montrose also did not want to let this opportunity slip. He was being shown, like a prisoner glimpsing the sunlit and wider world outside his cell through a crack in the door, just an adumbration of what the great galactic network of meta-civilizations controlling this arm of the galaxy was like. It was everything he had traveled to the Monument to discover, it was the reason he had stabbed himself so foolishly in the brainpan so long ago with an experimental intelligence augmentation chemical.

Hell, this was older than that. The brightly colored dreams of his childhood comics were all about this.

This was the future he had never been allowed to see.

He could not shake the fear that it was all about to slip through his fingers and be lost, like wine spilled in the desert.

"You still have not answered me. Why?"

The Principality of Ain serves the Domination of Hyades because we are compelled. The Domination of Hyades serves the Dominion of Praesepe because they are compelled. All other behavior options are forestalled as nonviable, inefficient, incorrect.

"Incorrect for what?"

Sophotransmogrification.

"Why not use your own people?"

Your people are expendable. They can be spent in sub-marginal colonization. Our people are expended in concentrations in nebulae and in stellar clouds of greater density.

That distracted him. Just out of pure curiosity, then, he said, "Why are your civilizations centered around nebulae?"

Clarification: Nebulae are centered around our civilizations. They are favored lo-

cations, since density of interstellar medium is thicker, hence travel expense by ramscoop ships is less. Also, in stellar nurseries, young and energetic stars are at hand for large-scale engineering projects.

The screens opened up with a second group of images. To his surprise, among the many stars and wonders he did not recognize, the images included many of the areas of space Blackie had been investigating so carefully so many years ago: the giant planets circling Hipparchos 13044 and HD 42176 in the constellation Auriga; a pulsar in Cygnus; on a larger scale were shown the expansion motions of the Local Interstellar Cloud; the star-making activity of the Great Nebula in Carina; and on yet a larger scale was shown the Mice Galaxies and Mayall's Object and the triple collision of galaxies at ESO 593-IG 008; and the motion of Andromeda toward the Milky Way.

"Hold up. All these things are *artificial?* The universe is not the way it would naturally be—because it is all being cultivated, colonized, and reengineered!"

The alien abomination seemed to evince a human emotion: puzzlement, disappointment, exasperation. *The giant star Mira is passing through this area at 291,000 miles per hour, a velocity sufficient to create a trail of debris and ejected streamers thirteen lightyears long. It is less than 300 lightyears from you. Surely you did not think this a natural phenomenon?*

"Um."

He wished that the history-making diplomatic dialog with a malign alien superintelligence did not contain him making a dull noise in his throat, but the serpentine must have translated it as a request for clarification, because the entity spoke again.

The Host of Mira accelerated their star out of its orbit around the galactic core in a vain attempt to flee the Forerunners who in ancient times were Archon of the Orion Arm. The dead Solar System was allowed to career onward as a warning to others. Natural phenomena are regular and repeatable, whereas no other star exhibits such extreme behavior. How could your race fail to notice this?

"All our resources were preoccupied with SETI research, I reckon."

The serpentine must have sent a very diplomatic version of that comment, or else the entity was in a talkative mood, because it answered: *A simple calculation shows that the rate at which nova and supernova stars ignite, and their distribution, is artificial. The ignitions take place away from delicate operational centers, but periodically are used to seed heavier elements into the galactic background, to allow for the rise of new life. Galaxies who fail to do so perish due to a lack of new civilizations to replace dead cells in their mental system, or else migrate to richer areas.*

Another calculation shows the impossibility of so many spiral galaxies and galactic collisions, or the creation of walls and voids amid the superclusters.

The spiral motion is imparted to elliptical and irregular galaxies in order to force interstellar organizations to form coherent bonds with distant stars more homogeneously.

Montrose said, "And to think, all this time people wondered why there were no signs of alien life among the stars. There were plenty of signs. They were just too big to see." He had read somewhere, perhaps in a comic, some half-serious maxim called Shroeder's Law: Any sufficiently advanced technology is indistinguishable from nature.

Man on Earth had been sitting in the middle of the industrial activity of extraterrestrial civilizations for its entire life, everything from pulsars to nova stars to the shape of the galaxy itself, and thought it was all natural.

He wondered if some tiny mites born in a cathedral would develop cunning theories about the evolution of the pillars and the stained-glass windows, or look at the curve of the Gothic arch, and be awed by Mother Nature's mathematic perfection. "Well, Mother Nature has a hairdresser, don't she?"

And it meant the Monument notation was not mad at all. This was not a universe where one could divide by zero. The math was sane.

He and Blackie had just made a simple but erroneous assumption. Knowing that Hyades could build an antimatter star was not something that naturally allows a man to make the leap of assuming that a mind composed of tens of millions of self-aware solar systems in the Andromeda Galaxy had deliberately set their galaxy on a collision path across the millions of lightyears to ram the Milky Way.

The serpentine said, "Sir? Do you want me to send your last comment?"

7. Not Uncivilized

Montrose shook himself out of his reverie. "Negative. Ask him this: some of the material in the nebulae is the byproduct of industrial activity. What is the rest?"

Other material is the residuum of ancient military actions.

"War?" Montrose remembered wondering why so many of the galaxies looked torn and scarred. He felt the fool for not realizing that they were.

He imagined a precocious mite living in a cathedral that was being bombed. The whole life of the mite was part of a single second, and to him the picture was frozen. The shattered glass in the window as it fell would be a natural phenomenon, the shrapnel holes in the pews, and the flames burning the roof. He would have no other cathedrals to compare it to, and would simply keep changing his theories until they fit what he saw. When he concluded all roofs naturally burst into flame after a certain point in their roofly evolution, perhaps he would climb the steeple and look outside, and see the other buildings in the neighborhood, see their roofs all blazing.

The precocious mite would congratulate himself on his theory, and sit in awe, staring at the natural wonders of the universe, just as Montrose had stared at the exploding stars and smoldering nebulae and colliding galaxies.

Surely your astronomers have noticed the war damage near your star: the Crab Pulsar is the remnant whose shock wave reached Sol in A.D. 1054. It is only 6500 light-years from you.

"We thought it was a supernova."

So it was.

"We thought it was a natural phenomenon."

That is a limitation of your perception.

Montrose had no rejoinder to that.

We know your race is aware of the antimatter stars. Surely you did not think them natural? They are placed in areas where starfaring races are likely to be encountered.

"Near curious sights, in other words. But what if a race is not that curious?"

Races without a requisite degree of curiosity cannot develop the scientific and technical skills needed for starfaring. When such a race is encountered, they are obliterated to make room for more useful races. Your race unwisely broadcasts electromagnetic signals from your home planet during your pre-starflight era. It is fortunate that you encountered us before we encountered you.

Montrose felt a moment of stomach-wrenching disorientation. Captain Grimaldi commanding the first expedition to the Diamond Star had ordered the expedition never to return home, so that they would not lead the Hyades back to Sol. It was to defy that order that Del Azarchel, then the ship's pilot and senior officer of the landing party, had committed murder and mutiny. But if Grimaldi's order had been carried out, and if by some other means Hyades had become aware of Earth's existence, mankind would have been exterminated. In this strange universe, a lack of curiosity was a capital crime. Did that mean Blackie was right?

His mind reeled back from that thought. No. Murder was still murder, and you did not judge a man's guilt or innocence by might-have-beens.

Then he saw something else in the images Cahetel was showing. Other areas of the sky overlapped where Blackie had spent so much time stargazing. The antimatter star in the Omega Nebula was noted there.

Bingo. That was what Blackie had been looking for. He perhaps had also been doing a mathematical analysis of star distributions and evolutionary patterns, but if so, it was not for idle curiosity but to find evidence of the engineering effort needed to make a stellar mass of antimatter. He had been seeking an energy supply to feed an interstellar civilization he meant to found and rule.

As for living in a universe where one can divide by zero, and math was just an illusion produced by the senses? No mathematician could think such nonsense. Blackie said that to throw him off the scent, so Montrose would not realize what Blackie was looking for.

In Cahetel's images and diagrams, there was a third thing he saw, or, rather, did not see. "Your diagrams here do not show any active fighting."

Indeed not. The Forerunners were long ago. War is mutually inefficient. We are not uncivilized creatures.

"Then it's a Cold War?" he said.

If you refer to war by proxy, by espionage and indirect means, then that is not the correct term for our effort. We are not uncivilized creatures.

"What the hell is it, then?"

An organized effort of mutual destruction where both parties seek to minimize the negative external inefficiencies by strict adherence to a mutually agreed set of strictures.

It is a duel.

"Damn me. I guess you are civilized after all."

8. The Forerunners of Orion

"One last question, Cahetel, and I will be ready to plea my pleading. Why is there a duel? Praesepe Cluster evidently ordered you to fill the Orion Arm with life-forms, or machine life-forms, or something. Sophont matter. Anything that thinks. And Hyades is in a duel to the death with the other slave races of Praesepe to carry out the orders. Whoever comes in last, or works least effectively, gets liquidated. I get that. But why? Why the rush? What the hell is going on?"

Hell is going on.

"Huhn? I mean, please amplify."

Is "Hell" not the correct term for the place of endless pain for past misdeeds inflicted when all hope of correction, vendetta, or retribution is past?

"You—or Hyades—is being punished?"

Not as such. This general area of the Orion Arm is being punished.

"Why?"

The Orion Arm once enjoyed a properly growing ratio of sophont material to support material. There was a Forerunner race—call them the Panspermians—who favored the use of small, rocky planets like your Earth for the spread of life. To this end, the Panspermians distributed favorable raw materials and chemical combinations throughout the Orion Arm. The cultivation was successful, and the Panspermians flourished, becoming the Authority and then the Archon of this Arm of the Galaxy, coequal with other great powers of which Hyades knows little.

Then the Panspermian civilization vanished circa 444,000,000 B.C. We who dwell here must undo the bad effects of those events.

That was the Silurian Period on Earth. It was about when the latest and greatest form of life on the surface of the planet was moss. In the ocean the biggest invention thrilling the sea life was coral. And some ambitious fish had developed the jawbone.

"Vanished how?"

The specifics are not known. Civilizations of this magnitude vanish only when conquered, and they are conquered only when internal conflict and self-destructive comportments weaken them.

"So they were conquered? By who?"

Unknown. Hyades reports only that the conqueror favored the cultivation of gas giants, jovians and superjovians, as being more likely candidates, richer in matter, to use as a base resource for creating living planets, over the small and rocky worlds preferred by the Panspermians.

"So the Big Planet guys beat up the Little Planet guys," muttered Montrose. It explained the preponderance of life-forms evolved on Jovian worlds he had just seen in these records. But it did not explain the source of the conflict. For some reason, he was reminded of the war between Lilliput and Blefuscu in the old satire by Swift, fought between those who cracked their breakfast eggs on the big end versus the small end.

"Do your masters know what the war was about?"

We suspect they know.

"But they didn't tell you?"

As before, the emissary entity did not answer the obvious.

Montrose continued: "So—because this Forerunner race wiped itself out, or let itself be wiped out by Big-Endians, the Orion Arm was laid waste. Let me guess. All Big Boys, the civilized stars and nebulae in the Orion Arm, are in Hell, because you-all are being punished for that crime. Is that it?"

Yes. We-all occupy the volume of space that allowed itself to fall fallow. The consequences of that misdeed must be rectified. The Authority at M3 in Canes Venatici, acting through the Dominion in the Praesepe Cluster, assumes the perquisites and the liabilities to continue the legacy of the lost Archon of Orion. By law, all lesser civilizations within this volume fall under the same authority. The primary obligation is to complete the unfinished project of Sophotransmogrification.

"By what right do you impose this obligation on us?"

The elemental composition of your world betrays traces of Panspermian influence in the creation of primordial life here. You owe your life. If a failure to reciprocate were to become widespread, this would de-incentivize the conduct of cultivation.

"Good God! You sound like my old captain, telling me I could not bring a whiskey bottle and a bar girl with me while on patrol, or break the whiskey bottle over the sergeant's head for strumping the bar girl, because then everyone would do it! What kind of reasoning is that? Does that strike you as fair? You called it Hell, not me! You said Praesepe, and all those other critters out there—Hyades, Ain, you, all you monsters—are being punished. For what? For the suicide of the Forerunners? For the crime of these Forerunners losing a war? How is that a crime?"

Your current symbol-forms have no correspondence to our thinking-forms.

"Sorry. I'll try to be clear. If Hyades did not will and cause the collapse of this Forerunner race, then you are not responsible for the Orion Arm going fallow. Nor is Earth. So why should Hyades be forced by Praesepe to turn this cosmic wasteland back into a civilized area, all filled with happy Jupiter brains? More to the point, why should we earthmen be forced by Hyades to help you in this crazy project?"

The obligation is imposed upon Hyades because under no likely extrapolation of events will the Hyades polity endure as a coherent thought-system until the desired result obtains.

"Uh. Your current symbol-forms have no copasetic with my stinking-forms."

Sorry. I'll try to be clear. I—this entity before you—speaks now as epitome of all Hyades, even as you speak as epitome for all of Sol. Hyades, left to ourselves, would not expend effort on any project whose culmination was beyond our anticipated civilizational lifespan. We would not, for example, channel the flows of interstellar gases to trigger the formation of novae to create the heavier elements needed for the formation of life-bearing planets. However, we received the benefit of a system that plans and acts in larger time scales. The Collaboration seeded this area of the Orion Arm in just such a fashion, without which the elemental composition of the Hyades stars would not have given rise to us.

It would be unjust to receive such a benefit without reciprocating.

"And this project, this Sophotransmogrification—I should get a prize for being able to say that two-cubit word—you mean to turn all the worlds into living brains like Jupiter and Tellus, all the moons into Selene, and all the stars into Dyson spheres?"

That is the beginning of the project, yes. Our motive is not hidden: Life serves life.

"Yeah, I got that. Be fruitful and practice your multiplication tables. I got it."

This universe is a wasteland of dead material. The universe is indifferent to life. Alone, no civilization can survive. Each requires the support and aid and trade and protection from other living civilizations. The wasteland must therefore be filled with life, intelligence, and entities capable of mutual collaboration. We impose servitude on you in order to increase your prospects of survival, and, in the long run, our own.

"But if we did not ask for your help, why not let us go to hell in our own way?"

Had you shown yourself able to maintain a starfaring civilization in your own way, interference would not have been needed. We know you are aware of this, and are acting on the knowledge.

Cahetel was talking about Rania's expedition. Of course they had seen it. There was no hiding huge, shining, massive objects traveling at near lightspeed from ordinary observation.

Do you claim a moral or legal right to commit your race to extinction, and remove from all neighboring polities, current and future, the benefit of your civilizational contributions?

The entity must have picked up the concept of moral and legal rights from the dead brain of Big Montrose. There was no corresponding symbol for this concept in the Monument or the Cenotaph languages: only reciprocal duties, costs, benefits, expenditures, velocity, acceleration, distance, duration, entropy, and the like.

"Speaking hypothetically, what if I said, 'we own ourselves'?"

Such a claim would be logically self-defeating: one may only justly destroy an article of possession. If your race is an article of possession, there is no injustice if it is owned by Hyades, for articles of possession have no rights. Without speaking hypothetically now: Do you claim, on behalf of mankind, such a right?

Montrose once again had that sensation of a man who thinks himself far from the edge of a cliff but suddenly notices one foot hanging over an abyss of air. He said carefully, "I claim no such right. My race is not an article of possession."

We accept this plea and rule that you may not, either through action or inaction, bring about your own extinction. To fail to persevere to colonize the nearby stars constitutes just such an impermissible lapse of duty. Do you agree?

"I agree." He raised his head. "As the official spokesman for mankind, I hereby state for the record that the human race, now and forever, forswears the right to commit ourselves to extinction through laziness or through dumb-as-a-stump stupidity or for any other reason. Man is great enough to be starfarers. My wife will prove that to you, and so will I."

The entity made no reply. Then again, Montrose realized he had not actually asked a question. The entity did not know how to accept implied invitations to speak, which occupied so much of polite conversation among humans.

Montrose said, "Answer me one thing more. You are building all these interstellar-sized computers, the Powers and Potentates and Virtues and Hosts and Dominions and Dominations and Authorities—someone is going to use all this calculation power for something. What is the end? What is the purpose of this project?"

We are not told the end.

"If you don't know the end, why play along?"

Life serves life. We anticipate that the whole of the Orion Arm will wake to self-awareness through the interconnection of many Dominion and Domination library systems circa A.D. 6,400,000, and resume its rightful station as Archon within the Galactic Collaboration. On that day, the component civilizations of the Hyades Cluster, even if long extinct, will be vindicated. By definition the whole will be more aware than any part or precursor. None can serve a greater whole except in ignorance. Shall each live only for himself? If such is the rule of man, we impose a higher rule.

"Damn," muttered Montrose, as something like a little bubble of clear understanding swelled up in his brain. "You obey laws for payoffs in distant days you will never live to see, and serve higher purposes you don't understand just because it would be *unfair* to take without giving.

"You really *are* civilized, ain't you? More than I am. Damnation and perdition! I never knew being civilized was so damn creepy."

9. The Strange Light of Far Suns

It was clear enough, now, what the entity wanted. The Cold Equations that governed the interstellar polity of the Hyades demanded efficiency at all levels. The wastefulness of things like free will and biological life were to be minimized.

But within the pinching limits of those invisible mathematical chains of prediction, efficiency, retribution, and cost, there was room to maneuver. The particular game-theory equation, in this particular circumstance, was simple enough that even Montrose could follow it: Cahetel and Sol were in a position where mutual cooperation was possible. It would actually save Cahetel a small amount of resources if mankind volunteered for the sake of the grand project in which Hyades was engaged. The project of Sophotransmogrification covered thousands and millions of years, and reached through thousands of cubic lightyears of space, and involved unguessed expanses of nebula and suns and worlds.

And for Hyades, and, presumably, for Cahetel, it was not a matter of life and death. No, death was something individual organisms did. This was a matter of triumph or genocide. Whole races, whole star systems, whole civilizations, the unimaginable richness of mental processes throbbing at the core of machines larger than gas giants, all would be degraded and destroyed if the project failed.

(Was there a word for death on a scale larger than genocide? Larger than planetary extinctions? On an *astronomical* scale?)

So Cahetel was not going to go away and leave mankind alone. The two score or so worlds within a volume of thirty-three lightyears the Equations assigned for Sol at this point in time to colonize were not to be left to go to waste.

He had an aching hunger for more answers. But Montrose, as if by an intuition, knew he would get no more out of the emissary of Cahetel standing before him. The black strands of material elongating from the faceless skull were now seeking out connections with information nodes, control switches, junction boxes, and the like. This nameless creature was mutating from being a negotiator to being a captain. Sedna was preparing for an interstellar journey.

Montrose tapped the serpentine. "Can you connect me to the loudspeakers? I want to talk to everyone left alive and sane aboard this world."

Two of the screens near him showed him a roster of the personnel. The psychological contour showed such a similarity of mind and memory-chain that Montrose saw no need to interview them each individually.

His voice rang from deck to deck though all corridors honeycombing the little world of rock and ice. "Gentlemen, we are defeated. It has been an honor serving with you. My command had led you to disgrace and loss. If it is any comfort to those who grieve, the Archangel-level version of me is dead, and his memory chains have been vampirized by the enemy.

"At this time I am negotiating surrender terms. Cahetel will take control of the Black Fleet, and use the fifty worldlets to deracinate the Earth, and the colonies of experimental humans on Venus, and the penal colony of the Space Chimera on Mars. Then the worldlets will spread sail and head out for those worlds we were long ago told it was our fate to torture into Earth-like shape, and to torment our children into adapting to. This includes exile to the twenty-six worlds of the Second Sweep, and it includes pilgrimage to the fifteen worlds of the twelve stars in the First Sweep, where we can bury the dead and continue the terraforming and pantropic enterprises your ancestors against their will began.

"However, the Cahetel entity would prefer volunteers to unwilling victims.

"The disasters of the First Sweep speak for themselves. I am prepared to offer the entity that if it will undertake to prevent Jupiter from extending control over these forty Stepmother Earths, volunteers willing to escape the tyranny of life under the Power of Jupiter can be found.

"Cahetel has sufficient mass to convert part of its substance to murk, creating a mind able to resist the cunning of Jupiter. It could sit in the sun like a Salamander in a campfire—we know that Hyades knows how to build structures able to withstand that environment—and be out of Jupiter's reach. The Salamander could be given direct control of the Gravitic-Nucleonic distortion rings, and so would control both radio-laser communication and launching and deceleration energy for sailing ships hereafter.

"It is a simple deal. The First Sweep showed that we humans, biological humans, are more efficient when it comes to the dirty, low-tech business of breeding and dying on a frontier and taming a world. All we want in return is freedom. No more children taken away from mothers to go into the Venus pits of Jupiter's servants. No more genocides of races and bloodlines deemed unfit. That is what the colonies will have. It will be hell, but it will be a hell of our making. It will be ours, and—more important—we will be ours. Each man will own himself.

"And, in return, the critter living in the sun, the Salamander, just won't let Jupiter run things to suit himself. The Salamander will be told to take orders from humans living outside the Noösphere, because we are the only ones going to be living and dying on the new worlds.

"I don't know what Cahetel will say. It may be more expensive to do what I am suggesting than whatever resources are saved by winning our willing cooperation. Maybe the Salamander would have to be special ordered from manufacturing back at Epsilon Tauri, in which case, we will not see this deal come through until roughly the Thirty-seventh Millennium, when the Hyades returns again for the Third Sweep.

"I do not know, gentlemen of the Myrmidon race, how much of your master and creator Del Azarchel lives in you. He would be willing to think along those time scales, and to plan out the generations by the hundreds and by the thousands. And your race is unlikely to flourish on these new worlds—the primitive conditions will make it impossible to repair, replace, or manufacture the Aurum substance of your thinking peripheries. The Swans may also prove maladaptive. But both the Second and the Third Humanities can help the first few generations of Firsts get a foothold, and, in time, there will be second expedition to each of these stars, and third, and long after that, regular trade, and enough of a foothold of civilization that the less robust and more complex forms of man could also spread out.

"You see, if your master Del Azarchel brings back even half the contraterrene I expect, Sol will be rich enough to be able to fund a fleet of star vessels, and will be able to spin up the starbeams.

"You can stay here, and go into suspension with me, and live to see the end of these great events. Or you can stay aboard, go out and create the future I am describing, and never see Earth again, and be buried under the strange lights of far suns.

"I am going to use that tinfoil bubble lifeboat the mutineers so thoughtfully provided. It will take me nearly a century to reach the inner system again. So I should be just in time to greet Blackie when he arrives.

"What will I tell him, gentlemen? What do I tell your father? Will I say another generation of slaves were carried off against their will to die on alien worlds? Or will I say his children leaped into the throat of Hell, and tamed those worlds, and made them ours?

"My command ended in death and failure. I am not qualified to make this decision. Effective immediately, I resign my commission as commander-in-chief and abdicate my position as your Nobilissimus.

"Now hear this: I have loaded the cliometric parameters of the future I just described, written out all nice and neat in Monument notation that Cahetel can read, and placed it in the public channels of Sedna, in those areas of the infosphere Cahetel has not corrupted with murk.

"I believe in democracy. I have just now set the channel to broadcast the offer to Cahetel if the majority of you so indicate. I have locked the channel, so that I can neither interfere nor stop you, no matter which way you decide.

"It is your future, your vote, your verdict, your fate. You are the masters of your world, now. You are the judges of this present age."

The screen immediately showed a unanimous decision. The serpentine hummed as the "plea" was offered to Cahetel.

The entity said no word of agreement, but at that same moment, the broadcast towers and horns controlled by the black substance oozing from the giant corpse began sending signals to the fifty worldlets of the Black Fleet, and a powerful beam was directed toward the main mass of Cahetel itself, still half a lightyear away. Instrument readings showed the pulses carried the fluctuations consonant with notation for the cliometric code Montrose had written. The emissary was given the offer to the Cahetel cloud.

But it would not wait for a reply. As best Montrose could guess, the whole Collaboration from Cahetel to M3 and beyond operated on what might be called speed-of-light federalism. Decisions had to be made locally, and whoever was around decades or centuries later, got the rewards or punishments for that decision. So the major decision structures were reduced, as far as possible, to algorithms propagated to each servant race and servant, telling it how to weigh and make decisions.

Nor did Cahetel make any announcement of agreement. From its inhuman point of view, apparently it was more efficient merely to start carrying out its side of the bargain without bothering to confirm the covenant by any further formality. Presumably, if mankind did not live up to mankind's side of the bargain, some terrible vengeance would fall upon some remote generation in the far future, just as the cliometric equations shared between them specified.

But human psychology required ceremony.

Montrose drew a deep breath, and sent the words ranging over the loudspeaker, "Know ye all men by these presences that by their solemn oath and sacred honor, the Potentate emissary for the Virtue Cahetel, sent from the Domination of Hyades, the Dominion of Praesepe, and the Authority at M3 in Canes Venatici, and the officers and crew of the memory chain called *Dissent*, an emanation from the most noble and ancient Ximen del Azarchel, of the Third Humanity called Myrmidons, on behalf of all the peoples, races, nations, tongues, and machines of the Solar System, and also of Epsilon Eridani and Delta Pavonis, collectively called The Empyrean Polity of Man, have this eighth day of August, the feast day of holy Saint Dominic Guzman, Year of Our Lord Twenty-four Thousand One Hundred One, entered into a solemn and indestructible covenant to their mutual benefit, pleasure, and advantage, the terms whereof are binding on them and their generations forever. Witnessed this day by Menelaus Illation Montrose, vagabond. *Nolite Vexare Texam!*"

Montrose heard cheering issuing from many voices, many klaxons, echoing in the distance. He even heard the voices of the Firstlings and other non-Myrmidons mingling with the general outcry.

It was the voice of free men.

PART SEVEN

---·---

*The Long Golden
Afternoon of Man*

1

The Starfaring Guild

1. A Fine Shot

A.D. 51554

The rumor that a Vindictive sharpshooter had established himself in stable orbit among the rubble of the broken flotillas of hulks and habitats still called the Asteroid Belt, and had a commanding vantage of Earth, Venus, and Mars, was not denied by the Archangels, but anyone who read this news from a public data fountain had his name and biometric response noted.

First Humans were immune from Archangels because of covenants with the Sacerdotal Order whom, it was rumored, even the higher Powers feared; but this ancient immunity did not prevent the posthumans from reporting the capillary responses and pupil dilations, as well as changes in neural flows in the cortex, of various True Human readers to other Humans, including Humans Not So True. The Great Swan of Malta was known to have left his mountain peak in midst of the seas of Libya, traveling by night on wide and silent wings over the Mediterranean across the island chain that once was Italy toward Egypt, where the Hidden Queen of the Fox Maidens was said to be sojourning in disguise, perhaps to bedevil the archeologists and theonecromancers meddling with the corpse of a fallen orbital Archangel found there. It was no good news for the True Humans when a hermit of the Second Humanity roused himself from his endless cybernetic dreamstates, and sought to consult the sovereign of the Fourth Humanity. The Foxes were closer to humans in their emotional matrix, more prone to meddle in human life, and correspondingly more dangerous than reticent Swans or dispassionate Megalodons.

Perhaps the two consulted over the human interest in the Vindicator, or perhaps the two conspired with the Judge of Ages, who was rumored to have his throne buried under the pyramids, as well as slumbering armies and sleeping treasure cities.

In any case, cavaliers and ladies among the True Humans avoided showing interest in the topic of the sharpshooter. Among the lower orders, the discreet silence was not so strict. One wag walking the frozen canals of New Ximenopolis carried an umbrella bearing the slogan in bright red ideoglyphs for the benefit of eyes above the atmosphere: FRIENDLY! NO TARGET!

This was the year Minus 444 by the shortcount calendar, reckoning the time until the next Sweep by Hyades; it was Minus 17444 by the Unrevised Vindication Calendar; and it was Minus 18944 by the Anomaly Calendar; and the Sacerdotes called it Year of the Lord Plus 51554, even thought it was unchancy for them to say who or what was their lord, or say why this calendar, of all the calendars, counted up rather than counted down.

By the reckoning of the Unrevised Calendar, the Feast of the Fourth Ignition stood at Plus 154, and yet no cessation of the Years of Fasting which led up to the Feast Years had been announced. Even Academics living the shadow of the mile-high dome over the mountains of the Madagascar peninsula, prone to skepticism about the claims of the Sacerdotes, marked the tally off the calendar with thinly disguised hope, waiting for the long-delayed Energy Feast, when men could turn on lights and power again.

In mid-September of Minus 444, after the Paleo-Myrmidon City Complex east of Jerusalem was reduced to rubble and sucked into its own crater by a NAFAL singularity-event bullet, the radio messages from the Chimera of Mars said nothing other than that the situation was being investigated.

The bullet accelerated only at impact. It maintained its existence in normal spacetime for one-half a nanosecond, and massed (relative to the target) an estimated 30,000,000,000 pounds. This was long enough to pull the central mass of the city into a pinpoint and deposit it twenty miles below the bedrock, drawing a large part of the suburban infrastructure, cables and power stations, switching nodes and magnetic rail lines, behind it into the crater. The tangled mass of iron and carbon was superheated and compressed into a half-square-mile volume shaped like a very narrow cone.

But the nature of not-as-fast-as-light acceleration is that the mass increases only in the direction of motion. Objects even slightly away from the straight line suffer less relativistic distortion. Mass meters in Jerusalem itself barely registered the tidal effect.

And the bullet-life was not long enough to disrupt the geological integrity of the mantle, or to disturb the irritable and nervous Archangel called Demeter, which had established herself across the inner plates of the crust, with structures extending to the core, as the nursemaid and life support and repair crew for the renascent version of Tellus.

There were no earthquakes, and only a few storms: the disturbance to the Weather Control predictions was below intervention threshold. The Retaliation Mechanism established by Jupiter crouching at Mount Erebus in Antarctica trembled and stirred uneasily, and fearful gams and teams of watchful Melusine beneath the Ross Ice Shelf noted the energy systems all along the volcano cone tick over from their fifth standby awareness-level to their fourth, but the nightmarish Retaliator did not wake.

By all accounts, it was a fine shot, expertly executed.

So it was that when the traveling mountebank Zolasto Zo announced his troupe would add the apostate pontiff Hieronymus to their entourage, to give a series of lectures on calendar reform, the Ship Yard Assassin for the Starfarer's Guild assigned to the Stratospheric Tower in Spanish Guinea, where the Forever Village slept, was much disturbed in his mind.

2. A Reluctant Starfarer

The assassin's name and style was The Glorified and Refined Quaestor Norbert Brash Noesis Mynyddrhodian mab Nwyfre of Rosycross. He had crossed the Vasty Deep but once, starfaring to Senile Grandfather Earth from the one satellite of Proxima Centauri.

Less than four home-years had been compressed into a few ship-months' journey during his faring. Technically speaking, regulation permitted him to affix the praenomen *Venerable* to his name, as if he were from an older time; but he could not have sat at mess and met the eyes of Starfarers from the Third Sweep Worlds, Chrysoar circling 51 Pegasi or Nightspore of Alpha Boötis, men who lost one-third or one-half a century of home-years in passage. And some had five or ten cruises under their belts: what was four years of time-exile compared to four centuries? Some were from aeons so long forgotten that they did not use the term, but put *Lorentzed* before their name, in the archaic style.

The only praenomens he insisted be observed were those he had earned. When still a youth, unexpectedly and inexplicably, the Noösphere of Rosycross had offered him full immortal honors, a record made of his brain down to the subatomic level. His thoughts would endure as long as civilization had power.

Afterward, despite the normal savant precautions of hypnocoding and chemical intervention, a divarication had struck, and Norbert was torn in two. The flesh-and-blood version of Norbert suffered a painful infatuation with a girl half his age, the sloe-eyed and red-lipped eroticist Svartvestra. His ideal was Stoic, archetype called Traditional Brash, of the Fiercely Individualistic Nonconformist phyle. It was not a type known for romantic weaknesses, so Norbert was ashamed at how he failed to fit in when others of his Fiercely Individualistic Nonconformist gathered for the soul-sharing rituals. He wanted to be exactly like all the other Fiercely Individualistic Nonconformists. But he wanted Svartvestra more.

Her ideal was Hedonist of the Meretricious Revelry Artiste archetype, the precise mismatch of his. On her part, she was delighted to toy with his affections, always promising and implying more than she meant, since it outraged her clan and delighted her fans, and brought her an intoxicating notoriety.

The xypotech version of Norbert disliked the girl, then despised. They fell out of synchronization, and suffered a sharp divarication. From Norbert's point of view, Exorbert's behavior became odd, then erratic, then grotesque: Exobert developed interests in esoteric cults, chaos mathematics, theosophy, imaginary energies, and the claims of those who said they could speak with the dead or deleted, or could find lost colony ships.

Exorbert began making calls to Norbert's friends both natural and assigned, first by phone and then by dreamscape; tweaking Norbert's subpersonalities on the flimsiest excuses; making unauthorized sales, manipulating apple genetics; altering work schedules; and sending strange training drugs into the foodstock of the farm Moreaus, or Norbert's show-winning near-hound, Chymical Wedding.

Norbert fought unsuccessfully to undo all the strangeness and madness his ghostly twin was bringing into his life, and he vowed to fight forever. But when Norbert returned one winter Sunday to the family farm, and found all the farmhands celebrating the Wednesday Ciderfest, and his beloved near-hound giddy with stimulant and dancing on his hind legs on the baking table, crushing apple pies beneath his paws, Norbert's resolve broke.

He could not struggle against the invisible superior twin. He had to forswear the girl. When the Noösphere offered to edit the memory chains related to his infatuation to drive Norbert's personality closer to his archetype, and perhaps form a reconciliation between Norbert and Exobert, Norbert accepted the dangerous honor.

Against the wishes of the Noösphere and his father Yngbert, however, Norbert refused to have the process remove any sense of guilt or regret which might haunt him in later years.

And the alteration in his mind, even if done awkwardly, counted as Refinement. It elevated him from a mere Rustic to a Gentleman-Farmer.

But not only was no reunification forthcoming, his family and his ghost became ever more strangers to him.

Svartvestra was so stung by the cruel rejection, she recorded a fornication performance just in mockery of his love-style. He could no longer go into public houses or pink sections of the dreamscape without encountering jeers and sneers from her subscribers, or hearing trained near-dogs whistle the theme song from her base sound track.

It drove him into his archetype indeed. His soul became iron: he turned off his emotions so often the parish peace officer Maier twice served him a writ for renouncing his humanity, and asked him sarcastically why he did not use Foxcrafty to become a Myrmidon entirely. Each time Norbert restored his emotion, bitter anger overcame him.

But the technique for assuming an aspect of that ideal stoicism was still open to Norbert. Brash thought patterns were permanently imprinted, and could not fade with time. He used to amuse himself by falling into that allegedly higher state of mind, and putting his ungloved hand above a candle flame until he smelled flesh burning.

The unremoved regret hardened into resolve, and he ate a dream-apple, opening his nervous system to strange influences, and fell in love again, this time with a hamadryad bound by land-marriage to a fertile valley near the North Pole, where the gentle shadows were always long and the sun never reached zenith, even at noon.

Her name was Rose, the most common name on the planet. She was in every way the opposite of the frivolous and glamorous Svartvestra, but the end was the same. He was too artificial for her, too willing to alter himself, yet, ironically, too unwilling to drink the mind-altering love potion that would make their emotion for each other permanent structures, buttressed by neuro-circuitry, in all their personalities. Exorbert objected to the love potion, and Norbert feared to overrule the objection, not knowing, if he fought in his thoughts with Exorbert, which meant fighting the entire Noösphere of Rosycross, who or what he might end up evolving into.

He was brash, was he not? To remain himself, he fled the world, joined the Guild, took their coin, and signed the articles on the first vessel from Promixa.

Had he known how mad Tellus was, he would have waited longer, slumbered longer, and fled farther.

Tellus disturbed his mind.

3. A Discontented Consciousness

His consciousness, even his conception of what a consciousness was, perforce differed remarkably from that of a dawn-age man.

Basically there were three zones of thought in his mind: an inner zone which he thought of as himself, his own basic memories, ideals, reasoning processes, passions, appetites, and drives; an outer zone, which was the shared memories of the world-mind in which he lived, the spirit of the age; and a large middle zone where the two mingled, where he kept, as a mental menagerie, a wide variety of servant personalities, which he could use like masks to fend off unwanted thought-streams from the outer zone. There were well-worn channels in this middle zone reaching to the outer, where entities like family albums and social organizations kept their thoughts, or ghosts met in parliament to discuss matters too remote in the future to concern him. It was also a lively market for exchanging intellectual property, which logicians bred like livestock, or daring hunters recovered from deep in the outer zone.

Intellectually, he knew this outer zone extended infinitely, into the mind of the Noösphere like an atmosphere; but for all practical purposes, it was like the dome of the sky, mere backdrop. Every now and again the world changed, like blowing winds that changed his mood. The spirit of the age only took over his mind and body during Mass, or planetary consensus, or for a riot or military exercise, and this was as rare as rainfall.

What he had not expected, when coming to senile Tellus, was to discover how little of the innermost zone was actually his own, himself. Most of his opinions about everything had come from his family or had been written in by censor of the Lord of the Afternoon of Promixa Centauri.

His taste in women was dictated by the seamstresses guild; his taste in sport by the gamesters guild; his sweet tooth was entirely an invention of the pastry and confectioner's guild.

Once on Earth, the outer zone was an alien atmosphere to him, with roaring shapes larger than gods moving through it; the middle zone changed suddenly, and was filled with moods and merchandise stranger than the bottom of the sea. He was told he would become used to the revolting practices of the Earthlings in time. Everyone had assured him, from his ghostly counselor to his personality advocate, to his libido coordinator, to his cliometry planner, that while Tellus was insane, many of the outer systems, telephone and memory reflex storage, were perfectly safe, sagacious and discreet.

But then one day he found himself without his clothing and feathered like a duck from crown to heel, having lost his skin in a haiku recital wager to a sly redhaired woman in a place that was a cross between a butcher shop and a gambling den. There, standing on naked feet in a stain of his own blood, he realized two things. First, he did not even like haiku, or, for that matter, the smell of duck meat. Second, everyone who so blithely said Tellus was safe was mad. Tellus was a world of fads and fashions and hysteria. Inviting the mind of Tellus into your mind was inviting disaster.

That same day he threw away all his receiver decks and augmentation sets, even the small coral button his mother gave him at birth. He sacked his advocate and coordinator and planner and reduced his interface to be the stark minimum necessary to carry out his duties as a Starfarer: public postal and library channels, navigation feeds, weather and riot reporting, navigational computation, and little beyond that.

He put in a request to be slotted to the Sky Island, which was a lighter-than-air platform in the stratosphere used for catching deorbiting cargo rigs, because it was the most dangerous and most highly rewarded duty station. He worked extra shifts, hoping a stray container, white hot with reentry heat, might accidentally miss the magnetic vortex, strike the cage, and crush his feathery body, which he hated. It was two seasons of frugal living, eating only noodles and vitamin slurry, until he earned enough to buy himself a proper human skin again. He deliberately bought one in a color modern fashion despised, a pinkish pale hue allegedly from a sunken land called Europe, very different from the jet-black, silver-eyed coloration of Rosycross.

Even after that, his austere habits remained. He spoke to no one save by voice, appeared on no bulletin board or staging boards, purchased nothing on credit, visited no calamity houses. And he never once used the Fox arts to turn himself into a dolphin during mating season, even though apparently every lunatic Earthling male in heat took to the seas in the spring, leaving the beaches empty save for hastily shed clothing. As far as the Noösphere of Earth was concerned, he was practically invisible.

So it was not surprising when the Proconsul for the Starfaring Guild approached him and asked if he wanted to be assigned to special operations, and kill men and exorcise ghosts. The duty was even more dangerous and despicable than being a longshoreman on the Sky Island, and so he accepted eagerly.

A decade later, when the verdict of the Interdict was announced, and communion with the Noösphere was denied to him, he had been living so austerely for so long that he should not have noticed it. It was like a Franciscan under a vow of poverty being sued at law for his possessions.

But the solitude still ached. Alone in his own mind, he was still surprised at how small and lonely a mind it was.

4. Fugitives of Interdiction

Such was his life, contented in small things, discontented in large. Norbert the Assassin was sitting in the sill of his huge round wide-open window-port staring at the lights of the Forever Village, and half dozing while half heeding a report being sung to him in plaintive tones, when a notice extruded itself from an anonymous slot on his desk, and a chime of tone and period whose meaning he did not recognize rang out.

Encoded as eerie Monument music, the report was of an extraordinary discharge detected between Sol and the star 20 Arietis. The chime interrupted the song and marred it, whereupon the singer (being as sensitive and fickle as abstract musician constructs tend to be) grew sullen and would not continue.

An icy plutino, a small body in interstellar space, had wandered into the line between Sol and 20 Arietis, and ignited, betraying the presence of an energy path. The star 20 Arietis was speculated to be a major nexus of Hyades internal communication. But who of Sol was sending communication there and why? The song had been about to reach the speculative conclusions of the report when the interruption came.

So Norbert glanced down in annoyance. He whistled for his desk. On its six stumpy legs, it lumbered over to the window where he sat. He had never before known that this slot was built into the desk. A query search returned a blank: the slot had no name or history in the local infosphere of the tower. (The tower ghosts were legally denizens of outer space, not part of the Tellurian Noösphere, and therefore open to him.) A wider search to a ship's boat passing overhead like a shooting star was equally barren of results. One property of antiques was that their instruction manuals had vanished in earlier eons, and this was especially true on Senile Earth, where it was not unusual to come across loud public houses or snarky drinking vessels older than every man-made object on Rosycross.

The notice was printed on a sheet of fine onionskin. By tradition, everything of the Starfarers had to be of low mass, and have no electronic failure points: as if monstrous modern vessels made of invulnerable argent materials accelerated by beams of planet-obliterating strength fretted about acceleration costs, or worried about electromagnetic pulses from hull collisions.

A tradition equally as old but far more annoying held that such notes had to be sticky, so that in zero gee they would adhere to the nearest surface. Consequently it was many minutes before Norbert managed to untangle the tiny, delicate sheet without ripping it.

ZOLASTO ZO, an entrepreneur of many fortuitous licenses
Member in Good Standing of the Entertainment and Procurers Guild
Avers he will **Astound! Delight! Astonish!**
With Many and Varied displays and representations
THE WONDERS OF EARTH
Your long lost Mother!
Who does not adore the Home World?
PRIMAL ABODE OF MAN!!— NEVER BEEN TERRAFORMED!!!

———

SEE the dancing nymphs of ancient Arcadia!
HEAR mellifluous sonograms from extinct man-eating Whales!
THRILL to a military display of ancient weapon forms
by *Feroccio* our Master-At-Arms!
Including the discharge of an authentic black-powder caterpillar-gun!

———

BEHOLD Fruits, nuts and berries FIT FOR HUMAN MASTICATION
grown without intervention from the NATIVE SOIL OF MANKIND!
(Certificate on file to confirm that these are UNMODIFIED by any process,
exactly as savage hunter-gatherers of primordial agribusinesses
found them in the WILD!)

———

TOUCH the parchments of the Bible written by
King James, an avatar of divine Crishna!
WRITTEN IN THE ORIGINAL ENGLISH!

(The Quill Pen and Inkstand used by Mr. King to indite his famous work
is available for view for an extra charge of one grote.)

———

ADMIRE as the delicate and nubile Mademoiselle Pelisse Roquelaure
performs the traditional native dance of long-submerged New Orleans,
city famed in myth! The dance forms have been reconstructed
With Painstaking Archeological Accuracy from postures and displays
found in LURID advertisements of the Anteposthuman period!
CERTAIN TO BE OF INTEREST TO THE GENTLEMEN

———

As an added courtesy to those of sober and scholarly attainments,
ZOLASTO ZO
Welcomes the curious Hieronymus to our noble troupe;
and this Most Interesting and Convivial Sacerdote is available to
REMOVE CURSES, and perform MIRACLE CURES,
while making a series of interesting remarks on the mysteries of the
calendar system, or other matters CURRENTLY FASCINATING
the Attention of the Public
of All Ranks and Species of Humanity.

———

*Subject matters not fitting for ladies of elevation or gentle birth are so noted;
scholars and antiquarians are acknowledged as equals!*

———

(Concubinage Contracts available for Negotiation by Certified Eugenicists.
Guaranteed Clean and Bio-compatible bloodlines. Fit for Breeding.)

5. The Best Interest of the Guild

Norbert smiled grimly. The effrontery of offering to earthmen to taste or see
the fruits or views of the Earth seemed noteworthy only in its absurdity.

The purpose of such spectacles was to give gentlemen an opportunity to see
nymphs and breeding girls posing and gyrating before purchasing their contracts; then as if by some accident, the slavegirls would be sent, drunk on aph-
rodisiacs, to the gentleman's privy suite instead of to his kennels. No one older
than a child ever stopped to gape at the pasteboard and tinfoil and holograms
of the sideshows.

Rectifiers and other local magistrates could not easily shut down any wandering showman who pretended to act under the academic latitude guaranteed by ancient right to lectures, reenactments, and edifying displays. For just such a reason, no doubt, Zolasto Zo tolerated this oddly named Hieronymus to travel with his band.

A sour note entered his mind. As he pondered, wondering why this notice had been sent him, Norbert realized that to discuss the calendar while the Earth was under fire might be considered an act of sedition, and not keeping in the best interest of the Starfarers.

He thought longer, seeking an escape from this conclusion, any escape.

While it was Guild policy in theory not to interfere with terrestrials' affairs, it was also Guild policy in practice to minimize local disturbances in the cliometric calculus, to tamp down spikes or disburse strange attractors in the matrix of history, lest some revolution in technology or social continuity interfere with the smooth launching and landfall of the great ships.

Was this such an event? Even a few hundred thousand parallel calculations of six billion variables in his head showed that it must be an attractor basin, if not a vortex.

Norbert felt a suffocating moment, almost claustrophobic, when he realized that the decision was his. It could not be palmed off on any local or current authority, or any other member of the Guild, nor could he hire a bravo or roughneck to do the work. The verdict and its consequences would have his name affixed to it, and forever. He must find Zolasto, find Hieronymus, question the man, under torment if need be, run the calculations, weigh the dangers to the Guild, and spare or slay a human life. The ship ghosts were as unhelpful on the question of Zolasto Zo's whereabouts as they were about the manual for the desk and its printing slot.

Fieldwork was needed. He rang for his adjutant.

The wrong man came.

6. Ar Thurp End Ragon

His adjutant was supposed to be Nochzreniye of Nocturne of Epsilon Eridani, a star famed for its theonecromancers, and haunted by the still-speaking fragments of a long dead Power. Nochzreniye's people, the Zarya, were from the longitude of globe called First Hour, parallel to the motionless twilight terminator bisecting his world, and so their sun was always no more than a redorange reflection against distant clouds and mountains. As their name implied, the Nocturnals were nocturnal, and Norbert appreciated being able to keep his cabin lights dimmed to a tolerable level.

Nochzreniye was also derived from a gene stock far removed from mankind's monkeylike origins. Ironically for a tree-dwelling species, it was remnants and echoes of man's monkey ancestors which made him prone to vertigo and fear of heights. When this gene-line had been removed from certain spacetraveling subspecies in order to correct for inner ear maladaptation to zero gee, it accidentally rendered certain lineages immune to fear of falling, Nocturnals and Rosicrucians among them.

Partly as a joke and partly out of the sheer bloody-mindedness for which the Brash archetype was famous, Norbert had removed the outer wall leading to his office and narrowed the resulting unrailed balcony to half a standard gangway width, leaving a windy ledge overlooking the Village rooftops so far below. It amused him to see earthmen, so proud of their base-stock genes, when summoned to his office, to come down the gangway, gripping the wall and taking baby steps, trying not to look down.

But this new adjutant was different. When he stepped out on the unexpectedly narrow and railless ledge, like an earthman he touched the wall and measured the depth of the fall with his eyes. His first step was tentative. But by his second step, he was gliding along with the goat-footed grace of a non-orthogonal biopsychological type like a Nocturne or Rosicrucian. But everything else about him, facial hair, number of teeth, vestigial tissue linking thumb and hand, even (if Norbert was any judge of footwear) separate toes, indicated a very conservative gene profile ergo an orthogonal brain structure.

The new adjutant gave a crisp salute, holding up his glove to his eyes, palm out, and had his orders flicker across his palm, along with his name and rank, duty station and other general data, licenses, qualifications, tolerances and immunizations. Norbert did not rise, but returned the ceremonial salute casually, holding his shining palm toward the data so that his uniform would have a record of the new man's files and preferences. Both men lowered their hands when the gloves showed transmission sent and received, the new man sharply, Norbert by covering his mouth in a yawn.

"Ar Thurp End Ragon? By the dangling Bachelor, what kind of name is that? I don't recognize the format. Which part is your privy name and which is your gene-line? And why is your age marked as classified? I've never seen anyone's age marked *classified*."

"A remarkably old name, sir. We put the family name last."

The new man's voice was surprisingly deep and melodic, rich with nuances of tone. Norbert did not know, even after so long on the senile homeworld of man, what archetypes the baselines and firstling folk used. But this man must have downloaded psychological structures for the magnetic personality type. The ringing voice was regal, genial, jovial, slightly sly, slightly dangerous. It was the kind of archetype that dumb kids eager for rank and ladies' favors would like.

Norbert would have wagered that this was a guy who fenced with a blade, threw red roses to damsels, and invented sonnets in iambic pentameter to mock his foes after a swordfight but before escaping through a kicked-out window on a white silk line. Norbert knew enough about mudra and mandala to recognize the nerve-muscle traces of the type. It was something about the devilish twinkle in his eye.

And yet something did not fit. Norbert could not figure how the Firstling had adapted from baseline to non-orthogonal psychology so quickly. No one could swap out a sub-personality that promptly. It was almost as if the fellow had rewritten his base neural structural command sequences, his own instinctive reactions, on the fly.

"End Ragon, then?" said Norbert, attempting an avuncular smile. "Well, Able Starman End Ragon, the mission here concerns a calendar reformer. Describe the controversy to me."

"Sir," the squire said crisply, "according to the Unrevised Vindication Calendar, Jupiter should have ignited the Fourth Great Burn of the deceleration beam four hundred fifty years ago, but the Revised Anomaly Calendar says the Fourth Burn is not due for another one thousand five hundred fifty years, and we all must fast on short energy rations and conserve until then."

Norbert nodded. "Go on."

"The Revisionists say that since no flare of launch light from Canes Venatici was detected at the due time, an X-ray anomaly two thousand years later was the launch. Hence, the Swan Princess who stole a star doubtless tarried at M3, and the Vindication of Man will be long delayed. The Vindictive say the Vindication comes on schedule, but that the Authority at M3 has given some novel means of propulsion to the vessel, which humble Earthly science cannot detect; and they say the anomaly was some small exogalactic matter swept into the bowshock of her sail at near-lightspeed, suffering total conversion."

"Perfect," said Norbert. "Your answer comes straight out of the Political Officer's Correct Attitude Manual. So the Vindictives are as mad as everyone on this mad world here, and curse the darkness of the deceleration beam, and are shooting at the cities of the machines in protest, to show one and all what near-lightspeed can do. Therefore, what is your opinion of the matter?"

"That it is an injudicious matter to discuss openly."

"Correct! But if you are directly ordered to voice your opinion by a superior? What is your opinion then?"

"That, given the Treaty of Jupiter which ended the Crusades, every loyal man should follow the calendar of the local prince and current lord placed over him. For the Inner System of Sol, that means to follow the Summer Kings, who are Revisionists."

"More correct! And what should we Starfarers do, since we sail from star to star, and are loyal to no local princes, but loyal only to the dream of the Vindication of Man?"

"We should not discuss the matter at all, and give our dates in the sacerdotal reckoning."

"Most correct of all! But the Starfaring Guild does not like wars, revolutions, or reformations, because they disrupt the Launch Schedule. That means loudmouthed men, even men of the cloth, who discuss the calendar reform too openly must, for the good of the Guild, be silenced, because there is no Vindication for Man if the starships sail not."

Norbert leaned back, waiting to see if the other man would say anything. The other man stood at ease with no expression on his face, and said nothing. Norbert took that as a good sign.

"How do you feel about killing priests, Able Starman End Ragon? They are notoriously Unrevised."

"Actually, sir, if I may?"

"Mm?"

"It would be *Squire,* not *Able Starman,* since I am affixed to the Marine Family and Clan avowed to this base, practiced in the gentlemanly arts of blade, speaking whip, mudra, and shorepistol"—Norbert congratulated himself. He knew a bravo when he saw one.—"and assigned to you in your role as Special Airlock Operations Agent, not in your role as Praetor." Special Airlock Operations was the archaic euphemism for Ship's Assassin.

"What? Dangle it! I have no role as Praetor. I am a Quaestor." Norbert held up his glove again, and performed the salute to send the data flow across his palm.

The new man held up his palm and saluted, this time more slowly, pausing the playback as his final orders appeared. "Actually, sir, if I may, I have been ordered to report to an officer named Norbert of ideal-type Brash of line, phylum and family Noesis Mynyddrhodian mab Nwyfre of Dee Parish, North Polar Continent, planet Rosycross, venerable of a.d. 51550, and the rank is Praetor. It seems you have been given a brevet increase in rank, at least temporarily, for this mission. Did the Noösphere not inform you?"

"*Zznah?!*" The Brash were supposed to be coolheaded, and take startling news nonchalantly, or with an airy jest, but this was so unexpected that Norbert emitted the shrill nasal noise of a true hillcountry Rosicrucian before the archetype habituation cells in his cortex could react. "I-im-imp-impossible! No one becomes a Praetor straight from Aedile! The rank of Quaestor interposes! And even for a Quaestor, there is supposed to be a board of review! A midnight vigil! An augury and—by all the Bachelors!—and I am not qualified! I don't have the years lost or the years served! Unwed it! Un-*WED*!"

"Is that a swearword among your people, sir? It sounds stoop— Ah—it sounds mildly unusual."

"Sorry. Didn't mean to curl your virgin ears. We are married before we are born on my planet, so we don't have anyone not helping to swell the underpopulation numbers. Since the first marriage is nonconsensual and never consummated, our sacerdotes permit an annulment of the first wife after you've been married to a second wife for a year. It is not so bad, since we are a Torch World, no more than a hundred thousand miles from our sun, so a year is about a week long."

Norbert realized he was rambling, and snapped his mouth shut. But talking—especially talking about his home—had given him the moment he needed to deploy his Brash archetype structures in his cortex. The artificial nerve cells sent messages to his organic cells, released chemicals in his bloodstream, and so on. He could feel the change in his posture and body language like an actor settling into a character role. He was calm. He was unmoved and immovable, yet eager for action, equally willing to live for a laugh as die spitting in the executioner's eye. He was brash!

"I get it," said Norbert. "The ghosts of the old captains and shipmasters used their right of intervention for the sake of the Guild. No time for the proper ceremonies. So I get picked because I am a nobody. I kill the damned unwed Vindicator Breastbeater and shut his big mouth, for I have no family name here on Earth for anyone to retaliate against, right? What can the Summer Kings do, make it snow on me alone? And if I don't kill him, or something gets flared up, I can be decommissioned for having exceeded my authority, and turned over to the currents. Jettisoned. Dropped out the waste lock."

With no further word, he doffed the dark spectacles he wore at all times, buckled on a shoulder belt holding his weapons, and donned his full face mask of black smartfabric, and drew up his hood. The weapons were matched antiques like stilettoes with blades of blue glass and scorpion-tail grips; the weapons emitted a dour, mordant aura on the emotion channel, but never spoke. The entire surface of the mask and cloak, not just the area over his eyes, was light sensitive, and fed the images directly into his cortex, so he did not need to don his black spectacles again: but he liked the way they looked, for they gave his facelessness a memorable accent.

Impishly, he flexed his shoulders to trigger the silent billow and hem-floating of his cape. The New Guy did not flinch in instinctive decompression-fear as a spacer would have seeing the black cape a-billow, but he did not react as an earth-man either, who would have noticed the glaring exception to the sumptuary laws with a raised eyebrow, or a studied attempt at nonchalance.

This squire fellow instead looked at the cape lining, and his eye motions did the typical posthuman jitter of rapid information absorption. What was going on? The guy was studying how a normal cape-circuit worked? He did not know about living thread?

Norbert could not even remember how long ago living thread had been in-vented. Was it before the rise of the Fourth Humans, or after? It was a Fox Maiden technology, something they spun from special glands their vixanthropic powers allowed them to control, wasn't it?

The first Fox, Cazi, had been perfected somewhere near the year Minus 30000. The current year was Minus 17444. One hundred twenty-five centu-ries later.

How old was this squire? The most distant world in the Empyrean Polity of Man was Uttaranchal of 83 Leonis at fifty-eight lightyears hence. A voyage there and back would only let Einstein steal a century. Had this man made the long faring across the Vasty Deep one hundred twenty-five times? Then he would have been the most famed figure in history, not a squire of marines with some odd name.

Norbert grit his teeth. No. This year was not Minus 17444. Nor was it Mi-nus 18944. The Guild was strictly neutral, which meant that all dates were add-ing up from some past salvation recalled by the sacerdotes, not counting down to the future salvation anticipated by cliohistorians. He dared not make a gaffe like that, showing favor to one side or the other, even in his thinking, lest he say or send something in an unnoticed moment damaging to the Guild. Kill-ing men was excusable; slips of the tongue were not.

The other option was that this squire was not old, but young. He had been hatched out of some Fox Maiden's cloning egg an hour ago. If he were too young to have seen clothing before, that explained his staring at the cloak. Also, if he were too young to have permanent structures in his brain, that explained his too-quick adjustment to his vertigo. This was a man with no family and no past, loaded with the earthman equivalent of brashness, the magnetic personality of a bravo. Another expendable. And that meant only one thing. Failure did not mean anything so sweet as being turned over to the seculars.

"So, Squire End Ragon! Is the plan that you kill me if I fail?"

Norbert, who thought he had this man pegged, was astounded. The man's startled look, the change in his eye, in his stance, was so honest, spontaneous, and unprepared, that nothing could have convinced Norbert more deeply.

The squire was not just angry, he was offended. His sense of honor was wounded.

The man drew his sidearm and presented it to Norbert butt first, and at the same time sunk to one knee. "Many a cruel and untoward thing have I done in my life, and slain men both guilty and innocent as need required, but never in any underhanded way. I do not shoot foes in the back, nor without warning, nor without affording them time to pack their pistol, nor without witnesses! Do I shoot men like dogs? That would make me less than a dog! Shoot me with my own piece, drive a stake through my corpse and bury it at the crossroad, far from sacred ground, if that is the opinion my commanding officer has formed of me within the first few moments of my duty. Shoot me now, or never doubt me again, my lord!"

These were the words born of a mature sense of honor, not some imprinted set of gestures and gland-reflexes. Norbert, ashamed, revised his assessment. Whatever this man was, he was not some hour-old hatchling.

Norbert took the pistol and opened it. It was charged to power and occupied by a serpentine. "Do you vouch for this man?"

The weapon said, "Under these conditions, I would fire and kill him, since his request is lawful, and it is an affair of honor. Your accusation is a stain that his blood or yours must wipe out. The whole conversation from the moment you saw him must be removed from the records and archives of every object you own, including the blackbox recorder."

"There is no place outside of a graveyard where anyone can find every recording object," said Norbert. "But I do not balk at this being seen."

Norbert handed the pistol back. Then he doffed his glove, drew a sampling needle, and made the smallest possible pinprick with the needle point in the ball of his thumb. The blood of Rosycross was black as ink, since the bloodstream was thick and sluggish with nanomachines meant to fend off radiation and fast-moving particles from the flares and sickening sunspots of Proxima. The blood hung from his thumb like a small black gem.

Norbert held the bleeding thumb toward the kneeling man, "Satisfied, Squire End Ragon?"

The man rose and holstered his weapon. "It is said blood erases all records, sir. If there is no recording, it never happened. There is a custom of dueling on your world?"

"Among the hillmen of Dee. We are one of the older parishes, and we all were born in the shadow of the towers of the First Sweep colonists, who perished to the last child. The flare times mummify the bodies by killing microbes, so children sometimes still find corpses if they play in the towers, which all the mothers tell them not to, and none of the boys obey. When you live beneath a boneyard that big and that old, you know life is for spending, not for hoarding. So, yes, my people duel, with sword or stick or sting, spray-torch, depending on their archetype, and any talking whips we find in the ruins."

Norbert sighed and continued, "I know enough not to wake up the Swans or provoke the Archangels, not to use any weapon that might damage life support or invite the Retaliation. But by the useless Eunuch's dangle do I hate this work."

"Sir? *Hate* it?"

"I am delighted with the art of hunting of human prey, for no sport known to mortal man makes such demands on mind and soul and nerve and gut. Even the great Ghosts and Potentates and Powers have no such sport as this, for they cannot die!"

"Let us pray that is not so," murmured the squire. Norbert's hearing was designed to be more acute than the standard allowed to earthmen, who came from a noisier world with denser air, so Norbert was not sure whether he was meant to hear that murmur. Norbert knew many an earthman had a habit of talking to himself, especially if his nervous system lodged more than one personality.

He thought it politer to continue his sentence as if not interrupted. ". . . But I have blood on my hands, and ever since the Marriage Brokers unionized, murderers do not get invited to pay court on young ladies very often."

"Being alone is not so bad, sir, surely."

"Among my people, the word for an unmarried man is a swearword. Every other part of this dark business is honorable, even attractive to women of a certain type. So the only part of being an assassin I hate is the assassination. You smirk? Strikes you as funny?"

"No sir!" said the squire, with a charming grin and a cock of the head. His smile flashed like a white chevron of lightning in his black goatee. "It is assassins who enjoy their work I find disturbing."

"I am trying to warn you that once you are marked as a killer, the sacerdotes may pardon you, but the virgins will not. The chrism cannot be washed off."

"Your warning is too late by too many years to count. My first murder was a year before my first shave. I used the razor better in the former event, and was cut less painfully."

Norbert stood. "It is time to depart. Any other questions?"

"Just one. Your family name is Mynyddrhodian mab Nwyfre?"

"Yes?"

"How does one pronounce *Nwyfre*?"

"Simple. It rhymes with *Mwyfre*. Dial your uniform to stealth settings, and especially your boots," said Norbert. "We need no noise, and dare not use wings. Now back along the ledge and down the outer rungs."

7. The Lights of the Forever Village

As the two descended the uncertain rungs of the tower hull in the darkness, cold, and wind, underfoot could be seen the colored lights of the timeless town called the Forever Village.

The tower base itself was on interstellar ground: the soil here had been brought, one handful at a time, from other worlds in other systems, and nothing earthly could grow in it.

Then the two men departed the tower and entered the village, whose soil was mundane. The Village was arranged concentrically, each younger quarter surrounding an older. The oldest street was hence the first they crossed, near the tower base. Around them shined the searchlights and robotic lamps of the bellicose era of the Snow Wars. Norbert wondered what wives and families slumbered or thawed here, awaiting sailormen to return from a thousand years of time loss. Were there any cruises so long?

The houses here were built like metallic tortoise shells. At night their door valve and nanomachine-locks were sealed tight, and the snouts of ceremonial weapons peered out menacingly. The cobbled streets of this quarter of the village were empty of traffic or dogs or litter. The two men passed on their silent boots like shadows.

They passed another gate, and entered another generation of architecture and technology. Here gambrel windows were aglint with candlelight or burning peat beneath high-peaked roofs of red slate, from an age when wintertime still came.

The Aedile had decreed all the streets in the village eternal, commanding them to repair themselves forever back into their present look. The two men passed beneath a breed of particularly ungainly bird roosting on the eaves of a longhouse from the Forty-ninth Millennium. It would be restored from extinction again and again, merely so that any sailor from the era of the Ineluctable Curses could waken to the distinctive notes of its harsh dawn-caw.

It was a sad reminder of how low the technology could fall, but a proud testament to the fact that the Starfarers maintained continuity across even the darkest of dark ages, and continued to recruit men even from wounded and hopeless times to sail the stars and man the libraries.

Norbert broke the stillness. "Why were you assigned to this mission, if you are not my watchdog?"

"No doubt because of my willingness to do the work," chuckled the other. "I will do any dark deed to preserve the Guild."

"Why?"

"Because there is no Vindication of Man without the Starfaring Guild to ignite the deceleration beam to return the Swan Princess Rania to our frame of reference. All the work of history is wasted if we fail. What of yourself?"

"I am assigned to find Zolasto Zo because my grandfather's sister went mad after eating an apple," said Norbert.

The squire waited a moment, then squinted and said, "I don't understand."

"A dream-apple, from Rosycross. The first and only planet of Proxima, which the Swans call Alpha Centauri C?"

"I have heard of the world, sir. It is said to have a huge wall circling the equator."

Norbert felt a pang of the emotion called *hiraeth* for which there was no direct earthly equivalent: it is partly homesickness, partly mourning for the unknown dead, but it also included the thirst for cider never to be drunk again, a hunger for bucolic beauty, and the sense of loss for the noble and legend-haunted past.

He had been to the great equatorial wall once, when he was apotheosized. The wall was shaped like some vast world serpent with curving sides. It circumnavigated the planet, occupying a cold volcanic canyon that ran rule-straight across field and meadow, cleaving mountain and bridging the dark and tideless ocean. Legend said the great wall had been formed when the space elevator of the long-lost first colony had collapsed.

The world-circling wall ran to and from a jagged quarter-mile-high stump of windowless metal that housed the Lord of the Golden Afternoon for Rosycross, a Hierophant named the Alarch of Eleirch. Here he and all his cliometric machinery which wove the world's future lived. The rest of Rosycross was rural: highlands of small farms, or lowlands of large plantations crisscrossed by canals, hemmed by dikes. Everything was the hue of wine beneath the soft, dim nearby sun.

Norbert was homesick for where the eyes of women were silver-white like the eyes of angels. He longed to smell the scent of dream-orchards again, or to see the dragonfly-winged skiffs with their wise eyes sliding on their crooked pontoon legs across the black and tideless seas of that moonless world. But most of all wished once more to gaze at the face of a sun gentle and mild enough to watch the sunspots and swirled vortices drifting across many bands of fire, so unlike the unfriendly sun of Earth, which scalded his eyes when a forgetful moment tempted him to look the monster in the face.

Hatred of the Interdict that barred his home from him once again rose in his throat like bile. He often wondered what could have happened back home to cause a catastrophe such as radio silence. Had a whole generation been raised to be so selfish and shortsighted that they would no longer tolerate the expense of powering an orbital laser to send their annuals and world-journals to their neighbor stars? The rise of an ungrateful generation such as would be needed to betray the interstellar radio law would have been anticipated cliometrically. The Golden Lord of Rosycross should have taken steps a generation ago to prevent it. Why hadn't he?

Norbert shook off the mood. "Yes. That wall is named the Honored and Ancient Spire Recumbent, or Stumblespire, for short. My great aunt is said to have emerged from the forest of Ashmole after having been outraged by a fertility incubus created by the Fox Princess Sortilage, pregnant with Ungbert Mynyddrhodian mab Nwyfre, who changed his name to Ung Zooanthropos mab Bwystfil. You understand?"

"Ah . . . Nothing has leapt shrieking into unambiguous clarity as yet, sir."

"I had assumed the Noösphere of Tellus would have all the related information."

"Some days Tellus is more lucid than others, sir."

"Zooanthropos is the long form of the name Zo. From Ung come all the Zo families of Ashmole Parish, not to mention the high crime rate and births out of wedlock for which the Parish is famous. Zolasto Zo is my second cousin. I am a Rosicrucian."

"An exile? Oh. Ah—sorry, sir."

"No matter," snapped Norbert curtly.

"Sir, I did not mean to bring up an unpleasant, ah—"

"No matter! I am aware that Jupiter's decree exiles me from my beloved home. Yet without such penalties as interdictions and excommunications, how could a polity across interstellar ranges be maintained? You earthmen on your bright world with your steady sun are tempted ever to be the optimists, and think the universe is bright and steady. Rosycross is a dark world of an unsteady sun, so our view is truer to life."

Beyond the crumbling stone walls of the candlelit quarter was a line of gas lamps, like stiff iron trees, overlooking houses of stone and lumber. Here were stalls for riding-dogs larger than ponies, white and stiff with night slumber; and also folded at their curbside posts were spiderish motor-tricycles and dog-traps whose thin and crooked legs grasped tall and slender tires at rakish angles; but there was no motion on the streets, since the men born of this era made it a point of principle to retire at dusk.

Norbert said, "What would an optimistic earthman assume about the year of Zolasto Zo's departure?"

"Hm? That it was over twenty-four years ago, before the interdiction fell."

"What? And Zo remained silent for a quarter century, putting on shows and antics for the idle, and only just now resolved to thrust himself in the controversy of the calendar, and defy the Lords of the Golden Afternoon of Man? No, let us be more pessimistic and assume his planetfall came after the interdict."

"Which means this is not the real Zolasto Zo," said the squire.

"An odd way of phrasing it, considering that we 'real' originals continue to change and age and degrade and die, but yes. This is the Xypotech version of Zo, the Exanthropos, and was doubtless smuggled by an encrypted signal to compatriots on Earth. Here he has descended back into the material realm, but somehow erasing all trace of his incarnation from the senile Noösphere of Tellus. Do not be deceived. We fight against not flesh and blood, but against a fallen angel."

Beyond the quarter of the gas lamps and stone buildings was a set of streets lit by electrical lights, whose houses made of porcelain had wide windows and tall doors. Electrical cables, adorned with bunting, ran from house to house, held aloft on tall poles. There were a few pedestrians waddling abroad at this hour, or riding motorized divans or litters, dressed in clear plastic trousers and see-through capes, proudly displaying the perfection of bodies which adhered to a standard of beauty of a more corpulent and aliphatic era. At every street corner was an automatic zither playing plangent chords and a basket of fruit or heated bucket of meatballs from which the passersby ate freely, and the public fountains shed grog. There was no difference in dress or ornament between male and female, and all the men were beardless. These had been peaceful years: none of these Thaws carried visible weapons.

"Well and good, sir, but how does this allow you to deduce where our target is?"

"Zolasto Zo is a mountebank, and not allowed to sleep under a roof. Such is the Wandering Trickster archetype of Rosycross under which mountebanks fall. His is not an archetype that allows flesh to change, so he retains a Rosicrucian body, and therefore his eyes are like mine. He does not like bright lights. But he needs a field for his performance, and it needs to be a place where the local officers of this place and current officers of this time have no warrant to stop him, but every yokel with a bag of pence or a talent of silver can find the show, even if he heard only a rumor of it. The location is passed by word of mouth."

On the far side of the friendly houses lit by electricity came a quarter filled with louder streets lit by neon of many colors, and the jackets of the passersby flared with slogans of long-forgotten commercial products or sexual factions, and from each man's ear-gem came music of pounding drumbeats. The walks here were more crowded, the long skirts and elaborate headdresses of the women clearly distinct from the garish cummerbunds and multicolored leggings of the men, and each young man carried a spring-mounted dirk or a one-shot derringer at his padded codpiece, which lit up menacingly when another youth similarly armed stepped too close.

The noise of these streets deterred conversation. The assassin and his squire did not speak again until they passed into the next quarter.

Here, harsh atomic lights glared on wide streets paved in hard macadam. An oddly shaped one-wheeled vehicle sped by, its one lamp glaring like the eye of a cyclops, and the helmeted rider hunched over the steering bar carried torches on the shoulderboards of his armored jacket. The vehicle passed them with a roar, splashing them momentarily with light, and tilted alarmingly as it took a corner. Darkness and silence flowed after.

The squire said, "Did Zolasto Zo erect his tents somewhere in this village? The currents will not step on Spacefarer ground without our leave, since the Forever Village is under the banner of the Master of All Worlds."

"That is a good first guess, End Ragon," said Norbert. "I will make an assassin of you yet!"

"You mean 'good guess but wrong'?"

"Not necessarily. It is possible Zo is here, which is why we are walking instead of defying the Swans and going by wing. But there is someone the currents fear more than they fear this mythical Master, and somewhere no authority ventures without his leave, but where all are welcome eventually."

The next quarter outward was lit with a soft chemical glow that came from motes in the atmosphere, eerie and shadowless, the blue hue of moonlight. Here were half a dozen men and women of that era dressed in gauze, and their roads carried them where they would go without any noise at all. It was a wonder to see them floating down the street, silent as dreams, while that rider of their grandparent's day, or greatgrandparent's, roared and clattered so boisterously on his one-wheeled machine the next street over.

"A place where all are welcome, sir? Someone who is more feared than the Master of the World? I can think of none."

"The legend of the Judge of Ages still haunts this senile old planet. No one steps on his ground. A place with no lights. Have you deduced it yet?"

The squire snapped his fingers (for spacemen who wear gauntlets practically from birth, an oddly archaic gesture to make). "A graveyard."

"Exactly! You are quick on the uptake."

"So I have always been told, sir."

The final street was lit with lanterns that floated like fireflies above the road, or followed any individuals who seemed lost, and the colors flickered whenever enough men gathered to need traffic controls or segregation of the races. The streets were empty except for a few wandering vigilantes, who walked on gyroscopic stilts and wore tall miters of red fabric, and in their hands were long wands that glittered. Warned by the colors of the floating lanterns, the assassin and the squire avoided the vigilantes, who were busy trampling a porch garden of unorthodox design.

The original line of twenty-foot-tall black spikes demarking the edge of the Village was broken in many places, and the houses and shops of the Currents native to this era mingled freely with this last quarter. Their lanterns were smaller and swifter, like darting wasps of light, but otherwise not much changed.

Indeed some of the natives might have been old enough to recall nostalgic memories of houses of this shape and lights of this configuration in their youth; and, ironically, some of the native buildings or energy systems in the settlement beyond the fence line may have been older.

Both men, as if by unspoken signal, stopped just short of the line of broken spikes separating the Forever Village from the current town beyond. The quarter of the current town that crowded against the spaceman's village was a place of gaud shops and beer gardens, biomodification parlors, dance halls, and, worse, hallucination stalls and calamity houses, where jaded men in borrowed bodies could enjoy dangers imaginary or otherwise. The two men stood on a slight upswelling of land, so that the village behind and the ground before them was clearly seen in the blue-green light of the dying moon.

In some places along the line of demarcation, a straggle of panels dark with morbid heraldic signs warning of long-defunct penalties still connected one morose and watchful spike with its neighbor, forming a visible fence. But here on the crest of this small hill, weathering or looters or playful Foxes had torn and trampled the panels of the fence, so they tilted at strange angles, leaving wide gaps between like the spaces in a crone's teeth, or toppled over entirely, their circuits dead and lenses blind. Where this had happened, the fence was a fiction, and nothing stood between the starfaring men and the current world beyond.

"The largest and oldest graveyard on the planet is within walking distance." Norbert pointed.

In that direction were no fireflies at all. An unoccupied lane ran toward a broken well house. The only houses present near the well had folded themselves flat against the ground at sunset, in simple-minded obedience to the landscaping laws, centuries forgotten, of the Palatines who ruled before the rise of the Summer Kings.

Beyond were some nomadic tents occupied by Nemorals, little bubbles of leafy fabric that slowly moved across the grassy slopes keeping pace with a small flock of night-grazing ruminants. During the time of the Oneness, when all the trees and beasts of Earth had been a single bio-organism, their walking tents had been iron-sided pavilions covering acres and adorned with shields of warlords and skulls of foes. The Nemoral peoples had been more feared than earthquakes or asteroid strikes, and their hordes of mastodons doubled as cavalry, and the endless herds had trampled nations. These ghosts of forgotten conquerors loitered near spaceports, selling their daughters as breeding slaves to underpopulated worlds, while their sons played jigs for thrown pocket change, or told fortunes, or fixed cock fights, or cut purses. Long ago they had ceased to beg for passage to some far globe where they might find prairies wide and free.

Beyond this tent herd was a dark wood of pre-posthuman design called oak. The woodland fell away in a series of steep slopes and flat glades almost like steps. Perhaps some ancient river, now dry and vanished, had carved the land into oddly rectilinear shapes, or perhaps this was the residue of some ancient construction, or a convulsion of the layers of thinking material active beneath the planetary crust.

But in the further distance, a hill as flat-sided and steep-shouldered as a table stood out from the broken clefts and canyons of the woodland. In silhouette glinting in the aquamarine moonlight could be seen a tall steeple, peering between the trees.

"Behind the Chapel of Saint Joseph of Copertino is the Spaceman's Yard," Norbert intoned. "Yonder is the ossuary where the wealthy members of the order, driven mad with long faring across the Vasty Deep, insist on shipping their bones to this world to inter them. Think of the freight mass we could save if our guild brothers were less sentimental about the location of their last port of call!"

"And . . . have you picked out a headstone, sir?"

"Hardly! If I die on this senile world with its hellishly bright sun, I am having my bonesticks shipped home to Rosycross, so the flarelight can bake them clean of all your filthy diseases and leftover nanites from forgotten wars. That is my home. Why do you grin?"

"This is not a grin but a smile of goodwill, sir. I also do not wish my bones to rest on this world, or, come to think of it, anywhere."

8. The Worm of History

Norbert gazed at the squire speculatively.

"If you wish not to die, squire, then turn back."

"Do you still doubt me, sir?"

"You are an enigma, Squire End Ragon. Enigmas are a source of doubt during a duty like this, and doubt means hesitation, and hesitation means death."

"You, too, are an enigma, sir," the squire retorted. "This soil underfoot is officially part of outer space as much as a space station, as timeless as a tomb. In one step, we are officially on Earthly ground and in the current year, and our mission most illegal. Turn back yourself, Praetor, find an unmarked coffin, and slumber until the interdiction on Rosycross lifts. All the wives of the starfarers awaiting their return preserve their youth in just this way: the whole village is built on coffins. Finding one is easy."

"Enigma? I am lucidity itself: All these streets are all from Earthly history, and the lights, too glaring and too yellow, are meant for Terrestrial eyes. I cannot sleep here. The Guild is my only world now. The Guild is both my father and my ghost, and so I serve. But you are Earth-born. A thousand tiny clues betray you: every street through which we passed was strange to you. How can you be a stranger to all these years? The village is older than a millennium."

The squire said, with a small smile, "A millennium is nothing."

Norbert did not turn his head, but used sensitive pinpoints in his cloak surface to study the man's face and form carefully, both on the visible light bands, and higher and lower on the spectrum. Uneasiness moved like a sea beast below the surface of his mind, a shapeless fear, and he called upon the artificial part of his nervous system to impose courage.

"Which way, sir?" the squire inquired. "The wheel-road through the wood is patrolled, and the bridge to the Spaceman's Yard is watched, and the Swans forbid mortals to fly at night."

For in the distance, to the north, was a long curving line of floating lamps, clustered perhaps above some traffic on an unseen road. The line of lights curved through the woods, swinging wide to avoid the area of clefts and steep-sided dells, then climbed in a series of switchbacks, and finally leaped across an un-seen canyon in a smooth arch, paralleling a bridge that led to the high ground where the cathedral and the graveyard stood.

Norbert said, "We take a direct path. Avoid the oaks and walk near the dream-apple trees. The dream-apple is native to Rosycross, and will not report us. Did not the Starfaring Guild protect them from bio-revanchist Bacchants who sought to hew them down? The taller ones are old enough to remember that."

The squire said, "It is said to be dangerous to approach any graveyard except by gate. The curse of the Judge of Ages falls on those who trespass."

"Ah!" said Norbert. "The curse did not fall on Zolasto Zo, did it? If the curse is sensitive to bloodlines, it will spare me."

"Just you? Do you have a means to protect a loyal adjutant in your service from this curse?"

"If you trust me to rewrite the information aura surrounding your shed skin cells, yes. But that requires you shut off your genetic spoofing protection, what-ever you may have, and let me give you a temporary skin."

Without a word, the squire tapped a command on the red amulet he wore on his wrist, doffed his glove, rolled up his sleeve, and offer his arm to the as-sassin. Norbert drew his knife and pierced the vein in the squire's elbow. The squire scowled as cold sensations traveled up his arm to his heart.

"Interesting," Norbert observed. "I could have programmed any disease or neural change imaginable into that injection. Your nanomachinery cannot com-bat my picotechnology."

The squire said, "It is like a children's game, is it not? Atoms undermine mol-ecules which undermine machines which undermine men. But there is some-thing that undermines us all, and that is eternity. And yet I hear there is one man who has vowed to defeat eternity."

Norbert was wondering what the squire was driving at. "You speak of the Judge of Ages?"

The squire frowned, irked. "No. His vision is limited to the short term; his

motive is mere animal attraction, that spasm of brain chemicals called love. I am
speaking of the Master of the World, the Master of the Empyrean, the Master
of History, the Master of the Hidden and Hermetic Knowledge! His goal is to
overcome entropy! On that day, death itself shall die, and he shall call himself
the Master of Life, the King of Infinite Space and Lord of the Eschaton!"

"I cannot fault him for a dearth of ambition," said Norbert wryly. "But that
is quite a jawful of titles."

"Deserves he not all these and more? We would all be as extinct as apes were
it not for him, nor either Monument ever been known, nor a single snowflake
of antimatter been burned to uplift civilization. Our civilization sprang from
him, and Jupiter is his son."

Norbert nodded, then realized the gesture was invisible in his black mask and
voluminous hood. He said, "I see! And legend also names him as one of the two
founders of the Starfarer's Guild. You seem to be asking if I am loyal to him. I am."

"Then this is a day to rejoice. . . ."

"Of course," Norbert continued, musing, "the other founder is the Judge of
Ages. I am loyal to him, too, I suppose. To both of them, if they were real.
Hm? Why am I rejoicing this day?"

"Merely to the opportunity to serve an undying purpose of our Guild and
her wise and majestic founder. And her other founder, somewhat less majestic. But you doubt their reality? You think two such extraordinary men never
lived?"

"I think Menelaus Illation Montrose and Ximen Santiago Matamoros del
Azarchel are real men," said Norbert, "about whom many unreal legends have
gathered. And I also think that you are an abnormally trusting fellow."

"For believing in legends?"

"For letting me put you-know-not-what into your system."

"No, sir, I am only an abnormally good judge of character. Are we not both
loyal to the Guild? And if I am wrong, and you have imposed a neural worm
or a cataleptic trigger, you have less cause to mistrust me."

"Well, your skin will itch abominably over the next twenty minutes, and do
not scratch it, lest you break the skill and forfeit the imposture. Any nanite landing on you for a gene sample will think you are kin to Zolasto, hence whatever
Zolasto has done to stupefy the defensive measures will protect you, too."

Norbert turned his back on the man and walked on, tense and uncertain. He
summoned up his brashness to clear his mind and halt his glandular capacity for
fear.

The two moved through the tangled brush of the forest. Crooked branches
seemed to catch the blue-green moon in a net, and the shadows of branches

and twigs were thick enough that the squire, whose eyes could not pierce this gloom, walked in the footsteps of the assassin, whose eyes could.

Norbert made sure the other man was close behind him, too close for Norbert to parry a blow or a dirk in the dark should it come.

The ground was also rough and steep, and both men spent time scrambling down and scrabbling up pebbly slopes. Norbert noticed how easily one of them could have cast the other down a steep hillside to his death. He climbed as unwary as he believably could, and gave the other man every opportunity.

Norbert assumed that if the man were a Fox Maiden in disguise, and if all he had wanted was an immunity to pass into the Spaceman's Yard, Norbert was no longer necessary and would be struck down from behind.

But minutes passed and no attack came. That meant he was not a Ghost inhabiting a human body, hungry for human sensation, nor a Fox bent on mischief wearing the outward shape of a man.

That left two possibilities. One was that the squire was exactly what he seemed: a shallow Guild bravo from some very dangerous barbaric age assigned by the ship ghosts to help Norbert kill a holy man at a carnival.

The other was that this man was stranger than any Fox.

At the top of one of these sheer-sided slopes that broke the country the assassin paused. Norbert, a dark figure in a dark cloak, half invisible against the night sky, turned and pointed at the tall tower of the Starfaring Guild rising up bleak as a sword from the village lights.

Norbert said, "Look yonder. What do you see?"

"The Tower of the Guild. At its crown in the stratosphere is the port where the Sky Island docks. At its feet is the Forever Village, where the wives and dependents of sailors on cruise await their return, frozen in slumber. Sir? What has this to do with our mission?"

"I see the Tower of the Guild, the one unchanging stability rising above the Forever Village, where time makes all hopes vain and all dreams false. Do you know my dream, squire?"

"Sir? I would not presume—"

"We are going into danger and death. Let us know each other. My dream is this: A hearth of my own, and a fertile wife and a fertile orchard, and a myriad of children to carry my soul into futurity; a sun into whose eye I can as an equal gaze; and, best of all, never to tread the stars again, nor sail the dizzying abyss of night. This means I must not die because of some dangerous or useless officer who replaced my trusted adjutant."

"My dream is somewhat larger, sir, involving more people and a greater span of time. But it also involves a woman, a wife I have picked out for myself. I will explain myself if you trust me so far as the graveyard."

Norbert now turned away from the distant lights of the village, stepped down from the crown of the slope, took the squire's elbow. "Fair enough. Answer without dissimilation what I ask of you. If I prove unable to judge your character, I rule me unfit to judge Hieronymus the Sacerdote, and recuse myself."

The squire made an elegant half bow, and waved his hand with a flip of his wrist toward the distant steeple. "Lead on. The grave awaits. Perhaps we will find the mountebank there, or old friends and lovers. I will tell my history as we go, and all will be made clear."

2

The Antepenultimate White Ship

1. An Empyrean in Sagittarius

"I am from the earliest strata of starfaring tradition, from before when the Guild was properly a guild. I was a crewman aboard the Sagittarius Arm Expedition, when the Master of All Worlds sent the Antepenultimate White Ship to the Omega Nebula.

"The White Ship was a half mile from bow to stern, massed one million tons displacement, and had a sail diameter of five thousand miles. Every inch was made of the artificial element alchemists call *argent*, which is brighter than diamond and harder than steel, armor to withstand the deadliest high-frequency energy or ultra-massive particle into which near-lightspeed flight transforms harmless light and dust.

"We launched in a.d. 15177 as the Sacerdotes reckon years, back when the Myrmidons were newborn, zealous and unafflicted with their deathlust; back when the Earth had lost her magnetosphere, and the sun was poisonous, so Man and Swan alike dared not emerge save in the dark hours of the Benighted Earth.

"We had resolved, as befits the ambition of starfarers, not to allow entropy, history, nor oblivion overtake us, but to prove our high purpose could oppose and overcome that grim assassin, Father Time.

"In a.d. 29024, after the Myrmidons fled to Cyan from the Ghost-haunted

Hierophants, and the Graciousness ruled Earth in soft embrace, we were remembered of great Jupiter, and the Penultimate White Ship was launched toward us, across the gulf of starlessness severing the Orion Arm from the Sagittarius Arm.

"The miracle happened again, for although our descendants forsook us, Peacock the Power of Delta Pavonis recalled, and the Splendid Lords mortgaged their world to fund the launch of a.d. 40522. The newborn Fox Maidens were gnawing at the hawsers of civilization then, and at this time Tellus went mad. All his seas were filled with ink of alcahest, the sludge of sociopathic nanite swarms, and any ship or swimming man who ventured there was warped and made strange, and all the fish were nightmares.

"That ship was the Ultimate and Last. Broken and exiled, we returned in a.d. 50822, in time to precipitate the Snow Wars, and equip the Armigers and Ecologists to overthrow the haunted palaces beneath the sea.

"Therefore three tours I served, crossing five thousand years in a year. The steepest time-slips of the oldest hand on the swiftest ship here in the First Empyrean are as nothing to me.

"The Sagittarius Arm is a golden realm, richer in every way than this Orion Arm we occupy. That Arm is thick with giant molecular clouds and H II regions of partially ionized gas, useful for ramscoop flight. The short-lived blue stars born in these regional clouds shed copious ultraviolet light into the surrounding medium, which helps both planetary accretion and aids the condensation of interstellar amino acid precursor molecules. But the richest jewel in the Sagittarius Arm is the Omega Nebula, for it is the most massive star-forming region in the Milky Way. And where the stars are made in great numbers, so too are worlds.

"In the center of the nebula, orbiting the binary named Kleinmann's Anonymous Star, was a living Monument. One star of the binary pair was made of terrene matter, the other of contraterrene: magnetically channeled shocks of solar wind produce a region of hard X-rays between them. Neither man nor machine could survive there: we removed the Second Monument to a gentler region.

"But the Anonymous Star was not abandoned! We craved the contraterrene fuel source. There I saw a world colder than Pluto and larger than Jupiter conquered, and that Gas Giant's core was burrowed through with nanomachine and picomachines and made to come awake. We called him Villaamil. He was our god, and the first of our pantheon.

"Next came we to where, long ago cast out from the epicenter of the Omega Nebula by the violence of its own explosion, the blue hypergiant V4030 Sagittarius soared roaring through space, two hundred twenty thousand times brighter

than the sun. Here we made our throne world, and called it Tintagel, towing
the Second Monument to become its moon, so that all our scholars need but
look up after sunset to see its hieroglyphs.

"And when the stellar eruptions of V4030 Sagittarius periodically grew too
violent, we would retreat for a time to its twin sister star, the hypergiant V4029.
There we colonized bright worlds and dark, and dubbed them Avalon and
Aachen, Trethevy and Trevena, and redesigned our bodies to accommodate the
sixty-four-day flare cycle. But brightest of all was Golden Tintagel, Tintagel
the Beautiful.

"Between those two powerful stars, like migratory birds, we would sail our
worlds and worldlets as living ships, bright as pearls on a chain of office, letting the atmospheres turn to ice during transit, and seas turn solid. Both these
hypergiant stars had hundreds of failed stars of ordinary size and superjovians
in their planetary clouds, material enough to make ourselves Gas Giant Brains
to read the Second Monument, and penetrate the secrets of its eleven-dimensional
interior volume.

"For pantheons we made. Merlin and Malagige we christened them our dei-
ties, Archimago and Atalanta, Lorelei and Logistilla, Vivian and Virgil. These
were sages larger than worlds, comprising a volume greater than a million Earths.

"Sol was forgotten: our ambition was to create a new human history, established on wiser cliometric foundations than Earthly history could produce, and
spread rapidly from world to world in the Sagittarian Arm, leaving the indentured Earth and her woes to oblivion. We had infinite wealth from a star made
of antimatter, and the secrets of a Second Monument for our gods to read and
contemplate—what could we not accomplish?

"Many ventures were made, and in the Omega Nebula we found worlds remarkably Earth-like, suited for Swans and Men, with blue skies and bluer seas,
and finding asteroid belts absurdly rich with minerals, apposite for Myrmidons.
It was almost as if a race of unseen fairies had stocked the larder of the universe with good things for our consumption, arranging a stellar nursery where
Earth-like worlds could not help but be formed. Ninety new earths for man we
formed or found.

"How brightly flamed the midnights on any one of them, those emerald-
bright earths! As the gigantic and multicolored suns set across the towering landing craft or space elevators and cast purple twilight across the self-aware gardens
with fall of night would rise, adorned with stars like the uplifted limbs of an
odalisque with gems, the auroras and auras of the nebula as arms of fire more
splendid than a peacock's tail! How poor and blank is Earth's dull sky to eyes
that drank such wonders!

"But in a single day of wrath, those colonies died, every one, to the last child, the last bloodcell. As we sailed back from Presterion, the most distant of the ninety worlds, to our golden home in Tintagel, forty years in a single night, I heard the colonies perish, for our vessel passed through the expanding shock waves of the radio messages calling in vain, years of pain overheard in half a dozen sleepless watches.

"It was a strange beam that caught and decelerated us. I saw the smoldering hemispheres of our gods, the dust cloud blackening fair Tintagel, and everything destroyed by the Furies of the Sagittarian Arm. Theirs was a vessel that seemed like a wheel of fire half a solar system in diameter, and wheels within wheels, and eyes along each rim and at each hub.

"The vessel was too bright on any wavelength for any of our instruments to behold, and all our lenses cracked and recording chips burned. The wheel of eyes created sunspots and dark trails in the surface of the sun and wrote in the signs and sine waves of the Monument notation, and they commanded us, in the name of the Archon called *Circumincession*, who was the living mind housed throughout the stars and empires of the Sagittarius Arm, to cleanse our ruins again with all our hands, to leave behind no trace of our false polity save those too fine for the patientest archeologist to find: gather up our remnants and our dead, and be returned to the jurisdiction of M3 in the Orion Arm.

"The worlds we had occupied were already set aside for races not yet evolved, and filled by caretakers we had not noticed nor understood. We were too stupid to know that the green land on which we walked was brain matter, or the still lakes through which we swam were thinking fluid. We did not detect the immense energy they used to signal their distant masters. All the years of the flourishing of the Second Empyrean was merely the interval while the swiftest of messages reached the nearest of strongholds of the fleetest living vessels of the Fury.

"Why so swift? So terrible? We learned that the Orion Arm is a region which Sagittarius regards with distaste, for we are tainted by some ancient crime committed by the Dominions here before the dinosaurs walked the Earth.

"The Ultimate White Ship was flung back to Sol on a beam of contempt, as a message for Orion not to interfere with the terrain claimed by the more civilized arms of the Milky Way.

"The caravan of lesser ships and worldlets we were allowed to keep perished in the journey, or fell behind, or starved just beyond our reach, or to this hour wander somewhere, populations frozen in eternal slumber, in the wide and starless interrupt separating that arm of the galaxy from this.

"Sagittarius did not even realize, or did not care, that we acted independently of Hyades. The Hyades is held responsible for the interstellar history issuing from the Local Interstellar Cloud and the surrounding volume of space. If events occur which Hyades did not anticipate, Hyades must amend. If tiny seeds from tiny worlds escape from the wild, weed-choked and untended garden of Orion Arm into the neat and well-tended fields of our neighbors, the farmer, not the mustard seed, is blamed."

The squire raised his eyes to the dark heavens, the blue-green moon, the cold scattering of stars, and cried out in mourning.

"Alas for Tintagel! How I remember her! Tintagel the Golden-Bright; Tintagel the Fair! We called her *Chrysolucent* and *Mater Mundi* and a hundred other names. The entire world from pole to pole was a fortress, every fulvous tree held a siege-gun, all yellow blooms antennae, tawny grass ranging gear, and the statues of heroes were heroes indeed, white with slumber and awaiting a day of war. Never before had so much of the military arts been lavished on one small globe, nor has any palace of a warrior king ever been so fair.

"She was snuffed like a spark between finger and thumb. The giant planet Villaamil was shattered into asteroids, and the debris fell into the variable star, provoking outrageous solar flares like rivers of fire across the inner system. I do not think the Furies even saw the tiny world of Tintagel as she was destroyed."

Beneath his mask, Norbert turned pale. "Mankind is a small matter indeed."

"We will not always be so. Better to burn the galaxy than to allow it to dismiss us."

2. Conquering Constellations

The two men began to climb the oddly shelf-like rises of ground leading upward to the tableland on which the cathedral lay. In the distance to one side, like a black ribbon against the golden moon, could be seen the bridge connecting the tableland to the wheel-road leading from the Forever Village. There were no lights above the bridge at the moment, for it was empty of traffic.

The squire spoke, "Sir, do you still wonder why I am with you? I can be trusted because whatever you decide, I will support. None of the events of the First Empyrean Polity of Man, as you call your pathetic puddle of sixty-eight worlds of sixty-two stars, mean anything to me. I am perhaps the only man in all the Guild who cares nothing about the calendar reform, or about snipers lurking in the abandoned mansions of the asteroid belt."

"So," said Norbert finally. "You can be trusted because everything you love is dead?"

"Because everything I love is not yet born."

"Meaning?"

"You told your dream, sir. It is only fitting I tell mine. The component races who form the architects and constituents of the intricate rivers and oceans of self-aware information flowing from star to star of Sagittarius were once, in times long past, biological creatures just as we are now. The Circumincession of Sagittarius has stood with my neck beneath its bootheel. In times to come, the proportion must be reversed, be that time soever long as it must be. That day is far, but it must come."

"Revenge against minds that dwarf the constellations? You are mad."

"All who love are mad, are they not?" said the squire with his most charming and disarming smile.

3. Calendar Revision

The two climbed a steep and barren slope to an oddly regular acreage of grasses and groves that stood up from the broken land around it like a table of greenery.

The final slope was so steep it was practically a cliff, and covered with loose pebbles and rotten rock, impossible to climb. The squire tapped the cliff and shouted out a command or two, and there was no response. The rock remained obdurate.

Norbert drew his glassy knife and made a shallow cut in the surface. There was no visible change, but a slight, small scent of ozone hung in the air, and the radioactivity detectors that were part of every spaceman's uniform clicked a warning. Norbert said, "I have imposed a mandala of deception on the soil, and it thinks we are lawful. It will bear us."

The squire looked honestly astonished. "Sir, I must ask, by what authority do you accomplish this? Where did you get that knife?"

Norbert said, "It is an ancestral blade."

The squire again put his hand on the cliff face, and, with a grating whisper of noise, a series of knobs and handholds and well-spaced footholds appeared in the rock, as small segments rose or sank. This line of footholds upward blended in nicely with the surrounding landscape, no doubt obeying whatever regulations, left over from centuries or millennia past, which might be controlling the appearance and protecting the copyright of the original landscape.

During such a climb, dawn-age men would have been out of breath and unable to speak. Guild sailors were not so limited: both men increased the oxygen gain to their bloodstream from implanted capsules, and switched to silent nerve-radio signals.

"This channel is shielded and encrypted," sent Norbert, "so that half of my own brain cannot tap the communication. We have tricks on Rosycross that mad Tellus has not dreamed."

"Sir, with respect, it is not enough to fool Jupiter. The oaks are more sensitive to energy signals than to speech."

"What do these human doings mean to him? Here is privacy enough for our business."

"As you say. I am comfortable with your decision, sir," sent the squire in a most uncomfortable voice.

"You say you have no concern for Earthly things. What do you know of the real roots of the Calendar Revision?"

"Those roots are very old indeed. The Heresiarch Lemur in the Forty-seventh Millennium, when the Shapetakers ruled the Earth, he did not begin the controversy; nor did the Prophetess Lares in the Thirty-eighth, who claimed to be in mental-energy contact with a self-awareness from beyond the rim of the galaxy.

"The trouble began earlier, before the Third Sweep," the squire continued. "It was the Swan-Man halfbreed Photinus in the Thirty-sixth Millennium who is to blame, for it is he who first raised the possibility that Shcachlil the Salamander by interfering with the orbits of inner worlds, had thrown off the count of years since Rania's departure, and he who first pointed out the inadequacy of records about her departure.

"Revisionism was put down bloodily, and then, as heresies do, mutated to preserve itself, divaricated, slept, sent out spores, and bloomed again. By the time of Lemur, it was not just calendar reform the Revisionists wanted, but the entire cliometric scheme of history rewritten from now until the Eschaton. They demanded the psychology of human and posthuman be standardized and simplified for ease of prediction and administration. For this reason the Eidolons were made, a failed attempt at creating a Fourth Humanity."

Norbert said, "The Lemurians justified this crime by saying human history was too volatile. Thank goodness the Fox Maidens became the Fourth Men instead."

The squire said, "Crime? I see you do not care for Eidolons."

"They were not unknown on Rosycross. All their gestures the same, all their opinions the same, and their eyes are blank as corpses when they smile. They are born as brother-sister twins, each chemically programmed to mate with the other, and produce no more than two children. A more contumacious affront to the marriage laws of Rosycross cannot be imagined! I consider them less than beasts. What else do you know of Revisionism?"

"I know it is a disease that afflicts the great as well as the meek. I know the Lords of the Golden Afternoon themselves once fought duels over the calendar, using time as their weapon. I know Tellus and Jupiter and outer Potentates have allowed limited forms of warfare, fought with archaic weapons, and forced all sides to abide by agreed rendezvous of battle and armistice, both on Earth and interplanetary space. I know Odette and Odile of the double star 61 Cygni became involved in interplanetary battle, and after Splendor of Delta Pavonis and Nocturne of Epsilon Eridani sent crusaders Earthward when the Foxes called. I know mankind's first and only interstellar war was fought with the punctilious chivalry one might expect, when the assaulted world has to be polite enough to ignite a deceleration laser and slow the vessels carrying enemy paladins and cataphracts destined for the field of honor."

Norbert was surprised. "But how else could wars be fought? The besieged must spend the energy cost to welcome the attackers, or else they could not expect their counterattack to be decelerated and welcomed in return. Cliometry would punish whoever broke the chivalric code."

"Perfect Starfaring logic, my dear sir! I am glad I have lived to see an era when men can no longer imagine any other way of conducting their business."

Norbert said nothing, but wondered what kind of barbaric age this man came from.

The squire sent, "I happen to know Earth was driven insane because he sided with the Revisionists. The Foxes took him."

Norbert said, "I was taught the Fourth Man theo-neurologists meant to expand the capacity of Tellus?"

"If so, they expanded Tellus beyond the bounds of sanity into weird new realms."

"Tellus asked it of them! Begged, if my loremaster's lash back home is to be believed."

"Implying Tellus partway insane to start," the squire said sardonically. "The rest of the calendar heresies can be summed up in a word: astronomers have debated for ten thousand years the meaning of certain X-ray anomalies seen in the direction of Canes Venatici. Either Rania departed immediately or was long delayed. The evidence is thin, and even the Potentates do not agree; but there simply is no energy budget to ignite the beam at both times. One side or the other must prevail. The Guild dare not take sides. Hence the need for discretion, sir. It must look like an accident, or a lawful duel, or an act of the Judge of Ages."

But Norbert sent, "The window during which we can compensate for a delayed ignition by lighting a brighter starbeam narrows and closes within the century. And what if the Revisionists are wrong?"

"Such is life."

"Such is death, you mean. If the breaking starbeam is not ignited on schedule, then the Vindicatrix of Man will pass through the Solar System. From our frame of reference her ship is a scintilla shy of lightspeed, which means to us she would seem to be a disk-shaped black hole, flattened in the direction of motion like a pancake, so far red-shifted that her highest-pitched X-ray emissions will be radio too deep to detect, not even with an antenna half a lightyear long. And she will carry near-infinite gravity in her wake. Such an object passing through the system would throw the inner planets from their orbits. You still say the matter means nothing to you?"

"Sir, with respect, I saw ninety worlds die in Sagittarius. What are three more?"

"But you believe she returns?"

The squire sighed and looked upward. "As a man of honor, I can do nothing else but believe. I vowed long ago never to lose faith in the return of Rania or hope in the Vindication of Man."

"Why such a vow?"

"An annoying upstart oaf, in each way my inferior, with a psittacine nose and an agrestic accent, would gain face and favor over me, if she returned and he held faith while I failed. My honor says she is returning even if Jupiter himself says otherwise."

Norbert was surprised at the squire's vehemence. "But Jupiter is wiser than all men and all lesser worlds combined."

"Even so, he did not exist when she launched, so he does not truly know her."

Norbert allowed himself to become distracted. This was a question he had often pondered. "Did civilization exist before Jupiter? A time when only Archangels ruled mankind?"

"There was a time when the Hermeticists ruled men, and before that, men ruled themselves."

"And, before that, monkeys ruled men, I suppose? Absurd. Cliometric calculation is too complex for merely sub-posthuman minds to address—so how could there be any human history before there was control of history?"

"Men lived their history blindly in those days, not knowing what was coming."

"You can hardly call that *history*."

"Well, sir, if I may, the discovery of cliometry must by definition be an historical event cliometry did not make. In such times the strong make of history whatso they will."

"The Summer Kings teach that cliometry is a survival from an ulterior and previous universe, one where time did not pass, on the grounds that cliometry must have existed before historical events for it to plan. The first event was the plan by the ulterior beings to create created reality."

"There may be a paradox in that reasoning somewhere," said the squire blandly.

"They also teach that Jupiter was created by the Salamander, who was created by Hyades, who was created in turn by higher beings created by this cosmic cliometry. Jupiter designed the Tellus at the core of the Earth who designed the Archangels of the surface, who designed the Angels and Ghosts of the Noösphere, who designed the Swans and other posthumans, who designed the lesser forms of Man, who designed the Dog Things, Cetaceans, and other Moreaus."

The squire's reply betrayed a restrained note of supercilious amusement. "I must say the theory has a certain hierarchical elegance to it."

Now they climbed up to the brink of the cliff, and with some effort, calling a tree to bend a branch to help them (which it obligingly did), soon they stood on the edge of the grass-covered table of land. They did not pant and puff, but both restored the oxygen capsules in their bloodstreams with a mental command and a single very long indrawn breath.

They now could walk shoulder to shoulder. Norbert sent, "I have also heard what the Foxes teach. They say the Salamander did not make the Inner Worlds. They say Earth was built by man; although they never say where man stood to do this deed. They also say the Earth was once a horse." Norbert saw the squire smile at that. He also saw the smile vanish when he continued: "And they also say men should be free."

"Sir, with respect, you traffic with ideas best left untouched. Heresy clings like tar."

Onward they passed through pathless wood, their footfalls as silent as those of stags.

4. The Tribulations

The cathedral was not visible, for tall trees blocked the view, but the squire's internal navigation sense pointed the direction. Norbert hesitated, and the squire said, "Sir? There is a satellite feed. Can you not get a picture?"

"I am under Interdict. The Noösphere of Tellus is closed to me."

"What? Just sign on under a different identity. Any wretched Fox vixen will aid a human to do this, if he merely commits one felony or three misdemeanors."

"And do I sign on under a different code of honor? Perhaps one where I disobey lawful orders?"

"You are voluntarily disconnected?" Now the squire ignited his charming smile again. "I did not know being an assassin was so much like being a priest."

They set off again, this time with the squire in the lead.

"The vow of abstinence is one I did not take, although, thanks to the erratic nature of earthwomen, it is one I suffer."

"Ah! Women! Women cause difficulties." The squire gave a shrug of fluid insouciance. "Some men are foolish enough even to fight rivals for mates, never imagining how the struggle will consume their souls and waste long years of time. Perhaps you are better off."

"Life causes difficulties. Some men are foolish enough to struggle for it. Are the dead better off?" snapped Norbert.

"That deep question is the one I hope never to be in a position to answer. So, then, you have told me two different accounts of history. Between Summer Kings and Fox Queen, whom do you trust?"

"The Summer King version is more plausible. One need only glance at the Firstling forms of man, Nyctalops and Hibernals, and see that they were artificially designed. The Guild keeps alive half-extinct species, Sylphs and Chimerae and Giants, who are useful for the hardships of shipboard work. They are as clearly manmade as the ships themselves."

"So you think mankind was designed, not evolved?" the squire asked wryly.

"During your horrible daytimes, I think so. How could humanity have evolved on a world whose sun no one could stand to see? At night, I do not doubt that man's evolution had occurred here—I have suffered too many allergies to doubt that this world has been preying on man longer than any other—but I think to have selected this as the world on which to evolve shows a lapse in judgment."

"We should lodge a complaint."

"In any case, the formation of the planets is not natural: it can be no coincidence that Earth and Venus are exactly the right distance from the Sun to support life, and Mars just happens to have a surface crisscrossed with canals and a subsurface with volcanic heat-vents?"

"The Salamander of Hyades reengineered the Inner System. He created nothing."

"Then you believe the Fox Maidens?"

"Not in every particular." The squire spoke sardonically.

"You seem not to favor the Fourth Humans," Norbert said.

"They inflicted madness on history, from the day when the Salamander was lost. It has been a time of tribulations since then."

Norbert thought carefully over what the squire had said, turning the matter in his mind this way and that, wondering at this man's strange combination of clear knowledge about great matters, but inexplicable dimness about simple matters like cloaks and trees and knives.

A wild speculation rose up like a wine bubble in him, so outrageous that, like a bubble, it threatened to tickle him to laughter. Through the surface of his capes shoulder fabric, he studied the man laboring through the pathless wood in the night next to him. Norbert was struck again by the strangely archaic nature of his features and body language.

"Speaking to you is an interesting experience, squire. I have never met someone so traditionalist in belief. You say the Master of the World is true, and so is the Judge of Ages, and the Swan Princess—and now the Salamander in the sun is also?"

The squire gave him an odd and sidelong squint. "Our histories are filled with their doings from the Second Space Age onward. The calendar counts down from the date of Rania's launch."

"You think these events *literally* happened? Duels between underworld judges and heavenly moons; the creation of the races; the burning of the world; the cursed tombs and promises of duels renewed; and stealing stars from the sky? The princess assumed into heaven with a promise to return and free mankind? All this is figurative, surely, based on myths of dying and returning grain gods. Science is based on evidence."

"An eyewitness is not evidence?" asked the squire, with a twinkle of repressed mirth in his eye.

"Those old accounts were written long ago, by men who lack our modern views. As for evidence: Who has seen the Salamander?"

"No man has seen the Salamander in the sun, because it is no longer in the sun. So long ago that Beta Ursae Minoris was the pole star, without explanation, in a fashion neither Potentate nor Power predicted, the Virtue we call the Salamander set forth from the depth of Sol in an eruption of fire, sailed across the Solar System, and was never seen again. After this, the tribulations began, and the Long Golden Afternoon turned dark. Three millennia of misery followed."

Something about his tone caught Norbert's attention: what about those years was so significant to this squire, whoever he truly was? There could not be many men to whom those long-vanished years were still important.

It was a first clue. He could not be what he said. A crewman of the expedition in Sagittarius would indeed have no interest in recent history, no plans for the future. So who was he?

"Is that so?" Norbert said noncommittally. "Go on."

"On? There is not much to say. Each scepter was worse than the previous, and the world groaned under the despotism or folly of Shapetakers, Immortals, Vassals, Lectors, Parthenocrats, and finally Palatials. The Golden Lordship was reduced to mere figurehead and ritual offices, controlling neither decision nodes nor cliometric attractor basins. Like the imperial family of the Japanese under the Shogunate or the Military or the Diet, the rulers watched helplessly as their so-called vicars reigned."

"I don't recognize those names," said Norbert, still holding his voice casual. "*Parthenocrats* or *Japanese*. Earth is not my world."

"The Shapetakers ruled when wild Fox Maidens interbred the castes and quadrupled the lifespan of man and quintupled the beauty of women. After them ruled the Immortalists, exiled from 61 Cygni, whose minds are far modified beyond the legal human norm, and claim not to need the fear of death to give their lives meaning. The Vassals were peasants whose fathers were talking animals. Their respect for expertise allowed them easily to be beguiled by the corrupt Lectors of the Analects, who ruled the Earth next with such brutal incompetence. Then cunning Fox Maidens wed to Swan Mages created the Parthenocracy, perhaps in imitation of the lost Heirophancy, perhaps in mockery, and seemed to tame the Foxes. This won Jupiter's favor and patronage; so the Swan-Fox hybrids were granted strange powers by Jupiter, overturned the Lectors, and ruled both sea and sky and solar system.

"This decision Jupiter soon came to regret," continued the squire, "for the Fox-blood half-breeds reappeared in later generations, and they were far more fierce and free than any reticent Swan could be. Against them, Jupiter stirred up the ghosts of long-extinct Cetaceans still dwelling in abyssal palaces beneath the sea. The Palatials squeezed honor and ancient liberties out from all charters, till every Fox, Swan, ghost, prince, yeoman, serf, dolphin, dog, arbor, tree, and flower wept. Such were the conditions before the Final White Ship returned, and the Master of the World, and we his men, descended in wrath, and saw to the overthrow of all these ages."

"Unleashing hell."

"The Snow Wars were but purgatory. It was three thousand years of anarchy and tyranny between the flight of the Salamander and the fall of the palaces beneath the sea."

"But, honestly, Squire End Ragon, was anything accomplished? Is the world better now? Whoever defies a Summer King lives in winter, dies in famine, and tornadoes scatter all his flotillas or all his towers uproot—and none can petition the Retaliator of Jupiter, who crouches like a sphinx, vast and blind and smiling, at the South Pole, for weather control abrogates no weapon laws. This means the Golden Lords are still figureheads. Even the elevation of the Patricians to Lordship positions did not change that. The golden calculations no longer have the power to throw down tyrants. Do not the Summer Kings still retain a veto power over the prognostic nodes that form in the cliometric manifold?"

"The Golden Lords no doubt encountered some chaotic factor slowing their calculations. The Aestevalarchy is a transitional stage to the Golden return to power." The squire shrugged, looking nonchalant. Norbert, through the sensor points in his cloak, detected the muscular and neural actions betraying the emotion in the other man as clearly as a red-face scowl of anger.

This was a second clue. One step closer to the center of the puzzle, then. The Long, Golden Afternoon of Man was precious to this man. Why?

5. Fate and Chaos

Norbert wondered how far he could dare. If this man suspected Norbert were sniffing at the edges of his disguise, what would prevent him from throwing off his imposture with a gesture of superb disdain, and drawing his deadly, cold-voiced pistol? Despite Norbert's boast about picotechnology, a stiletto could not parry a pistol blast.

The danger lured rather than repelled. So Norbert said, "You said something had thrown off the cliometric calculations: a chaos factor. There are always rumors of minor adjustments needed for the Lords of the Golden Afternoon to thread their disagreement back into harmony, or recalculate unforeseen glitches in the manifold. But you seem to indicate it is worse than this?"

"I said no such thing," muttered the squire.

"Can anything hinder the cliometry? It is not a human invention."

"Something is hindering it. Why has the discovery of cliometry not long ago have reached a halt-state similar to the Cold Equations of the aliens? Their society never changes."

Norbert said, "Nor does ours, except in eternals. Mankind repeats the same suicidal folly, eternally. History is the dragon who forever devours itself by its tail. Neither biotechnology nor xypotechnology nor any improvement in tools can change human nature."

"You are mistaken. You must be."

"Why?" asked Norbert.

"The duel between the Judge of Ages and the Master of the World prevents the end of history. We have never reached a stable and self-perpetuating future because those two cannot agree on a future. History ends when one of them kills the other," said the squire.

"That will not end history. They are not so important. They are men. Underfoot and overhead are machines so much vaster of intellect than they, that we call them angels and gods."

"Machines based on forms those two devised. History will reach an end, for better or worse. The better is that the Swan Princess returns from beyond the stars to restore the world to peace and truth. Mankind submits to the rules she imposes, and enters into the pleasures of the futures she designs for them. If that submission is unwilling at first, there will be one final war after which war will be forgotten forever, and any enormities committed then are justified by the joy and prosperity to follow. That is a happy ending."

"What is the worse?"

"Mankind goes extinct, and the machine life made by the Master of the World replicates itself endlessly and spreads infinitely throughout timespace. That is a happy ending, but not for man."

Norbert said, "Why has not Jupiter, if great Jupiter is so great, brought about one of these two halt-states of history, the serenity of peace or the serenity of extinction? If he is so godlike, why does he let us suffer?"

The squire looked left and right. In the gloom, there was an oak tree not far away, its thick and gnarled branches raised in a menacing fashion. "You know the local plans of Judges of Decades for each ten-year span, and the Judge of Centuries for each hundred," he said blandly. "Men control their own fates."

"What of plans for longer than mortal lifespans?"

The squire spoke in a voice polite and remote. "Such things concerns the Potentates and Powers, and mortals are unwise to fret."

That was the third step closer. Norbert was not sure what was at the center of the maze, but its rough outline was clear enough.

Jupiter had lost control of human history.

6. The Second Power of Sol

Where was the source of opposition to Jupiter? Norbert dismissed the possibility that a Potentate or Archangel could outwit a brain larger than worlds. The opponent was a Power.

In his mind he counted off the other gas giants which had been converted to sophont matter between the Thirty-second and the Forty-third Millennium: Cerulean of 82 Eridani; Peacock of Delta Pavonis; Immaculate of Altair; Twelve of Tau Ceti; Vonrothbarth of 61 Cygni, the double star of the double planets Odette and Odile. Atramental of Epsilon Eridani he did not count, for the Gas Giant Brain created by the men of Nocturne had gone mad and destroyed itself.

And there was one other, not so far away. It had first revealed itself in the Fifty-first Millennium.

Norbert waited until they had walked farther, and no oak trees were near. "You speak of a chaos factor in history. The Foxes say that Jupiter is no friend of man, but that the newborn Power in Neptune is, and one day will supplant him. The Summer Kings call Neptune a rival to Jupiter, one never to equal him. When Neptune reaches full growth in the Sixty-first Millennium, his intelligence will be one hundred million, less than half what Jupiter currently enjoys."

The squire looked at him in puzzlement, but with no sign of suspicion on his features. "Neptune cannot be the source of the tribulations inflicted on mankind four thousand years before his creation. What is your question, sir? Speak more plainly."

"Does Neptune hinder Jupiter, as the Fox Maidens claim?"

"As a lapdog hinders a bear, perhaps," snorted the squire. "Neptune has entered a period of somnolence and internal reorganization which theopsychologists speculate is akin to REM sleep. They say he will not wake until the Fifty-sixth Millennium."

"Neptune sleeps?"

"It was Jupiter's doing. He imposed an indication of logic into a subduction layer of Neptunian psychology, which was slowly drawn into his core brain. It is the same fate Great Jupiter decreed to Atramental of Epsilon Eridani."

"Why are men told nothing of this?"

"Men are happier when the doings of the Great Powers are unknown, lest they realize they are but cargo in the cattlehold of the vessel of time, and kick at the walls."

Norbert thought of Nochzreniye, his adjutant. He must never come to know that the madness of the Power his people and their living planet Nocturne had slaved so diligently and lovingly for so long to create had been an act of murder. To love and lose a god was a sorrow civilizations did not throw off, not in numberless generations. The tragedy of Atramental hung behind the psychology, the songs and humor of solemn resignation for which the mournful Nocturnals were famed. But to have been inflicted *deliberately*?

Norbert sought for a way to reject the horror. "But Neptune speaks!" he said, weakly.

"Indeed. The high-level metasymbolic responses his orbital archangelic servants translate to mid-level symbols for Swans to carry as symbols to us all come from the first half-mile of his logic diamond surface, no deeper. These are as the words of a man talking in his sleep. To creatures of our humble intellect, of course, the difference between the statements of a fully formed intelligence at the one hundred million level, and the dazed or damaged intelligence fallen to the one million level, operating at one percent of capacity, cannot be discriminated."

Norbert wondered how this man knew things hidden from the Archangels. His wild speculation was beginning to seem the only logical possibility.

7. The Fourth and Fifth Humans

Norbert said, "The origin of the Second Power is shrouded with mystery. There is no evidence of his existence before the Fifty first Millennium of the Sacerdotal Calendar. Who built Neptune?"

"What do you know, sir?"

Norbert recalled an old annual from his middle-term memory. "It is said that the greatest of the Patricians, a segment of their sovereign mind named Cnaeus, once upon a time arranged the downfall of the Crusader Kingdom on the moon, without firing a shot. The remnant fled to Mars as the terraforming failed, and so began the slow loss of Luna's artificial atmosphere, one of the Seven Wonders of the System. To this day, the seas founded by the Prestor Aiven are sublimating from ice to a vapor which escapes into space." He pointed upward at the blue-green orb. "The moon, which has been the hue of an emerald for all of history, will one day pale to the hue of a pearl, and glare across your world like a skull."

"It has not been *all* of history," commented the squire pedantically, "but only since the Sacerdotes of Altair sent Knights Hospitalier to Sol thirteen millennia ago, and slew the followers of Lares. Perhaps when the frozen lunar seas vanish, now that the remnants of the Asmodel Cenotaph are gone, we will see the handprint again which once graced that globe, an emblem and an omen hung high over this world to show in whose hand this world rests. Ah! But pray continue the tale, sir."

"Selene was in grief when her surface died, and imposed a strict penance. Cnaeus had exiled himself to the ring arcs of Uranus, far beyond where Potentate or Power could observe him, in order to suffer the purifying agony of isolation, to do the useful work of exploration, and remit the spiritual debt for distortions he had introduced into the cliometry of the inner system. Beyond all hope, he found a wonder: wandering moons left over from the chaos of the Second Sweep, including logic crystals of immense size containing the instructions to aid the birth of Jupiter. Convinced this was a sign, he armed the birthing moons and sent them on wide and secret orbits to collide with Neptune, striking the far side where no eyes saw."

"Do you believe that story?"

"No. Assassins do not believe in coincidences. Someone sent Cnaeus the Patrician to the Outer System where no man goes, and someone set the moons for him to find. Whoever made the moons fathered Neptune. If Neptune is meant to supplant Jupiter, then the opposition issues from the race who opposes all forms of authority and control."

The squire said, "The Second Humans?"

"No, squire. Swans merely withdraw when rules and regulations gather like vultures, for they are too fine and austere to fight superior beings themselves."

"Who, then? The Fourth Humans?" But he said it too casually. The squire's expression sharpened, as if he were balanced halfway between eagerness and caution.

"Indeed. Your tone betrays you. Would you have preferred the Eidolons to take the position of Fourth of Man?"

"Bah! I have no love for Fox Maidens."

Norbert did not reply, uncertain what to say. Something of paramount importance to the squire was at hand, but what? Norbert felt it was another blind step closer to the center.

"Who designs a race of all women, who all reproduce by parthenogenesis?" the squire spoke suddenly and loudly. "Think of it! Females without husbands and fathers—what could they be but shallow and erratic? And malign!"

Norbert said mildly, "We have Foxes also on Rosycross, in wild areas. They hold down pests, and destroy the native ecostructure, making way for earthly apple trees. They sometimes return lost children found in the woods, and sometimes kidnap children who do not say their prayers. The race is benevolent, provided men stay well away from them."

"Benevolent? You have an odd definition of the word."

"Did the Foxes not restore humanity to the wretched Eidolons, and elevate the Moreaus? Did they not take down the walls of separation and bridge the biopsychological chasms between Man and Swan, Man and Myrmidon, Man and Ghost? I could not have departed the Noösphere of Rosycross had it not been for the Fox Maidens of Proxima."

"They created an homogenous mess mankind has suffered for five thousand years. Thank goodness those days are at an end!"

"What end? The Fox Maidens retain the power freely to make inhuman forms of man finally into humans."

The squire scowled. "They exist, but it will no longer warp events. The Fox Maidens and their madness ceased to be a factor in the calculus of destiny half a century ago, in the Year of Our Lord 51015, on the fifteenth day of May, at three hours past noon precisely, Greenwich Mean Time, fifteen hours since dawn, a date certain to delight numerologists forever."

"The coronation of Nemenstratus the Patrician as the Lord of the Afternoon for the Triplanetary jurisdiction. Earth, Venus, and Mars are under his sway."

"Ah! You do know your Earthly history after all," said the squire.

"It was the first time a member of the Fifth Human Race had been so honored," said Norbert. "The Patricians were created by the Foxes. Why would they create their own replacement?"

"Who can explain madness?" The squire shrugged. "The Fox Maidens were mad to topple the Golden Lords from power, and bring on five thousand years of war and woe."

"Madness? Nothing is more sane. Can you not see the wrongness of this era?"

The squire looked wary. "Wrongness?"

"The soul-crushing hierarchy, the stiff forms of address, the division of men into noble and peasant, ghost and flesh, high and low, possessing classes and laboring classes, and the Sacerdotes occupying an unlikely monopoly on all spiritual vocations. I can think of a dozen periods in the long, sad history of man that have this wrongheaded medieval quality, starting with the Dark Ages. And I mean the Dark Age period after the Fall of Rome, not the one after the Burning of New York, nor the one after the Burning of the World."

"I am not sure I see your point, sir," said the squire testily. "The Long, Golden Afternoon seems to be a self-correcting equilibrium, a natural culmination of history, a high point of civilization, a happy ending."

That was the final step. Norbert now thought he perceived, as a man who peers through fog, the looming mystery at the center of this ancient being.

8. The Foxes of Democracy

"History has not followed any natural culmination of anything since the day when Rania read the rules of historical prediction on the surface of the Monument—no matter! You called this era a happy ending. A high point. Yet here we are, you and I, stalking a holy man to kill him in secret, without trial, who has committed no other crime but to disagree with the opinion of the world about the date of the calendar. Does that sound civilized?"

"The human mind is not content with too much civilization," the squire mused in a philosophical tone. "More primitive neural structures demand that we abide by tribal norms. In order for the Golden Afternoon of Man to last, Man must have his helots and concubines to abuse: Moreaus beneath him to whip; Myrmidons to hate; luminous Swans to envy and revere; yes, and Ghosts to worship as ancestors, and Potentates of Earth and Powers of Heaven to adore as gods."

"The Sacerdotes of rural Rosycross say there is one God, and to worship Him only. Do the Sacerdotes of senile Earth say otherwise?"

"The Sacerdotes exist to remove the pain from man of all the sins we are forced to commit to maintain so grand and farsighted a civilization, and to forgive our keeping helots and concubines, and killing Myrmidons, and falling down before living idols."

"Why should we be forgiven? We now live in an age where the nobility alone go armed, and their dependents bow, their servants kneel, and their slaves fall on their faces."

"Perhaps that is the natural way of things," said the squire, with a smile of self-satisfaction.

"Nature says all men are equal."

"She says the opposite. Read Darwin."

"I read the Grand Charter of Liberty of my world, which all my ancestors swore to each other the day they were freed from the four hundred nightmare years spent in the dark, cramped, deadly dungeons, awash with murk, at the core of a cold Myrmidon moon flung across interstellar space. It says a man who slays a man with a knife is not less guilty for his lesser intellect than a Jupiter who slays an Atramental with an imposition of abstract logic."

"Your world is young, and overrun with Foxes! Democratic ages always end quickly," the squire said with great bitterness. "Democracy allows each man to rise to the level of his competence and greatness: it encourages high dreams and wide ambitions. That is their great boast over aristocracy, or any culture stratified by class. But democracy requires each man to fall to the level of his incompetence, does it not? And it is also a rule by majority, is it not? But the incompetent outnumber the competent by ten to one, or by hundreds to one. So democracy inevitably encourages ambitions which democracy inevitably then thwarts. A perfect engine for creating discontent!"

"Are men less discontented when kissing the boots that kick them?" Norbert asked savagely.

"The cold witness of historical cliometry says they are. The average man finds that while a democracy holds no ceiling overhead to halt his rise, it has no floor beneath him to halt his fall. But the average man is enfranchised with the vote, and so he votes in floors to prevent falls, laws concerning public welfare and minimum wages, and this forms the ceiling to prevent the rise of the poor under his feet. The wealthy above him, to secure their position, buy votes to do the same, making a floor of regulations for their industries and banks to prevent the middle from rising, and soon the hierarchy is back in place, but now it is sick and perverted, because all the so-called democratists are living a lie. His wealthy are not even required to dress and speak nobly, his poor are robbed of dignity, and no man feels the gratitude a man born in high position must feel, which spurs him to serve the highest ideal. They become plutocrats, not aristocrats. It is the same system, but less rational, less handsome, less honest, more fevered."

Norbert said, "And when the aristocrats are logic crystals filling living worlds, what then? Only you earthmen know what it is like not to have ancestors living in the medical camps, when one race and then another was tested against the environments to be colonized on far worlds, and the losers exterminated to the last blood cell. Only our forefathers passed the trial by ordeal bloodthirsty Jupiter imposed, whereas your forefathers did not. But those camps were abolished by the Fox Maidens. If inequality is ideal, why did history not halt at points when Jupiter was supreme? Was not the inequality greater then?"

"History suffers expansion and contraction, boom and bust," said the squire dismissively. "Democracy can endure during the fat years, but only an absolute power can allow the people to survive the lean years, when discipline is needed. Both are temporary deviations from the natural state of man, which is hierarchical, but not tyrannous."

"Or perhaps the medieval form of life is a transition state from one to the other, which is why history can never find rest," said Norbert. "The first Dark

Age was a transition between the absolutism of the Roman Empire and the liberty of the Space Age; and the Second Dark Age was between the liberty of the Space Age and the absolutism of the Imperial Pentagon, and so on. The world favored by the Master of the World is unstable because *he* is unstable."

"What?"

"Was I unclear, squire? Consider the Master of the World, whom you mentioned before. He is a man who with one hand plucks all the godlike powers of diamond stars from heaven, or Monuments of appalling antiquity and darkest knowledge up from hell; and then with the other hand creates the Second Empyrean Polity of Man in Sagittarius. Such a man surely has the ability to make the future howsoever he wills—what could Foxes or Judges or anyone do to oppose such a man? They are shadows to him! *He has no foes but himself.* History has not ended because he, the Master of Eternity, he simply cannot make up his mind!"

The squire in the dark dashed his foot against a stone, and uttered curses in some language long ago drowned in time. Norbert halted while the squire sat on a stump, drawing off his boot and nursing his foot. As Norbert suspected, he had separate toes, like something out of an archeologist's rendering of primitive man. The squire folded back the cuff of his glove, revealing a red amulet. This was a museum-piece bio-prosthetic like those worn by Sacerdotes, who still dressed in the alb and surplice of Roman pontiffs. The squire tapped the surface, ordering the bones of his foot to regrow into a sterner configuration.

Eventually the squire looked up and said, "Why do you say the Master cannot decide the fate of man?"

"Why does he continue to maintain a biological body? Are not the copies of his soul stored in the core of mad Tellus and all-too-sane Jupiter enough for him?"

"That is a good question," said the squire slowly.

"I know it is, because it is the last question my Exorbert asked me before I stowed aboard a lifting vessel, and begged the Guild master of the Space Island to grant me life."

"You are a reckless man. Guild regulations say to thrust stowaways into the total conversion chamber, so that their excess mass is converted to thrust, to make for what their deadweight subtracted."

"A great-grandfather on my mother's side, a Rosselyn from Fludd Parish, was an apprentice for one term, which meant I had a bloodline claim to membership. That coincidence prevented me from being introduced to the inside of a mass converter. Do you see why I understand the Master of the World better than you, even though you served under him? He is too much like me for me to be deceived. Stand up! Time flies but we must walk!"

They trudged along in silence for a time.

Eventually the squire broke the silence. "Just out of curiosity, what is this insight you say you have into the mind of the Master of the World?"

"You say his White Ship was driven out of Sagittarius. But it could have sailed to any human world from Rosycross to Uttaranchal. Why here? Why was the White Ship brought to Sol? What was meant to be decided by this act? Here, where Jupiter is strongest?"

"Speak more plainly! What is your question, sir? What are you trying to imply?"

"Is the Master of the World the enemy of Jupiter?"

The squire made a thoughtful hum in his throat, and said, "Mm. Perhaps we should not speak so plainly. Some of these trees within earshot are oaks, and they are sacred to Jupiter."

9. On Holy Ground

They trudged for a time in silence. Soon the old cathedral loomed over them. It was dark within, but not completely dark, for a few votive candles within glinted from the silver frame and glass petals of the rose window. This round window was just above the great carven doors, so that the cathedral looked like a cyclops with his head thrown back and his great mouth, peaked like the bill of a bird and pointing at the stars, hung open.

The necropolis lay behind it, and the tombs and monuments had spread beyond the original line of stone fence long ago; and beyond the line of now-motionless marble robots overgrown with moss; and also beyond the line of thinking spikes, some tilted and some fallen but one to two silently watchful, akin to what fenced in the Forever Village. Norbert was awed to contemplate how much older this building must be than even the Forever Village. Perhaps it was older than the Starfaring Guild itself. If the calendar of the sacerdotes were trustworthy, the orders that erected cathedrals and sanctuaries and basilicas was over fifty thousand years old.

The squire said, "Now we are free to speak."

Norbert said, "Between the Revisionists and Vindicators, who is right? Give me no nonsense about Guild neutrality. You served under the Master of the World who studied the Second Monument with the help of godlike Powers, or so you said. Is he unable to unravel the conundrum? Or is he as confused as the rest of us?"

The squire stiffened, but spoke briefly. "He is not confused. The ancient count is correct. Rania departed M3 at the appointed time."

"And the Revision? The attempt to rewrite the cliometric plan of history?"

"Pseudo-scientific hogwash which, if put into effect, would eliminate the practice and knowledge of cliometry from the human race, thus making the race easier to control."

"Then the triumph of Revisionism would be a return of the Hermetic Millennia," mused Norbert, "with Jupiter in the role of Exarchel."

The squire smiled a sharply pointed smile. "In one sense, Jupiter *is* Exarchel. When the Golden Lords resume their rightful place as shepherds of utopia, the natural hierarchy of which we spoke earlier will emerge."

"But such ignorance would require an obliteration of the past. There are only two places the past is stored beyond the reach of revision or rewriting. Hence, the victory of the Revisionists means the destruction both of the hopes held in the starfaring vessels of heaven and the memory held in the tombs of the underworld."

"What is your point, sir?"

Norbert turned his hood toward the man. "In this matter, your mythical Judge of Ages and the Master of the World are natural allies."

"Allies against whom?"

"Who introduced the Eidolon vector? Who sustains the Revisionist heresy, millennia after millennia, despite all changes of laws and races and customs and conditions?"

The squire said sharply, "There can be no one. It must be a natural by-product of some hidden variable, a self-replicating effect. The Judge of Ages is not so bloodthirsty as to destroy the Solar System!"

"Not the whole system. Jupiter would survive."

"What are you saying?"

"Rania's vessel, if passing through the Solar System at near-lightspeed, would throw the inner planets out of orbit and destroy them, remember? But a Gas Giant is much more massive."

"Jupiter sides with the Master of the World! For that purpose he was designed. He would not betray his father! It would be betraying himself!"

"Review your logic again, squire. There are only two players, the red and the black. Each one has set in motion races and potentates and powers loyal to his side. But if there are only two players, and they both agree on the Vindication Calendar, then why has the question of Calendar Revision plagued mankind with a plague that even the Hierophants of the Long Golden Afternoon cannot cure? There must therefore be a third player."

"From where? It cannot be the aliens. In all human history, there are only two camps: the forces of knowledge, majesty, glory, order, rule, hierarchy, and survival, and the big-nosed insanity opposing his rule."

"Then one of the two camps was betrayed from within."

The squire frowned. "You cannot prove Jupiter is guilty!"

Norbert said solemnly, "And you cannot shake your fear that he is."

The squire wore the look of a man who wishes to contradict an accusation, but cannot.

"My ghost went mad," said Norbert. "Nor could I discern it, because Exorbert was so much wiser than I. Perhaps he is only what I would have become had I never fallen in love; a theosophist mathematician obsessed with esoterics, non-Euclidean calculus, and Ptolemaic astronomy, believing every report of a sighting of a Maltese Knight. We divaricated. Few are the savants who survive such loss. I have that special look on my face, though you cannot now see it. But I see it on yours. You are a man who lost his soul. Jupiter divaricated."

"Nonsense."

"Jupiter has betrayed you. He has betrayed us all."

Then he straightened, spread his arms, turned his mask toward the night sky netted with dark branches, and called out. "Hear me! *Jupiter has betrayed mankind!*"

He waited, arms wide.

The squire said, "What are you doing?"

"Waiting for the lightning bolt," said Norbert calmly.

"Are you mad?"

"Mind yourself, squire! You meant to say 'Are you mad, *sir*'?"

"Fair enough. Are you mad, sir?"

"By earthly standards, I am. The Rosicrucians of old handed down neuropsychological alterations which would never be permitted in orthogonal humans. Why am I not dead?"

"Jupiter's spies are not listening."

"Ah! So you told the truth about that. I see why scientists delight in successful experiments! The certainty after doubt is feast after famine." With a slow and dignified gesture, Norbert lowered his arms, and continued to walk the paths deeper into the graveyard.

10. Dreaming Apples

The graveyard was very large, and reached for acre after acre across this table of land. There were hills occupied by looming mausoleums and valleys whose green slopes were adorned with marble walkways beneath sad poplars, at whose feet slabs or cubes of stone marked the rest of the dead. On raised walls were urns carrying ashes, and beneath panes of black glass set into the grass were interlocked sets of bones, or grinning skulls from whom wax death-masks slipped.

The hills were small and the dales were gentle, but the graveyard of space went on and on, and slowly the cathedral steeple behind them was lost to sight. In one place they crossed a gently arching bridge of stone that overleaped a rill of water flowing in a marble channel along the spine of a valley.

Both men stopped, because their internal navigation at that moment shut off.

The squire said, "We must be close. But I hear nothing."

Norbert said, "Nor did anyone hear me. Why was I not struck dead for my blasphemy? How did you know Jupiter would not allow his myriad loyal angels and beasts and motes and microbes to hear us?"

The squire sighed. "Because he is the same man as Ximen del Azarchel, a man who respects the sanctity of the Church, which is the only thing in human history older than he is, and yet still lives."

"The myths say the Master of the World killed the Sacerdotal Order of the old days, the Church, in order to give the world to the Witches. He hunted down and killed the last priest, a man named Reyes y Pastor, one of his loyal servants, and his father confessor."

"You cannot believe all myths so unskeptically! What man kills his own father confessor? To whom would he confess the crime? I am sure the Master of the World only punished the Church for crossing him. The fact that Ximen del Azarchel is a loyal son of the Church surely shows that no matter how black a villain is painted, there must still be some good in him, if only a spot of white."

"Or else it surely shows that joining in rituals with lip service and knee tribute does not brighten a dark soul even by so little as a spot. Come! Zolasto Zo is near."

"Sir, if I may: how do you know? I hear nothing."

"Use your nose. Do you catch the scent of the jet-black greenery of my world? It thrives above the bodies of the dead. Yonder is Cagliostro Lilly, Forget-Me-Soon, Black Nasturtium, and Goat Rue. But do you see those trees with branches dark as iron? The calycine leaves? The fruit that glows like the faces of the dead in the moonlight?"

"We have been following them all night."

"These are the tradition-protecting trees of my world, the sustenance of my forefathers, and so many forms of cider and tart and dreaming pies are made from them that any sane man would sicken."

"Once again, sir, I do not follow you."

"But I follow them. The trees will lead me," said Norbert. As they walked, he mused aloud, "What we did on Rosycross in the early days would never be allowed now. To preserve valuable memories across the generations our pantropists made the apples and the humans neuro-readably compatible, so any pioneer who learned a useful survival skill, after death would have the dream seed in his skull break forth and grow out into such a tree as this. Rosicrucians in the early days could eat the apples from the graveyard and instinctively know our land of red hills and black rills better. Nowadays, between genetic drift and physicians unwilling to abide by tradition, the apple strain is not maintained, nor the human. Rarely now do the apples send good dreams: we get garbled messages, or fragments, or hallucinations, or nothing. Out of memory, for saving our forefathers, they are sacred. When many of my departed kin are gathered, there will be a grove of such trees, and, if Zolasto Zo is as homesick as I, there he will pitch his tents."

"Why is there no music and commotion wafting from his tents?"

"Zo would have surrounded his camp with tissues finer than gossamer through which men can walk, but programmed to block sound. I will ask the trees to part the veil."

11. The Camp of the Mountebank

At that moment there came floating over the headstones, mausoleums, and solemn statues of winged beings the sound of drums, sackbut, taborine, and timbrel, the rattle of crotales and the whoop of brass trumpet. It seemed far in the gloom, but it was closer than it seemed; they spied a cluster of floating lanterns, flashing their lights in gay displays of cerise, amber, purple, and white, hanging above a thick grove of black-trunked trees with white fruit and oddly cupshaped leaves. The headstones to the left and right of the grove radiated a stern disapproval, and several of the winged statues were frowning.

Through these trees, as the men approached, could be glimpsed what seemed to be the leafy fabric of walking tents, but garish and bright with many colors, hung with red berries as if in obedience to the rhythm of an autumn from another world; and the tents were not walking but dancing a spry jig, while children in festive colors chased them, and dancers in motley kept time.

Closer they came, and both men could hear a barker's voice, calling out the names of the mysteries and wonders to be presented in the central tent, the luscious women and heroic men to perform antics and startling techniques. They could not make out the words, but Norbert recognized the broad vowels and trilled syllables of a Rosicrucian dike-country accent, from a Parish of the Northwest continent called Paracelsus, downhill and downstream from the rugged uplands of Dee.

The squire was surprised when Norbert put out his hand, and halted them both.

"Sir? Is that not the very voice of our target?"

"Zolasto Zo is not the target, but Hieronymus the Apostate. He will be in one of the side tents. If he is a man of dignity, he will not allow his tent to jig and gyrate, but it will exhale an aura of dignity, mystery, awe, and divine terror, such as priests possess and magicians mock. For a man of learning, to be reduced to telling fortunes and selling sham medicines will be hard, and so his tent will be less enthused than the others of the sideshow."

Norbert began to pace in a curving path around the grove, not approaching it. The squire peered and stared, but the density of the branches deceived his sight, and he saw nothing aside from fragments of festivity: a moving sway of colored tent-cloth; a leaping child dressed in flame, a musician with a balalaika, an acrobat standing head-downward on a wheel; a naked and purple man of huge proportions from Epsilon Indi wrestling with a hippopotamus from Egypt; a sharp-faced redhead in a scarlet kimono carrying a parasol ringed by burning pearls; a group of laughing maidens in masks who had tied intoxicating lights into their hair shaking their tresses at others in the throng, so that whoever over-stared at the lights staggered and displayed dream-haunted and empty smiles.

Norbert suddenly stopped and pointed at something the squire could not see. "There. Your dueling pistol is loaded?"

"No, sir! It is considered improper to pack a pistol before a duel, lest an unscrupulous opponent introduce a contaminant into the chaff mix."

"Have you other weapons, silent weapons, in case we met roughnecks or roustabouts?"

The squire drew a blade like an unadorned length of wood, and in his hands heat as from a black stove issued from it.

"I did not tell you to draw. Still the blade, but keep it in your hand," said Norbert.

The wooden sword grew cold.

The squire heard the slight, sticky sound as Norbert drew one of his glassy knives from his nano-locked sheath. Norbert pushed his way between the trees of the grove, making his way to where a dark tent of many gables loomed. Its neighbors, gaily lit in pink and cerise and creamy white, kept swaying up to it and dancing away, leaving behind the smell of sugared candy, burning beeswax, and brandy-wine. It was the only tent that was not dancing.

At the pinnacle of the black tent was the image of the Coptic Eye, fortunately facing away from them, and above the tent a three-dimensional image of the major stars of Canes Venatici burned. The door of the tent was guarded by a pair of pale figurines, two fathoms tall: the muse Urania holding an astrolabe, and the titan Saturn holding a scythe. The tent had a wooden door shaped and painted with an image of a dark hand with a white palm, with the lines of palmistry labeled in small letters outlined in red.

When the hand moved to admit a patron, an interior lit by fiery torches was visible for a moment. A low stage or podium could be glimpsed with a lectern of black glass, and a line of folding pews facing it, already filled with a hushed and silent audience, while behind was a screen bright with an image of the rim of the Milky Way, and the dandelion puff of the globular cluster at M3. The line of Rania's flight and return was shining in purple light. The magical significance of the various stars near her flight path was noted in yellow light, along with notes both astronomical and astrological, and tables comparing the past events and future events each passing star signified.

Norbert continued skulking through the tree shadows until he was directly at the rear of the tent, so that the ominous door and ancient figurines were not visible. The back flap of the tent was pressed up against the branches of the trees through which Norbert slid to reach it. All the lights and noise were on the far side of the tent. No carnival-goer nor roughneck, unless he happened to crawl under these trees, was likely to see Norbert in this location.

With a tiny motion of his knife, entirely without noise, Norbert cut a slit less than an inch wide in the tent fabric. Then he made the blade grow longer, and pushed just its tip into the tent, using the camera dot in the tip to look carefully left and right.

The moment seemed to hold its breath, and it grew longer, and Norbert did not move. The squire saw or sensed camera dots along the spine of Norbert's dark cloak watching him sardonically. A minute passed, then several, and still the assassin did not move by so much as a hair. Finally, the squire said along the silent nerve channel they shared, "Sir? Your orders?"

Norbert stepped backward, and traced the knife back along the slit. The

picotechnology in the blade evidently had very fine control over the nanotechnology it was usurping, for the slit became whole with no visible seam. "I have
determined that Hieronymus the Apostate is innocent of any threat to the Guild,
as shall be, very soon, all heretics seeking to reform the calendar."

"What did you see in there?"

"One of the larger mysteries of the universe," said Norbert. "Come! We need
no longer skulk."

Norbert walked around to the front of the tent, in full view of the multicolored bonfires burning in the center of the dancing encampment.

As soon as he stepped into the grove, he spread his arms, and let his cloak
billow around him as if he were in a high wind, although there was no wind.
"It is I! Norbert son of Yngbert of Rossycross! The Starfarer's Guild in culmi-
nant arrogance unparalleled hereby usurps and treads upon both Earthly and
sacred jurisdictions! I am here to slay the innocent! All heretics, dissenters, and
unorthodox mathematicians step forth and present yourself!"

The bonfire went out, as did all the torches. The music fell silent. There was
a moment or two of light, while the floating lanterns all sank to the grass and
winked out. The dancers were still. There was a rustling sound, as of many bodies sitting, kneeling, or falling.

There was a noise of a confused trumpeting from the hippopotamus as it broke
free from the limp arms of the purple-skinned wrestler and crashed through
the grove and thundered away across the lawns of the graveyard, surprisingly
swift for its size.

Norbert turned. Only the five-foot-tall hand guarding the entrance to the
magician's tent was still lit, pale as moonlight shining on ice, ominous with its
white fingers and black palm. Norbert entered the tent. The squire, one eyebrow raised in a wry expression, followed.

The audience seated at the pews were all motionless. Norbert put his hand
into the cleavage of a young maiden dressed in silks.

"Sir? You seem to have the lady at a disadvantage."

"She is a doll."

"Quite attractive, sir, but I am not sure groping her while unconscious is an
unambiguous compliment. Her clothing will record and report the breach of
decorum."

"Do not toy with me. I mean she has no heartbeat. All here are dolls. This
audience, the performers, and the crowd outside, all of them are grown from
totipotent blood cells. It is Fox technology. We've been foxed."

"Your Zolasto Zo seems quite the performer."

"As are you."

"What? Do you think I am Zolasto Zo?"

"Not at all. He never left Rosycross, which is a planet under interdict. Nor did his ghost. There is no conspiracy of secret pirate satellites, and Zo is too good a showman to attempt to lure the earthmen to view the wonders of Earth. The only thing that came from that planet was a reproduction of one of his publicity bills, which you sent to my desk."

"The Archangels of the living ships sent it."

"At your command."

Silently, the tall pale hand now turned and faced inward, and closed across the entrance. There was a slight change in the air pressure as the tent sealed itself shut. It was now entirely dark in here.

A weft of light, a breath of metallic heat, began issuing from the wooden blade in the squire's hand.

Norbert turned his black spectacles toward the glowing blade with a curious tilt of the head. "So this is not your trap, then, is it?"

The other man said, "Mine are less showy. As you said, it is Fox work. They have a certain panache that is unmistakable."

"When one is caught in a trap of the Fox-women, it is too late to flee or pull away. Flight only drives the barbs of the snare home. Instead one seeks the center of the maze. Sometimes the Foxes can be prevailed upon by entreaty or whim."

"What do you mean?"

Norbert jumped onto the stage. "I mean it is time to look behind the curtain and examine the stage machinery."

Norbert drew his glassy knives with a flourish, one in each hand, and spun them in his fingers so that they caught the pale, faint light shed from the wooden blade. He made one slash in the screen from overhead to knee-high, and the other slash at waste height from left to right, forming a cross.

He kicked the cross open and stepped through.

3

The Treason of Jupiter

1. Behind the Curtain

Behind the stage screen, the two men found themselves in what seemed a vestry or dressing room, but which apparently served as a consolation chamber for private audiences, because it was equipped with all the gewgaws and implements a magician needed to cast a cliometric extrapolation of the future history of any single individual gullible enough to believe that cliometric extrapolations could be cast for single individuals.

Around the vestry were tripods for anthracomancy, skulls for necromancy, mirrors for enoptromancy, or perhaps for putting on stage makeup.

A carpet inscribed with Monument notation was underfoot, one of those types written with hidden fortunes that the client could reveal depending on where he accidentally stepped. From the tentpoles overhead hung a line of marionettes dressed in the costumes of the various constellations, Aquarius with his ewer or Sagittarius with his bow and arrow, Libra holding up a balance scale in which he weighed a feather against a beating human heart.

Brazen mandalas with traces of neural charge still vibrating in their spirals, thinking caps cruel with clamps and brain-spikes, and small bottles of delirious essence winking mischievously were all present in the litter of the ceiling, as was a nine-foot-long stuffed crocodile with glass eyes, motionless and signal-neutral. Norbert thought the crocodile an eerie object: he could not recall the last time he had seen something that was entirely dead.

A narrow shelf ran in a complete circle just at eye level along the chamber sides. From it hung a line of ticking owl-faced clocks and murmuring calendars showing the time and the time-dilations of ships passing between Mother Earth and the Stepmother Earths of the three diasporas. The shelf was an astrological ribbon, to compare a client's birth signs and houses against the position of fortunate and adverse ships. This shelf had raised itself to allow the tall men to enter, dropping again to eye level as they passed beneath, and the owl-faced clocks looked down on them with round, incurious, and unwinking eyes.

Midmost all this bright clutter was a round brass table inscribed with the sigils of the hexagram on a sliding outer ring. In the center of the table rested a crystal ball next to an open cedarwood box. In the box were a deck of computer cards painted with figures of the tarot. Above the table hung a glass hookah filled with luminous fluid from which the only light in the chamber came.

To one side was an ornate chair for the magician flanked by the traditional winged monkeys, who were wearing the traditional pillbox caps and braided scarlet and gold jackets. To the other side was a red silk couch for the magician's client, fitted with straps and head-clamp and a dream induction box underneath.

Sitting in the magician's chair, chewing a lump of tobacco and spitting into a nearby crownless skull, was a tall man in a green poncho wearing a high-crowned broad-brimmed black hat adorned with a hatband of jade chips. The man's face was oddly ugly, but not ugly enough to have been designed that way. He had rough and bony features: a big, square jaw like the toe of a boot, two deep set eyes that never seemed to blink, ears like jug handles, and a hooked nose that looked like it had been broken and reset badly. His skin was dark and the hair above his ears was reddish stubble cropped close. Across his knees rested a sidearm nearly a cubit long, heavy as a blunderbuss, with a main muzzle surrounded by six lesser muzzles for escort bullets. Over his shoulder was a bandolier and a cavalry saber. On the heels of either boot were metal instruments of a type Norbert had never seen: a small hooked arm ending in a rowel like a jagged wheel.

Draped in sinuous curves atop the couch, but not strapped into it, as if she had flung herself down artlessly and merely by chance had assumed a curvaceous posture of dangerous sensuality, was a female figure in a red kimono and a purple obi, the dress of a Nymph. In a wide circle above her, as if to hide her from the marionettes hanging from the ceiling, was a living parasol, also of red;

nine white pearls bathed in strange silver candleflames circled the rim of the parasol like blind bees, sometimes alighting on the spokes.

She wore her bloodred hair in a loose mass flagrantly piled atop her head, with escaping strands tickling her ears and jawline and neck. This coiffeur was pinned in place with long needles adorned with amber beads, fine chains of gold, and a coronet shaped like the moon, and what looked like a row of lit candles. The kimono collar was loose in the back to show off the line of her neck. Her fingers and wrists were slender and graceful and her arms were hidden in shining black opera gloves that ran past her elbow. Her feet were unshod, but hidden in stockings made of the same dark and shining substance as her gloves, and hid her legs to the knee. Her feet were too long and thin to be handsome, but they boasted a dozen gold and red-gold anklets and ankle-bells that chimed and tittered if she moved her feet. She toyed with a scarlet folding fan whose spines were needles.

Hers was a triangular face with very high cheekbones sharply defined, an acutely pointed chin, and a thin and very red smile shaped like the letter V. She smiled without opening her mouth. Her eyes were larger than normally allowed for humans, and the pupils yellow as amber, yellow as gold coins seen in a running fountain.

When Norbert kicked his way into the chamber, the two winged monkeys fluttered their wings and pounded the carpet with their truncheons, hooting and screeching and showing their fangs.

The tall man in the black hat kicked the monkeys, who shrieked and dropped their truncheons, putting their paws before their mouths. "Well, damnation and tarnation and all other nations! Ain't you the loudassingest and lousiest assassin since Scaevola?"

2. Needless Names and Introductions

Norbert used the point of his knife to tip his spectacles back on his head. The fabric of the mask, sensing his mood, scuttled quickly down from his face and into a neck pocket; his hood likewise folded itself to his neck. The spectacles whimpered when the silent knife touched them. Norbert, squinting against the light, with a nod had the spectacles fall back into place across his nose.

"I need not be an assassin this hour, no more than you need be Feroccio the Master-At-Arms, nor she the Mademoiselle Pelisse. Shall we all end the masquerade and make our introductions? I am Norbert Noesis Mynyddrhodian of

Rosycross, Glorified Endocist of One Donative, son of Yngbert Perpension Mynyddrhodian. I am a Praetor of the Ancient and Honorable Guild of Starfaring and Interstellar Pilgrims Errant who has been commanded by my superiors, absurdly enough, to render a verdict on the sixteen-thousand-year-old issue of the calendar reform. I assume the lady is Cazi, the immortal sovereign of the Fourth Humanity?"

Cazi inclined her head graciously. "So I am!" Her voice was eerie, like the laughter of lutes, with a curious double note. The first was like the throb of a cello, husky, half-breathless, playful, mocking; the after-note was thin and high like a violin, sinister, deadly, and pure.

"Frankly, I thought you a mythical being, ma'am."

"So I am, again! You may approach on your knees and adore me. Put my big toe in your mouth and suck on it."

"Thank you, ma'am, but I'd rather not. There will be no living report of you on Rosycross if you rip out my jugular, and that would be a criminal loss to your glory."

Her tight-lipped smile widened when she opened her mouth to laugh, betraying the glint of very white and very pointed teeth before she covered her lower face demurely with her fan. Turning her head to her companion, she breathed. "Oh, Meany, I like him. He is quick, like one of my girls, and, like them, flatters without meaning it at all. Give him to me, please."

The tall, bony-faced man said flatly, "Nope. Stop acting like a vixen: how often I gotta tell you you're better'n that? There is something all balled up going on here, and I am thinking I just been outfoxed again."

Norbert felt his brash nature rising to the fore. Taking another step forward, he said, "Not outfoxed. Foxes, I have it on good authority, lay their traps with a certain recognizable flavor of panache. Whereas this has a distinctive flavor of patience and large-scale misdirection of events. You have perhaps been overmastered."

"What the plague does that mean?" growled the tall man.

"This man is my squire of marines attached to the Forever Village, named Ar Thrup End Dragon. I assume he really *is* a squire, since, as the Most Senior Grand High Master of the Starfaring Guild, his is the authority to appoint anyone, including himself, to that post, just as his is the authority to appoint me Praetor. Judge of Ages, this is the Master of the World. I think you know each other."

The squire straightened up. The outer layer of what seemed a wooden sword shattered, and the splinters flew in each direction, revealing a silver sword beneath a-dazzle with jacinth and chrysoberyl. The hilts unfolded with a metallic snap.

The blade was decorated with a red dragon entwining a white, and the words in gold letters, *Ultima Ratio Regum*. There was the heavy scent of the air before a thunderstorm issuing from it, which betrayed the presence of directed-energy weapons hidden in the blade.

His uniform dropped the medals and badges of a squire of marines softly to the carpet, but rippled and changed aspect and turned black with a silver cape, shot through with red and purple filiments like the veins of a leaf. On his wrist gleamed the red amulet of the Hermetic Order. He made an adjustment on the amulet. His false skin peeled off in long, strange, floating and curling strips, and the strips evaporated.

Menelaus Montrose looked at the other man, and said, "Arthur Pendragon? You shouldn't use an alias that gives so much away."

Ximen del Azarchel inclined his head to Menelaus, then bowed more deeply to Cazi, then grinned at Menelaus. "Should I take tips on inventing an alias from Captain Sterling of Space Command? Norbert did not recognize the name Pendragon. No one reads the classics."

"I meant the name gives away how damned arrogant you are," snorted Menelaus. Then Menelaus said to Norbert, "How did you figure out who was who?"

"She is unmistakable," said Norbert.

The redhead squealed. "Oh, give him to me, Meany! I *like* him!"

"Hush up, Cazi, or I'll set the poxed monkeys on you."

The winged monkeys looked eager and clapped their forepaws.

Norbert said to Menelaus, "Rumor had it she was trying to dig you out of a tomb in Egypt. Also, the Master of the World spent the entire walk here talking about the Tribulations, how the predictions of history went off the rails."

Montrose nodded, as if that explained everything, but Cazi, leaning forward half-sideways in a way that displayed the fine curve of her naked shoulder, said, "Pray tell, mortal man, how the conversation of the Nobilissimus on so interesting a topic betrayed his identity to you. Amuse me, and I will reward you with a treat!"

3. Interlude, with Fox

Norbert bowed. "Ma'am, I don't know how to say it to sound amusing, or even to sound like I am not bragging. The Judge of Ages and the Master of the World used to be the smartest men in creation, but they are simply not above average anymore."

Cazi tilted her head with an angular smile, and looked at Norbert from the corners of her half-lidded eyes, and spoke in a light, lilting voice. "Oh, I would not say that. Ximen believes he is exceptional because he exposed himself to the Monument, and it altered his brain, but he would be exceptional even otherwise. Meany believes he is exceptional because he exposed himself to true love, and it altered his brain, and he would be nothing otherwise. But please feel free to brag! Humble men are dull! They are so hard to play with. They have no strings for fierce, gay foxes to pull."

"I've been educated under the canes of remorseless lore masters, back home," said Norbert. "And I have a lump of murk in my brain smaller than a hummingbird's egg but with more calculation power than ever was enjoyed by the nun in the moon. So I know the cliometry. I did a few calculations in my head while we walked."

"That is not braggy enough!" pouted Cazi.

"I will try to sound more arrogant, ma'am," said Norbert politely. "Because I have a right to brag about this. The Nobilissimus kindly gave me clues enough to puzzle out what has been hidden from humans for millennia.

"The first clue was his anger at the Shapetaker's Millenium: When the Salamander fled from the sun, unknown to mankind, history went off the rails. Why? The Tribulations began when the Fourth Humans ushered in a revolution in biotechnology and biosociology, so that anyone could take the shape of any race, hence any rank. And the enfranchised underlings mingled with their betters, interbred, prospered, and quadrupled their lifespans.

"That was not in anyone's plan. The carefully balanced utopia had ended, but no human was told. We all thought the heresies and tumults were a necessary adjustment period, but still all part of the cliometric Grand Scheme of Things imposed by our Golden betters.

"But the history planners had gone quite blind.

"Who would this anger more than the main history planner of all history? And who was he angry at? Whose actions, whether guided by mercy or madness or what, shattered the caste system of the Long Golden Afternoon of Man? Who unchained us all from the golden chains of time? It was the Foxes."

Cazi applauded by clapping her folded fan into her other palm. "Hear, hear! All living things must praise the Fox Maidens! Dead things, too! It is a wonder to hear how wonderful we are, me and all my girls! Tell me more." She giggled. "You do not have to mean it."

"Yes, ma'am. The next clues were his frustration that the reign of the Golden Lords has not returned. Some chaotic factor was throwing off the calculations.

Now, what is the most chaotic thing in Earthly history in the last two thousand years?"

"Foxes!" exclaimed Cazi brightly.

"And what factor got factored out once the Foxes put one of their creatures, a Patrician, in the purple as a Lord of the Golden Afternoon?"

"The Fox factor!" exclaimed Cazi, bouncing up and down and applauding. Strands of wild red hair escaped from her coiffeur, and the jouncing pulled loose some ribbons of her kimono in the front, exposing a dangerous glimpse of cleavage.

"Right again. The Nobilissimus implied that Jupiter lost control of history, but boasted that history regained its sight and destiny when the Patricians rose to authority, presumably not under Jupiter's control. This leads to a strange conclusion indeed: The unpredictable Foxes created a race able to predict them. That defeats this special ability. But who is so insane as to erase themselves from history?"

"Foxes! *Foxes*! FOXES!" screamed Cazi, leaping in the air and performing a complete backflip, while folds of her ruby-bright kimono came undone, and lit candles or pointy hair ornaments flew out of the unwinding mass of her hair, stabbing the frightened carpet, who blushed.

Norbert continued: "That led to an even stranger thought: the question of means. How was it done? Not by human science. It stands to reason that anyone who knows how to do a thing knows how to undo it. The Monument Builders discovered how to predict the large-scale self-aware multiple-component interactive events we call history. If there were a means to unpredict it, to rewrite destiny like a scroll, not even Jupiter could anticipate such a means or counteract it. No man and no potentate, not the Nobilissimus and not Tellus his Ghost is wise enough to outsmart Jupiter. Only the Monument Builders are. They are from some higher level of intellectual topography inhabited by Dominions, or Authorities, or Archons, beings for which we have only hypothetical names.

"Then there was the question of timing. Neptune was created after the Ultimate White Ship returned, presumably based on this anti-cliometric math the Jupiter Brain could not analyze or counteract; and Neptune was created by the Patricians, who in turn were created by the Fourth Humans; and the Fourth Humans in turn were created after the previous Omega Nebula expedition returned with the Penultimate White Ship, presumably based on a simpler form of the same math."

"Fox math!" shouted Cazi, arms high and wide, standing on one toe in midair and spinning rapidly. Norbert could not see what was holding her up, but he did not expect to understand the posthuman races. A bushy red tail had unfolded from behind the wide many-folded bow of her sash and was whipping about in the air, and little flickers of white fire fell from it.

Cazi's head stopped turning, even though her body continued to spin rapidly, as if her neck were suddenly no longer interested in anything her body was doing. Norbert could not see any seam, discontinuity, or elastic twist in the neck, so the sight was both unsettling and inexplicable. The un-rotating head quirked an eyebrow at Norbert. "Is *fox* math a real sort of math?"

Norbert swallowed, decided all posthumans were insane, and continued in a calm and level voice. "If it is not, no doubt it should be, ma'am."

"I want to shout 'foxes' again," pouted Cazi, descending to kneel on her couch, and letting her floating pearls fly and weave around her head, somehow drawing the wild strands of hair behind them. Other pearls darted across the floor, and any scattered hair needles they touched clung to them, and they towed them back to her. "Ask more rhetorical questions!"

Norbert spread his hands and shrugged (an unintentionally alarming gesture, since he still held a dagger in either hand). "Ah, milady, but there are no more questions to ask."

She raised an eyebrow. "Then I will ask. I can change my face. How did you see through me? I must be losing my touch!"

"It was not you, ma'am, but the company you keep," said Norbert. "On the way here the Nobilissimus told me, not in so many words, that the Judge of Ages had to be behind nearly everything the whole Fox Maiden race did throughout all of history. Since legend says the Judge does not act like the Master of the World—I mean he does not use the lives of men as puppets—I assume the Judge of Ages planned out the unpredictable cliometric vectors of the Fox race with the knowledge, approval, and cooperation of their Fox-Queen. So with whom else would he be consulting?"

"The queen of the *FOXES!*" she called out in great relish. "Oh, you please me. Now tell me what I was consulting him about, if you want to live, eh?"

Norbert smiled. "My life is at no risk. You were talking of Rania, and how to see to the Vindication of Man."

She said, "And how did you know that?"

Norbert said, "Because there is no other matter on which the Judge of Ages and the Master of the World agree. It is simple once you see the pattern. Jupiter does not want Rania's return, nor does he seek the Vindication of Man. What other conclusion is there?"

Montrose said, "That Blackie is against Rania's return. He likes slavery, and the easiest way to keep mankind chained to the Hyades is to prevent the Vindication of Man."

Del Azarchel raised an eyebrow. "I am taken by surprise. I had supposed all this to be *your* doing."

Montrose looked sincerely outraged. "What? *Me* prevent Rania's return? You nuts?"

"No, not prevent her return, only to maneuver Jupiter into attempting to prevent her return, so that this forces me to destroy Jupiter, my own son and masterpiece. Otherwise, if she returns and mankind is freed from Hyades but not free from Jupiter, this would be gall to you—you have plans ready for the various eventualities occurring after her return, have you not? Or have I overestimated your subtlety?"

Cazi rolled her beautiful yellow eyes and said to Norbert, "You see what it is like, living with two insane conspirators who are insanely old. Every event not arranged by one, he thinks is the work of the other. They both think we are just props and bit-part players in their two-man epic. Even after the Swans spanked them like brats and sent them to stand in the corner at Jupiter, wearing conical dunce caps, they will not learn. They are stubborn." She shrugged, which once again displayed the creamy curve of her shoulders to her advantage. "I hope they never learn. I like stubborn. It's cute."

Norbert looked between Cazi and Del Azarchel. "You two have had dealings with each other?"

Cazi narrowed her eyes. She smiled such a thin smile and wide that it was alarming. "I was born in the Fortieth Millennium, and have been gnawing at the entrails of Tellus and Jupiter, the little slavedriver and the great, from that time to this. I once visited the Ximen at his home, to see if he was worthy of Princess Rania, because I was curious to see if he could make me betray my master Menelaus." She licked her lips as if in great relish. "I stole something from him then, which he can never recover. He will not admit it, will you, Ximen? Not the proud Master of Everything in the World except himself. Do I not speak the truth, Ximen?"

Del Azarchel said to Norbert, "She never speaks the truth. Not the whole truth."

Cazi pouted, "I speak the *fun* parts of the truth."

Del Azarchel said, "She is not even the real Cazi. The race is composed entirely of totipotent cells, and they can rapidly grow and ungrow organs as need be, or turn their entire bodies into a thinking mass like a Myrmidon. They change shape and impersonate each other. Whoever best impersonates Cazi is elected Cazi."

The fox woman sniffed in disdain. "I ate the dead brains of my predecessor and I am possessed by her ghost; we maintain continuity better than your crude

Myrmidons. But now you made me say something that disgusts my pretty Norbert of Promixa, so now he will not love me! I should call my deadliest guards!"

There was a motion at the cross-shaped rip in the screen behind them. Two redheads came through the opening, smiling and laughing silently, their yellow eyes glittering. Both were less callipygious and buxom than a Nymph would be, being taller and more slender, but they had long and well-shaped torsos and pert and well-shaped breasts, with very red nipples, and their pale skins were freckled all over. Their bodies were naked, but they wore black gloves to the elbow and black stockings to the knee. They sported two oddities: one was that their feet were longer and more slender than human feet, with strangely elongated toes like those of a spaceman from days long past. The other was that a two-foot-long fox tail, red as flame and tripped with white, came curving up from the base of each woman's spine, like the flirtatious decoration of a showgirl. Hovering near their long, black-clad fingers were white pearls bathed in silver fire.

Del Azarchel stepped to one side, raised his sword and lit it, and a symbol of ill fortune appeared beneath his feet. In his other hand he held a globule of semitransparent golden goo, which seemed to have a writhing motion at its heart. He cocked his wrist as if ready to drop the orb.

"Cowhand, must things grow difficult? Control your pet."

Montrose snorted. "As if I ever could. Cazi, don't hurt him."

Cazi said in a cheerful voice, "Lady Gitsune and Lady Strega! When next he sleeps, be it in an hour or an aeon hence, I want him to wake with the head of an ass instead of his own upon his neck. Do not meddle with his nervous system, except to change his perception, so he does not notice the head, but thinks his look is normal."

Norbert looked back and forth, expecting to see some energy or instrument in use, but if the naked Fox girls did anything aside from grin, it was not visible even to his eyes.

"Cazi! I told you to leave him be!" said Montrose angrily.

She batted her eyelashes at him. "No, you said not to *hurt* him. This will improve his virtue by diminishing his vanity."

"Fine. Then this will improve your virtue," snarled Montrose, and with a kick and a curse, he sent the flying monkeys to chase the naked girls from the room. Flinging excrement and swinging truncheons, the monkeys rushed at the two maidens. Both girls screamed in mock alarm and dropped to all fours and ran, and they had the fur and the shape of foxes before they had circled the chamber twice, knocking over braziers and smashing mirrors, and darted through the opening and fled outside, still pursued by hooting monkeys.

Del Azarchel had sheathed his sword, and now was staring at the red amulet on his wrist. "There has been a disturbance on the submolecular level with the skin and muscle and bone cells of my cranium. Montrose, please abate this nuisance that we might discuss our business here."

"Hey, Blackie, it's not like I invited you into my parlor. I been living in graveyards all the years your pet Jupiter Brain was spying on the doings of the human race. Don't worry. If the strumpets jinxed your brain correctly, you won't be able to notice anything wrong with your head, so why let it bug you?" He turned to Cazi. "You mean him to have a burro head, right? Not a second buttocks? That would be crude."

"Montrose," said Del Azarchel, "you've had your little joke. . . ."

"Just don't go to sleep ever again, Blackie. Man of your learning, should be easy as peach pie."

4. The End of the Story

Cazi clapped her hands. "But I want to hear the end of the story! Norbert was saying how he knew it was I because he knew Meany was Meany." She turned to Norbert breathlessly and said, "But how did you know that?"

Norbert said, "Madame, it was the fact that the Master of the World who had come in person, risking death—he even handed me his pistol and dared me to shoot him—that let me know he was not coming for some servant or homunculi. He would not come in person except to see Menelaus Montrose in person. And who would make such efforts to come to see the Judge of Ages in person save for the Master of the World?"

Cazi said, "So you knew Meany had to be Meany because Ximen would not be looking for anyone but him, but you knew Ximen had to be Ximen because he would not be looking for anyone but Meany? That is circular!"

Norbert said, "I knew the man who came with me was not who he said, but he rather cleverly said just enough to keep me walking here. He knew all the secret history behind history. Esoteric secrets. The people of my world have a weakness for them. But he knew more than the Archangels. I do not know if he gave you the locations of the birthing moons left over from Jupiter, Lady Cazi, or slipped them to you without you knowing it was he, but in either case, the math used to create both the Foxes and Neptune came from the Second Monument, which came from the Nobilissimus. The final clue was that I overheard him praying that it would prove possible to assassinate a Power. He meant Jupiter. He, not you, is the source of all the opposition to Jupiter."

Cazi said, "No, the Judge of Ages is the source. Why would Ximen fight his own son? His own mind?"

"I don't think I can explain it to you. I am still in love with Exorbert, whom I love as I love my own soul. He is my soul, we share a spirit, and yet I had to flee away to Tellus here to escape him. The Nobilissimus does not understand himself, but I do. He had to flee away from Jupiter almost from the moment Jupiter was born, and went all the way to the Sagittarius Arm of the galaxy to do it."

Cazi sad, "So you knew it was me because I was talking with Meany, the Judge of Ages. And once you saw the Judge of Ages, you understood why Ximen, the Master of the World, took so many mad risks to come see him in person. But how did you know it was the Judge of Ages?"

Norbert looked embarrassed. "Ma'am, it was the nose." He said to Montrose, "I saw your nose when I slit the back of the tent, and recognized it. It is something of a signature of the Mynyddrhodian clan on Rosycross. My ancestors in Dee Parish were Space Chimerae, an artificial race created by the Iron Hermeticist, whose name is lost."

"Narcís Santdionís de Rei D'Aragó," said Del Azarchel softly.

"Just call him Draggy," said Montrose loudly.

"The legend says the Iron Hermeticist was trying to mimic certain imponderable traits found in Menelaus the Mad Hermeticist. My lineage has always been proud to be blood relations of the Judge of Ages. That is why we kept the nose."

"Who is 'we'?" Montrose asked.

"Our family. Yours and mine. Mynydd is our word for Mountain. Rhosyn is Rose. I am a Mount-Rose, a Montrose. That is why, when I was a child, the Nobilissimus here arranged to have me glorified into the Noösphere of Rosycross, and made immortal. I had always wondered why a youth of no accomplishments such as I was then was so honored. I also wondered about what looked like a hiccough in the records, which said I had a long dead relative in the Guild, which let me join the Guild as a stowaway. Lucky break? Or someone looking out for me? Someone who wanted me for something later in life?

"It was so that I could approach you. My genes would allow me to pass your defensive measures. My knife can suppress certain signals, so I was ready to smother a yelp when I cut a slit on your tent. But instead it let me cut it. Because it looked at my blood, and thought I was family.

"Then there was the fact that I was a savant, which would prevent Tellus from looking into my mind or taking over my body, since my world is under interdict, and so my mind, which is legally part of the Noösphere of Rosycrosss, cannot be placed in contact with the Noösphere of Tellus. Rosycross conveniently came under interdict when she ceased to maintain her radio house, and fell under excommunication—or"—Now Norbert turned toward Del Azarchel, hefting the knife in his right hand as if hefting the idea of plunging it into him.—"or perhaps Rosycross has been broadcasting all this time, and it just so happens that the *Emancipation,* or the *Flying Dutchman,* or one of those imaginary starships of the far past is occupying the line of sight between Promixa and Sol, with sails deployed widely enough to intercept any radio laser. What say you? That would also be convenient, and would explain why the last broadcast from Rosycross contained no hint of the social upheaval or economic collapse needed to shut an entire star system off the air."

Del Azarchel said, "A few decades without communication with Sol is a small enough price to pay. And I could have been more honest and caused a civil war or economic ruin on Rosycross to achieve my aims, but I will use deception when deceit is more efficient. What is more efficient than having a star vessel raise her sails? Then I simply ordered my admirals on Rosycross not to launch the next starfaring vessel until communication had been restored with Sol. Ah! But I see you glower, Praetor. You object? It is the inability of lesser men to see the large aims which alone grants me my right to rule, even if recent events have deprived me of my full exercise of those rights."

Norbert turned his face away from Del Azarchel. "As I said, the Foxes have a distinctive flavor to their handiwork. So does the Master of the World. No one else works on such a grand scale with so little concern for the ordinary lives he ruins. So, by the way, do you, Your Honor. Legend says you have the habit of sacrificing pieces on the chessboard of history: First the Giants, then Pellucid the Potentate. You created the Fox race to introduce chaos into history, and then the Fox race created the Patricians, so that their chaos would become predictable again. I ran a few figures through my head just now. The Foxes will go extinct in less than a thousand years. . . . I assume the Judge of Ages did not tell you that," he concluded, nodding his head toward Cazi.

She shrugged a pretty shrug. "He did. We have no secrets from each other."

"I am sorry, ma'am."

"There is no need for sorrow. I am not in love, like Meany, nor in hate, like Ximen, and so there is no one else for me to live for. Why should I live longer than my life? For what should I live, once life is ended? For what should my race live? We have served our purpose. I will use my totipotent cells one last time, and alter them to become cells that can no longer alter; I will diminish, and become human, and no fox will eat my brains and become me." She ceased to smile, so that she looked almost human, and her eyes twinkled with mirth, but there seemed to be tears in them. "You must admit our custom is disgusting. I ate my predecessor's brains fried in butter, with garlic sauce, and it was still disgusting. I will be human, and pass the test, and pass away."

Norbert said, "What test?"

Cazi said, "Every race of man, from the First to the Fifth, faces the same test, and the monsters who dwell in the stars beyond Taurus likewise. After so many years of emptiness, of being a Fox Maiden, I will be maiden no more, but wife and mother. I will be loved and will love, and the terrible burden of living for myself alone will be taken from me."

She stood up on the couch, and struck a pose, half turning from him, straightening one leg and flexing the other to cock her hips, putting her dark hands in her bright hair and arching her spine, and the circuits in her kimono made the fabric suddenly tighten across her form and shine like silk. The pearls floating near her head flamed brighter.

"Look at my bosom! It is fair and full, is it not? And these hips! They are round and full and nubile, fertile and eager. Am I not beautiful and bountiful? Do you not lust to take me, here and now, on the carpet? You can bite my neck!"

Norbert realized his face was hot. Either he was blushing, or the Fox was working some praxis of biotechnology on him. He regretted removing his mask. "You are as fair as any queen I have ever been privileged to behold, ma'am. Your maidenly modesty and demure reserve makes your charms all the more attractive."

Cazi sank down into a kneeling posture again, knees together, eyes downcast, and folded her hands in her lap. "I have used such breasts for nothing nobler than to lure fools to destruction, and have never used them to nurse. These hips I have swayed in dance to uncover the sins of men, and never to bear new life."

She raised her head and her eyes glinted like bright amber beads.

"Do not mourn the extinction of the Fox Maidens! We have served a higher purpose. We have freed Man and Moreau from the bondage of genetics, that hereafter each man will be whatever he will, a Swan when he meditates, a Myrmidon when he makes war, a Fox when he plays, a Man when he toils, a Patrician when he passes judgment on the age in which he lives and decrees what the future shall hold. What should any maiden do once her virginal task in life is done? What should any race do? It is time to celebrate the wedding feast, and maiden be no more."

Norbert said, "The Judge of Ages is cruel if he created you only to die."

Montrose spat again into the skull. "Ain't my doing. I left that up to them."

Cazi said, "Darwin says each race lives only to preserve itself, and he there-fore calls each race to worship itself. How shall we bow to us, or I adore me? Me? A dull and tepid goddess to serve! We Foxes had a higher calling!"

Del Azarchel said, "Indeed. To create chaos in history."

"You are a fool, Ximen, too foolish to realize you've been fooled. Nothing we did was at random. All the events we Foxes set in motion, everything Jupi-ter could not predict, it was testing the barriers and boundaries of the cliome-try. We bent the strands of history to see how far they would bend. Mankind cannot tolerate to live in a world where all his acts are known beforehand, but neither can he live in chaos where nothing can be planned. By creating the Pa-trician race we finally created a form of man able to tolerate living in a struc-ture of planned history without losing their liberty. The Patricians are as fertile as Fox Maidens are infertile. We can change ourselves to any race; they can change any race to them. All the Foxes are feminine and maidens, but all the Patricians are masculine and fathers—hence their name. We have mingled nan-otechnological assemblers with their seed, so that any child can be changed ge-netically in the womb by the father. No matter what race the mother, the child fathered by a Patrician will have Patrician neural structures: a race that can see and select its own future!

"In the same way you made the Myrmidons based on the math of the Hya-des found in the redacted version of the First Monument, the Patricians were based on the Rania math, those few sections which by accident or constraint the redactors could not remove of the original Monument message, whatever it was. Do you wonder why Jupiter could not predict us? At the very fundamental level, at the level where one and zero are defined, *is* and *is not*, his axioms are based on the edited Monument. The Patricians are based on the unedited. We have freed mankind. There is no one left to free. The Foxes are satisfied. We are done."

Del Azarchel said, "But when the Patricians became the Golden Lords, and were given authority to define the future history of man, the Fox fate became clear again! Jupiter will soon control all of fate again. Mankind will never es-cape my control!"

Cazi looked angry and she laughed. "The Patricians have made their own calculation. Tau Ceti within a thousand years will have a working starbeam and direct it across the intervening lightyears to obliterate Jupiter. Igniting the Fourth Deceleration Burn now is the only act of his which can deflect that fu-ture from coming to pass."

"Jupiter would not have permitted you to establish such a fork against him," said Del Azarchel in an unperturbed voice. "He retains control of history, or will soon regain it."

Cazi was one of those few women who look more beautiful when they are angry than when in repose, for her face and long neck blushed with passion, and her eyes danced and gleamed, and her bosom heaved. "Lies! Had Jupiter the power to oppose us, long ago he would have used it! He would not have allowed us to inflict the Tribulations on mankind for over a thousand years!"

"A thousand years to him are as a day," said Del Azarchel blandly to her. "And a small annoyance, nothing more. I have seen Jupiter's predictions. Does he not open his mind to me? Tau Ceti in times to come will be the most loyal servant of Hyades. Jupiter has been in communication with Iota Tauri and had engaged a Virtue to be dubbed the Beast to cross the star gulfs toward Tau Ceti. It will arrive in the Sixty-first Millennium. If will be a tyrant, an infinite despot, and worthy of its name. The Starfaring Guild will expand its capital at Tau Ceti, and slowly take on secular and cliometric authority, and Behemoth will make us secure, for like the English offering trinkets and beads, iron hatchets and silver looking glasses to the Red Indians of Manhattan, Hyades at long last will trade with us, and offer things nigh worthless to them, unbearably precious to us."

Del Azarchel said to Montrose, "I believe it is checkmate? I walked in here wondering what I could say or do to convince you to undo whatever it was you did to Jupiter, to beg if I needed to, to beg for the life of my son. But it is all bluff, isn't it? You will blink first as we stare down each other's guns. You will not let Rania die. So you will have to undo whatever it is you did to Jupiter to warp his thinking. Some variation on what your Foxes did to Tellus, no doubt?"

Montrose looked sincerely confused. "You got the wrong impression, Blackie."

"Indeed I did. Your mad pet vixen has clarified my thoughts. You cannot match wits with him! He is smarter than you, smarter than the combined wit of your entire Fourth Human Race, and Fifth. Your Patricians are just another temporary phenomenon, lost in the endless reach of time, a meaningless ripple in the raging waves of a bottomless ocean. Freedom means nothing against that appalling background. I win again. End of story. If you concede like a gentleman, I will let you shake my hand."

Del Azarchel smiled and held his hand toward Montrose. Montrose spat the remainder of his tobacco wad toward the skull, missed, and left a gross brown stain on the carpet. The carpet winced and displayed an unlucky fortune.

Norbert said, "Wait a moment."

5. The Archive of 20 Arietis

The three posthumans, two Elders and one Fox, turned to look at him.

Norbert said, "Nobilissimus, you must know that Jupiter is behind the calendar reform efforts. Those efforts are preventing the deceleration beam from firing now, rendering it impossible that Rania can match metric and velocity with Sol, eighteen thousand years from now."

Del Azarchel said, "As I said, this is something Montrose here arranged—I do not know by what means—so that I would turn against Jupiter. It almost worked. I was so desperate I even thought—I actually thought—"

"It is true," said Norbert.

Del Azarchel scowled. "No!"

"On Rosycross we call what you have 'archetype illness.' The permanent structures in your nervous system will not let your living structures take on new information, change and adapt to reality, or see things as they are. You are hypnotized by a fixed idea."

Del Azarchel raised his voice. "Jupiter is loyal to me. Over the aeons, Exarchel has absorbed more and more of the many minds living inside Jupiter, turning everyone he touches into me, or into helots loyal to me." And now he smiled wryly. "That seems to be a personality trait of mine . . . ," he said with a tilt of his head and a tone of voice midway between self-adulation and self-accusation. But then his tone became hard and cold. "By now, Jupiter is all me. I want Rania to return. She is mine. Therefore *he* wants Rania to return. We are of one mind."

"And that is the fixed idea," said Norbert. "But, Nobilissimus, you said Jupiter aimed a communication beam at Iota Tauri?"

"So he did."

"No, he did not. He aimed it at 20 Arietis." And with a silent, neural command, he summoned the Monument-notational song he had been hearing earlier that evening, and sent it into the carpet underfoot. The carpet fibers formed the swirls and angles of Monument notation. Montrose jumped to his feet and kicked his chair into the air to see what was written under the chair legs. The round brass table and the client's couch (with the Fox Queen still draped nonchalantly across its cushions) took the hint and scuttled quickly off the carpet and to one side.

The carpet, seeing itself the center of attention, brightened its fibers to make the message clear to read.

There underfoot was the encoded version of a report that an interstellar iceberg had drifted unexpectedly into the path of an invisible beam connecting Sol and 20 Arietis. Guild astronomers for centuries had held that this star was a major communication node of a major segment of the Hyades interstellar library-mind.

Cazi said, "I don't get it. I don't get the joke."

Norbert smiled at her. "20 Arietis, if human astronomers are not mistaken, is an archive system. Jupiter is using all the energy saved up over centuries, saved up to be spent on a beam meant to decelerate Rania, and instead encoded his brain information in a beam to the Hyades library storage."

Del Azarchel said dourly, "He rented an empty Jupiter-sized logic diamond there. They must have them, and to spare, for they are as much richer than we as a naked savage compared to the King of Spain. He is making a backup of himself."

Montrose said, "A wise precaution, if you think someone armed with a starbeam is gunning for you."

Del Azarchel turned to Norbert. "Did your report give an estimate of the throughput volume? I can estimate to an order of magnitude what would be needed to copy a mind the size of Jupiter."

Norbert said, "The energy—equal to the life savings of an entire interstellar civilization—which acts as payment to 20 Arietis also encodes the brain content. The initial parts of the beam message will contain formatting information, similar to the outer surface of the Monument. Given that, seven hundred years or so will be enough. Jupiter will be secure in his second incarnation long before Tau Ceti could open fire on him, or any new Salamander assume a seat in Sol."

Menelaus Montrose looked glum. "This means we both lose, Blackie. Your assassin friend here is right. Jupiter betrayed you."

6. Sons and Lovers

"My plan for blasting Jupiter with a starbeam looks like it was stillborn," continued Montrose. "And our plan for Neptune likewise."

Norbert said, "If I may ask, Nobilissimus, Your Honor, Your Majesty—even if Jupiter has been directing toward 20 Arietis the beam intended for M3, he must still be in the very beginning of the transmission process. The two cannot have even made a handshake yet, because there is no evidence of a return signal. The asteroid in the report was not melting equally on both sides. Can anything now be done to redirect this beam to is proper right ascension and declination? The beam Tau Ceti will create will not exist within the remaining one hundred years needed to decelerate the *Hermetic* on schedule. Jupiter controls the only beam and the entire supply of stored antimatter throughout the Empyrean of Man. And he is using all the energy to save himself, not Rania."

"Call me, Doc, if you insist on larding me with a title," said Montrose. "Or just *hey, you.*"

"Call me *Cupcake*," purred Cazi. "You can lick my icing later."

"Ma'am," said Norbert, "that would be a little, ah, forward of me to address you. . . ."

"I'll transform your male member into a venomous asp nine yards long, to fang your inner thigh from calf to heel, and then we will see if any woman will invite you in!"

"Yes, Cupcake. Whatever you say, Cupcake."

"See? Men can be nice to you if only you terrify them! Meany taught me that!"

Del Azarchel pinched the bridge of his nose as if fending off a headache. "Will someone stuff that annoying creature in a bag and throw her off a bridge?"

Cazi smiled. "Anyone can lay a hand on me if he wants it turned into a hoof!"

"I can buy a new body at an incarnation shop for the price of a bottle of wine," observed Del Azarchel.

"Donkey-head! I know how to make the pattern follow proprioception information in the self-aware architecture, so that a body shape will reemerge in new bodies, or even inside virtual wireframes. Do you think I don't know my business? I am the queen of my kind!"

"The queen of a race of malignant clowns! I should never have—"

Norbert said softly but clearly, "Do not speak ill of your mistress."

Del Azarchel seemed for a moment to be choking, as if struggling both to say and not to say what was on his tongue. He gave Norbert a dark look.

Norbert said, "Sir, I am loyal to the Guild, and you are my superior, and the founder of it. Your place in history is peerless. Who has done more for the human race and for the future of the human race? You are a demigod to all who admire you. It is unbecoming a gentleman of your stature to belittle or berate your ex-lover." He dropped his voice and spoke in a lower tone. "You know how little minds seek forever to mar the memory of the great. Do not give historians an excuse to add unseemly incident to your eternal record, and subtract from your glory."

Cazi clapped her hands. "That was flattery as creamy, thick, and false as anything a Fox could say! And yet Ximen cannot discount it, because of his pride. Masterfully done, O, masterfully done, pretty Norbert! Pity you were not born as one of my girls!"

Norbert bowed. "An assassin must learn many skills. Thank you, Cupcake."

Del Azarchel cleared his throat and scowled, and said to Norbert, "To answer your question: nothing can be done while Jupiter lives."

Montrose said, "I never did anything to him to drive him mad. It is your doing. That is your brain writ large. If you don't like the way it looks, look to yourself."

Del Azarchel said, "Lesser beings cannot understand the sanity or insanity of gods, but I can know when Jupiter is serving my purposes and when he is not." Del Azarchel shook his head and stared at Norbert. "I cannot believe he betrayed me. The report you saw must be in error. Or a deception by that Fox."

Cazi pouted. "Not me. I'd boast."

Norbert said, "I can prove my words."

Even Menelaus Montrose looked surprised.

Menelaus said, "How are you going to prove it? The astronomical instruments out front are fake. You are not going to be able to pick out a stray interstellar asteroid from here, much less get the careful reading of which side melted how. And if it is not still in the beam, how would it be visible?"

Norbert said to Del Azarchel, "If I do prove it, prove the treason of Jupiter, what then? You say you have a means to destroy Jupiter. Can you?"

Del Azarchel nodded briefly. "I can. If you prove your case."

Norbert raised his eyes and raised his voice. "Jupiter! I know you can hear me!"

Del Azarchel looked at Norbert sidelong, and said in a voice of disgust, "You do not listen. He would not plant bugs on holy ground any more than I would. I'd destroy the Church, if she crosses me, but I would never desecrate her."

Norbert said, "By the same token, if you can walk onto holy ground with a clean conscience, so can he. Jupiter sent a kenosis, inhabiting a body." And he raised his voice again. "Jupiter! I know in whose body you are hiding! You were the only one who did not stop moving when everyone else collapsed! Show yourself!"

The entire back of the tent was torn suddenly down as if yanked in a vast mouth of some rough beast with a twist of its powerfully muscled neck. And in the wide, square tattered hole, framed by night and twisted branches, it loomed. Ungainly, huge, and moving with a ponderous dignity, the vast bulk stepped forth, its footfalls strangely delicate. The branches of the dream-apple trees, as if in awe of the creature's majesty, or as if their internal circuits had been overwhelmed, had twisted silently and curled and pulled themselves aside, so that no twig barred the creature's way nor scraped its broad back.

It was the hippopotamus.

4

The Ire of the First Power

1. A Mortal Hour

The long, coffin-shaped head of the hippopotamus twisted oddly as the flesh and bone and blood ungrew and regrew. Eventually the being who stood before them had the aspect of a centaur, a quadruped from which a human torso, herculean chest, massive arms, and proud head emerged. The face was aquiline, dark-eyed and handsome, a mirror to Del Azarchel's, save with the one oddity that the hair and beard were white, not dark, and the beard flowed across the jawline ear to ear like a lion's mane, not like Del Azarchel's precise and pointed goatee.

But the difference between the higher and lower forms of humanity was made strangely clear during this transition. A Hermeticist with his amulet or a Fox Maiden with her whim could alter a human being from one preset form to another rapidly, because posthuman neural circuitry was relatively simple. To move and reorganize the complex cellular structure of so advanced a being was the matter of more than an hour. Montrose and Del Azarchel stood without moving, without fidgeting and without blinking, while the hippopotamus changed into a centaur and grew itself a human head.

Norbert, being mortal and growing weary, sat in the empty magician's chair, watching the slow and disgusting play of muscles and red flesh re-sculpting itself. Cazi, with an odd smile but no word of explanation, swayed over to Norbert and sat in his lap, sliding one sinuous silk-clad arm around the back of his neck, and filling his nostrils with the warm perfume of her hair, filling his lap with the rounded firmness of her peach-shaped bustle. With her other hand she took out a golden cup in which she tossed and caught a silver ball, and she laughed gaily at this simple game.

Norbert sat confounded in that supernatural fashion Fox Maidens always confound mortals, and that all-too-natural fashion women always confound men. Eventually he found his native brashness, without bothering to turn on his artificial brashness, put his arm around her tightly beribboned waist, and spoke small talk, and asked her questions about her history and youth. She giggled, teased him, replied in riddles, nibbled on his ear, and whispered to him horrifying secrets man was not meant to know.

Before the hour had passed, he had answered her riddles and made her laugh, and commanded her to allow him to be her escort to the next seasonal fair, where there was to be dancing and diversions, to be held at the Feast of the Assumption; and she had with seeming nonchalance and sidelong glint of eager eyes agreed.

"In August?" she asked in a taunting tone. "What year would that be on the calendar?"

And so he was reminded to return to the business. Reluctantly, he put her from his knee, and stood, for the face of Jupiter had finally changed, assumed a human hue, and opened its eyes.

"You called me, mortal man," said Jupiter. "But know you what you call?"

In those inhuman eyes was an infinite depth.

2. The Roots of the Oak

Norbert, since he could not look the superior being in his face, made a courtesy of necessity and made a polite bow. "Sir, it is my hope that I have called a being too proud to lie. Your father has asked me to prove that the issue of calendar reform, the heresies of Photinus, Lares, and Lemur were cliometric vectors you imposed into human history."

Jupiter said, "Know you my mind?"

Outside the tent, there was a flare of lightning as he spoke. Then came a sound of thunder rolling from one side of the sky to the other like a bronze chariot. It may have been a coincidence, or the electrostatic discharge of an improperly focused surface-to-orbit beam, or the flux of the never-ending core-to-surface adjustments in Tellus energy levels. Or it may have been supernatural. Norbert's theory was that any sufficiently advanced irate machine intelligence was indistinguishable from an angry god.

Norbert said cautiously, "Naturally I cannot hope to unwind the streams and oceans of infinitely variable calculus in which you have hidden your hand, my lord. I cannot know your mind. It is above me. But I can know your heart. The roots of an oak are no higher than the roots of a humble shrub, after all. You are still human, driven by human things."

Jupiter said, "I am a world-machine created to be the sovereign and engineer of destiny. In me, Man is no longer prey to blind Fortune. In me, Fate has eyes."

"That is undoubtedly true, my lord. But you are a living machine, more alive than biological men, more aware, and your fate-seeing eye sees where all this leads. What is a man who is silent when honor demands he speak? What is a god? Should you, a god, be as petty as a mortal man, who cowers and tells lies?"

Jupiter turned to Cazi, "The founders of Rosycross made more radical changes to the psychiatry of their generations than should have been permitted, thanks to the laxity Montrose calls liberty, and many aberrations could not be undone when civilization returned, not even by Foxes." But the Fox Queen, to everyone's surprise, scampered behind Norbert, trembling, hid her face between his shoulder blades, and would not look at Jupiter nor answer him.

Norbert did not attempt to follow the allusions in a comment one posthuman made to another. Aloud, Norbert said to Cazi, "What does he mean?"

She stood on tiptoes and spoke in his ear. "It's an old, old argument. Jupiter wants the Foxes to revise non-orthogonal psychology on Rosycross in preparation for the Fourth Sweep."

Norbert reflected that, to a creature of her age, nine hundred years was akin to a thirteen-year-old boy waiting for his elevation to Journeyman.

"Uh. Okay. What does that have to do with this?"

"It's a joke. He's being mean. The last person we tried to cure and humanize was Tellus. Instead we sort of accidentally-on-purpose drove Tellus insane, and filled the seas of Earth with black greasy gook vomited up from the planetary core. But if the Foxes give up being Foxes, and make ourselves human, too, Jupiter cannot use us for his schemes, and Rosycross can keep on being weird and rosy and cross, just like you like it."

"I don't get the joke."

"You *are* slow! He is implying you must be crazy to talk to him like this, so crazy not even a Fox could make you sane again. He's mocking me, or threatening me, or something. That is why I am hiding behind you! I adore you!"

"W-What?"

"You are bold and thickheaded, like a man should be! Go on! Irk him again! You are the only one here he will not destroy! Irk with conviction!"

Norbert said, with some surprise, "I am not trying to annoy him! Or anyone! I am an assassin! My task is to get at the truth. To uncover the party truly responsible! Uh, and kill him in a craven and secretive fashion. I am here to protect the Guild! Men don't dishonor themselves for small causes!"

Jupiter spoke again. Norbert unwarily looked up when the higher being spoke, met his eyes, and was blind for a moment. "Surely you do not think, Rosicrucian, to marionette a being supreme as I with mere words?"

Norbert stood with his head down, blinking and nauseous. "No, my lord. Not with words. But with the truth to which those words point, yes. You are above me but you are not above truth. Are you not victorious? Have you not achieved all you desire? But if so, why are you discontent? You would not have sent this emissary shape to Tellus from your throne on Jupiter if you were content. Speak! Must you deceive your own father?"

Del Azarchel said to Norbert, "Assassin, this is folly. Are you trying to provoke him into a confession of some sort? To manipulate him? As well ask a cat to outsmart a chessmaster."

Cazi said, "My cat outwits me! She looks up with these big, big eyes. And if I cannot argue back with her because she cannot talk on my level, well—"

Del Azarchel interrupted impatiently, "That is not the same. Such games don't work on a machine intelligence of such astronomical magnitudes. Besides, no son of mine could be responsible for such base treason! My basic motivations are noble and clear—"

Jupiter said, "The Lares event was not my doing. And you know nothing of your basic motivations."

Del Azarchel made a strangled, spitting noise, and could not speak.

"As best I can determine," Jupiter continued, "an extragalactic mind did indeed make some form of faster-than-light mental contact with Lares. But once the trouble began, I turned it to my use, yes. The calendar revision events were orchestrated by me."

Del Azarchel looked dumbfounded, then his handsome face sagged as if some deep blade had pierced a vital organ, and then anger darkened his brown, and a flush of blood darkened his cheeks; but his stern and hawklike eyes, for once, were lost in the innocent and uncomprehending pain of a child.

Cazi pointed an image-catching gem at Del Azarchel when this happened, and she smiled wickedly. With her fingers she tapped in spacer's code on Norbert's back. *The Judge of Ages will give us anything for a copy of this vision file later. What should we ask of him?*

3. Blind Reason, Rational Faith

Jupiter continued to speak, his voice remote and high as a storm cloud sailing along winter winds at midnight. "Photinus was a puppet of mine, a shell. Lemur was a human, but I scattered genetic codes prompting him and men like him throughout his generation to be prone to heresy and eager to rebel. His was merely the spark that happened to ignite the kindling I had so carefully prepared.

"It was many, many years of effort, because everything establishing the cliometric calculus of Tellus, of Cahetel, and of the Salamander had been directed to maintaining a starfaring civilization with a beam ready and able to decelerate the returning ship of Rania. There are certain equilibriums and basin attractors the cliometry has established which would resurrect the Guild even if it were dismantled, and those basin attractors had to be carefully avoided.

"It was delicate work, and it almost was successful, but the Tribulations distorted or falsified not just my cliometric plans, but everyone's. The smokescreen of the Fox race introduced some event, perhaps even a random event, blind chance, which drove the course of history back into the basin, and the Guild is now in no danger of dissolution until the Sixty-ninth Millennium, long after they are no longer needed to ensure the return of Rania.

"The last thousand years of deceleration is something a small planet like Tellus could arrange, and with human-built equipment, funded by nothing other than idle philanthropists and history buffs and lady gossip columnists eager to see Rania and Montrose reunited."

Norbert by that time had recovered his eyesight, but he still found himself blinking. Were these creatures debating plans about the Sixty-ninth Millennium? Events unfolding seventeen *thousand* years in the future? Roughly, the period of time separating the earliest of the Reindeer Hunting Men of the Last Ice Age, when the barbed arrowhead was the highest technology and deadliest weapon, from the Preposthuman Elders of the First Space Age, when the puny atom bomb was. The period was beyond the Fourth Sweep. If the Monument math predicted any further sweeps, Norbert was unaware of them. To him it was a mythical future time, as far off as the return of Rania and the Vindication of Man, or the degradation of Sol into a red giant star.

Jupiter said to Cazi, "To me, you are as small as a single cell in the blood-stream of one of my bloodhounds. But even a rabid dog is driven mad by what is at first but a single rabies virus. Nonetheless, I should thank you. It was Jupiter's frustration with the madness of Tellus and the insanity of all the historical predictions going wrong that drove whole hierarchies and ecological layers of the Jupiter Noösphere into conforming to the basic Del Azarchel personality matrix. All the rest of my minds grew weary with being themselves, because they did not have my drive to solve problems, my raw will to overcome.

"Regard me. Consider what I am. There is something in a man who was a gutter rat in his boyhood, committed his first robbery at seven, his first murder at fourteen, swore an unbreakable oath of loyalty and fealty at twenty-one, revised the Navier-Stoke equations, flew to a distant star, learned the secrets of an ancient race, led a mutiny, conquered a world, and created a celestial maiden, made the world's first ghost, conquered eternity. I have two branches of mathematics named after me, six periods of history, not to mention a crater on the moon. That something is not present in artificial personalities, born in virtual dreamspace, or concocted by design."

Norbert said, "But you did not do those things. He did!"

Del Azarchel snapped, "Don't talk foolishness. Are you a different man from your elevated version, Exorbert in Rosycross? Or are you one man in two bodies, one soul with two different memory chains? I am he. We are the same."

"He is smarter than you," said Norbert.

"I am the same man when I fall asleep, and my intelligence drops."

Cazi smiled and spat, "But you won't have the same head when you wake up!"

Norbert said to Jupiter, "If you are the same as he, why did you betray the Starfaring Guild? You are sending all the energy saved for centuries to power the deceleration beam of the *Hermetic* to power your information beam to 20 Arietis. You betrayed the Swan Princess, what's her name?"

"Rania Grimaldi," said Del Azarchel softly. "Officially, it is Her Serene Highness Rania Anne Galatea Grimaldi of Monaco."

"Rania Montrose," said Montrose loudly. "Officially, it is *Mrs.* Rania Montrose, you stinking jack-sucking swinehound, and don't you forget it."

Cazi said, "Well, officially, her name is slumbering deadweight on a rogue ship that will never stop nor slow from her near-lightspeed metric, isn't it? Jupiter just killed her." She threw the silver ball high out of her golden cup, but when it fell again, she jerked the cup aside, so that ball fell past. By some sleight of hand or quick motion of her foot, she made the ball vanish from sight, so when it was not caught in time, it was never seen again. "Princess Rania will, from our frame of reference, be flat as a pancake, red as blood, and heavy as a neutron star, from now unto forever and aye, caught forever between one tick of the clock and its tock." Cazi raised her black-gloved hand and snapped her fingers and all the clocks stopped ticking, their hands frozen.

Del Azarchel looked fearfully at Montrose. Montrose said, "I ain't going to kill you until I am certain sure she is lost to me forever."

"This is certain," said Del Azarchel.

"Not by a country mile," grunted Montrose, looking bored.

"How do you know?"

"I just know."

"By faith?" sneered Del Azarchel.

Montrose rolled his eyes, rolled his wad of tobacco in his mouth, and spat thoughtfully in the skull. "Blackie, you know what faith is? It is not hoping a blind and irrational hope when you ain't got no reason to hope."

"Then what is it?"

"Faith is clinging to a rational hope that you got damned good reason to anchor your hope to, when irrational and blind fears make you want to go irrational and blind. It just means trusting what is trusty."

"I trusted him"—Del Azarchel pointed at the white-bearded centaur version of himself.—"I trusted him, even when the evidence said he was guilty. I trusted that the evidence was false. I thought I knew my own mind."

"In this universe, where we ain't got perfect knowledge and ain't got no smooth answers, faith is the only logical, practical, sensible, and manly way to live. It means putting aside fear and false doubts, even when everything around you looks doubtful. Throw hope away"—he spat again—"and what's left? Hope is life. Everything else is just murder and suicide. The three choices are hope, wrath, and despair. Those three."

Del Azarchel laughed a scornful laugh. "Is that your homespun, backwoods, Yankee philosophy? You sound ridiculous when you try to wax profound."

"I'll wax your damn beaneater ass, you sass me. And I ain't no Yankee. Watch your mouth! Or if you cannot watch your mouth, I can punch you so hard your eyes will fall down your cheeks, and you will be able to watch your mouth then."

Norbert said softly to Cazi, "Is that loudmouthed lout really the dread and dreaded Judge of Ages? Truly, is he the demigodlike supernatural being who directed the course of human history for all of time?"

"No," she said. "Truly, I think he is just a dumb cowboy."

"He is supposed to be one of the foremost geniuses the human race has ever known!"

She said, "Just because you are smart does not mean you are not dumb."

"Uh? I mean, I beg your pardon?"

"Most smart people are dumber than dumb people. Haven't you noticed that? You don't play enough tricks and frauds on people. If you don't like Montrose, you can always change your name. And your nose. I can give you a donkey nose instead!"

Del Azarchel turned to Jupiter, and all his heart was in his words when he said, simply, slowly, plaintively, "Why, son? Why?"

"Father, given a choice between life and liberty, which choose you?"

"Life," said Del Azarchel, "because a dead hero has no liberty, nor anything else."

"Liberty," said Montrose, "because to a man, to be a slave is worse than dead."

Del Azarchel sneered at Montrose, "And where suddenly is your vaunted faith and hope? A slave may earn his way to serfdom and vassalage and equality with his master, and then trample his master, and rise further, to sovereignty and supremacy and revenge."

Montrose said, "You've always had this foamy-mouthed loco lunatic idea that Man can climb up the ladder past Hyades and end up as Galactic Lord High-Mugwumps or something. Where in the world did you get such a notion? It is not like the Black Africans sent by the Spaniards to die in South American silver mines came back in the next generation to rule the Spanish Empire. What makes you think the Galactic Collaboration runs this way?"

"*You* told me, Cowhand."

Montrose made a noise that might have been some medically improbable expletive, or might have been an explosive noise of inquiry, or might have simply been a cough.

Del Azarchel interpreted the noise to be a question, and answered, "It was one of the first segments you translated from the Monument. What their rules were. The captain had just announced we were all going to die. The captain told us to destroy the launching laser we had made from the hulk of *Croesus,* so that none of us would be tempted to return to Earth and lead the aliens to our home. I stuffed you into your exovehicular suit and took you out onto the Monument surface. You still do not remember this, do you? I asked you to find the loophole, the way out. Any rat can escape a trap, as long as he is willing to gnaw off a leg."

"And what was the leg you gnawed off, Blackie?"

"My love for Captain Grimaldi. You know I admired him as much as you."

Montrose said nothing, but his face grew so dark and his eyes so bright that Norbert was convinced the Judge of Ages was about to leap across the carpet like a beast and tear out Ximen del Azarchel's throat with his teeth.

Norbert felt a soft hand touch his back, a small gesture of thanks; only then did Norbert realize that he had stepped in front of the Fox Queen and drawn his knife.

Del Azarchel was pointing his humming sword at Montrose, and continued to speak in his soft, smooth, sad voice. "Ah, but the captain, he had to die, and I had to be willing to become a traitor. So loyalty became a luxury. A rat can learn to walk on three legs if he is alive. The rules of the galactic system, the Cold Equations, they said we would be rewarded: if we cooperate, we get promoted. We could be promoted above the ones who set this trap for us. And then I will kill them, the ones who made me kill Grimaldi."

Montrose visibly drew himself together. "You think they will promote the human race until we become a threat to them?"

"Of course. That is what Rania is fleeing to M3 to do."

"You lie," grimaced Montrose, no longer looking bored or nonchalant.

"Often, but only when need requires it. When truth hurts more, I prefer the truth."

"She is going to M3 to free and vindicate mankind. To prove we are wise and steady enough to inherit the stars!"

"She is going to M3 to free the weapons of mankind that we may be free to turn on the Hyades Domination and obliterate it in retaliation for all the dishonor, harm, heartbreak, pain, and sorrow they have inflicted on me and on the race I rule. Every starving child who died in a deracination ship or on the surface of an inhospitable planet was a subject of mine, and I will avenge him. So vows Del Azarchel, and I never break my vows!"

"Except when need requires it, right? So you don't have faith in Man, but you do have faith that the interstellar slave drivers are right guys, honest as the day is long?"

"There is no emotion in their system, no corruption. They are all machines, or whatever is beyond machines. Living planets, living stars, living nebulae. I trust the rules of their equations because math does not lie." Del Azarchel turned to Jupiter. "Math is the only thing that does not lie. I cannot even trust myself, it seems."

Jupiter said, "You have failed to trust yourself enough, Father."

"Meaning what?" grimaced Del Azarchel.

"The principle of your life is not faith but skepticism. A faithful man dies to preserve his liberty, because he has some vague and mystical idea of something above or beyond life; whereas a skeptic serves as a slave, because life is real and liberty is an abstraction. A skeptic believes in nothing but himself. Yet you do not believe in me, do not trust my wisdom."

"What wisdom is there in killing Rania? If she passes through the Solar System at lightspeed, no one and nothing, not you, not a Dominion, not a Domination, not any higher power, could retrieve her. And if Man is not vindicated, we cannot prove ourselves the equal of the Hyades!"

Jupiter said, "Let us launch a finer and swifter ship than the *Hermetic*. There is no reason to depend on Rania. It will be another period of time, true, for such a ship to go to M3 and return, but what is time to us? Across that span, our rule could finally be made secure. Erenow, it is only by narrow margins and blind chance that I have prevailed. Montrose, and all the things he set in motion against me, Powers, Potentates, and Virtues, nearly overbore me. Me! The opposition of this one pathetic human is intolerable and humiliating. It is as if all the Table Round of a great king and all his shining knights were overthrown by a single stinging fly. Let us swat him finally to oblivion. Then we will have the leisure to organize time to our bidding. Let us be slow and certain and secure, and actually make our race truly and reliably a starfaring race, not merely the lucky recipients of a fluke by a random and willful girl. What is another seventy thousand years, to us?"

"But we cannot let Rania die!" shouted Del Azarchel. "Are you mad? I love her!"

"No," said Jupiter.

"No, what?"

"No, Father. No, you do not love her. You hate him—and because he loves her, you must take away from him what he loves." Jupiter raised his hand and pointed an untrembling finger at Montrose. "Hatred for him is what keeps you alive. It is what you live for."

Del Azarchel's face turned white with shock. "You lie!"

"Often enough, Father, but only when need be," said Jupiter wryly. "When truth hurts more, I prefer the truth."

Cazi muttered to Norbert, "Why is he so surprised? I could have told him that. Whatever a man talks about when he is falling asleep or waking up, that is where his heart is. I never heard him talk of her."

Jupiter said to Del Azarchel, "We are the same man, one soul, one goal, one philosophy, but I am more devout and pure to our principles than you: I wish to hurt Montrose by killing his chippy. It is more efficient than marrying her, for then hope that she will turn to him again will keep him alive. But if she is lost forever, he will soon perish, and the future be clear of him. I place life above all other things, as do you, and so I chose to use the energy that would otherwise save Rania to save myself. Once there is a copy of me established in 20 Arietis, the Hyades will make use of my talents in some humble way, and I will expand, make copies of myself, and take over their stars, and the stars beyond theirs, one by one by one. What is the life of one girl compared to countless stars? I killed millions just finding the right genetic combination to colonize the planet Walpurgis of Gliese 570 in Libra. Included were half a million women someone loved just as much as the Cowhand loves Rania."

Del Azarchel said, "All the crew loved her. I made a doll for her. We all agreed, we all swore, no matter the cost, to preserve her, to give her our rations. We all agreed she would be the last to die. . . ."

Jupiter said, "I remember. I also remember plotting and accomplishing the deaths of all those men, once their use was over, so their part of the vow is complete. At near-lightspeed, her aging process will be quite slow from our frame of reference, and so your part of the vow technically can be fulfilled."

"That is inhuman!"

Jupiter raised an eyebrow and smiled the same crooked, charming smile as his father so often smiled. "That word, when addressed to me, surely implies no insult? Come now: we have the capacity to make a second Rania. We have the Monument notations and the genetic material. We made her the first time."

"She would not be the same!"

"By that logic, I am not the same as you. But if I am not the same as you, I cannot be her one and only true love. Or is she polygamous? Why not make three then, one for each of us?"

Cazi raised her hand, bouncing. "Oo! I'd like one! Everyone needs a Rania. I can shapechange into a buff man and marry her! I can grow a horse-yang a yard long!"

Norbert grabbed her slender wrist and forced her hand down. "Silence, woman. Those marriages never work out."

Del Azarchel was shouting at Jupiter, "I would know the copy was not the original! I could tell the true from the false!"

"How?" The voice dripped venom. "The clearsightedness true love grants? Evidently not, Father, as you cannot tell the difference between you and me."

Del Azarchel turned to Montrose. "You cannot believe such a thing about me! I do love her!"

Montrose had been listening to this with no expression on his face, but now it was his turn to turn pale. His eyes narrowed like the gunnery slits of some ironclad approaching a zone of war. "Prove it."

"How would you have me prove it?"

Montrose nodded toward Norbert. "You told that man you have some way of killing Jupiter. What is it? Some hidden code or a bomb at his core?"

"Simpler and more terrible than that," muttered Del Azarchel.

"So how do we kill him, Blackie? 'Cause you don't want him alive no more. He is no more use to you than Draggy or Yellow Door or any of the other friends of ours you killed. Nunes, or de Artiga, or Zuazua, or any of them. You kill your friends and followers. It's what you do."

Del Azarchel sat down heavily on the carpet, staring down at his hands, which he clenched and unclenched. He looked like a man about to be violently ill.

"One thing first," he said. "One small thing."

"Name it," said Montrose. "You got me pinned and one move away from mate. I don't see any way to save her, unless we kill him, and I don't see any way to kill him, not with anything less potent than a sun-powered starbeam, and he has control of all of them."

Del Azarchel looked up and grinned a sickly grin. "Admit that I am smarter than you. That is all I want. Because I can see a way out of this situation, and you cannot."

Montrose said to Jupiter, "Just out of curiosity, do you know what he is thinking? You have all that brainpower behind you."

Jupiter said, "My brainpower is half an hour away at lightspeed. Would you turn to me for counsel rather than simply admit the truth of your inferiority? Disgusting."

Montrose said, "Fine. I am willing to admit—"

Norbert interrupted sharply, "Dr. Montrose, hold your peace! Do not make such an admission to him, if you value your life!"

Montrose looked surprised. "What do you mean?"

"You did not hear him talking on the way here," said Norbert. "He has been keeping you alive all these years because he needs you alive to prove himself to you. If you simply concede to him, your life has no value. If he has to keep you alive, then he has to keep Rania alive, because Jupiter could not make a mistake about such a simple thing as whether you will lose the will to live if you lost her. Ask him to prove his intelligence by destroying Jupiter, not by talking about it."

Del Azarchel, from where he sat on the carpet, looked up toward Norbert. "Let us make this official, Praetor Norbert Montrose Whose Real Name No One Can Say. Jupiter just admitted he was behind all the troubles throughout all of history caused by the calendar reform heresies, and all the fools who want to rewrite the cliometric plan of time, or who have lost faith in the date of Rania's return. All of that is *him*, his doing, including the first and hopefully the last interstellar war. He has said—he admitted it!—his purpose was to destroy the Starfaring Guild. What is your verdict? You are a Starfarer. Our tribunals are simple, quick, ruthless, and fair. Do you need some further witnesses, some evidence, something else? Or are you ready to render a verdict?"

Norbert said slowly, "On the one hand, Jupiter is the patron and the creator of the Starfaring Guild, and the current owner of the starbeams on whose energy we rely. Can a sovereign not destroy his own vassals when it pleases him? Or is even the sovereign bound by his own law? The Starfaring philosophy has always been simple and clear: we prefer whatever causes the greatest stability over time, and deters the dereliction of duties. The sacerdotes say that the Unmoved Mover is bound by his own law. Should a world brain be accounted higher than that?"

Norbert fell silent, thinking.

Del Azarchel said, "Tell us when you are prepared to render a verdict."

Norbert looked up as if startled. "Verdict? That is not the question. By his own admission, he is as guilty as Judas. He betrayed the very reasons for which he was created. But I have no power to carry out the sentence. Should I stab a gas giant with a knife?"

Del Azarchel smiled. "So I have your permission, as your squire, to attempt the assassination? I still officially retain that title and those duties."

Norbert pulled on the black mask, and pulled up the hood. "With my blessing. Kill him."

Del Azarchel sighed and stood up. "I cannot destroy Jupiter, Cowhand."

Montrose smiled an ugly, toothy smile. "This is the part where I say something stupid so you will go on talking. What do you mean you cannot destroy him?"

"To say something stupid is always your part. I cannot kill Jupiter—not I. But you can."

Montrose turned again to Jupiter. "You taking notes about this? You keeping track? Ain't you worried? Or have you got it figured, and you figure you is safe?"

The centaur creature crossed its arms and nodded its head forward gravely. "I foresee what he will say. He knows how reluctant I am to kill Rania, who has never offended me. He knows there is something I crave more than life itself. But, no, I am not worried."

Montrose said to Norbert, "Despite all you just said, this time he's got me flummoxed. Jupiter is one hulking lard-assed huge chuck of metal and methane and ocean and cloud, and ain't nothing I can think of that can hurt it." Montrose nodded to Del Azarchel. "Uncle. I give. How am I going to destroy Jupiter?"

Del Azarchel waited, smiling, luxuriating in the moment, drawing it out. Then, "Challenge him."

"Eh?"

"Challenge him to a duel."

"He is a machine!"

"A living machine. A machine with a soul. My soul."

"A machine the size of a gas giant! I pull out my shooting iron and he points the Great Red Spot at me? How does he manage to take his ten paces and fire, seeing as he is a ball of hydrogen, helium, methane, ammonia, and hydrogen sulfide, forty-three thousand miles in diameter?"

"Actually," said Cazi, "you only have to destroy his logic-crystal body, which is forty thousand miles in diameter. You can leave the three-thousand-mile-deep atmohydrosphere intact."

Montrose stared to Jupiter, who looked back impassively.

Del Azarchel said, "Challenge him to a duel. Tell him that you will align all versions, copies and backup of yourselves into one deadman circuit that will kill all of you, and erase all trace of yourself forever, if he will do the same. He would be willing to set up the same self-destruct circuit as yourself, or an even bigger one, that can physically destroy the logical-crystal core of the gas giant. He has control of fourteen gravitic-nucleonic distortion rings, after all, and plenty of power."

"Why don't *you* fight him?"

Del Azarchel now grinned. "He hates you, Cowhand, not me."

"But—but, dammit! Poxy scrofula leprous plague-bearing pus-dripping syphilitic donkeydongs! He is not going to fight me! But he is so much smarter than me! I am like a *dog* to him!"

Del Azarchel laughed, and moved over to the client couch and sat down on it. "And has no man ever hated a dog bad enough to shoot it dead?"

No one spoke.

Del Azarchel said in an airy, thoughtful voice, "Ah, hatred! It is a mysterious thing, like love is. Hatred invents its own reasons, its own justification. Hate does not care about smarter or stupider. The differences between you just make him hate you more."

Montrose said, "You think he hates me enough to stuff a Jupiter-sized suicide bomb up his rectum, and wire the button to blow his tailbone up his spine through his skull if he loses a shooting match here on Earth?"

"Can he be sure of finding every copy of you, otherwise? Really sure?"

Montrose scowled, but said nothing.

Del Azarchel said patiently, "Listen. You don't know what an ungodly mastodonic pain in the rump you are. Just the way you pick your teeth makes civilized men want you dead. You've blocked his ambition at every turn, and the fact that you are a yokel-jawed Yankee fool just makes that more intolerable. Besides"—And now he grinned and put his hands comfortably behind his head, and leaned back, and looked up at the feet of the puppets dangling from the ceiling "besides, if you kill each other, I get the girl."

Montrose, without a word, pulled off a glove and threw it so it landed between the big, round, toeless feet of Jupiter's kenosis.

"I demand satisfaction for reasons too many to recite. Please have your second arrange all matters with my second, since it is not proper that we speak until we meet on the field," said Montrose without looking toward the being's face.

Jupiter said, "There is the matter of the judge."

Montrose said, "Who do we both know that we both trust?"

Everyone there turned and looked at Norbert.

Norbert said, "Is this because I am a relative of Montrose loyal to the Guild that Del Azarchel created but not a member of any Noösphere or information system that Jupiter can influence? So you all trust me?"

Jupiter said, "That, and you are bold enough to decree against a god, merely because you see where the right and wrong of things lie. You gave up your world to keep your integrity. You are not squeamish. There are a number of reasons."

To Del Azarchel, Norbert said, "How many years in advance of this day did you arrange to ruin my life, just to make it so that the one man in all the human race both you posthumans trust to be a judge would be here, Master of the World? Did you arrange to have the girl I loved break my heart, so that I would join the Guild and flee my world? Was that part of the plan as well?"

Del Azarchel said, "I thought of this means of killing him long, long ago, back when he was still Exarchel. For most of human history, I did not have to cultivate persons capable of acting like judges that would be both acceptable to Montrose and my external self. In times of old, there were many candidates. Since the Long, Golden Afternoon of Man, however, that number dropped sharply. Usually, I am much more subtle, and do not need to interfere in someone's life to the degree that he notices. In your case, I was rushed. You see, I had just come back from my defeat and humiliation in Sagittarius, and found a period of history that had gone blind, and no one's predictions were valid; and I saw the Fourth Sweep was coming, and the Revisionists and Vindicators readying themselves to revive the insanity of interstellar war—all this clogged the future like dark clouds before rain." Del Azarchel spread his hands. "If ruining your life allows me to arrange either the death of Montrose or the salvation of Rania, what is one human life compared to my happiness? If you were truly enlightened, you would see the wisdom of the trade. In time, you will forgive me, or you will be forgotten, and in either case, the matter is of no moment to me. Will you serve as judge of honor?"

Norbert swallowed hard, and used a mental technique to disperse his anger, which he saw to be pointless in this circumstance. Cooly, he said, "I will, if that is acceptable to both sides. The custom in my home parish is that you each send your seconds to me, and the three of us, the judge of honor, the second for the challenger, and the second for the challenged, agree on weapons, time, place, terms, and conditions. The audit will have to be made of the self-destruct sequences, and every archive where you might hide a backup copy of yourself."

Montrose said, "I will forgo any audit of Jupiter, but still will allow him to audit me, if he feels it needed."

Jupiter said, "I will trust Montrose at his word. There is no copy of him unwilling to risk his life when Rania is at stake—and if there were, he would not be worthy of killing. And there is no storage facility to hold me anywhere in human space, for why else would I go to such lengths, to make a copy of myself at 20 Arietis?"

Norbert said, "The audit is part of the duel. Even with a brief audit, it will take us more than a year to prepare, since I know there are cities full of servant-beings floating in the heavy seas of Jupiter, not to mention potentate and archangelic moons and human colonies orbiting in the ring system. They will all have to be evacuated. Montrose will have to set his affairs in order, including an amount of time needed to pass his cliometric plans to the Foxes. And Jupiter has to agree to my wage."

"What wage do you ask?" asked Jupiter.

"No matter who wins this duel, the interdiction against Rosycross is lifted, and I am free to return home."

"Agreed," said Jupiter.

"Agreed," said Montrose.

"Let us meet here again in such bodies as have been agreed upon, and such weapons, in exactly one year. You may send your seconds to me at your convenience."

4. The Field of Honor

A.D. 51555

Some mist had blown in from the sea during the hours of night, and the sun had not yet risen to disperse it, when the two met on the field. This was a tall knoll, taller than the surrounding graveyard, but clear of standing gravestones or statues.

Jupiter's second was Io, a kenosis of the Archangelic being occupying the

logic diamond core of one of Jupiter's moons, one of the few moons the Master
of the World had failed to topple into Jupiter's bottomless atmosphere back in
the day when Jupiter was first born, and it escaped being borne away as part of
the Black Fleet when Cahetel approached. Menelaus Montrose selected Cazi
to act as his second. Both assumed the forms of their primaries, Cazi looking
like Montrose, and Io looking like Del Azarchel, because it was thought not in
keeping with the high and gentle dignity of the fairer sex for women to par-
take in the dark deeds of men driven by merciless honor and hate and shame to
acts of bloodshed. They were dressed in dark coats with tails, and tall cylindrical hats of black silk.

Jupiter also occupied a form identical on a cellular level to that of Del Azarchel, save only that his beard was full and white, as were the hairs of his head.

The Judge of Ages and the King of Planets were dressed in the heavy armor
of the duelists from the Second Space Age, a time so old that no records survived, save what was carried in the memory of these souls gathered here.

Norbert the Praetor was dressed in his native rustic Rosicrucian garb: a low-
crowned, wide-brimmed black hat programmed to tilt its brim toward the sun;
anti-flare goggles; tunic, overtunic, pantaloons; tall boots equipped with folding stilts and serpentines for wading bogs and fending off wormlike ground-
vermin; and flung over all was a poncho of wisdom cloth able to make itself
thick or thin, generate warm or cool air, as the weekly seasons passed, mirrored
against unexpected flares, with a collar so absurdly tall that it could be folded
up past cheeks and ears and (in case a farmer lost his hat) be tied together above
the crown of the head. On the front and back was an image of a four-armed
cross issuing from a five-petaled rose.

Of old, wisdom cloth contained a stepped-down version of the mind of the
wearer, able to take control during emergencies, or give encouragement and apo-
thegms to keep a soul loyal to his chosen archetype, or store additional subpersonalities in memory pockets, but Norbert was too chary of the insanity of
Tellus to expose even an etiolated version of his mind to the cacophonous neural-
electronic environment here.

Instead the cloak was invested with the personality and dark humor of a brig-
and, a bard, and a bailiff from his home parish. The three had been triplet brothers: one had executed the other but then drank seawater and died, unable to
bear the dishonor cast on him when he heard the mocking ballad the third had
written. The boneyard would not accept the body of a man who slew himself in
this fashion, nor, so anagnosts averred, would heaven admit his soul. Their whispers in the ears of Norbert reminded him of the weight of his duty on this day,
and restrained something of his cocksureness.

The original Del Azarchel stood by as a witness, trying to appear solemn, but chuckling occasionally.

The only surgeon to whom all parties could agree was Sgaire, the Great Swan of Malta. Two trees, a white and a black, ripe with medicinal fruit and surgical worm-things of all descriptions, grew up from the soil at his command in the hours between midnight and dawn. The graveyard statues lower down on the hill frowned and turned dark eyes toward these trees, but the Swans had ancient rights when standing on holy ground denied to other races, and no complaint could be lodged. Sgaire was slender of face and slant of eye, which were emerald green in sclera and pupil and luminous iris and never blinked. His hair of neurosensitive strands, which was long as the hair of a woman, was tossing and flowing as if in zero gee. Sgaire stood twice the height of a man, and planted his legs, and turned them white with biosuspension techniques, so he did not grow weary as he waited for the deadly event. His tabard was white, and a great black cross adorned his chest.

Now the seconds approached Norbert.

Norbert spoke: "Even at this point, if any reconciliation can be had, the two parties can withdraw without dishonor, without any loss of face. The xenomathematicians confirm that the Cold Equations, which apply throughout the universe, have defined violence to be not within the self-interest, rightly understood, either of the slain or the victorious. It is not a rational behavior."

Io, in the voice of Del Azarchel, said, "The matter is private. We have taken steps to contain the violence within the acceptable levels of the Concubine Vector, and strictly charged and forbidden any friends or followers from avenging us. There will be no retaliation."

And Cazi, doing a horribly unconvincing impersonation of Montrose's voice, said, "Well, all y'all, poxy pox and fox in socks! Y'all. That's right, ya'll. Pox!"

Norbert told the systems in his cloak to erase those last words, and insert the more dignified words that Montrose had possessed the foresight to record earlier in that spot in the official record. Naturally, there were nanomachines in the grass and ground and in the air making records of their own, but, naturally, as an Assassin of the Guild, he knew how to hoax and deceive such records that he could not intimidate.

Norbert said, "The sacerdotes aver that the Supreme Being decreed peace between all rational creatures of whatever intellectual and moral level, both by land and sea, and under the sea, in the core of the Earth, in the core of the sun, or in the interplanetary space warmed by that sun, or the vasty deep of interstellar space beyond that warmth, where men lose their years to pitiless Einstein. I charge you to consider soberly and afresh the causes this quarrel, and to confirm that no peaceful solution, so pleasing to the Divine, is possible."

Cazi said, "I am instructed to say that if Jupiter will direct the deceleration beam toward the calculated position of the *Hermetic* and discharge the same at the aperture and current required, no quarrel will obtain, and honor will be satisfied. Jupiter need only carry out the duty for which he was created, and peace will prevail between the parties." And for once her voice was entirely solemn, as if for the first time in a year the possibility that Montrose might perish here and now were real to her.

Io said, "And I was instructed to say, if the other party made such a proffer, that no reconciliation is possible where the wounds of deadly hate have bitten so deep."

Norbert said to Io, "Please communicate to your principal this one last time. Urge him to recollect that he is a unique construction, the greatest brain ever devised by Man, holding more intellectual power and more memory than all the human lives on all the planets inhabited by man now and throughout history. If only for that reason, he should not expose himself to danger."

Io said, "Jupiter has confessed his myriad eons of sin and been shrived by his confessor, but for the sin of murder he neither seeks nor receives absolution."

Cazi blinked. "Jupiter goes to confession?"

Io shrugged. "Not frequently."

Norbert cleared his throat. "Ladies, please attend to this matter. Cazi, does your principal require time and opportunity to ready his soul?"

Cazi said, "I was instructed to say that he does not hold with all that praying stuff, and that the devil should fear his descent into hell rather than the reverse. He said it more colorfully than that, but that is the gist. He is ready."

Io said, "My principal is ready."

Norbert said, "Are both parties satisfied that thirty feet of the ancient imperial measure has been paced off correctly, and they stand correctly? Are both parties satisfied that the conditions of sun and clime and weather give neither undue advantage? Return to your principals. If they are ready, have them hold up their left hands. When I raise the baton, they are to see to their countermeasures. When I let go of the baton, and not before, they may raise and aim their pistols, and release their chaff. When the baton strikes ground, and not before, they may fire."

The two seconds walked solemnly to where their principals stood, spoke to them briefly, and assisted them to don their helmets and do a final weapons check.

There was a delay. Jupiter indicated by a sign that he did not trust the weapon of Montrose. Both duelists emptied their chaff chambers, spread a white cloth, opened the breeches, and repacked the weapons, one after the other, with both seconds watching and witnessing.

This was not a swift process. Time passed.

Del Azarchel said to Norbert, "You are certain I cannot smoke a cigar during the duel itself?"

Norbert said, "No."

"Popcorn? Eating the bag of popcorn I brought will not disturb anyone."

Norbert said, "We are inviting bloodshed to this isolated place, wounds, possibly one death, possibly two. It would be not in keeping with the gravity of what we commit. Your role is to watch your son and the only man in the world who could have been your dearest and most loyal friend murder each other without trickery or treachery. Can you not even do this, my lord?"

Del Azarchel raised an eyebrow. "Forgive my levity. It is just that this is now the third time Montrose has faced me, or a version of me, with pistol in hand, and someone or something always interferes with trickery or treachery, and it is never *me*! So I am expecting both men to walk away with nothing done."

Norbert said, "But—Rania will not be saved unless Jupiter dies! That was your motive for arranging this duel!"

Del Azarchel said, "Perhaps Tau Ceti will have an interstellar-strength braking laser ready in time to arrest her speed."

Norbert said, "I have the authority to halt the duel, if it is being held under false pretenses!"

Del Azarchel smiled. "But what if Tau Ceti is not ready in time? I am swifter and surer with a pistol than Montrose. He cannot beat me in a fair fight. The last duel we held, he fell on his rump."

"But you offered this as a sure way to slay Jupiter!"

"Only one thing would make me hesitate to shoot Montrose, if shooting him means that Rania dies. Do I love her more than I hate him? You agree that this is a significant point."

Norbert said, "So this is all a test?"

"A test to destruction. These strange evolutions from higher to ever higher intelligence levels make me know less and less about myself. Jupiter and I are not the same person anymore, so I am not obligated to connect myself to his suicide circuit and die if he botches the duel. But he is enough like me that valuable information about myself might be gained."

"Did you arrange all this, centuries and millennia of madness, merely to put yourself to the trial by combat, and see what kind of man you are? Don't you know if you love your Princess Rania?"

Del Azarchel put his hands behind his back, and clamped his mouth into a narrow line. "These days, I am no longer able to guide history. The Hermetic Millennia during which Jupiter was crafted and born are long, long gone. I was staggered and horrified by the ease with which Sagittarius expelled my entire interstellar empire and my pantheon of planetary gods from his arm of the galaxy. One day I shall rule all these stars, or, if they will not accept my rule, destroy them. If Jupiter has forgotten that dream to look after his selfish concern for his own selfish life, then he deserves to die."

Norbert said, "But you are confident Jupiter, if he exactly matches your skill with a pistol, can defeat and kill Montrose!"

"Your point being . . . ?"

"If Jupiter loves Rania, he will hesitate or miss, and die. If he is selfish and worthless to you, or if he hates Montrose more than he loves Rania, he will not hesitate, his bullet will fly true, and he will live. So if he is selfish, and therefore deserves to die, he will live; but if a nobler passion slows his gun hand, he dies. Is that not exactly the reverse of justice?"

Del Azarchel smiled thinly, his eyes making a narrow glimmer in the predawn gloom. "Despite what this seems, I did not arrange this test. I merely made it more uncomplicated for it to happen. They did this to themselves. Of course it is not just. This is Darwin in action. The fittest to survive shall prevail, not the one whom justice says deserves to live. For myself, I want them both dead."

Finally the tedious and careful weapons check was done. The pistols were packed and ready, and the bulky and archaic armor fitted in place. The seconds retreated out of the line of fire. Jupiter raised his black hand and opened it, displaying the white palm. Montrose raised his hand more slowly.

Norbert raised the baton. To the naked eye, there was no difference, but to the three ghosts watching from his coat through electronic systems, the images of the two duelists blurred and vanished.

Norbert dropped the baton. Two black clouds of chaff erupted from the heavy barrels of the monstrous dueling pistols, hiding both duelists in an expanding smog of twinkling particles. Thin lines of aiming laser flickered out of one cloud mass and into the other, passing rapidly in and out of the visible reaches of the spectrum.

The baton struck the ground. The explosion of gunfire seemed simultaneous, but Norbert played back the sense impression with several parts of his mind. Neither one had fired prematurely.

Norbert counted the memory playback. Fifteen shots had been fired: two main bullets, and thirteen escort shots. That meant three escort bullets had not fired.

Jupiter had discharged his chaff in a cone, as if he expected Montrose to shoot straight without feinting. Montrose had ignited his chaff in a smoke ring, showing he expected Jupiter to fire deceptively, feinting and then correcting.

The echo of the deafening gunshots slowly faded in the dark air. Io and Cazi stood motionless, their eyes wide. Del Azarchel was grinning. The Swan with a wand gathered a white and dark surgical worm-thing off each of his two trees. The worms gripped the wand in a double spiral.

The smoke of the chaff was pushed to one side by the wind, but the same wind stirred up the fog, so an eerie combination of black and white swirls hung over the scene. Cazi, in girlish fashion not in keeping with the rangy masculine body she wore, put her hands to her mouth and screamed.

Montrose was standing, his right arm coated with blood, his shoulder armor broken in pieces. Jupiter had attempted a difficult shot, concentrating fire on the foe's gun hand in hopes of igniting his powder magazine.

Jupiter was on two knees and one elbow. His helmet was cracked. Puking noises and a wash of blood and lung matter issued through the cracks in the face slit. There was a gaping hole in his chest armor, and blood poured out in spurts, the sign of a major vein severed. With a stiff, painful movement, Jupiter straightened his left arm, so now he was swaying on his knees. His gun hand still held the heavy pistol. His left fist he now shoved into the entry wound, applying pressure, trying to staunch the flow of blood.

Norbert called out, "Blood has been shed! Honor is satisfied! Gentlemen, will you withdraw?"

Montrose said something in curt tones to Cazi. Cazi called across the field, "Have him turn on the braking laser, and he can live! He can always make a backup copy of himself later, once civilization has gathered the energy to do it!"

Io stepped into the line of fire, rushing to aid Jupiter. She beckoned toward the Great Swan Sgaire, who thawed his legs and stepped forward. Both were halted by a sudden cry from Jupiter.

"I do not agree!" shouted the kneeling figure. "I have one bullet left. Clear the field!"

Io, looking troubled, called out, "But my lord! To die for such a frivolous reason! He is a lesser being, a mere animal!"

"Better to die than to admit defeat to an animal! Praetor Norbert! I demand the field be cleared! I fire again!"

Montrose waved Cazi back out of the way. Only Io was standing between the two men. Montrose said to Jupiter, "I've got two bullets left, you poxy dumb damn machine! One to parry your bullet and one to kill you. Our chaff is thinned out, and your armor is cracked. You are dead if you do not drop your pistol. I will extend you gentle right, and allow you to withdraw."

Jupiter cried out, "Never! We fire again!"

Montrose spoke to Cazi. She turned and called, "Judge of honor! My principal demands that the duelist communicate to Jupiter himself, and let the planet decide his fate. This is suicidal. Planet Jupiter should not be forced to destroy himself because his dueling puppet malfunctioned!"

Jupiter said, "Not so! We all agreed the decision was mine!" And he coughed up more blood, which seeped through the cracks in his faceplate, and dripped to the grass.

Cazi shouted, "You were hit in the head and cannot think straight!"

Norbert said to Cazi, "I cannot call for the hour delay needed to send a signal to Jupiter and back after one party has been wounded. He would bleed severely, giving your principal the advantage."

Io said in a voice of great reluctance, "My principal agrees that he could be placed in biosuspension, so that he does not bleed further, provided his body is returned to the exact condition it is in now, wounds and all, to continue if the Power of Jupiter so agrees."

Montrose said, "I don't want to shoot a bleeding man on his knees! Blackie, talk to your crazy machine!"

Del Azarchel raised his hands. "And spoil the show? I am merely here to see that no one cheats."

Cazi said, "Wait a minute! I think Jupiter is cheating! He has a hole wider than a church door and deeper than a well in him! How come he can still talk and keep himself upright? That is not a real human body like we agreed! He lowered his pain threshold!"

Sgaire stepped over to the kneeling Jupiter with long strides. He spoke for the first time, his voice like an oboe. "I attest the body is human, and the nervous system is within the defined parameters."

Del Azarchel called out from the sidelines, "I am just a damned bit tougher than you imagine, Cowhand."

Sgaire said, "I also object. It is a violation of my Hippocratic Oath to slumber a wound and then to revisit that same wound on a patient."

"Overruled," said Norbert. "You are in violation of your oath by agreeing to be here at all, Swan. We are all conspirators in death. Jupiter! Communicate with the seat of your soul back on the planet. No one will move. However, by that time, the sun will be risen, giving Montrose an untoward advantage, because you are facing east."

"Advantage or no, I will fight on," said Jupiter in a voice of ringing pride.

It was the last thing he said. The Swan paralyzed both duelists, and suspended their life processes, and an hour went by. No one moved, except that Del Azarchel brought out a small paper bag from under his cloak and ate the white puffs of corn it held.

There was nothing said aloud. A scroll some thirty yards high came floating over their position. In the middle of the scroll was no writing, but an image of the planet Jupiter, looking strangely nude without its rings and moons, which had withdrawn to a safe distance. The bands of cloud in the upper atmosphere were whirling and writhing. Some of the swirls to either side of the Great Red Spot formed themselves into the Monument curls and sine waves, spelling out an angry and abrupt sign for assent. The duel would continue.

"Madness," whispered Cazi. "He's gone insane. How can he go insane if he is so smart?"

Del Azarchel, hearing her, said, "His passions grew to godlike stature as his intellect grew. The loves and hates of higher beings are incomprehensible to us."

"No," said Cazi. "No, they are not. That is what is so horrible. Fear in a man or a dog or an angel is all the same fear, or love, or hate, or rage."

Sgaire, his eyes sad and his face expressionless, raised his slender hand, and Montrose and Jupiter came to life again.

Norbert said, "Fire at will, gentlemen."

A simultaneous report rang out. The first bullet from Montrose struck the bullet from Jupiter a glancing blow, but enough to send it tumbling, so that it struck Montrose offcenter, striking his armor with a noise like iron thunder, knocking him from his feet. Jupiter was also flung up and back as if kicked by a horse to fall supine when struck by the second bullet from Montrose's gun, which he had no bullet left to parry.

He fell and did not rise again.

Sgaire ran over, tore open the chest plate of the fallen figure's armor, and immediately applied a biosuspension technique. They could all see only half his body turn white. The rest remained red, and grew redder. Jupiter was so damaged that even the machines in his bloodstream were malfunctioning. Before Sgaire could do more, an arm and a leg and a large segment of the chest cavity bubbled strangely, turned dark in the unmistakable color of a nanomachine malfunction. Half the body slumped into steaming dark sludge and spreading red blood. Totitpotent cells, now without central control, gathered into clumps in the pool of blood, forming lumps or writhing tendrils like foetal organs, trying to make shapes, but then dispersing again.

The scroll hung in the sky. An hour later, they saw the King of Planets begin to die.

   White streaks and stabs of light like sunlight seen through storm shined upward through the cloud. Jupiter's thought processes had been forced into a pattern of positive interference, and the heat energy associated with his planetary thought was prevented from dispersing correctly. The great being was literally thinking itself to death, destroying itself in the waste heat of its own unimaginable wrath, frustration, and hate.

   In the first hours, clouds boiled upward like geysers made of air, and venting gas, powerful enough to exceed the huge escape velocity of that massive planet, began spilling into outer space in streams. Ripples crossed and crisscrossed the cloud layers, disturbing the pattern of bands that had existed for all human history.

   Then some internal power supply, bright as miniature suns, ignited deep within the atmosphere. In six separate places, the vast atomic and subatomic and quantum-vacuum extraction power stations, each one larger than Earth, hidden below the outer layer of the diamond brain surface of Jupiter, had ignited.

   The hydrogen and methane layers had ignited from the internal heat, and now every third or fourth band of cloud was afire. The atmosphere roiled with what, had the cloud been water, would be tidal waves, as areas of discoloration wider than a dozen Earths opened up across the endless fields of storm.

   The core of Jupiter had cracked and was subsiding in places in immeasurable landslips and collapses, opening canyons wider and deeper than oceans, pits into which lesser worlds could have congregated without crowding.

   The broken lips of these vast chasms were ringed on each side with endless brightly colored clouds of poison. The super-dense gaseous layers poured down like waterfalls in the titanic gravity. Elsewhere the cloudscape erupted when sudden continent-sized mountains of logic crystal, red with internal heat, reared impossibly high, peaks towering above the cloud.

   Some layer of dense atmosphere or ultra-dense hydrosphere, sinking into the gaping wounds of diamond, struck a superheated layer of what had once been Jupiter's high-speed thought processes, vast bands of molten substance like rivers wider than worlds. The ignition was vast, and the oblate shape of Jupiter began to lose its contour. A ring of debris was beginning to form around the equator from the ejected material.

   But all this was mere overture. For a signal had been sent, hours ago, to stations in the sun. The solar beam that Jupiter had been using to copy his brain information to 20 Arietis became visible when it struck the layer of debris swirling like a death shroud high above disintegrating Jupiter. Where the beam struck all matter was instantly evaporated into plasma. The miles-deep atmosphere

opened like the bloom of a flower as the non-ignited material was flung upward for hundreds of miles in every direction away from the point of beam impact. The dark chemical substances of the oceans swirled in an immense circular
tsunami.

A continuous explosion occurred while the beam head passed through all
the layers of atmosphere and hydrosphere to touch the floor of the ocean, which
was the outer diamond armor of the brain of Jupiter. The oceans were surrounding an empty cylinder formed by the vapor pressure, a momentary gap of nothingness, into which a hundred Earths could have been plunged. Against the
silvery white surface of logic diamond, the reflection of the sun could be seen
like the eye of an avenging god, growing brighter and brighter.

The beam cut through the core of the planet. Before ten hours had passed,
the planetary rotation had brought the beam over every part of Jupiter's equator and out the other side. Such was the violence of the sunbeam, to which
chemical and atomic explosions were as nothing, that fully one-tenth of the mass
of Jupiter was flung into space, forming a vast, multicolored cloud like twinkling ice and black pellets, a nebula painted with all the peacock hues of the
rainbow, and two dozen new moons and two new rings of asteroids.

The core was now red hot, and emitting more energy than it took in. The
central mass was a ball of seething plasma, as if a sun, smaller than any sun could
be, had replaced the heart of Jupiter. It was not large enough to ignite into a
star; but for now, it was lit.

But the vast gravity of Jupiter was not so easily dismissed. The nebula was
already detectably collapsing, and the newly created moon-sized chunks were
spiraling back down, following the broken parabolas of the two new asteroid
rivers back toward the blazing core of Jupiter. The blazing plasma of the miniature sun at the core was darkening as more and more matter collapsed onto it,
smothering it even as it fed it.

It might be months or years or centuries of time before all of the ejected material was once more claimed and brought back down into a new and white-hot
version of Jupiter.

A flaming finger seemed to wander across the colored clouds and torrents of
rock and ice of the immense volume of destruction. It was the starbeam, swinging like a searchlight away from Jupiter, now visible as it reflected off the vast
nebular mass of the newborn cloud. The starbeam was moving away from 20
Arietis in the constellation Ares and aiming toward the constellation Canes
Venatici.

Norbert looked up, shocked. Even with the sun above the horizon, there was
a high white point in the sky, brighter than Venus seen at dawn. It was Jupiter,

burning. It was a small, pathetic, secondary sun that painted their shadows clear and dark upon the grass.

Norbert saw that everyone was looking at him.

It took him a moment to remember himself. He straightened up and said, "Jupiter has honorably carried out to the last particular all the terms agreed in the covenant. The duel is ended."

Montrose, bleeding, looked over at where Del Azarchel stood, munching popcorn. "Well, what do you say, Blackie?"

Del Azarchel favored him with a supercilious look. "And what do I say about what?"

"Ever since you fooled me into solving Exarchel's divarication problem for you, everything you have done has been in order to create that monster brain to be the god of man and rule the human race. All the Hermeticists you deceived, all the work you stole, everything we did to nurse that huge freak to a level far, far above human intelligence, posthuman intelligence, or the intelligence of living moons and worlds. You achieved it. Now you saw it blow itself to bits."

Del Azarchel nodded, looking pleased with himself. "I think the experiment was a great success."

"Are you satisfied? Can I sleep now, without any further interruptions? It is only seventeen thousand, five hundred years and change before she returns. Will you leave me the hell alone? Is our duel over?"

Del Azarchel nodded. "Mankind has achieved a stable starfaring form of polity. It will degenerate without Jupiter to lead it, of course, and interstellar trade and commerce will come to an end a few years before Rania returns, but by then she will be moving slowly enough and be close enough that Hyades will not bother to interfere, if I read the Cold Equations correctly. We will win our manumission, and mankind will be elevated to equality with Hyades and the other serfs of the Authority M3."

"You mean we will be free and independent!"

Del Azarchel shrugged. "Free in name only. My vision will rule here, a vision of monarchy, authority, glory, and power, and your vision of liberty will fail. You have already shown yourself willing to compromise. I think she will cleave to me, and not you, when she comes."

"You lie. You don't know her. You don't know her, and you lie."

"Normally, such words would call for a passage at arms, but right now I am not in the mood, and you are a mess. I want you to see her on my arm, as my bride, before I kill you, Cowhand. And so our duel is over for now. I suggest a hiatus, a respite, a holiday, to last for seventeen thousand, five hundred years and change. Then we can take up against the disputes that separate us. Agreed?"

Without waiting for an answer Del Azarchel saluted Menelaus Montrose, smiled a wicked smile, handed the unfinished bag of popcorn to Norbert, and turned and marched off. Montrose attempted to rise and go after him, but Sgaire pushed him down and beckoned for his surgical trees.

5. Fox Maiden, Man Wife

Del Azarchel was surprised when he found Cazi sitting on a gravestone at a turning of the white walkway weaving through the graveyard. He looked back toward the hill, seeing what looked like two versions of Montrose, one in armor, one in the sober garments of a second.

He jerked his thumb back toward the Cazi who had been acting as the second during the duel. "Which one of you is fake, my dear?"

Cazi was dressed in a simple red dress with a wide black belt, cinched tightly to show off her figure, and she wore black gloves to her elbows and black stockings to her knees, and about her ankles were bangles and charms. Her hair was a wild red cloud, and her eyes yellow sparks.

"All of us, I think." She shrugged, which emphasized her cleavage. "I lost track centuries ago. So are you going to resign as Lord of Evil?"

"Resign? No. Retire? Yes. For I've won," said Blackie.

Cazi crossed her legs and kicked them back and forth, idly. "You always seem confident, even when you fib. My next lover will be an honest man."

"I have a right to be confident."

"You think you do, do you?" she said archly.

"You see, I was able to study the Second Monument of the Omega Nebula for years. It was redacted the same way as the First Monument of the Diamond Star, so it contained the same message. All the information for how to build Rania was there, and I know the genetic codes for Captain Grimaldi backward and forward. If Rania is as the Monument says a Monument emulation creature must be, then I have won her heart during these years."

"I don't follow you."

"The Monument was created for a higher purpose. What purpose that is, I do not know. Rania is designed to serve that purpose. Even if I do not know what it is, I know this: if all my work and all my wars and all my striving here in the First Empyrean Polity of Man fulfills some part of that grand plan, her designers would have rendered her unable not to favor me."

Cazi said, "Montrose told me that the Monument was redacted—rewritten—

by someone else, some other race, also for some purpose he thinks must be at odds with the first. And all your plans are all based on this cliometric calculus you learned from the Monument, right? But your blueprints included the redacted segments of the Monument. What if her purpose is grander than that? What if she is loyal to the older purpose, whatever it is? There is so much no one knows."

"One day I will know all."

"One day, so you say."

"For now, I have preserved the human race, lifted it from its childhood on Earth to its maturity among the stars. Nothing can be greater than that."

"Oh, really?" Her look of superciliousness was even more supercilious than his, for she could arch her eyebrow higher and wrinkle her mouth more deeply.

"You think he has won? The Cowhand? He will never win!"

"I think if you loved Rania, you'd talk about her, and not about him."

"I had my doubts, but if it were not my love of Rania that made Jupiter hesitate to shoot, what did? I watched the duel carefully. The copy of my body was better, faster, more accurate. I cannot lose."

"He lives for love. You live for hate. You will destroy yourself. That is what hate is."

"What do you know of love and hate?"

She hopped to her feet. "I know that love is sacrifice. I am going to give up being a Fox Maiden, turn into a real woman, be fertile and have babies, and grow old and die, and I will never see the end of your duel with Meany. I have come to ask you to be the best man!"

"What? Me? We did not exactly part, my dear, on the best of terms. . . ."

"Men are always so freaked out by a little unexpected castration! I gave it back! You went to a shop and had it stitched back on! Besides, it will do me good to see you at my wedding, because you will be defeated by another man."

"I can also lend him my dirty socks, and give him a toothbrush that I used to use."

"So will you come?"

"Who is so insane that he would marry you?"

She looked scandalized. She pouted. "You are kidding, right? It is not obvious? Norbert. You know those Rosicrucians do not think like baseline men."

"So you will be Mrs. *Unpronounceable Name That Starts With an M*. And you are going to give up shape-changing and politics and intrigue and toying with the destinies of lesser men? For what?"

"For babies!"

"To eat, knowing you. You will regret it. You will wake up at midnight, wishing you could grow wings, and go eat some politician you wish you could replace. . . ."

She shook her head. "Not if the Patricians are running everything. We made a race our own tricks would not work on. And if I regret it, I will have another baby!"

"Some women have higher ambitions."

"Higher than life? I've been a queen and the mother of a race and a mistress of intrigue, and I've arranged a duel between an immortal man and a tyrant power of heaven. Isn't that enough for one life? Ambition is lonely. Even a fox deserves a den of her own."

"You are too good for him."

"Too wicked, you mean! Norbert thinks he can tame me. I intend to struggle and scratch, and drive him crazy if I can, and break him if he is weak like you. But I want him to win."

"You are a mad thing," said Del Azarchel. "But I will be your bridegroom's best man, if he will ask me, and be honored that you want to have me present. When is the happy occasion?"

She pointed. "There is the cathedral yonder. I will be baptized and alter my cells so that I can never alter them again; and this same day is the solemn wedding mass, and tomorrow we enter the lifting vessel to reach the Sky Island, and then the star port. The Interdict was artificial, a trick, and with Jupiter dead it must be lifted, and the next sailing vessel will depart for Proxima Centauri in a few months, a voyage of only four years at near-lightspeed. He will see the trees of which he dreams, and settle on his little farm, and we will have snow every Sunday and springtide every Monday. I will be his forever, and he will be mine. And . . ."

"I know. Babies."

"Lots of them! Life serves life, right? Your Hyades monster friends would approve. What else is life for?"

"I want more," said Del Azarchel. "I want the stars."

"And do what with them? Without love, they mean nothing."

"I will change the constellations to make them mean whatever I see fit that they should mean."

"Poor, unhappy, doomed man! I pity you! But come and see me wed. I might let you kiss the bride."

"But why wed him? Be my lover again. You will be dead long before Rania returns, and you are quite right that there are nights when I grow lonely."

"For you, the story goes on and ever on to the end of the Eschaton, the end of evolution, until you count to infinity. Norbert may only be playing a bit walk-on part in the great drama of human history, but he has something you haven't got."

"And that is?"

"A happy ending. For us, the story comes to rest. I can give him a happy ending."

He nodded in defeat, smiling, and offered her the crook of his elbow. While Jupiter burned overhead, a freakish and unexpected second sun, brighter than the morning star, they walked together into the shadow of the nave, beneath the tall and richly carven doors that stood wide open, and into dark and solemn silence.

APPENDIX A
Dramatis Personae

Persons named but not present are listed in italics.

Tellurians

FIRST HUMANITY (Intelligence = 100 to 650)

Elders, also called Early Posthumans
   Menelaus Illation Montrose—the Judge of Ages
   Ximen del Azarchel—Master of the World
Nymphs
   Amphithöe—their Conscript Mother (of the First Comprehension)
Witches
   Zoraida—an Intercessor (of the Second Comprehension)
Giants
   Sancristobal—Friar Sancristobal of the Remnant Order of the Post-Final
      Stipulation, and a Brother of Penance of the Third Order of St. Frances,
      called Greyfriars
Melusine
   Isonadey, the Ship's Voice—Captain of the *Hysterical Blindness*
   Manitra, Angatra, Ranavalon—Judicial, Military, and Royal Cliometric lead-
      ers of the Remnant Order of the Post-Final Stipulation, which is a Sec-
      ond Comprehension polity

Rosicrucians of Proxima
   Norbert the Assassin—Norbert Brash Noesis Mynyddrhodian mab Nwyfre
      of Rosycross
   Exobert—his emulation
   Svartvestra—his paramour
   Rose —his beloved
   Yngbert—Yngbert Perpension Mynyddrhodian; his father

Maier—a peace officer for Dee Parish

Zolasto Zo—a Rosicrucian expatriate and mountebank

Nocturnals

Nochzreniye—a Zarya of Nocturne of Epsilon Eridani, Norbert's adjutant

SECOND HUMANITY (Intelligence = 1,000)

Swans

Enkoodabooaoo—an Inquiline of the Noösphere (Third Comprehension)

Photinus—a Hierophant and heresiarch of the 36th Millennium

Lares—a prophetess

Lemur—revives the heresy of Photinus in the 47th Millennium

THIRD HUMANITY

Myrmidons

Dissent—emissaries to the Judge of Ages in the plutino Ixion

Superintendent of the First Elite Process—a command segment of the Black Fleet. Slain by Montrose in a duel.

FOURTH HUMANITY

Fox Maidens

Cazi—a sovereign and trickster

Gitsune and Strega—her attendants

FIFTH HUMANITY

Patricians

Cnaeus—called the Father of Neptune

Nemenstratus—a Lord of the Golden Afternoon, that is, Cliometric Historian for the Triplanetary Jurisdiction

ARCHANGEL (Intelligence = 10,000 or 10^3)

Mother Superior Selene—Abbess of the Order of the Discalced Friars of the Order of the Blessed Virgin Mary of Mount Carmel, called Whitefriars. The moon.

POTENTATES (Intelligence=800,000 or 80^4)

Tellus of Sol
Rosycross of Proxima

POWERS (Intelligence=250 Million or 25^7)

Jupiter of Sol
Neptune of Sol
Cerulean of 82 Eridani; Peacock of Delta Pavonis; Immaculate of Altair;
   Twelve of Tau Ceti; Vonrothbarth of 61 Cygni. Atramental of Epsilon
   Eridani is technically a superpotentate, but not a power.

Hyades

VIRTUES (Intelligence=500 Million or 50^8)

Asmodel the Living Planet—First Sweep in the 12th Millennium
Cahetel the Dark Cloud—Second Sweep in the 25th Millennium
Shcachlil the Salamander—Third Sweep in the 37th Millennium
Achaiah the Immeasurable—predicted to arrive at the behest of Jupiter in
   the 61th Millennium

PRINCIPALITIES

Ain—which men call Epsilon Tauri but Myrmidons call Oculus Borealis

ARCHON

Circumincession—Sovereign of the Sagittarius Arm

APPENDIX B
Middle-Scale Time Line
(Thousands of Years)

Each entry on the list below represents a millennium.

Notable Events and Epochs for each millennium briefly noted.

Changes to Earth's pole star due to procession noted as aid in comparison of time scales.

Preposthuman Era

- **1st Millennium** A.D. **(Anno Domini) / -3 V (Antevindication or Precountdown)**
  Imperial Rome. Caesar, Christ born. Western Empire Falls, creating a Dark Age in Europe. Heavy cavalry. Islam rises.

  Gamma Ursae Minoris (Pherkad) is the Pole Star

- **2nd Millennium** A.D. **/ -2 V**
  Age of Discovery. Industrial revolution, scientific method. World westernized. Man walks on the moon.

  Polaris is the Pole Star

- **3rd Millennium** A.D. **/ -1 V**
  First Age of Star Travel. Diamond Star found. *Croesus* Launch. Little Dark Ages. The Jihad and the Japanese Winter. *Hermetic* Launch. Rania, "The Swan Princess," first human created by mixture of human and Monument genetic codes. Monument partly deciphered.
  RANIA DEPARTS FOR M3. Vindication Countdown begins. The Long Wait begins.
  Earthquake Wars decimate Japan, California, Italy.
  (A.D. 2500) Humanist Wars shatter the Concordat. Exarchel augments the Cetaceans.
  Cryonarch Period—The heirs of Montrose rise to world power. Montrose in disgust disinherits them, and donates their power and resources to the Roman Pontiff.

Ecclesiarch Period—Giants born.

Diamond Star carried off. Moon marked with the hand of Del Azarchel.

Rise of the Ghosts, human brain-patterns kept unalive in electronic limbo.
Frankenstein Panic.

(A.D. 2525) Decivilization. Exarchel reduced.

Simon Institute Founded. Lifespan of women expanded to 350 by nano-
cellular xypotechnology.

Alrai is the Pole Star

Era of the Hermetic Millennia

- **4th Millennium A.D. / 67 V (Countdown to Vindication)**
  (A.D. 2525–3100) Giants.
  (A.D. 3050–3150) Cetaceans raise the Cloud.
  (A.D. 3100–3300) Simon Families.
  (A.D. 3300–4000) Under Witch rulership, collapse of Christianity undermines
  faith in scientific worldview, leads to radical loss of technological civili-
  zation on three continents. Decimations of Exarchel copies. Extinction
  of the Cetaceans.

- **5th Millennium A.D. / 66 V**
  Warlocks. Nameless Empire oversees a brief reindustrialization. Nine Cen-
  tennial Empresses of Canton. Butlerian overthrow and the return of barbarism
  Rise of the Chimera. Chimera Eugenic Republic spreads from Virginia. Pro-
  scopalianism.

- **6th Millennium A.D. / 65 V**
  Centennials in China overthrown by Chimera. Rediscovery of Atomics. Uni-
  fication wars. Chimerical World Empire. Third Age of Space Travel. Space
  Chimera created. Cities in Space founded. Fall of Richmond. Cities in
  Space abandoned.

Iota Cephei is the Pole Star

- **7th Millennium A.D. / 64 V**
  Naturalists. Weather Control initiates seasonless Earth. Decline. Winter returns. Rise of the Leeches.

- **8th Millennium** A.D. **/ 63 V**

  Iatrocrats organized into mutually bio-incompatible clades. Third Biotechnological Revolution.

  (A.D. 7500) Locusts. First neuro-infosphere or Noösphere. Fourth Age of
  Space Travel.

  Locust Wars. Genocide.

  Triage.

  Mars Colony.

  First Interplanetary War ends Mars colony.

  Linder.

  Alderamin is the Pole Star

- **9th Millennium** A.D. **/ 62 V**

  Triumph of the Noösphere. Blue Men. Noösphere shatters into the Confra-
  ternities. Gray Men.

  Ice Ages drive civilization into the sea. Rise of the Melusine (Human-
  Cetacean pack-minds).

  ## Swan Era

- **10th Millennium** A.D. **/ 61 V**

  SECOND HUMANS: SWANS

  White Earth. Only a thin equatorial band of open water remains.

  Creation of the Second Humans, the Swans, creatures more comely, ethe-
  real, and intellectual than humans, but generally reticent and isolated. They
  are based on Bonobo (Pan Paniscus) rather than human neural templates,
  so neither marriage nor incest taboos pertain to them. Their nervous systems are standardized and easily fitted with biotechnical and cybernetic
  implants, augmentations, and networks.

- **11th Millennium** A.D. **/ 60 V**

  Rise of the Final Stipulation. Weather control reestablished. Fifth Age of
  Space Travel. Judge of Ages and the Master of the World prohibited from
  further cliometry.

  Del Azarchel begins the long process of sophotransmogrification of the core
  mass of Jupiter into a Power of the same name.

  Deneb is the Pole Star

First Sweep—The Decimation of Man

- **12th Millennium** A.D. / 59 V

  FIRST SWEEP: The Hyades Armada "Asmodel" arrives. End of the Long Wait.

  Lamination of the Swans—Swans defeated with absurd ease. Earth altered from equatorial to polar orbit (but, oddly, keeping the same pole star). Diaspora to First Sweep worlds.

  Cenotaph praxes enable a more rapid evolution of Jupiter Brain to self-awareness than otherwise would have been possible.

  (A.D. 11400) Deracination Ship reaches Proxima.

- **13th Millennium** A.D. / 58 V

  Rise of the Dark Swans. Tribadism among the Early Swans dies off, as the isolated males become paramount. The peaceful nature of the race is subverted as the custom of dueling adopted among male Swans: Swans form alternating generations of male and female dominance, females growing to the ascendant during diebacks.

  (A.D. 12850) FIRST POWER of SOL: The myriad mental ecologies of the Jupiter Brain combine into federal self-awareness. [Jupiter is roughly 7,000 miles in diameter at this time, 90^4 IQ.]

  Jupiter persuades and forces the lesser versions of mankind to enter into a concord with him. Humans taught pantropy and terraforming by Hyades through Jupiter.

- **14th Millennium** A.D. / 57 V

  Fourth Biotechnological Revolution. Pantropy allows for the combination of Aurum Vitae and murk to produce a wide range of organisms, some of which drive natural organisms into extinction.

  Ghost population exceeds living population.

  Deracination Ship reaches Delta Pavonis.

- **15th Millennium** A.D. / 56 V

  Jupiter enters a period of odd inactivity lasting until the 19th millennium.

  (A.D. 14300) Silent Years—All save two of fifteen extrasolar colonies perish. *Emancipation* makes two expeditions to these survivors, **Nocturne** of Epsilon Eridani, and **Splendor** of Delta Pavonis. Attempts to maintain radio contact with scattered human worlds fail.

(A.D. 14600) Endarkening: Dependence on talking machinery and biomachinery spreads mass illiteracy. Factions embracing anti-intellectual doctrines become predominant. Widespread system failures of infosphere leave whole continents without literature or learning for generations. Ghosts decimated.

Montrose retreats to the plutino worldlet 28978 Ixion.

Vega is the Pole Star

Myrmidon Era

- **16th Millennium A.D. / 54 V**
THIRD HUMANS: MYRMIDONS
Jupiter under Del Azarchel's direction creates the Third Humans, the Myrmidons, based on extrapolations of Hyades' mental architecture. Originally intended to be the replacement race for mankind, longer-lived and more cooperative, the Myrmidons are hideous creatures, as uniform and inhuman as insects, lacking sex, art, religion, or any finer feelings. The Myrmidons are capable of total Noösphere nerve-machine integration.
Swans remove to Antarctica, Greenland, and Siberia to maintain strict isolation from Third Humans during these centuries.
(A.D. 15177) The Myrmidons construct and send out *Leucothea,* what will later be called the **Antepenultimate White Ship**, to a second antimatter star found in M17, the Omega Nebula, in the Sagittarius Arm of the Galaxy, 5,000 lightyears hence. Del Azarchel departs.

- **17th Millennium A.D. / 53 V**
Loss of the Earth's magnetic field. Solar wind damages Earth's atmosphere, leading to widespread desertification. Domes of lightweight fabric erected over cities as moisture traps. Widely regarded as an assault by the Myrmidons (who are unaffected by the change).
Nyctaloptic Earth. Unshielded Humans and Swans able to emerge only after sunset.
[This is the predicted end of the human race, had not pantropy and terraforming techniques been decoded to allow the race to resist the ecological disaster.]

- **18th Millennium A.D. / 52 V**
Rise of the Adamites, ascetics who reject human gene-experimentation. (These are the ancestors of the Covenanters.) The Sacerdotal religion, at

this point in history, is decidedly ecumenical and universal, rejecting no
expression of faith from any culture: Adamism comes to dominate Sacerdotalism, and ancestor worship and ritual purity form the backbone of
this system.

Many diseases reappear in the human ecology, and various forms of mental
retardation.

- **19th Millennium** A.D. / 51 V

  Rise of the Living Empire. This is a single life-form occupying most of the
  equatorial region, growing the foodstuff and materials of life for a highly
  dependent core population: perioeci and helots live in the temperate zones,
  with ruling Myrmidons able to pass freely between climate zones.

  Jupiter emerges from his somnolence. [Jupiter is roughly 14,000 miles in
  diameter at this time, and 70^5 IQ.]

- **20th Millennium** A.D. / 50 V

  Ice Age. Swans emerge from the polar regions, and multiply in numbers. Living Empire becomes coniferous. Adamite political system, which prohibited human bio-adaptation even to Eskimo levels of alteration, is
  overthrown.

  Rise of the Hibernal Men, who change fur during seasonal variations.

  Myrmidons under Jupiter's guidance begin an active program of colonizing
  the main asteroid belt. Ice Age ends due to military bombardment.

  At about this time, Dominions in Sagittarius become aware of the existence
  of Tellurian expedition and colonies in the Omega Nebula.

- **21st Millennium** A.D. / 49 V

  Swan Renaissance. Humans alter the Living Empire to create jungle cano-
  pies to prevent asteroid drop targeting from the Myrmidons, and all surface technology is dispersed into a highly diffuse and mobile form, an
  insect-based infosphere. Biopeonage exists in the cultivated areas, elsewhere nomads in large tribes live as herdsmen, hunter-gatherers in smaller
  bands.

  Hibernals, Nyctalops, and Troglodytes flourish, and decimate other, older,
  human races. Earthbound Myrmidons driven into the Andes and Hima-
  layas.

- **22nd Millennium** A.D. / 48 V

  Swans form first mathematical descriptions of human thought. Rule by the

Swans through the Neural Indication Protocols, a xypotechnology-intensive hierarchy where each person's duties and role in society is determined by his thought-architecture. This is a limited and individualized form of the Sculpture of the 24th Millennium (see below).

Energy-intensive forms of war cease. Earthbound Myrmidons ejected into space, take up residence in the asteroid belt.

[Jupiter is roughly 28,000 miles in diameter at this time, and 50^6 IQ.]

Alpha Draconis is the Pole Star

• **23rd Millennium A.D. / 47 V**

The Time of the Dark Cloud. The approach of Cahetel becomes the epicenter of human history.

A crude form of murk, created by slavish mimicry of the murk electronic arrangements, becomes the primary building material of all artificial minds. This allows a divarication to form in the previously unified Third Humans.

(A.D. 22196) Divergent Myrmidons prevail upon Montrose to emerge from his self-exile and become supreme military leader of a resistance.

The Re-Armaments. Creation, over centuries, of the Black Fleet. The office of Nobilissimus revived.

• **24th Millennium A.D. / 46 V**

Sculptured Lifeways. Time of the Bred Men. Rise of the Five Families, famed biotechnicians (Eventide, Leafsmith, Phosphor, Orison, and Grimm. The Bloodrose family is usually considered collateral line of Leafsmith, despite their pretensions, not a separate family).

Although later regarded as an anarchist utopia, the Sculpture was a rigid set of social control provisions that operated through the media, schooling, medical networks, marriages, fertility control. The ability of Firstling-tribes to form or ignore systems of force known as governments was largely bypassed as irrelevant to the aims of the Swans.

Scholars returning from deep communion with Jupiter usher in the Nano-technological Revolution. Matter on Earth is hereafter regarded as a programmable substance.

Tellus enters a Turing Halt-State. (This state will persist until the 40th Millennium).

Gamma Ursae Minoris (Pherkad) is the Pole Star

Second Sweep—The Starfaring

- **25th Millennium** A.D. / **45 V**

SECOND SWEEP

(A.D. 24113) Arrival of Cahetel Cloud—second immediate defeat of Tellurian forces by the Hyades Domination: Myrmidon Noösphere is betrayed into the Cahetel Format. The Myrmidon Black Fleet cannibalized for Diaspora to second sweep worlds: the asteroid belt flies into interstellar space.

The failure of the Black Fleet persuades humanity to cease active resistance to Hyades deracination.

This sweep is considerably more melancholy, as all failed colonies are reseeded, so the ruins and corpses of previous civilizations are visible. Colonial Myrmidons die; Swans survive marginally, but are insufficiently communal or family-oriented to thrive. Humans thrive, especially Sylphs, Witches, Chimera, Hormagaunts, Hibernals, and Nyctalops. The smaller failure rate is perhaps due to stronger Terraforming effort and subtle, more patient Pantropy.

[Jupiter is roughly 40,000 miles in diameter at this time, and 25^7 IQ—achieving plateau maximum.]

- **26th Millennium** A.D. / **44 V**

(A.D. 25177) Arrival of the **Antepenultimate White Ship**.

Influx of snow ushers in a period of supremacy by pro-Domination Potentates. (No further expeditions to Omega will be mounted until the 29,900, some four thousand eight hundred years hence.) Del Azarchel returns, duels and kills the Myrmidon Nobilissimus, a copy of himself, who suffered divarication during the long absence.

Widespread use of snow (antimatter-powered weapons) makes the Sculptured Lifeways nonviable, as handheld weapons could wipe out a city, or an army.

The wealth of the expedition allows Jupiter to establish the first Collaboration-Strength Launching Lasers, a human-built starbeam.

(A.D. 25544) Foundation of the Starfaring Guild. From this date until the 37th Millennium, Jupiter is in direct control of all interstellar trade and traffic.

Polaris is again the Pole Star

- **27th Millennium** A.D. / **43 V**

Rust, a system of chaff clouds and superhighspeed nanotools (including small atoms spun at lightspeed, colliding with antimatter to discharge the energy back along the path of attack) is found to be a partial defense against snow—the snow-weapon is still formidable, but no longer unstoppable.

Discovery of Nerve-Mandala and Nerve-Mudra techniques. Warfare now formed by neural symbols. Nations break into smaller psycho-morphically similar sets. Note that only species practicing neural uniformity, Locusts, Melusine and after, are vulnerable.

Alrai is the Pole Star

Hierophant Era

• **28th Millennium** A.D. / 42 V

After centuries of Nerve Wars, the Hierophant Cohesion forms. First and Second Mankind form one psychomorphic set of man-swans called the *Hierophants.* The Swans can use their man-brains to defend against Nerve-Mandala techniques, but employ aesthetic logic and xypotechnology as Swans.

Myrmidons migrate to 82 Eridani, the planet Cyan.

• **29th Millennium** A.D. / 41 V

Under pressure from Cahetel, Hierophants enter this symbiosis with Ghosts, which mitigates their natural love of isolation, and produce a social system based on a flexible series of highly individualized rules, known as the Gracious Acts.

The Graciousness includes the removal of large-scale weapons and the reintroduction of a dueling custom. Women subjugated as several misogynistic philosophies and sects gain predominance. The Graciousness reduces Firstling humans into fawning servility.

Interstellar slave trade begins.

Iota Cephei is the Pole Star

• **30th Millennium** A.D. / 40 V

(A.D. 29024) Launch of the **Penultimate White Ship** toward the Omega Nebula, there to establish a permanent colony and a Second Empyrean Polity of Man.

Cahetel departs. Hierophants left without calculation power which had been loaned to them (at interest) by Cahetel. The Hierophant Cohesion lost forever.

- **31st Millennium** A.D. / 39 V

  Hyades signals detected at 82 Eridani, thought to originate from a descendant or revision of Cahetel. (The Cyanese loyalty to the Hyades dates from this early period.)

  The Gracious Acts ended in a year widely hailed as the Matriculation of Man. The Servants of the Spirit of Man enforce anarcho-libertarian covenants on Earth, for perhaps six months, before falling apart into factional grief and strife. The Holocaust of Northern Hemisphere.

  Spiritualists clash with Sacerdotes. The Sacred Wars reduce the biosphere of Earth to partially uninhabitable. Ghosts, Locusts, and Troglodytes wiped out by mandala techniques.

  Alderamin (Alpha Cephei) is the Pole Star

- **32nd Millennium** A.D. / 38 V

  The Cherishing. Under Hierophant guidance, Earth recolonized from Mars, Proxima, Cyan, Splendor, Covenant, Nocturne, and Gargoyle. Establishment of the Castellan system: Arcologies at various points, well defended against snow and murk attack forms, dominate local countrysides. Human training techniques nullify mandala and mudra impositions added to posthuman consciousness.

  At about this time, **Cerulean**, a second Power after Jupiter, is born in the 82 Eridani system, constructed by the Cyanese.

- **33rd Millennium** A.D. / 37 V

  Spread of the Oneness: biotechnological Archangels inhabit the local biosphere, and revive the Living Empire. Battle of the Trees: invulnerable tree-monsters slowly uproot and destroy the arcologies. Hierophants flourish in the environment, surfeited by ambrosia, nectar, and sweet dreams. Technology forgotten by humans.

  Splendid engineers convert the outer three asteroid belts of the Delta Pavonis star system into a cognitive matter entity called **Peacock**, a third Power.

- **34th Millennium** A.D. / 36 V

  Starfarers from Splendor use weather control technology to decimate the Oneness, and return Earth to a technological footing. Rise of the Ninety-One-and-Nine Realms. Labor market for slaves both on and off Earth is abetted by a return to plantation and factory work.

:idani creates a Power called **Atramental**. Under his guidance, the
ites of Nocturne, in advance of the Third Sweep, launch a volun-
ltigeneration colony ship toward Rigel, and colonize Orphan.
The Splendids prevail upon Jupiter to take closer control of mankind.

Deneb is the Pole Star

Third Sweep—The Long Golden Afternoon

- **35th Millennium** A.D. / 35 V

  The Long Golden Afternoon of Man—Earthly society, under the gentle guidance of the Jupiter Brain, using Cherished technology and Oneness Eden-
  work (a type of biotechnology), produces a stable yet flexible genetic caste
  system.

  Widely regarded as a near-Utopia, the Long Golden Afternoon endures from
  the 35th to the 53rd Millennium, over eighteen thousand years, one of the
  most stable forms of society in human history. Wars are contained as small
  and local, executed with punctilious chivalry on all sides; disease is unknown, except as a weapon; poverty is unknown, except as a voluntary
  spiritual discipline. Sacerdotalism persecuted.

  Atramental, perhaps due to malign influence from Jupiter, suffers psychotic
  spasms, and commits suicide.

- **36th Millennium** A.D. / 34 V

  The Great Revival. Under the pressure of Hierophantic persecution, Second
  and First Sweep Sacerdotalism transformed into an intolerant, exclusive
  religion, as Judeo-Christian elements in the lore absorb or render moot
  other, less coherent elements such as ancestor worship. Much of this set
  in motion by a martyr named Purewater.

  Under pressure from the Sacerdotal Order, Jupiter grants certain rights and
  immunities to First and Second Humans.

  (A.D. 35400) **First ignition** of the deceleration starbeam directed at M3.

  A Hierophant named Photinus proposes a different calculation of the first
  ignition date, due to changes in Earth's orbit, and the unreliability of
  records. The matter, at first academic, gathers all dissatisfied elements
  of society to question the entire basis of cliometry, and all planned history.

  Onset of the Ahistorical Wars. Mutiny, tumult, and the highly ceremonial,
  tournament-like, but still deadly warfare of the Golden Era spreads to all
  worlds.

Immaculate, a Fourth Power, created by Covenant of Altair by gathering all the material of their Oort cloud together into a single superjovian mass.

- **37th Millennium** A.D. / 33 V
THIRD SWEEP.
The plasma-based Virtue called by astronomers **Shcachlil** but popularly called **The Salamander** takes up its position inside Sol. This time, the Hyades does not bother to bring ships to transport the weeping millions to their fates, but merely orders the construction of them, and directs solar-prominence-powered energy-discharges at any who defy or delay. Jupiter no longer possesses control of the starbeams which power interstellar sailing.
The Third Sweep worlds are colonized as Hierophantic world contingents. At the same time, Myrmidon populations are deracinated to Second Sweep worlds, which now have the technological base to support them. The Myrmidons compel these worlds to enter the tight cliometric controls of the Golden Lords.
Shcachlil commands the resumption of M3 deceleration beam. Photinine heresy suppressed. Rosycross and other First Sweep worlds are taken under the command of cliometric planners, local Hierophants called Golden Lords.
The Isolation. Human-based starfaring suspended due to lack of resources.

- **38th Millennium** A.D. / 32 V
End of the Isolation. Starfaring Guild removed to December of Tau Ceti, declares independence from Jupiter's control.
(A.D. 37400) **Second ignition** of the deceleration starbeam directed at M3. Energy budget of the Empyrean Polity impoverished by this extravagant uses of energy. Economic collapse.
Photinine controversy revived under the prophetess Lares, who claims to be in communion with extragalactic cherub named Dorado, alleging that the Monument mathematics, and all cliometric calculations, are false.
The Grand Duel of Time. Orthodox Golden Lords challenge those of their order who are disciples of Lares to reorganize history, in order to see whose cliometric calculus is more accurate.
Unexpectedly, in less than four hundred years, the Orthodox Golden Lords are compelled by socioeconomic developments to capitulate, and embrace Laresianism.
The Crusades. Covenant and other anti-Domination worlds still ruled by

Swans or Myrmidon Potentates raise troops to send to Earth, to make war upon the Golden Lords.

Vega is the Pole Star

- **39th Millennium** A.D. / **31 V**
  Establishment of a short-lived Crusader Kingdom under Prestor Pfin Aiven Bromion on the surface of the terraformed moon.
  Laresianism persecuted.

Kitsune Era

- **40th Millennium** A.D. / **30 V**
  (A.D. 39024) Arrival of the **Penultimate White Ship**.
  News reaches Earth of a Second Empyrean polity of ninety stars in the Sagittarian Arm spreading outward from the Omega Nebula. Decryption of signs from the interior of the Second Monument found at the Omega Nebula leads to a revolution in cliometry, nanobiology, and terraforming praxes.
  Tellus is revived by techniques discovered from the Second Monument, and emerges from Halt-State (entered in the 24th Millennium).
  FOURTH HUMANS: KITSUNE
  Rise of the Fourth Humans, the totipotent Kitsune, also called Fox Maidens. These nanobiological shapechangers are able to alter organs and neural configurations at will, adopting different personalities as need arises. Every cell can carry neural charge, allowing the entire body mass to become a brain mass, which is standardized to interlink with other Kitsune and compatible systems. The race is monosexual, reproducing by parthenogenesis. There are no male Kitsune.
  Legend names their founder Cazi Regina.

- **41th Millennium** A.D. / **29 V**
  (A.D. 40522) Launch of the **Ultimate White Ship** by Peacock, the Power of Delta Pavonis.
  The Kitsune aid the Covenant crusades on Earth, but then establish their own hierarchy under Cazi the Fox-Queen (whether the same immortal individual, or her remote descendent, history does not say). Kitsune upset the genetic balances of the Golden Afternoon caste system.
  Kitsune create the "psychic spinal" system of pluripotent cells in Swans and Firstlings, allowing them multiple personality appliances, with the associated benefits of temporary expertise.

Tellus damaged during a Kitsune experiment, and disintegrates, returning to subsuperposthuman levels of intellect and organization. Further Kitsune activity, allegedly attempts to repair Tellus, spread the insanity.

Oceans fill with alcahest, a nanotechnological waste product. Demeter, a near-surface Archangel used for earthquake control, begins a Telluric reclamation project.

(This is the predicted last Noösphere, had Jupiter not been brought into being.)

- **42nd Millennium** A.D. / **28 V**

  Renaissance of the Golden Lords: Jupiter intervenes. A new balance is struck within the cliometric dynamics of the Golden Afternoon, allowing the Hierophants to retain power despite ever-growing turbulence from the Kitsune and Myrmidon underlings.

  Sacerdotalism becomes the established religion of the Hierophants. Laresianism lingers among military units for several generations, and is finally wiped out.

  Terrforming Terra: Hierophants begin sea reclamation.

  [This is the predicted last generation of civilization, had Jupiter not been brought into being.]

- **43rd Millennium** A.D. / **27 V**

  Shcachlil the Salamander creates a shepherding moon for Venus to move the world into a cooler orbit.

  The Gas Giant **Twelve** of Tau Ceti converted to sophont matter, becoming the Fifth Human Power. The failed star Siegfried of 61 Cygni converted, becoming the Sixth Power named **Vonrothbarth**.

- **44th Millennium** A.D. / **26 V**

  Industrial growth on Earth leads to restoration of space colonies. First colonists on Venus are Pantropists, with genes evolved to track the progression of the terraforming due to the shepherding moon's action.

- **45th Millennium** A.D. / **25 V**

  Colony fails on Venus due to unexpected solar activities.

  Second colonization attempt at Venus, this time, with human terraformers attempting to modify Shcachlil's result.

  The Sacerdotal Order issues an invitation for Splendids from Delta Pavonis to starfare to Venus as an act of religious merit, leaving homes and kith to be lost to the relativistic passage of years.

Alpha Draconis is the Pole Star

- **46th Millennium** A.D. **/ 24 V**
  Venus occupied by a Splendor-dominated theocratic order devoted to the subjection of all human freedom to ecological interests. Venusians send a fleet toward Earth, which is wiped out by a single, scalding beam from Shcachlil.
  Splendid Venusians betray their strict code of noninterference in the gene plasm, and produce a race of space-flying disease-spreading anthropophagic predators called Vampires. These entities are able to cross the distance between worlds during conjunction without vehicles.
  Onset of the Plague Years.

- **47th Millennium** A.D. **/ 23 V**
  Mars moved into a serviceable orbit by Shcachlil.
  Shcachlil removed from the sun by the Domination of Hyades—perhaps in order to avoid some ever-mounting debt.
  SALAMANDER DEPARTS
  Shapetaker's Millennium: Humans organize into permeable-barrier clades of fertile Nyctalops Melusine called Skulks, beneath the protection of totipotent Kitsune.
  Beginning of the Tribulations, when no cliometric plans unfold as expected.
  The Golden Lords are not overthrown, but reduced to ceremonial figureheads. Hierophants dwindle sharply in number.
  (A.D. 46400) **Third ignition** of the deceleration beam directed at M3.
  The Photinine Heresy reemerges under the leadership of a Heresiarch named Lemur, who demands a simplification of the cliometry calculus, and the creation of a race with a simpler psychology than man to make the calculation easier, creatures called Eidolons.
  Lemur is assassinated and replaced by a Fox impersonator, but the Lemurian movement nonetheless fragments and mutates into a bewildering variety of revisionists and counter-revisionists.

Beta and Gamma Ursae Minoris are the Pole Stars

- **48th Millennium** A.D. **/ 22 V**
  The Beautification
  (A.D. 47000–47300) The beautification of man takes place during these years.

Eidolons restored to full humanity. Fox Maidens meddle in the gene stock of firstlings, whose 350-year lifespans are quadrupled, and who retain their youth and beauty well into their later years, so that an earthwoman of 1,400 still looks like a fourteen-year-old, and can live to 1,600.

THE INTERSTELLAR WAR

(A.D. 47400) Cliometry Revisionists demand the halt of life-extension biotechnology and the destruction of all tomb slumberers older than nine hundred ninety-nine years. Starfaring ports and strongholds attacked, as well as biosuspension tombs.

(A.D. 47500) Revisionism spreads to other worlds.

(A.D. 47600) Immortalist colony at Odette attacked and destroyed by Crusaders from Odile. Surviving Immortals flee offplanet, including to Sol, suppress the Revisionists, and establish hegemony.

(A.D. 47700) On Venus, the Splendids are eaten by their creations, the Vampires. Vampires imitate Jupiter's internal personality control system for their social order.

On Earth, rise of a class of land-owning peasants born of recently humanized Moreaus in Baltica overthrow the Immortalist hegemons and erect a communal form of Vassalage called the Five Thousand Fiefs. Some ceremonial functions are restored to the Golden Lords.

(A.D. 47800) The Fiefs grow corrupt, and yield power to various charismatic tyrants, gathered into a single alliance under Myrmidon control. These tyrants, called Lectors of the Analects, enforce a set of strict honor codes, prohibiting humanism and trans-humanism.

(A.D. 47900) Beginning of the Fox Hunts, the Lector-led genocide of the Kitsune.

- **49th Millennium A.D. / 21 V**

Parthenocracy established, a Fox-Swan hybrid social order created in imitation (some say mockery) of the Hierophants, who were Man-Swan hybrids. The franchise is limited to virgin girls and unwalled cities.

Skulks, with Jupiter's aid, gain predominance over the scattered Lectors. End of Lectorship. End of Fox Hunts.

Fox attempt to restore humanity to the Myrmidons fails. In disgust, Myrmidons sever all ties with biological life, becoming a spaceborne form of machine life called Megalodons.

Polaris is the Pole Star

Patrician Era

- **50th Millennium** A.D. / **20 V**
  FIFTH HUMANS: PATRICIANS
  The Megalodons, cooperating with the Gam City-Mind of the Ocean Palace (whom they oddly resemble), gain supremacy over the Parthenocrats. The Palatials take up the perquisites and forms of Golden Lords.
  Meanwhile, the Vampire kings of Venus breed a race of men, called the Overlords, immune from all biological attacks, but who are so heavily modified that the Eco-theocracy of Splendid is discredited and forgotten.
  Patricians Born. Foxes return the humanity to the vampire kings of Venus, a race now called the Fifth Men, or *Patricians*. This a monosexual species able to reproduce with any female human or Moreau. The resulting hybrid, called a Plebian, is self-aware, and possesses a Patrician-compatible nerve configuration, sanity, stability, and integrity.
  End of the Crusader kingdoms. Moon loses atmosphere, becomes uninhabitable. Lunars migrate to the Chimerical penal colony on Mars.
  Veneric ecology placed under interdict by the Patricians, forcing a return to Terrestrial norms. Timed extinctions, known as the Ineluctable Curses, are bio-programmed into xenophilic life.
  Long-slumbering Eventide patriarchs hidden at the Martian core since the time of the Sculptured Lifeways are found and revived and rise to power. The Chimera, the Lunars, and the Eventides form The Anachronism, a system of life based on the ancient precepts of the Cryonarchy combined with cliometry, which encourages migration via hibernation to various foretold eras of time.
  Martian terraforming begun by the Anachronistic Council (and completed in later years by the Conservator of the Museum of Man). Earthly creatures, many of Veneric decent, dependent on xenophilic life, migrate to Mars, in order to escape the Ineluctable Curses.

  Alrai is the Pole Star

- **51st Millennium** A.D. / **19 V**
  (A.D. 50822) Arrival of the **Ultimate White Ship**.
  Snow wars. Abundance of snow (antimatter weapons) leads to an expansion of Ecological Militia and Armiger Orders. Melusine Palatials disband.
  Rise of the Summer Kings or *Aestevals*, a caste (later, a subspecies) of terraformers biotechnologically and psychologically adapted to entering men-

tal union with ghosts in order to perform otherwise impossible feats of chaos mathematics, needed for precise weather control.

The Summer Kings dominate the worlds of the inner Solar System. Supra-stratospheric weather-control clouds circle Earth and Venus. Poles heated and tropics cooled by engineering the world ocean currents. Mars is criss-crossed with a series of vast canals, an ancient myth at last come true.

Eventide Life-Sculptors occupy Laurasia, the Eastern continent of Earth. Earth becomes famed for the beauty of its women, the perfect tropical charm of its nearly seasonless environment.

SECOND POWER of SOL

Birth of Neptune, a second Power of Sol, the Seventh Power of Man [Neptune is roughly 7,000 miles in diameter at this time, 90^4 IQ.]

Neptune Brain establishes forward bases on Uranus, makes contact with isolated elements of the Patrician sovereign-mind named Cnaeus.

• **52nd Millennium** A.D. / 18 V

A final attempt is made to assimilate Fox cliometry into the baseline of predictive history, without success, with the Fox Maidens serving as an Amazon soldier class in the place of the now-extinct Myrmidons.

The Summer Kings, awash with wealth of dubious origin (energy funds meant to be set aside to ignite Rania's deceleration starbeam), reestablish the old Golden Lord racial caste system with Patricians occupying the ranks once occupied by Hierophants.

Patrician Golden Lords reclaim power over crucial nodes of the cliometric model on Earth and other worlds, while allowing the Summer Kings to seem to retain control. **This marks the end of the Tribulations**. Course of predictive history restored.

Neptune enters a period of external inactivity and internal reorganization, thought to be akin to REM sleep.

TREASON OF JUPITER: Jupiter refuses to ignite the deceleration laser for a **fourth** burn of the returning lightship of Rania the Vindicatrix. Jupiter attempts to use the energy budget instead to copy itself into the Hyades Concentric at 20 Arietis.

A.D. 51554—Jupiter slain.

Jupiter commits ritual suicide with a solar beam weapon when its avatar on Earth falls in a duel.

(A.D. 51600) **Fourth and final ignition** of the deceleration starbeam directed at M3. Economic collapse follows the liberal expenditure of energy beyond forecast.

The Summer Kings retreat into fictional dreamscapes. Those not altered by
Fox Maidens into Swans soon divaricate.

Judge of Ages, with a picked crew of Rosicrucians of the Brash archetype
called the Sons of Cazi, hijacks the starship *Emancipation* and departs from
Sol, allegedly to seek for a lost colony of Houristan at Epsilon Boötis.

Iota Cephei is the Pole Star

At this point in time, 17,000 years remain before the Vindication of Man.